SOON

A NOVEL

SOON

THE BEGINNING OF THE END

JERRY JENKINS

TYNDALE HOUSE PUBLISHERS, INC.
WHEATON, ILLINOIS

Visit Tyndale's exciting Web site at www.tyndale.com

Copyright © 2003 by Jerry B. Jenkins. All rights reserved.

Cover photograph copyright © 2003 by Brand X Pictures/Alamy. All rights reserved.

Author photo copyright © 2003 by Jonathan Orenstein. All rights reserved.

Designed by Dean H. Renninger

Edited by Elisa Petrini and Ken Petersen

Published in association with the literary agency of Vigliano and Associates, 584 Broadway, Suite 809, New York, NY 10012.

Library of Congress Cataloging-in-Publication Data

Jenkins, Jerry B.
   Soon : a novel / Jerry Jenkins.
     p. cm. — (The underground zealot series)
   ISBN 0-8423-8406-5 — ISBN 0-8423-8407-3 (pbk.)
   I. Title
PS3560.E485 S66 2003
813'.54—dc22   2003016337

Printed in the United States of America

09   08   07   06   05   04
8   7   6   5   4   3   2

To

BILL OUDEMOLEN

with affection

Thanks to

DIANNA JENKINS

ELISA PETRINI

DAVID VIGLIANO

RON BEERS

KEN PETERSEN

THE TYNDALE TEAM

JOHN PERRODIN

TIM MACDONALD

and

MARY HAENLEIN

Imagine…no religion too.

JOHN LENNON, "IMAGINE"
© 1971 BAG PRODUCTIONS, INC.

MANY PEOPLE WILL DIE IN IRAQ. A FEW OF
them, perhaps, bad people, but most of
them surely innocent. In a war, even if
the U.S. can kill 100 Iraqis for every
Westerner who dies, the economic, eco-
logical and moral costs are too high. In
Britain we have recently suffered cata-
strophic chaos on the rail network and a
frightful foot-and-mouth epidemic that
stripped the countryside of animals. In
other countries there have been terrifying fires. All these events were disasters
that di...

who are God...
enough to nurture their own r...
with God; they must also lash out and attempt to extinguish those who belong to
other faiths, whom they see as threats to
their own salvation.

MARK MILNE
Zurich

MANY RELIGIONS ASK YOU TO TREAT OTHER
people as you would want them to treat
you. But human failings, especially...

"...ban all these religions, cults, and
man-made concepts of how to worship
God. Bar the different religious leaders
from spreading their views as the only
absolute....Forbid religions, and there
will be fewer fights."

Jorma Kajaste • Espoo, Finland

conclusion: ban all these religions, cults
and man-made concepts of how to worship God. Bar the different religious
leaders from spreading their views as the
only absolute. Mankind can always use
religion as a casus belli. Forbid religions,
and there will be far fewer fights.

JORMA KAJASTE
Espoo, Finland

"THE LEGACY OF ABRAHAM...
teresting. I was unawar...
great influence on thre...
religions. It is disheart...
see the people of the f...
common "father" fighti...
pretations of Abraham...
Hindu, but I have no re...
religious stories to beli...
brought up to be Goo...

"If there were no religions, and only
empathy, altruism, and humanism to
lead the way, the world would truly be
an enlightened place."

Preeti Kumar • Harlington, England

of humankind. If there were no religions
and only empathy, altruism and humanism to lead the way, the world would truly be an enlightened place.

PREETI KUMAR
Harlington, England

ONE ELEMENT OF THE THREE RELIGIONS
mentioned probably makes reconcilia-
tion between them extremely unlikely,
and that is the tendency of some or many
of their adherents to insist on looking at

AT THE CONCLUSION OF WORLD WAR III

IN THE FALL OF 2009, it was determined

by the new international government in Bern,

Switzerland, that beginning January 1 of the fol-

lowing year, the designation A.D. (*anno Domini,*

"in the year of our Lord" or after the birth of

Christ) would be replaced by P.3. (post–World

War III). Thus, January 1, A.D. 2010, would

become January 1, 1 P.3.

PROLOGUE

11:05 P.M., EASTERN STANDARD TIME

MONDAY, DECEMBER 22, 36 P.3.

BRIGHTWOOD PARK, WASHINGTON, D.C.,
CAPITAL OF THE COLUMBIA REGION,
UNITED SEVEN STATES OF AMERICA

A COMMON CITIZEN would not have recognized the danger. But the lone occupant of the Chevy Electrolumina was retired Delta Force Command Sergeant Major Andrew Pass.

He touched the tip of his right thumb to the tip of his pinkie, activating cells implanted in his molars. He could have dialed with his other fingertips, but he opted for voice recognition and quickly recited the numbers that would connect him on a secure, private circuit to his brother in the underground compound.

"This is Jack, Andy," came the answer that resonated off his cheekbones and directly to his eardrum. "GPS shows you heading north on Sixteenth toward Silver Spring."

"Roger that. My ETA was eleven-fifteen—"

"Was?"

"Yeah, I—"

"Say no more. I see 'em. What kinda rig, Andy?"

"Looks like an extended Suburban Hydro. They're on to me."

"You sure?"

"And I'm unarmed, Jack."

"Can you lose 'em?"

"Snow's deep and packed, but I have to try."

"What do you need?"

"Just wanted you to get hold of Angela in case I can't."

"No fatalism now, Andy. Come on."

"If I don't see you in ten minutes, spread the word."

Andy pressed his pinkie and thumb tips together again and peeked in the rearview mirror. *Smooth.* The hydrogen-powered Suburban was hanging back almost three blocks. By now they had to know that he knew. Clearly they weren't going to blow this by being overeager.

He thought about calling his daughter himself, but he had to concentrate. Jack would know how to break it to her.

Andy took a right and then a left, dousing his lights. That wouldn't shake the Suburban, and with its colossal power pack, it could run him down in seconds, even in this weather. For the moment he was out of his pursuers' line of vision. Andy reached deep into his pocket and pulled out the flat, smooth, white stone that told those he wanted to know that he was one of them. He lowered his window a few inches and tossed it into the frigid night. He was going to have to ditch the Chevy too.

He wheeled into an alley, eyes peeled for a spot to hide the small car. Nothing. He leaped out and sprinted three blocks through icy flurries, darting in and out of shadows, keeping to alleyways. He was grateful his daily jog and workout afforded him such conditioning at fifty-six. But he chastised himself for leaving the compound without a weapon.

It had been months since Andy had had even a close call, but that was no excuse for laxity. If only he could distance himself enough from the Suburban, he could get Jack to have someone pick him up in a fresh, unsuspected car.

Another black Suburban whooshed past ahead of him and slid to a stop. Andy heard doors slamming and boots crunching. He whirled to head back out the way he came, but the original tailing Hydro roared up, blocking his escape. Andy slipped but stayed upright as he quickly moved left to use a window ledge, hoping to hoist himself atop a one-story building. Too late. His pursuers had filled the alley, and he faced the barrels of high-powered weapons.

A rawboned, thin-lipped woman with a shock of silver hair stepped forward. "Andrew Pass?"

He would not respond.

Another uniform, a young man, patted him down. The vapor rushing from his mouth told Andy the kid was excited. "Un-armed." He cuffed Andy's hands behind his back, the steel cold on his wrists. "I'll wand him."

Oh no.

He ran a detector over Andy's limbs, stopping when a high tone signaled the ID biochip beneath the skin of his right fore-arm. The young man studied an LED readout. "It's Pass, all right."

Silver Hair waved the rest of the uniforms into position. They guided Andy to a windowless truck and boosted him into the back. When the door was shut, Andy lowered himself to the floor. With his hands behind him he couldn't keep from pitching and rolling, banging into the door as the truck took off.

Would his family or his compatriots have a clue what be-came of him? Could he escape? He had to try. He had to do something.

Andy judged the ride at between ten and fifteen minutes, at a speed that sent him bashing from wall to wall. When the truck finally skidded to a stop, he wrenched himself into a sitting position by planting one foot and pressing his shoulder against the side of the truck. The doors opened, and he was yanked to the ground.

The icy pavement was gritty, and the air smelled of moldering brick. They seemed to be in a run-down industrial park. A few buildings were operational, judging by their outside lights, but no doubt were deserted at this hour. The others looked abandoned, black hulks beyond the headlights of the cars ringing Andy—the Suburbans and a new one, a sleek dark limousine. Andy strained to see who was inside, but its tinted windows were impenetrable. *Some big shot.* He shuddered.

The silver-haired woman stood by the limo, talking to someone in the backseat. She came into the light, nodding to an underling who directed one of the Suburbans to the front door of the dark ruin to the left. Two men pulled a fifty-five-gallon drum from the back of the vehicle and awkwardly rolled it into the building. Two others grabbed Andy's arms and hustled him toward the door, a third propelling him from behind. They shoved him through the door and into a cavernous room where the two with the drum were prying off the perforated lid. It clanged to the floor.

Andy closed his eyes and drew in a long breath, acrid fumes attacking his nostrils. Fear flared in him. He had imagined such a moment. He prayed he would remain stoic.

The woman loomed over Andy, her eyes as silvery as her hair. *Psycho eyes.*

She moved close and bent toward Andy's ear, her breath hot and wet. "Recognize those fumes, Sergeant Major?"

Andy glared, pulse raging, determined to stay silent. Surrender wasn't in his nature. A flying kick could topple this witch. A lowered shoulder and a head butt might take out one or two more. But the odds were ludicrous. Even if he could make it to the door, there were at least four men outside, plus the driver and whoever else was in the limo—all were surely armed. Was he willing to die their way or with bullets in his back? Time was running out.

"Actions have consequences, *An-dy*," the woman said. "Now others will get the message. The USSA does not tolerate subversives."

Andy wanted to spit in her face. *Stay silent. Strong.* His mind reeled. *Torture? Death?* He'd risked death on the battlefield but had never faced such personal horror. Was his faith strong enough?

"Here's your chance at bona fide martyrdom, Andy. Saint-hood."

So this was it then? Ignominious death without a fight? Andy had been taught that courage was not fearlessness but rather the management of fear. He wasn't managing well. *I'm actually going to die.*

Two enforcers lifted him over the barrel, which was lined with napalm. As they lowered him Andy tried to kick, but his heels caught the rim of the drum as his hands and back slid into three inches of the surprisingly cool, jellied gasoline. One of the uniformed men jammed Andy's feet into the drum. There he sat, pinned—feet above his head, chin pressed so tight to his chest that he could barely breathe.

"Ready, sir!" the woman called out.

Andy heard no reply but assumed her superior officer—the person in the limo?—was now in the building. *For what? To see me suffer?*

"Okay, hit it," the woman barked.

Someone pressed the lid down over the barrel, sealing Andy

in. Dim light peeked through the holes. None of his training had cured his claustrophobia. His breath came in great rushes through clenched teeth.

"Stand back ten feet, gentlemen."

The strike of a match. The tiny flame dropping into the barrel. The explosion of fumes. Andy willed himself to make no sound, but he failed. He had drawn in enough air to fill his lungs just before the conflagration enveloped him with a heat so hellish he could not fathom it. And he exhaled with a scream so piercing he could hear it above the roar of the fire.

He screamed as long as he could, knowing his next breath would draw in the flames and fuel for which his body had become a mere wick. Insane from the pain and unable to move, Andy finally sucked in the killing breath—the merciful, final invasion that roasted his lungs and heart and transported him from one world to the next.

1

WASHINGTON, D.C., STILL KNEW how to do holidays. Though the city was now merely one of seven capitals of the United Seven States of America, at times like this it harkened back to its glory days and reminded old-timers of the turn of the century—before the war changed everything, including the calendar.

Dense snowfall didn't slow traffic or seem to dampen spirits this December 24—Wintermas Eve—of 36 P.3. Lights bedecked the monuments, those that had survived the war or been erected since. Only the war memorials remained dark. While military heroes were acknowledged with appropriate burials, war itself had not been commemorated for more than thirty-five years.

The main thoroughfares of the historic city sparkled with blinking white lights that washed the trees with cheer. The West Wing, all that was left of the White House, shone through the splatty downfall. And behind it the Columbia Region's Wintermas tree illuminated the lawn. Santas dotted street corners, ringing bells and thanking passersby for donations, but not to the Salvation Army, for neither *salvation* nor *army* remained de rigueur. The money would go to international humanitarian relief.

On a tony, tree-lined street in old Georgetown sat a row of nearly identical three-story brownstones. In the driveway of one on a corner, snow slid off the steaming hood of a rented Ford Arc, and the car's electric power pack began to cool. Fresh footprints—of two adults and two children—led to the front door. While there were no outside decorations, the den window boasted a gleaming Wintermas tree.

Inside that den, Dr. Paul Stepola, Jae Stepola, and their young family from Chicago awkwardly settled in with her parents, the former army Lieutenant General Ranold B. Decenti and his wife, Margaret.

This was the first Wintermas Eve in their ten years of marriage that the Stepolas had celebrated with the Decentis. Traditionally they spent holidays in Chicago with Paul's mother, who was alone, while the Decentis—thanks to Ranold's postwar ascendancy in the National Peace Organization, for which Paul also worked—attended a ceaseless round of high-level year-end parties. But Ranold had eased out of the administrative fray, and that September, Paul's mother had passed away after a protracted and painful battle with brain cancer. Her death was expected and not unwelcome, so it wasn't sadness at the change of venue that made the holiday greetings so stiff. The four adults had greeted each other with handshakes. Daughter Brie, seven, and son Connor, five, were formally acknowledged.

Paul had never settled on how to address his father-in-law.

He had tried *Dad, General, Ranold,* and even the sixty-six-year-old's last title in the NPO, *Deputy Director.* This year Paul called the man *sir* and lied that it was wonderful to see him again.

Margaret Decenti might as well have been invisible. She smiled occasionally but rarely spoke. Her lot in life, it appeared to Paul, was to do her husband's bidding. This she did, largely with a blank expression. Occasionally she would ask Jae to tell the kids to stop doing one thing or another.

Complicating this year's festivities for Paul was that Jae was again on his case about the time he spent on the road—her code for not trusting him. He had been caught in an indiscretion, which she persisted in calling an "affair," more than six years before. At thirty-six, a muscular six-foot-three, and possessed of a quick wit, he had always been attractive to women. Often when traveling he would have dinner with a female colleague who, after a few drinks, would radiate the signals of invitation, sometimes even brazenly. If the woman was appealing—and not infrequently she was—Paul didn't say no.

These encounters were mostly onetime, no-strings flings that livened up the boredom of travel and, to Paul's mind, had nothing to do with his marriage. But Jae sifted through his luggage like Sherlock Holmes and quizzed him relentlessly. Her jealous obsessions and tight-lipped silences were wearing him down. Paul used to love merely gazing at Jae. Now he could hardly stand being in the same room.

They had met in graduate school at the University of the District of Columbia in 22 P.3., just after Paul had left the army's top secret, elite counterterrorist strike unit, Delta Force. He had joined the army to honor his father, who had been killed in World War III when Paul was an infant. Despite his obvious proclivity for it, the military wasn't much of a career since there was little armed conflict in the world anymore. So Paul had chosen to pursue a doctorate in religious studies, with the encouragement of his mother.

She had taught him that every war stemmed from the fairy tales of religious extremists and that the most rewarding career he could choose would be one in which he helped maintain an intellectual, humanistic society that eschewed both religion and war. "Study the major religions," she'd say again and again, "and you'll see. You'll find out what makes people follow despots like sheep. Study history or be doomed to repeat it."

It seemed everything Paul read of religion bore out his mother's belief. His religious studies program was a virtual military history course, especially when it came to World War III. It had been sparked by the Muslim holy war against Jews and the West, which began with the American World Trade Center attacks in 2001. The U.S. invasion of Iraq in 2003 led to an escalation of the Israel-versus-Palestine conflict, prompting devastating terrorist attacks in the nations that tried to quell it—in both North America and Europe—in 2008. Meanwhile, Catholics and Protestants continued to war in Northern Ireland, culminating in the destruction of major landmarks in London; the Balkans exploded with the mutual persecutions of the Catholics, Muslims, and Orthodox Serbs; Hindus and Muslims battled over Kashmir; and various Asian religious factions skirmished. Soon the globe was ablaze with attacks, counterattacks, reprisals, and finally, an all-out nuclear war that most thought signaled the end of the world.

Jae had been a local girl studying economics, and Paul's immediate attraction to her was returned. She was tall and lithe, a celebration for the eyes. He—she said—would easily pass muster with her father, an ex-army general and one of the founding fathers of the NPO. They married in 26 P.3., right after grad school.

Paul dreamed of a corporate job, but when his Ph.D. in religious studies didn't open those doors, Jae urged him to pursue the NPO. The National Peace Organization had risen from the ashes of the FBI and the CIA after World War III. Like the CIA, it was a foreign intelligence force—though a skeletal one, since in the postwar world the United Nations oversaw global peace-keeping. And like the FBI, it handled interstate crimes—which, these days, were as likely to be international—such as fraud, racketeering, terrorism, and drug trafficking.

Paul trained at Langley, Virginia, then spent his first few years in Chicago on the racketeering squad, where, surprisingly, his graduate work found purchase. Studying the world's major religions had introduced him to a broad range of cultures, back-ground that proved invaluable when investigations drew him or his colleagues overseas. Now he did much of his work abroad, on one of the consulting teams the NPO hired out to help other governments train their own peacekeeping and intelligence forces.

Ranold Decenti seemed to view Paul's work as a cushy desk job. Paul never felt put down in so many words, but his father-in-law's tone and demeanor were condescending. Ranold clearly considered the early years of the NPO, when he was helping build and run it from its original headquarters in Washington, as its golden age. "Back then guys joined the agency for the action, not to teach and consult. And no one wanted to get stuck in some regional capital. The best and the brightest came to Washington."

"Well," Paul said, "maybe that made sense when it was the capital of the country. Nobody listens to Washington anymore."

"Tell me about it. Now, instead of visionary leadership, a national director baby-sits a bunch of bureau chiefs who all set their own agendas."

"Task forces work across regional lines."

"Yeah, but—"

The kids burst in, trailed by Jae, now in their pajamas and begging to know whether Wintermas presents might be opened that night instead of the next day. Margaret expelled an audible sigh.

Ranold gave her a look that could have stopped the snow. "No!"

He growled with such menace that Brie backed away, but Connor kept staring at the Wintermas tree. "Why do you have a flag on top of your tree, Grandpa? My friend Jimmy's mom says when she was little people put stars or angels on top of their trees. She's still got some."

Ranold waved dismissively. "Not in this house. And not in yours either, I hope."

"Of course not," Paul said.

Connor climbed into Paul's lap and wrapped his arms around his neck. Paul sensed the boy's fatigue. "Why not, Dad?"

"We'll talk about it in the morning," Paul said. "Now why don't you and your sister—"

"But why not? They sound pretty, like they'd look better on a Wintermas tree than an old flag."

Ranold stood and moved to the window with his back to them. "That flag stands for everything I believe in, Connor."

"He wasn't saying anything about the flag," Paul said. "He doesn't understand. He's just a—"

"He's old enough to be taught, Paul."

"It's never come up before, Ranold. I plan to tell him—"

"See that you do! And you ought to check into that mother who's harboring contraband icons."

Paul shook his head.

"What's wrong with angels and stars, Daddy?"

"I promise I'll tell you tomorrow."

"Tell him now, Paul!"

"Ranold, give it a rest. I'll decide when and how to educate my son. . . ."

Jae stood and nodded at Brie, taking Connor's hand. "Right now he's going to bed," she said.

"Tell him in bed then," her father said.

• • •

Jae avoided Paul's gaze as she led the children to the stairs. "Say good night to Grandpa and Grandma."

Both singsonged a good night. Margaret formally wished them the same. Ranold said, "Yeah, yeah."

Great, Jae thought. *Paul and Dad are already sparring.*

When they were first married, Paul seemed to look up to her father, but there was always an undercurrent of competition. Paul had declined a good offer from the Washington NPO bureau, asking instead to be assigned to Chicago, his hometown, to escape his father-in-law's shadow. For Jae it was an adventure to settle in a new city, and she was thrilled to land a position with the Chicago Board of Trade. Then the kids came along and she became a stay-at-home mom. Now that they were in school, she missed the camaraderie of the office but didn't feel she could go back to work with Paul on the road so much. Even when he was home, he wasn't much of a companion. In fact, he was so distant and distracted that her old suspicions came flooding back. She had been looking forward to Wintermas in Washington as a break from those worries.

At the top of the stairs, Paul caught up with her. "What?" she said.

"You know what. I don't like your father criticizing the kids."

"I don't like it either," she said, "but you know how he is. And you know what he lost because of a bunch of religious fanatics."

"Jae, come on. He overreacted. Connor brought it up and—"

"He has a reason to be hypersensitive about it."

"We all have painful areas, Jae."

"Of course we do." Jae steered the children toward their beds and tucked them in. "But, Paul, he did lose his entire army and the population of a whole state. Hawaii was a state then, you know."

Paul bent to embrace Connor, who turned away, appearing upset by the tone of the conversation. "There were a lot of states then, Jae."

"What's that supposed to mean?"

They closed the kids' door and stepped into the hall. "Just that it's not like losing a whole region would be now. And it doesn't give him the right to tell me how to raise my kids."

"Oh, Paul, he doesn't mean it that way. He was a general. He's used to speaking his mind."

"So am I."

Tears welled in Jae's eyes. "Paul, please—I want this to be a nice holiday. Mom thinks Dad's testy because he's having trouble adjusting to his consultancy—being out of the limelight."

"That was his choice, to hear him tell it. He was tired of management and could be more 'creative' in special projects, whatever that means. And it's been more than a year."

"Yes, but for someone like him, it's tough giving up the big staff and the authority and the perks, even if he's doing what he wants. So go easy on him. Can't you go back down there and try to make nice?"

"How'm I supposed to do that? I'm not going to apologize because I didn't—"

"I'm not asking you to apologize. Just smooth things over. Have a drink with Dad. There's a lot you two could talk about. Let's not start the holiday off on the wrong foot."

"I guess I could do that. Whatever you think, I don't enjoy butting heads with the old blowhard."

•   •   •

Trudging down to the den felt like going to the principal's office. Paul was well aware that nothing upset his father-in-law more than religion. Ranold had been commander of the U.S. Pacific Army during the war. He was on his way back from Washington to his headquarters at Fort Shafter, north of Honolulu, when disaster struck. Conflict between Asian religious factions in the South China Sea resulted in the launching of two nuclear warheads. A colossal chunk of southern China, including Kowloon, was literally separated from the rest of the continent. Besides the devastation from the bombs themselves, which snuffed out tens of millions of lives, the violence to the topography caused a tsunami of such magnitude that it engulfed all of Hong Kong Island, swamped Taiwan with hundreds of feet of water, raced to the Philippine Sea and the East China Sea, obliterated Japan and Indonesia, swept into the Northwest Pacific Basin and the Japan Trench, finally reaching the North Pacific Current.

It was upon the whole of the Hawaiian Islands, swallowing the entire state before any evacuation could take place. Not one person in all of Hawaii survived. The great tidal wave eventually reached Southern California and Baja California, reaching farther inland than expected and killing thousands more who believed they had fled far enough. It changed the landscape and the history of millions of acres from the Pacific Rim to what was then known as North America. The global map would never look the same, and decades later the grief at the human toll still lingered.

A million times more destructive than the atomic bombs that had brought an end to the previous war, the killer tsunami seemed to sober every extremist on the globe. It was as if, overnight, every nation lost its appetite for conflict.

Antireligion, antiwar factions toppled nearly every head of state, and an international government rose from the ashes and mud. The United States was redrawn to consist of seven regions:

Atlantica in the Northeast encompassed ten former states, with New York City as its capital. Columbia encompassed nine southeastern states, with Washington, D.C., as its capital. The president of the United States was deposed and the vice president installed as regional governor, reporting to the international government in Switzerland. Gulfland took in Texas and five nearby states, with Houston as its capital. Sunterra was comprised of Southern California, Arizona, and New Mexico, with Los Angeles becoming its capital. Rockland was made up of seven states, and Las Vegas became its capital. Pacifica, with its capital in San Francisco, encompassed Northern California and four northwestern states, as well as Alaska. And Chicago became the capital of Heartland, which took in ten Midwestern states.

Paul's own father had died earlier in the war, when the Coalition of Muslim Nations attacked Washington, D.C. *Ranold's loss isn't the only one that matters. His whole generation still focuses on the horrors they saw. We're never allowed to forget how they suffered so we could enjoy a lifetime of peace.*

Paul felt an immediate pang of guilt. Early in the twenty-first century the world had been uglier than he could conceive, and the devastating war had left scars—personal and global, physical and psychological—that would never be healed. He shouldn't have let his father-in-law provoke him. He hated the old man's self-righteousness, but maybe he could cut Ranold some slack.

When he reached the den, however, neither host nor hostess was still there. Paul glanced at his watch. Eleven straight up. He turned on the big-screen TV and settled in a chair.

"Local police report tonight the grisly discovery of the charred remains of a decorated military man, apparently the result of a tragic accident. The body of retired Delta Force Command Sergeant Major Andrew Edward Pass was found among the ruins of an abandoned warehouse just north of the Columbia Zoological Park."

Paul stood, mouth agape, holding his breath. *Andy? Andy Pass?*

"Police spokespersons say they have not determined any reason Major Pass would have been in the building, but they have ruled out arson. The fire has been traced to an electrical short, and police speculate that Pass may have seen the fire and attempted to put it out. Pass reportedly has been involved in community service since his retirement from the military five years ago. Full honor guard funeral services are set for Arlington Regional Cemetery at 10 A.M., Saturday, December 27."

Paul crossed the room to his father-in-law's bar. He poured two fingers of Scotch, raised the glass, then added two more. Ranold entered in robe and slippers. "No ice, Paul?"

"No thanks."

"That's a pretty good slug of booze."

"I just found out my Delta Force commanding officer is dead. He was like a father to me, and—"

"Pass?"

"You know?"

"Pour me one too. Make it bourbon."

"The news said he was caught in a burning warehouse."

"Paul, don't believe everything you hear."

"What are you saying?"

"Just that it's debatable which came first: his being caught or the warehouse burning."

"Caught by whom?"

"When was the last time you heard from Pass?"

"I don't know—seven, eight years ago."

"So you don't have a clue what he's been up to since you were his protégé at Fort Monroe."

"No, but Andy was the finest—"

"Sit down." Ranold took his glass from Paul, gesturing toward a chair.

Paul sank into the padded leather.

Ranold leaned in close. "Pass headed up an underground religious cell right here in D.C., in Brightwood Park."

"Religious? What faction?"

"Christian."

"Andy Pass? That's hard to believe. He was a veteran, a patriot . . ."

"Those are the ones who turn, you know. The true believers. Only a man who's capable of faith can be converted."

"So they say."

"It's true. Paul, we've got cells popping up like snakes in the woodpile. You gotta catch 'em while they're small. Lop off their heads and their tails soon die."

"Their heads? What's your involvement here, Ranold?"

His father-in-law smiled. "I hate snakes." He clinked his glass against Paul's and took a sip. "Let Andrew Pass serve as an example to other subversives."

• • •

Paul headed to bed gnawed by doubt. How could Andy Pass become a subversive, religious or otherwise? People changed, of course, but Andy had always seemed rock solid. And Ranold was so smug. Was that whole story prompted by his trouble adjusting to his new job, an effort to keep himself in the limelight? Could he have cobbled it together from the gossip of his old agency cronies? Ranold was rabidly antireligious, and he loved being in the know. Maybe all those years in the cloak-and-dagger game had made the man conspiracy buggy.

Paul wanted to believe Ranold's story, but he knew better—and it filled him with rage.

2

JAE WAS SHOCKED at the news about Paul's old commander. She had met him only a few times—most recently at their wedding—but she knew how deeply Paul had admired and even loved him. She tried to console Paul but he remained withdrawn, civil but distant and seemingly depressed, even on Wintermas Day. He spoke so little that it was Saturday before Jae realized he was bent on attending Pass's funeral.

"We have a two-thirty flight," she reminded him. "Can we make it back by one?"

"I'm going by myself," he said. "I'll be back in time."

"Why can't I come?" she said.

"It's business."

"Business? Why would the NPO cover an accidental death? And if Andy was under investigation, wouldn't the D.C. bureau handle it?"

"You know I can't discuss my work."

"Are you sure there's no other reason you don't want me to go?"

"Stop it, Jae. I'm not in the mood."

"You have to admit that it seems strange—"

"Leave it alone."

Jae knew pushing Paul further was pointless. Secrecy was paramount in his work, but what could be so hush-hush about a funeral?

Then it struck her: *What if Andy Pass was in the NPO? What if he was killed in the line of duty?* Her reflexive mistrust filled her with shame. She reached out to embrace Paul, but he turned his head so her kiss landed on his cheek. "Okay," she said, backing off. "I guess I deserved that."

Paul shrugged.

She accepted that as forgiveness. *I've got to get a grip on these suspicions.*

• • •

Paul's mood was darker than he had let on to Jae. He could have told her the gist of Andy's situation without specifics, but he couldn't bring himself to speak of it. Ranold said nothing more about the case either, though Paul sensed his father-in-law studying him, and now and then they had exchanged loaded glances. Three days of brooding about Andy Pass had only stoked Paul's sense of betrayal. Attending the funeral was business, as he told Jae, but it was personal rather than official—to try to confront the enemy that had devoured his mentor from within.

In an angry fog, he drove south over the Potomac River into Virginia to Arlington Regional Cemetery, due south of where the Iwo Jima statue had once stood and slightly northwest of the

Pentagon Memorial Crater. The famed statue—destroyed by an Islamic terrorist dirty bomb early in the war—was now represented by a photo, sheltered in a kiosk, of the actual incident a century before when four United States Marines planted a flag on Iwo Jima during World War II.

The crater where the Pentagon had been was ringed with an ornate chain-link fence, on which visitors pinned mementos of the thousands of loved ones lost there during World War III. It took the largest warhead ever to land on American soil to obliterate one of the world's largest buildings, six months before the end of the war. It was a North Korean submarine-launched ballistic missile shot low enough to evade radar. It scored a direct hit inside the courtyard of the Pentagon and virtually vaporized the structure.

The cemetery itself, still a national shrine, had escaped war damage and was as beautiful as ever. Today it was covered by several inches of snow, making row upon row of veterans' white headstones appear to have grown from the icy blanket.

Paul was directed to a low stone building in the new, postwar section, where all headstones were rectangular—no crosses or Stars of David or any other ancient religious symbols. When he identified himself as a government employee, his car was parked by an army cadet.

Inside, the building was long, narrow, and plain. At the front a closed coffin was draped with a seven-star American flag. On the wall behind it the only decoration was a display of American flags of the past, from Betsy Ross's thirteen-star model to the fifty-star banner that preceded the present version.

Accepting a small printed program from a young officer, Paul thought he spotted NPO agents milling in the back. None of them returned his gaze. Paul noticed three former army buddies sitting together about midway toward the front of the hall. They greeted him with a warmth that made him envy their innocence. For them, Andy Pass was still a hero.

He learned all three had flown in from New York City, where they worked in the corporate world. Within the bounds of propriety for the occasion, they joshed Paul about still working for the government. "Not much call on Wall Street for religious studies," Paul said. "And academia is not for me."

The guy next to him leaned toward Paul. "It was the old ball and chain who pushed you into the NPO. Am I right?"

"It was my decision, but she's happy, yeah."

"Still married?" one asked, proudly showing his own bare ring finger. The other two showed theirs as well.

"Ten years," Paul said, flashing his ring.

"Poor boy," another said. "If I *was* still married, I wouldn't be tonight, here on the loose in D.C."

"Who'd have thought," the one next to Paul said, slapping his back, "that the babe magnet in our crew would be the only one still married?"

The others chuckled.

"And I'd bet cash money you've still got the old charm. Am I right?"

Paul rolled his eyes and, in spite of himself, grinned.

"You dog! The same old tricks! Am I right?"

Paul shook his head. "And you still say 'Am I right?' after every sentence."

"Like I say, some things never change."

"Except Andy," Paul said, solemn again. "Hey, listen, before this thing gets started, what do you know about his death?"

The three glanced at each other. "Just what was on the news. Why?"

"Just wondering. I hadn't heard from Andy in years. I was really shocked. Have you seen his wife yet?"

They shook their heads.

"And he had kids too, right?"

They nodded.

An elderly man in full dress blues stepped to the podium and called the service to order. "We come this day to celebrate the life of Andrew Edward Pass, born 12 November A.D. 1989, died at age fifty-six, 22 December 36 P.3. He decided on a military career following the first terrorist attacks on the United States in September of A.D. 2001, two months before his twelfth birthday. He later joined the Reserve Officer Training Corps, eventually became a distinguished military graduate, and graduated with honors from the United States Military Academy at West Point, New York. He excelled as a second lieutenant during the U.S. invasion of the Middle East and quickly climbed the ranks with outstanding and heroic service to his country during World War III. He reached the level of command sergeant major of the First Special Forces Operational Detachment—Delta, better known as Delta Force. Ladies and gentlemen, would you please rise if you served or trained under Sergeant Major Pass at any stage of your military career."

Paul and his buddies stood, and he was surprised to see about half the crowd also rise.

"Would the rest please stand and join me in singing 'America the Beautiful.'"

Paul knew from his course work that this was one of the religious-based patriotic songs that had different lyrics since the war.

> O beautiful for spacious skies, for amber waves of grain!
> For purple mountain majesties above the fruited plain.
> America! America! We pledge ourselves to thee,
> And crown thy good with brotherhood, from sea to shining sea.

After the song the host announced that Major Pass's daughter would deliver the eulogy and invited anyone else who wished to offer a word of remembrance to come up afterward. A beautiful young woman stepped from the front row to the microphone. She clutched a matted tissue in one hand and a tiny, wrinkled sheet of paper in the other. Her voice was thick; her throat sounded constricted.

"My name is Angela, and I am Andrew Pass's only daughter. It touches our family deeply that so many are here, though I confess we are not surprised. The influence Dad had on you that caused you to carve out the time to honor him in this way is not foreign to us. He had the same effect at home.

"Did you find him tough and demanding? We did too. Did you ever find him unfair or harsh? Neither did we. Did he challenge you to look within and yet beyond yourself for resources you never knew you had? Did he push you and inspire you to heights you never might have reached otherwise? Then you knew my dad.

"Dad couldn't hide his frustration and sometimes even his disdain for what happened to his beloved country before his children were born. But he was a man of deep, deep belief and conviction, and it was borne out in his life. We take comfort today that he lives on. In everything good about you and me, he lives on. And as long as people walk the earth who were shaped in some way by this unique man, he will live on."

Try as he might, Paul could not detect in anything she said any suspicion about her father's death. Nor did he perceive anything that hinted at Andy's subversive activity—though the line about deep belief could be taken more than one way. His anger flared, and he turned to scrutinize the mourners in the surrounding seats. The NPO agents he'd spotted earlier would be photographing and identifying everyone in attendance. Somewhere among them was the snake who had bitten Andy, injecting him with the poison that bred zealotry and violence and which ultimately cost him his life. If a staunch soldier like Major Pass could succumb to the lure of make-believe, no one was immune.

If I could get my hands on that fanatic—that killer . . .

A line was forming to the left of the podium. Paul felt the eyes of his army buddies on him. *I was Andy's favorite.* He wrestled to reconcile his fury with his undeniable debt of gratitude to Andy for being a virtual surrogate father to him in the army. Whatever Andy had become, Paul decided, he deserved to be commemorated for the past. He rose and took his place at the back of the line of speakers.

When Paul's turn to speak came, he noticed Angela's double take when he identified himself. He struggled for the right words. "The two years I served and trained under Major Andrew Pass remain the most pivotal of my life. Andy Pass represented everything the army had to offer, and he was the one we had to impress to remain among the select. But beneath his drill-sergeant style was a kernel of humanity that I, for one, never detected in other superior officers. When he recognized that I not only obeyed but also enjoyed every torturous task he dished out, he rewarded me—as he did so many others—with respect and friendship. I just want to say that he changed my life. He made me want to excel and to treat others the way he treated me. I hope I can live up to his model."

Later, Paul stood in line to file past the bier and greet the family. He was surprised when Angela broke from her place in the receiving line and approached. "So you're Paul Stepola," she said, smiling through tears and taking his hand in both of hers. "Daddy spoke so highly of you."

Her dignity and warmth had been evident when she spoke,

but up close her beauty was disarming. And she smelled of lavender. Despite his anger at her father and the gravity of the occasion, Paul's attraction to Angela was immediate, intense, and visceral.

"Oh, surely not," he managed. "Your dad had so many trainees and subordinates over the years—"

"I'm totally serious," she said. "You must have epitomized what he was looking for in Delta Force. I've always wanted to meet you."

Paul could barely murmur how pleased he was to meet her. Wild thoughts coursed through his brain. Though no stranger to the power of seduction, he had never before felt this kind of instant, overwhelming connection to any woman—not even Jae.

Good thing she's not here.

"Your remarks were perfect," Angela said. "It was obvious you really knew him."

"Well, Angela, he meant a lot to me—to all of us. I hope we get a chance to talk some more about him one of these days."

"Me too," she said. "I would love that." She let go of his hand to gesture toward two young boys. "Those are my sons, and I'd like to introduce them to you."

"Certainly," Paul said, sobering. So she was married. Well, so was he.

He shook hands with the boys, and both had to be coaxed to look him in the eye and tell him it was nice to meet him. Paul slipped Angela's business card into his pocket.

• • •

The burial was restricted to family. Walking to the parking lot with his buddies, Paul declined their invitation to lunch because of his flight. Their departure left Paul once again isolated in his anger. Unready to head back to the car, he veered off the pavement into the snow-covered cemetery. Tromping past the rows of headstones and the Robert E. Lee and John F. Kennedy memorials, Paul moved into a section where all the headstones were cross-shaped.

A plaque read: *Religious symbols were common before World War III, when it was the custom for every enlisting soldier to declare his denominational preference.*

Paul spat in disgust.

As he walked on amid the tombstones, his outrage mounted. Life had been torn from all these young men and women—so many barely out of their teens—and for what? Because fanatical Muslims waged holy war on the West? Because religious groups in Bosnia jockeyed for primacy? On and on it went, back to the dawn of history, people persecuting each other over abstract ideas. That their tombstones symbolized the ideas they died for seemed the cruelest of ironies.

And what were these ideas about? Outlandish notions of an afterlife. Sure, it was hard to imagine that this life was all there was. Paul could identify with the need to believe there was some form of nirvana in the end. He'd like to have known his father, and, short of that, to think he might still meet him one day. But were such wishes worth killing for? dying for? His mother was right. That these religious fanatics all thought they knew the truth—with many convinced that theirs was the only truth—proved they all were deluded.

Even worse than delusion was the compulsion to inflict delusion on others—to corrupt even strong-minded men like Andy Pass.

Paul's stomach was empty and his feet were cold. He had worn nothing over his shoes, not planning this foray into the dead zone. He headed back for his car, turning to look at the crosses that seemed to line up all the way to the horizon. *I hope it gave them some comfort. And yet here they lie.*

· · ·

By the time Paul got back, Jae had everything packed and the kids ready to go. Once the pile had been transferred to the car, the good-byes began. Ranold held Paul's arm to slow him as he approached the car. While Jae was getting the kids buckled in, the old man spoke quietly. "You may not have done the best for yourself, attending that funeral."

"Meaning?"

"Paul, the agency is focusing more and more on homegrown subversives. If it comes out—the truth about Pass, I mean—and it's known that you went to his funeral, that you were old friends—"

"I didn't go as an old friend."

"Whatever made you go, it was imprudent."

"You're saying it could hurt me inside the agency?"

"Of course."

"That would require my knowing the truth before I went, now wouldn't it?"

Ranold pressed his lips together. "You did know. I told you."

"Then I would be in trouble only if anyone in the agency knew that you had told me. Am I right? Surely I can count on you to sit on that . . . Dad."

3

PAUL WAS RELIEVED to wake up in his own bed in Chicago Sunday morning. The winter sun flooded through the windows and glinted off the clean, crisp snow. Jae was already downstairs with the kids, and he could hear them clamoring to go ice-skating.

"I guess they felt cooped up at my parents' house," Jae said when he joined them at the breakfast table. "It might do us all good to get some exercise and fresh air."

"Could you take them?" Paul said. "I don't feel like skating, and I want to make more headway at my mother's house. I want to clear everything out over the holidays and get the house ready to put on the market."

"We could all come and help you."

"No, thanks. You've done plenty. Most of what's left is that stuff she saved, which no one can really go through but me."

"That seems depressing after a funeral."

"It's what a funeral puts me in the frame of mind to do. "

• • •

The truth was that Paul had felt cooped up too. He craved an afternoon alone. After letting himself into his mother's house, he stood in the front hall and relished the quiet. His mother had spent her whole adult life in the neat suburban home where Paul grew up, with a live-in caretaker after she'd begun to lose her faculties. During her last few years, she was increasingly gripped by dementia, unable even to recognize her son and grandchildren. Last Wintermas, Paul had set up a tree for her, though he could tell she had no idea it was there.

Though most cancer was now curable, certain strains defied the best efforts of modern science. A century of study had yet to unravel the intricate mechanisms of the brain. For Paul's mother, cutting-edge treatments had served only to slow the virulent disease. All the doctors could do, Paul had been told, was keep her comfortable until the end. His mother's death, when it came, was anticlimactic, for Paul had said good-bye years before.

The upstairs rooms were now empty, but Paul had not yet tackled the basement, jammed with a lifetime of mementos. A trash can by his side, he began sorting through the dusty boxes. Financial transactions had been electronic for decades, so Paul was surprised to find a cache of checks used before the war— carefully filed and made out in dollars, United States currency when each country had its own. For all her tidiness, his mother was a pack rat. He plucked out a few checks to show the kids and jettisoned the rest.

By early afternoon he had cleared out half of the storage space. Now he started unearthing artifacts of his parents' marriage. His mother had given him many of his father's papers, photos, and possessions long ago, and he remembered seeing some of these, the ones she kept, when he was young. He came upon his parents' marriage license, their wedding invitation—

the celebration had been held in a hall on an army base—and a ribbon-tied stack of old-fashioned greeting cards, with graphics on the front and preprinted messages inside, congratulating his parents on his birth. Beneath these was a heavy, cream-colored vellum envelope with the remains of a flattened blob of a dark red wax on its flap—a broken seal, Paul supposed.

Clapping the dust from his hands, he picked it up and turned it over. On the front was the inscription, in strong black letters: "For My Son on His Twelfth Birthday." Paul remembered that one of his schoolmates had gotten such a letter, written by his parents on the day of his birth and expressing their hopes for his future. He had asked his mother about it, but she professed ignorance of the tradition. So where did she get this one? He slid out the letter inside and was surprised to see the date of his own birth at the top of the page.

My beloved son,

Your birth today was a miracle, filling me with a joy greater than I have ever known or thought possible. Holding you for the first time, I felt blessed . . .

Paul paused at the peculiar, antiquated word.

. . . with the ultimate earthly gift. One day you will hold your own child and understand the profound depth and breadth of a father's love.

The day you read this letter you will turn twelve. On the threshold of manhood, you will be old enough to understand another kind of love—the love of God. It is a much maligned love at the time I write. There have been persecutions and terrorist acts around the globe—supposedly undertaken in the name of God, as different groups construe Him—which have drawn us into world war. Many, your mother among them, have turned away from a God they see as the root of the world's misery. But you must not turn away, Son. First, God's love transcends all earthly gifts, even the gift of your birth for me. God so loved the world that He sacrificed His perfect, only Son, who died on the cross to save us. Accepting that love has been the most important and fulfilling decision of my own life.

The second reason is that God's Son has promised to return in glory to gather up those who believe in Him. The Bible tells us "He will lead them to the springs of life-giving water. And God will wipe away all their tears."

But those who have rejected God will face a very different fate: punishment and suffering beyond anything we can imagine or have ever managed to inflict upon each other. The end of the Bible, the book of Revelation, describes in vivid and terrifying detail what will befall those who incur God's wrath.

This may happen in your lifetime, Son. Many scholars see our current world conflicts as the fulfillment of the Bible's ancient prophecies. The Gospels tell us that we must be ready at all times, "for the Son of Man will come when least expected." And in Revelation, the Lord Himself reminds us several times, "I am coming soon."

I hope to be at your side when you read this letter. But if I am not, I hope I will at least have had time to educate you in these things as soon as you were old enough. Otherwise, you must seek the truth for yourself. I urge you to open your heart to the truth—to become not just a man but also a man of God.

Your loving father,

Paul Stepola Sr.

Paul stared, aghast. His father had died when he was too young even to have a memory of him. He had formed an image of the man from his mother's photographs and stories, as well as those of his fellow soldiers, who invariably depicted him as noble and brave, honest and warm—a hero and a trusted friend. Until last week, ironically, those were the same terms he would have used to describe Andy Pass. How could it be that neither of the men after whom he had modeled himself—the ones he had believed defined what it meant to be a man—was what he seemed?

This was the only direct communication he had ever seen from his father. And clearly his mother had kept it from him. She had to have been the one who broke the seal—she hadn't trusted her husband.

Was she afraid that at twelve Paul would be too susceptible to his father's words? Did she want to preserve Paul's illusions— and her own—rather than acknowledge that his father was so gullible and cowardly? Was she shocked—as Paul was—that instead of wisdom or inspiration, all her husband had offered his son was a myth about a man who died on a cross and was coming to punish those who didn't buy it?

I needed more from you at twelve, Dad. I deserved better. Thanks, Mom, for sparing me this till now.

And the idea that the Bible's prophecies were being fulfilled, that God's Son was coming soon—well, urgency was part of the come-on in virtually every fraud. "A onetime offer," "Get in on the ground floor," "Fire sale—prices will never go lower," "Something for nothing"—how could his father fall for that? Paul knew of the book of Revelation from his studies but had never read it, though he'd heard it was powerful and richly symbolic. The florid what-if pitch was another typical huckster tactic—fire-and-brimstone razzle-dazzle to throw in a scare and close the deal.

Didn't all religions threaten colorful punishments to keep the faithful in line? Was his father really that naive? After a lifetime of admiration, Paul was flooded with contempt for the pathetic dupe his father had turned out to be.

What kind of man fell prey to such lunacy—calling it "the most important and fulfilling decision of my own life"—and even tried to inflict it on a child? Maybe his mother, with all her rationality and abhorrence of religion, couldn't justify ever showing it to him—or was too ashamed to. He could only imagine what Ranold would say. He couldn't have had this planted, could he? Some coincidence, this and finding out about Andy Pass the same week.

The envelope looked rather pristine, considering it had been in a box for thirty-odd years. The sealing wax seemed darkened and brittle, but it would take an expert to tell for sure whether it was new or old. The same was true of the ink, which looked like the kind that had to be drawn out of a bottle into an old-fashioned pen. He could compare the handwriting by eye but computer analysis would be necessary to test it definitively against other letters from his father that his mother had saved.

We were in Washington long enough for someone to plant a letter, of course—but did I tell anyone I'd be clearing out my mother's basement this weekend?

Paul examined the box of mementos, which looked no less dusty than the others. It had been in the middle of a stack of boxes, so its lid was clean and offered no clue. But maybe the timing wasn't the issue. Surely Andy had been under investigation for months. During that time, people in his life would have come under scrutiny—including Paul, if Ranold, who knew he once viewed Andy as a father, was in charge.

Ranold would know better than to suspect Paul was a Christian, but the letter could be some kind of loyalty test—to see if

Paul knew the truth about Andy and looked the other way. If Paul suddenly discovered that his own father had been a Christian, it would be natural for him to turn to the one religious person he knew and trusted. So anytime during the three months Paul's mother's house had been standing empty, the letter could have been planted to flush him out.

Spinning the plot, Paul had to acknowledge it seemed like a stretch. Maybe he was grasping at straws to escape the reality that his father had been a crackpot, not the shining example of a man he had idolized for thirty years. But "a stretch" didn't mean impossible or even far-fetched. Paul knew well that fabricating and planting a letter was child's play for the NPO; and if the operation was one of Ranold's first special projects, his father-in-law would have pulled out all the stops.

The letter itself was probably the only key to the truth. Paul tore off part of the envelope flap, then folded the letter back into it and replaced the envelope in the box, beneath the stack of congratulatory cards.

He had hit the trifecta, Paul thought bitterly. Andy and his father and now even Ranold were tainted by the Christian threat. Tomorrow he would sound out his boss about the extent of the Christian problem—whether the activity was nationwide or localized in Washington—and try to detect any hint that he was under suspicion himself.

And if this infestation is swarming beyond Ranold's backyard, I want to be an exterminator. And not just for national security.

4

MIDMORNING MONDAY, Paul dropped by to see his boss, Robert Koontz, the National Peace Organization's Chicago bureau chief. Standing in the doorway, Paul recognized that, frankly, it was Koontz's office he aspired to more than his job. Large and handsomely appointed with a nautical theme, the office had banks of windows on two walls, offering sweeping views of both the Chicago River and Lake Michigan.

Koontz at sixty was a big man with a shiny pate and a rim of salt-and-pepper hair. He was fiddling with his computer but gestured for Paul to take a seat. "So how were the holidays?" he asked, eyes still on the screen.

"The usual. Except for Andrew Pass."

Koontz stiffened but didn't turn. "You knew him?"

"Bob, you know I did. I saw the NPO guys at his funeral. They had to tell you I was there."

Koontz spun in his chair and held up both hands. "You're

right, Paul. Yeah, I know. You spoke. You served under him. I'm sorry for your loss."

"Thanks. But why the agency presence?"

Koontz sighed. "Pass was a Christian fanatic."

So the word is out.

"That's incredible. What about his family?"

"We think his brother, John—goes by Jack—is in deep too, but he's not shown himself enough to be vulnerable."

"Anyone else? Wife, kids?"

"Apparently his wife divorced him over it. So we don't think so, but we don't know."

"Bob, did we take him out?"

"What did your father-in-law tell you?"

"Nobody stonewalls like an old spymaster. So that's a yes?"

"Well—"

"Why—he resisted?"

"You bet he did. I hear we confiscated an arsenal out of his car, and he tried to take a few of our guys down with him. One tough hombre—but you knew that."

"So the story about the warehouse fire—?"

"Strictly press fodder. His confederates got the message loud and clear, but we kept the public's nose out of our business. It starts getting out that this cult exists, it will only grow. And with martyrs? Don't get me started. Listen to this." He turned back to his computer and scrolled. "Over a hundred years ago Russia closed almost all its churches and disposed of more than forty thousand clergy. They turned city churches into museums and country churches into barns or apartments."

"Like we did."

"But get this. By the turn of the century—of course this is after the fall of communism—two-thirds of all Russians identified themselves as Christians."

"So insurrection was brewing underground."

"Bingo. Can't let that happen here. What happened in Russia and China and Romania decades ago could reemerge here, right under our noses. We haven't really eradicated religion unless we can contain the fanatics. If we let them get a foothold, we could see a full-blown religious uprising."

"Is there really an armed Christian cult?"

"There's a lot we're just learning now, Paul. We're putting together a task force to determine the extent of the problem—whether we have just a few isolated cells, or worse."

"It's a disease," Paul said. "An addiction. Religion gets hold of people, and they can't seem to keep it to themselves—they spread it and get other people hooked. Makes me sick—the waste of a guy like Andy Pass."

"Exactly," Koontz said. "And that's why we have to treat this like the war on drugs—expose the threat, flush it out, eliminate it." He shook his head. "This has the potential to destroy everything this country has worked for since the war. I'm old enough to remember how things were. It was religious extremists who persecuted homosexuals, assassinated abortion doctors—before we had childbirth grants to promote repopulation—and bombed stem-cell research labs that yielded most of our cures for disease. And after the terrorist attacks of '05, it was the extremists who defied the tolerance laws and rioted, killing Muslims."

Paul nodded. He'd studied all this in grad school. Naturally, people wanted revenge for the Super Bowl and Disneyland bombings and the gas attacks on the underground trains in Washington, Boston, and New York. The same thing had happened in Europe, when the Eiffel Tower, the London Bridge, and the Vatican were destroyed. And then the war came—life on earth nearly snuffed out because of religious fanaticism.

"We're lucky the war ended the way it did and woke us up,"

Paul said. "The abolition of religion has proved the best out-come of tragedy ever."

"Tell me about it," Koontz said. "Peace for more than a gen-eration. Not a single nation at war for the first time in history. But we can't take it for granted. Not now—and not ever again."

"What's this new task force?"

"We're calling it Zealot Underground."

"Bob, get me on that. You know I've got the background. The corruption of Andy Pass—and so many others—demands ven-geance."

• • •

The following week, Paul was dispatched to Mexico on a con-sulting job, returning the Tuesday following the Martin Luther King Jr. holiday weekend. The big news in Chicago was that a speaker at a King celebration had twice used the archaic and out-lawed term *Reverend* in connection with the martyr's name. One TV pundit suggested the city declare a moratorium on King Day observances "until organizers learn to control themselves."

Paul's secretary, Felicia, a tall black woman in her late forties, couldn't hide her emotion. "Dr. King died long before I was born, but no matter what you say, the man was a reverend. They go stopping King Day for something minor as that, they're going to have trouble. Tell me the truth, Dr. Stepola. You see any harm in using a man's title, one he earned and used himself?"

"Yes, I do, Felicia. And the organizers know better too. It's playing with fire to link religion with a hero like Dr. King."

"*Link?* Isn't that where Dr. King got his nonviolence philoso-phy?"

"If you're talking about his tactics, I believe he got them from Mohandas Gandhi. Think about it—what that title *links* him to is occultism and ignorance."

"I just meant—"

"Dr. King was a product of his time. Do you think highlighting that era's blindness serves his memory? When we want to honor Thomas Jefferson, do we focus on his slaveholding?"

Felicia looked stricken. Paul smiled. "Am I going to have to arrest you for practicing religion, Felicia?"

"Cuff me. You'll need backup."

"Oh yeah?" he said, chuckling. "We'll see about that. But seriously, I spent four years studying the major religions. And 'I ain't gonna study war no more.' That's what the history is like. Believe me, religion is the opposite of nonviolence."

Though he let it go, Paul was amazed that an NPO secretary would defend religion in front of her boss. But before Wintermas, he himself had given little thought to the likelihood of a Christian threat right here in the USSA. *We've forgotten that the price of freedom is constant vigilance. We take peace for granted. But not anymore.*

The river appeared in danger of icing over, a rarity. He stared at it past the picture of Jae on his desk and acknowledged that he had thought more about Angela Pass than his wife while he was away. He'd felt so relieved when Koontz said she wasn't a suspect. Angela had said she'd always wanted to meet him and that she'd love to get together to talk about her father.

Felicia buzzed. "Koontz wants to see you."

Paul pulled on his suit coat, tightened his tie, and grabbed a notepad. He paused for iris scans at two checkpoints, then was waved in by Koontz's secretary. "He's on the videophone, but he wants you to come in anyway."

Paul entered and shut the door, just as Koontz was saying, "He's here now. I'll call you back."

He clicked off but didn't offer Paul a chair. "That was the brass. Talking about you, Step."

Paul nodded, unsure what to say.

Koontz rose. "Let's go." He pointed down with his thumb.

The secure room?

Koontz smiled. "I have news."

"Okay," Paul said, more as a question.

Koontz opened his credenza and the DNA-coded lock on his safe, pulling from it a sealed document box.

Paul followed him to the elevator, and they rode sixteen floors to the basement. At every checkpoint Koontz's ID was enough for both of them. In the wing that led to the secure room, however, Koontz and Paul were treated like anyone else. Though they had known the uniformed guards by name for years, there was no small talk and no shortcuts. Their holographic-image IDs were scanned by computer and compared to their faces. Besides the iris scans, both put their palms against a screen for fingerprint and DNA checks.

They passed through a metal detector and were finally given two metal keys for the secure room, a touch that always struck Paul as quaint. The keys were supposedly a precaution against bugs that might be somehow encoded in the modern electronic locking devices. Koontz unlocked a three-inch-thick steel door that revealed, six inches away, a three-inch-thick wood door, also locked. Once they were inside and Koontz had secured both doors, a guard outside ran a final scan on the room. The results appeared on a small monitor on the wall. No evidence of bugs or microwaves or any other invasive device. Koontz hit a button next to the monitor, which triggered white noise, a barely audible hum that would interfere with any recording equipment and make their conversation unintelligible.

Six luxurious, deep burgundy leather chairs surrounded a round mahogany table. Otherwise the room was bare, save for a pewter ice-water pitcher and several glasses. Koontz tossed the document box on the table and poured two glasses of water, mostly ice. He set a tiny napkin beneath each glass. "Missed my calling," he said as he sat and pointed to a chair for Paul. "I'd have been a dynamite waiter."

Paul smiled and tried to act calm. Koontz, usually all business, seemed to be stalling. Paul wondered if his father-in-law had been right. Had he aroused suspicion by going to Pass's funeral? His plan was to claim he had no knowledge of Pass's activities since he'd known him in Delta Force—which was true. Or was this somehow connected to his father's letter? *Alleged letter.* He still had the scrap he'd torn from the envelope tucked in his wallet. What if he was searched? *Whether or not the letter is a plant, wondering about it is no crime. It would be weird if I didn't wonder.*

Koontz stood and removed his jacket, draping it over the back of his chair. He loosened his tie. "Get comfortable," he said. "We got us some work to do."

"I'm comfortable for now," Paul said. He had been in the secure room twice before and knew it was kept at a constant temperature.

"You kept up on your firearms, Paul?"

Paul nodded. "I can handle anything from a derringer to a howitzer. I'm at the range every two weeks, minimum."

"You own a double-action semiautomatic?"

"I've got an eleven-point-five-millimeter Beretta and a Walther Stealth."

"Got a preference?"

"Depends. What am I going to do with it?"

"Kill someone from close range."

Paul hesitated. "Beretta's hard to beat, Bob. Who am I going to kill?"

"Hopefully no one. But this job requires a side arm."

"This job?"

"The new task force. You asked for it, and you got it."

"That's great. But tell me—is Ranold involved?"

"The Special Projects Unit in D.C. is developing some kind of operation. It's classified—need-to-know only—and down the road we'll probably intersect. Here, at this point, we'll be more of an intelligence clearinghouse."

"What will my role be?"

"Actually twofold. I want you to be a wild card. Officially, you go along on strategic raids. You'll counsel us on what these Christians believe, and you'll help interpret what they're really saying when interrogated. You'll do some of the questioning yourself. Unofficially, you'll keep me personally informed as to the size and strength of the cult. We don't know yet whether these various factions are connected. How sophisticated are they? Is this thing nationwide, or are these independent groups that just look and act alike?"

"I'll need to brush up on their theology and beliefs and practices."

"We think some of them are into sabotage. Remember that incident with the Reflecting Pool in Washington?"

"It turned red, right? Wasn't that some kind of prank?"

"Not exactly. In front of a hundred tourists, the water turned to blood. Real human blood—we tested it. All it takes is one person in a crowd like that to claim it's a miracle—which is what happened, though we kept it out of the press—and you have a religious crisis in the making. Christians are staging these supposed miracles and using them to win converts, claiming they are signs the world is coming to an end."

Koontz leaned forward. "I hate to tell you this, but we think Pass was behind the Reflecting Pool thing. When we tried to interrogate him—well, the way he fought, it turned into 'suicide by cop.'"

Paul nodded. "Extremists will die for their causes."

"I have to be honest with you, Paul. It's going to be tough. More people are going to die. It can't be avoided."

"Whatever it takes," Paul said.

Koontz unsealed the document box and spent two hours showing Paul what they believed was evidence of some kind of Christian presence in all seven states.

"See what we're up against?"

"Shocking how fast this thing has snowballed," Paul said.

"I'm glad you're on board. In case you're wondering, it's a significant jump in level and pay." Koontz stood and began gathering his materials. "You'll stay in the same office, and you can inform Felicia, but first we'll have to upgrade her security clearance. That should be done by the time you get back."

"From?"

Koontz reached into his breast pocket and pulled out a thin folder. "Plane tickets, hotel reservation, and contact information," he said, sliding it across the table. "Your first assignment: San Francisco. Our people have uncovered a Christian cell led by an elderly, wealthy widow we have code-named Polly Carr."

Paul smiled. "So you do know a bit of church history."

"Well, I've heard of Polycarp, but that's the extent of it."

"So what's the assignment?"

"Apparently this woman lives in a ramshackle Victorian mansion in a formerly ritzy, now blighted, area called Sea Cliff. Half the places are abandoned, and she lives alone. We got a tip that every Sunday morning before daylight, a couple dozen people show up and slip into her place. They leave separately, and we're convinced it's some sort of religious gathering. I want you to go with the task force and monitor what's going on in there. If it's what we think it is, we'll rush them. You'll supervise the inter-rogations out of our San Francisco office."

"Doesn't sound like I'll need a weapon for that one."

Koontz shrugged. "Can't be too careful."

"When's this set for?"

"This Sunday, the twenty-fifth."

"I'm assuming I can tell my wife."

"Your new role, sure. Details of the missions, of course not."

• • •

On the way back to his office, Paul swung by the division lab. It was presided over by Trina Thomas, a vivacious redhead from the South who seemed to enjoy flirtatious banter as much as Paul did. Though she was married, Paul always thought it was the fact that they worked together that kept them from taking the next step.

"Dr. Stepola!" she said. "I've missed you. It's been far too long since you've honored us with a visit."

"Only the most pressing business could have kept me away."

"Mexico, wasn't it? And what do you have for us? Some precious artifact?"

"A personal favor actually. For Jae."

"Is she ready for me to take you off her hands?"

"Afraid not. No, it's more of a—it's a genealogy project, I think. She came across some document and wondered if its age could tell her who in her family produced it."

"I'll run it this afternoon—for a price. Lunch?"

"That's a price I'd be glad to pay. But not today, unfortu-nately. I'm leaving on assignment tomorrow."

"I'll collect when you get back."

• • •

Jae was guardedly impressed with Paul's new job. "I'm glad it's stateside. But since you just got home, I can't say I'm excited you're leaving again."

"Don't start, Jae. I know what you're worried about, and I'm sick of defending myself. If I had a desk job, you'd still be sure that I was seeing another woman."

"Paul, when you get back, do you think we should go to counseling?"

"You go. You're the one who's paranoid."

5

PAUL'S PLANE TOUCHED DOWN at San Francisco International just after noon on Saturday. His favorite city had grown from around seven hundred thousand people to more than a million during his lifetime alone.

He took a cab north on 101, which now ran seven lanes in both directions and looked out over the deep blue waters of the San Francisco Bay. Since the war, the skyline had bloomed with towers built to withstand the occasional tremors that still plagued the area. The glass O-shaped Pacifica Life & Casualty Building was a marvel, and the side-by-side regional and municipal centers—one shaped like an infinity symbol and the other replicating an ankh—drew photographers from all over the world. Downtown San Francisco, rebuilt following residual tsunami damage, boasted replicas of its quaint and colorful row houses. Even the cable cars had been restored.

Paul checked into the Presidio Hotel, equidistant between

the reconstructed Palace of Fine Arts and the National Cemetery in the new Golden Gate Park. As he settled into his room, Paul felt something new and strange, something he hadn't experienced in his overseas assignments. There had been nervousness, sure, excitement, anticipation of the unknown. But never a sense of real danger. It was thrilling.

A ping from the flat screen in the wall indicated a message. Paul aimed his remote control at it and called up a note from Larry Coker, an operative in the local bureau office supervising the next morning's operation.

"Looking forward to meeting you. Pick you up for dinner at six. Reservations at Smyrna's Sole Emporium. Call me if you don't like fish. We'll go somewhere else."

Paul was a steak man, but he enjoyed fish, especially in San Francisco. The no-nonsense message seemed to confirm what he'd heard about Coker—that he was a real take-charge guy. He was younger than Paul and had been a Navy SEAL. Paul felt sure they'd hit it off.

Coker pulled up in an agency sedan a minute before six and seemed pleased that Paul was waiting outside. He burst from the car and vigorously shook hands. He had short blond hair and red cheeks, stood about six feet, and was thick and solid. Paul guessed 225 pounds. "Hey, man—sir—I've heard great things about you," Coker said.

Paul smiled. They took 101 south, and when they got near the rebuilt Fisherman's Wharf, Coker began pointing out all the areas of interest, from the memorial to the destroyed Maritime Museum to the fully computerized interactive Fort Mason, and from the holographic Art Institute to the historic Cable Car Barn. He talked a hundred miles an hour, and Paul didn't have the heart to tell him that he probably knew as much about San Francisco as his host did.

"You know there aren't any fishing boats docking here anymore," Coker said. "They process the catches on freezer boats and deliver them directly to retailers and wholesalers."

"I know." To Paul, a city located between the Pacific Ocean on the west and San Francisco Bay on the east needed no promotion. It had once consisted of forty hills and was now made up of twenty. Coker insisted on driving up and down both Russian and Nob Hills, exulting about the sights, but still got them to the Wharf and Smyrna's in time for their reservation.

They were seated in a secluded corner, and Paul loved the ambiance—an old-world, dark-wood, linen-and-silver air of class. He could hardly believe Coker had chosen such an elegant restaurant. Maybe there was more to him than met the eye.

Over dinner they compared notes on their time in the military, with the usual jocular army/navy rivalry. "Now about tomorrow," Coker said finally, spreading papers on the table so Paul could get the right perspective. "These are aerial and land photos of the Polly Carr residence. That's her code name."

"So I've heard."

"Does it, like, mean something?"

Paul filled him in briefly.

"Weird. Wonder why they picked that."

"Not sure," Paul said. "Maybe because these people are asking for trouble, like Polycarp."

"I guess," Coker said. "Anyway, I'm gonna drive you by there tonight, give you the lay of the land. The neighborhood's mostly deserted, so we shouldn't have trouble with nosy nellies." He pointed to the aerial diagram. "We'll park nondescript vans here and here. You'll be with my squad and me in this one, about a block and a half south of her place on Twenty-fifth. You'll have a clear view of the house and people coming and going, and we have a monitoring card for you that will serve both as a tracking device and a relay of the audio from the bug inside the house to your molar receivers."

"Bug's already planted?"

"Two days ago."

"Great."

Coker gathered up the papers and packed them away. "If you don't mind, I want to go in with my people on the first wave, since we're used to working as a team."

"Makes sense," Paul said, disappointed.

"There'll be more than enough action," Coker said. "We're gonna have us some fun!"

"You expect resistance?"

Coker cocked his head. "Hey, the law's crystal clear—meeting to practice religion is forbidden. If they were unsure about it, they wouldn't be sneaking around in the dark."

"Any evidence of arms?"

"My instructions are to roust a widow and her group of anti-government plotters. I don't think we can just knock and expect them to come quietly. But if you're thinking 'excessive force,' don't worry. I got a team chomping at the bit, but everything will be by the book."

"I'm not worried. And the word's *champing.*"

"Huh?"

"The correct term is *champing* at the bit."

Coker laughed. *"Polycarp, champing* . . . that's another difference between the Army and the Navy. No vocabulary class in the SEALs, man."

"Sorry, I'm a bit of a wordsmith."

"I know, Professor. And tomorrow you'll get to see what SEAL training can do. My team and I will have these perps subdued quicker than you can say 'Delta Force.' Then you can play Scrabble with them, or whatever it is you're supposed to do."

• • •

Coker arrived at four the next morning in a plain white van with tinted windows. The damp cold cut through Paul, despite his hat, heavy overcoat, and gloves.

Coker rolled down the passenger-side window to let Paul know it was him, and when Paul climbed in, he noticed Coker wore navy from head to toe, including calf-high boots. His thick belt bore several compartments for everything from ammunition to Mace to handcuffs to a fifty-caliber Glock Century Three.

"Greet half our team," he said as he drove west on 101 toward Highway 1. "Ladies and gentlemen, Dr. Paul Stepola, our adviser from the Chicago office."

Four men and two women, all dressed like Coker and carrying Bayou Solar assault rifles, called out variations of "Good morning, Doctor" and "Good luck, sir." No one spoke further as Coker headed south on 1, west on Geary Boulevard, then north on Twenty-fifth Avenue, stopping short of California Street. There he cut the engine and affixed night-vision goggles to his head, handing a second pair to Paul and lowering his voice so his people couldn't hear.

"The other half of the team is in position with visual contact of the home. Two unit leaders, including myself, and twelve SWAT team members."

"How many attendees are we expecting?" Paul said.

"Most we have been aware of is twenty-three, sir."

"Paul."

"Here you go, Paul." Coker handed him what looked like a credit card with an embedded circuit board, which he had aligned with the frequency in Paul's molar-implanted receivers.

"You'll be able to hear all our transmissions, as well as the ones from the bug in the house. And it also tells us where you are, no matter what."

The fidelity was amazing. Through the night-vision goggles Paul detected no movement between them and the dark house. He heard an animal—probably a dog—padding around, whining quietly. He also heard the hum of what he assumed was the refrigerator and the tick of a clock.

About half an hour later he and Coker looked up when they heard more noise in the house. "Has to be the old lady," Coker said. "We're sure she lives alone."

The dog came to life when a light came on, and Paul heard running water as the woman fussed in the kitchen. She was clearly talking to the dog and filling water and food bowls.

Several minutes later, Coker said, "Bogey, three o'clock." Paul smiled at his calling the first visitor by the same term he would use for incoming enemy aircraft.

A tall, slight man in his early twenties approached the house. He wore modest-to-cheap clothes and a jacket too light for the weather. His hands were in his pockets.

The man knocked lightly three times on the front door. When the woman opened it, he said, "He is risen."

She responded, "He is risen indeed."

"Sounds religious to me," Coker said.

Paul recognized the phrase as an early church greeting, referring to Jesus.

What made two such ordinary, unprepossessing people—an old woman living with a dog in a ramshackle house and this nondescript shabby dresser whose very bearing seemed timid—join a forbidden group, given the danger? Neither seemed particularly bold or visionary or dangerous. *They're not firebrands*, Paul thought. *They're losers with empty lives they try to amp up with make-believe and the hope of some glorious reward after death. Secret meetings are their only excitement.*

But that didn't explain Andy Pass, who had a family, the respect of his colleagues, and an important, fulfilling career. And what about Paul's own father? He flushed at the thought.

"See something?" Coker said.

"No. These people make me sick. That's all."

Over the next fifteen minutes a score of visitors showed up, singly and in pairs. Paul noted a middle-aged couple, probably the oldest aside from the hostess. He guessed them to be in their late fifties. The man was thick and walked with a limp. The woman carried a large purse and appeared to be wearing a white uniform underneath a tattered coat.

"Could be armed," Coker said.

"Yeah," Paul said. "Bonnie and Clyde. What a couple of sad sacks."

"House could be a bomb shop, for all we know."

"Well, I think we're all here now," the elderly woman's voice said.

"All right!" said Coker, reaching for his helmet.

6

"LET'S START by passing around the Bible. Don't anyone take too long with it. As we wait for our turns, the rest of us can sing."

"That's it. The Bible is contraband," Coker said. "Let's roll."

"Wait," Paul said. "I want to hear this. We might catch what their game is."

It was as if Paul's textbooks had come alive. Meanwhile, those in the house sang.

Amazing grace! how sweet the sound—
That saved a wretch like me!
I once was lost but now am found,
Was blind but now I see.

"They'll see in a few minutes," Coker said. Paul heard him check with the other unit.

No question, a crime was in progress. But what was the point of it? What so gripped these people?

Now the woman was talking.

"Be encouraged, brothers and sisters. Here is the word of the Lord. 'Blessed are those who wash their robes so they can enter through the gates of the city and eat the fruit from the tree of life. . . . "I, Jesus, have sent My angel to give you this message for the churches. I am both the source of David and the heir to his throne. I am the bright morning star." . . . Let each one who hears them say, "Come." Let the thirsty ones come—anyone who wants to. Let them come and drink the water of life without charge. . . . He who is the faithful witness to all these things says, "Yes, I am coming soon!" Amen! Come, Lord Jesus!'

"And what is our instruction in light of this?" The woman read again, "'Therefore, go and make disciples of all the nations, baptizing them in the name of the Father and the Son and the Holy Spirit. Teach these new disciples to obey all the commands I have given you. And be sure of this: I am with you always, even to the end of the age.'"

"Protocol says we move now," Coker said. "The longer we sit, the more vulnerable we—"

"One more minute," Paul said. "She's getting down to it."

"So, dear ones, we are not alone," the woman was saying. "The Lord is with us, and many other believers are rising up, gathering, certain the end is near. We have all seen the signs that the coming of the Lord draws nigh. That's why we must be about our Father's business. We have critical tasks we must perform— despite the law, despite the danger—trusting God to give us courage. As Jesus told His disciples, 'The harvest is so great, but the workers are so few. So pray to the Lord who is in charge of the harvest; ask Him to send out more workers for His fields.'

"And why do we believe this, friends? Jesus Himself said,

'Look, I am coming soon! Blessed are those who obey the prophecy written in this scroll.' Later He said yet again, 'See, I am coming soon, and My reward is with Me, to repay all according to their deeds. I am the Alpha and the Omega, the First and the Last, the Beginning and the End.'"

These nuts talking about rising up made Paul's blood run cold. So they hoped to spread their poison all over the world—to "make disciples of all the nations." They were plotting something big, "despite the law, despite the danger," the woman said. And that idea that the end was near, that Jesus was coming soon—that was their justification for flat-out sedition.

"We've waited long enough," Coker said. "We're going in."

"Be careful. These people might be crazier than we think."

"Relax, Professor. We know what we're doing." Coker turned and motioned to his people to follow him.

He got out and moved around to Paul's window, giving him a thumbs-up. "Watch, listen, and learn," he said. He ran, leading his troops to join the others jogging toward the house.

In less than a minute, the house was surrounded. And from what Paul heard, no one inside had an inkling.

"I want to allow you all to be gone before sunup," the woman said, "so let's sing another hymn and close in prayer."

Coker raised his arm and swung his fist in a circle. No knocking, no announcement, no warning—as one, the SWAT team charged the house. Paul ripped off his goggles and leaped from the van to move closer. Windows were smashed, front and back doors rammed in, tear-gas canisters tossed. Screams filled the air.

Through his receivers, Paul heard the SWAT team members bellow encouragement to one another. Then a new sound—the unmistakable, unforgettable *whoosh-splat* of laser beams hitting human flesh. This was no raid; it was a shoot-out. These scruffy outcasts weren't just a bunch of deluded dreamers—they were armed with high-powered weapons.

Paul sprinted through the darkness, gun drawn. As he neared the porch, flamethrowers belched. The old woman came whirling out the front door, trailing a billowing sail of fire. The hideous, crackling, pinwheeling form and the smell of charring flesh stopped Paul. He dropped her into a hissing, smoking heap with a single shot.

An earsplitting cracking sound made the earth rumble. Low booms, growing in intensity, knocked Paul to his knees. *It's a bomb factory!*

"Coker!" Paul bellowed. "Get out!"

He caught a lurching flash of white at the side of the house— the white uniform he had last seen drooping from under a coat. The middle-aged couple had slipped out and were staggering away as fast as the man could limp. Paul fired and saw the white form sink, dragging the man down. Rocking forward on his knees, Paul fired again and the man was still.

The wood house twisted on its foundation, shrieking and splintering. A man burst through a front window, stumbling on the porch and staggering to the rail. As Paul took aim, the ground surged, knocking him onto his belly as he fired off a shot. He thought the ray caught the man in the chest as he vaulted off the porch.

Paul struggled to rise but the ground buckled again. It pounded against his belly like a huge heart beating at the earth's core. A crevasse burst open in front of him. He buried his head in his arms and rolled over the pitching ground into the street, down the hill—sliding, scrambling to his hands and knees when he could get purchase. He was more than halfway down the hill before he managed to stand and coax his battered limbs into a run, heaving and stumbling toward the bottom, now ringed with the gleaming blue lights of the San Francisco police Suburbans.

Two helmeted cops ran to help him, and he collapsed into their arms. Another deafening blast and a great underground heave knocked the three of them into a heap. As they disentangled, a final tremor and concussion sent debris raining from the top of the hill. They lay covering their faces until it settled. When at last they could stand, the top of the hill was invisible, clouded with smoke and dust in the foggy morning light.

As the cops helped Paul into an ambulance, he read their lips asking him what had happened. "Bomb," he choked out through puffy, bleeding lips, his ears too battered to tell whether he was making sounds. His eyes were swelling shut, and he could hardly bear to settle his bruised body onto the gurney. As medics hooked him to machines, one thought looped through the ache and ringing in his head: *What bomb could do that kind of damage?*

• • •

It was a miracle. That's what the doctors said about Paul's injuries—or the lack of them. "Nothing but cuts and bruises," one of them said. "You look a lot worse than you are."

Paul tried to remember that when he examined the purple mottling on his arms, legs, and torso through a pair of teacup-sized shiners. The coat and hat and gloves that saved him were in shreds before the doctors cut them off at the hospital. Paul insisted on saving the scraps.

His eardrums had ruptured, but with modern technology that required only a simple repair, done in the emergency room. He would need to be shielded from noise for about a week. That was a relief, because he was too banged up to endure more questions.

• • •

Jae's father had been enthusiastic about Paul's new job. "Exactly what he needs. Young guy like him, trained for the military— he's bound to get frustrated after a couple of years as a desk jockey. I wouldn't respect him if he didn't. I used to see it all the time in the agency. Jae, it will be the best thing for him."

So when Paul came home bruised and battered, Jae was dismayed but vowed to keep it to herself. It would be hard enough for the children to cope with an injured father—especially one as frightening to look at as Paul—without having to hear their parents fight about it. And what if her father was right? What if part of Paul's disaffection was the need for a new challenge, a chance to prove himself? He'd certainly shown his mettle. He was a hero. At this point their marriage was so rocky she was willing to accept almost anything that might revitalize it.

• • •

"A miracle," Koontz said, slamming the printout onto his desk. "That's what the subversives are claiming about the San Francisco explosion."

He and Paul sat in the safe room reviewing Operation Polly Carr after Paul's two weeks of sick leave. It had culminated in a kind of earthquake scientists had never seen, one that caused a panic even in a quake-protected city because it looked so much like a terrorist attack. The top of the hill had split, forming a crater into which the widow's house and a few abandoned ones nearby had disappeared. The strong wavelike tremors had uprooted trees and left cracks in the roadways, but had only minimally damaged other earthquake-fortified homes farther down the hill. Nonetheless these houses had to be evacuated until geological studies determined the hill was stable and, if possible, what had triggered the bizarre predawn convulsion of the earth.

"It was a bomb," Koontz said. "We just don't know what kind, and with the whole hilltop collapsed in on top of the house, I wonder if we'll ever find out. But it's obvious these people are more sophisticated and dangerous than we thought."

"What about all those NPO special weapons and tactics people?"

"All gone."

Paul shook his head. "That poor kid Coker. He was a real go-getter."

"We think the subversives all bought it too."

Paul leaned in closer. "There's something I want to tell you about that, Bob."

"Fire away."

"Coker and the team busted into the house—no announcement, no identification. They swarmed the place, attacked with flamethrowers, tear gas, Bayous with laser bayonets, and pulsar handguns—"

"That must have been something."

"It was! I heard shooting—friendly or not, I couldn't tell. As I ran to assist, the old lady came spinning out of the house. They had set her on fire. That was before I knew anything about a bomb."

Bob let out a big breath. "What are you saying?"

"Did we even know that they were armed? It was like those kids walked into a booby trap. So I shot the old lady."

"Sounds like you put her out of her misery."

"Then the bomb went off. Did we know it was there?"

"We had our suspicions."

"Why wasn't I informed?"

Koontz hesitated. "The commander of an operation like this

needs broad discretionary powers. Maybe the situation was too dicey for him to communicate much with you or the others. You just don't know."

"Well, I just kept shooting. I didn't even think about taking prisoners. I got three more of them—a nurse, maybe, and two guys trying to escape."

"Kill 'em?"

"Think so."

"Your first kills?"

"Yes."

Koontz smiled. "Rough. But don't let it bother you. You did what you were trained to do, and under fire. Listen, they would have died in the explosion anyway. You're the only survivor. In this day and age, few of us ever kill anyone. Look at it this way— the bomb went off. That's as close to proof as we'll ever get that there were terrorists in that house."

"Bob, I don't have regrets. It's about those kids, Coker and the rest. They didn't know, and they went up in smoke. They never had a chance."

Koontz nodded. "Guerrilla warfare. That's what we're up against."

7

THE MONDAY AFTER PAUL'S DEBRIEFING by Koontz was his first official day back at work. He arrived early to find Trina Thomas perched on Felicia's desk, legs crossed and a high-heeled pump dangling from one toe.

"Hey, good lookin'," she said. "I was just writing you a note. You look like you tangled with a cactus."

"Last week I looked like I tangled with a grizzly."

"Well, I'm sure you could lick a bear any day. But seriously, how do you feel?"

"Surprisingly good. Not even sore anymore, even if I am black and blue."

"It's very macho, I assure you. I came by to tell you I ran that sample a couple different ways while you were gone."

Paul unlocked his office door. "Come on in." When she was seated, he shut the door. "And so?"

"It's old paper of very high quality. Today what little paper we use is made of reconstituted fibers from the plastics that used to be considered indestructible. But at the turn of the century, paper had a high organic content—wood pulp, even cloth fibers. Cheaper papers were made of ground wood and tended to the acidic, so they yellowed and decayed quickly. Your sample is top grade, with a high rag or cotton content, which is why it's in such good shape."

"Is it possible to buy today?"

"Not that I know of. It hasn't been commercially available since the war. There's so much surplus plastic around, which is cheaper and easier to work with, and the final product is so much more stable. There may be craftspeople who produce organic paper in small batches for artwork or something. But spectroscopic analysis shows the fibers in your paper have started to break down to an extent that suggests that it's between thirty-five and fifty years old. The sample is gummed, too, treated with an adhesive activated by moisture. It's part of an envelope, right? They used to seal them by licking the gum."

"Ugh."

"Not as sanitary as our snap-dot seals and not as secure. Once you snap shut a modern security envelope, you can't open and reseal it without detection because the dots can never be exactly realigned. But back then, to be sure no one but the intended recipient opened it, they might also seal the envelope with a blob of wax. There are some traces on your sample."

"Interesting."

"So where does Jae think it came from?"

"Oh, ah, the genealogy project. Some relative during the war."

"Makes sense. Was a letter with it? Something important, I'd guess from the quality, and probably not electronically printed. Handwritten? Calligraphy?"

"I'll ask."

"You'd expect something that formal to be signed. And thirty-five years isn't that long ago. I'm surprised Jae's relatives can't identify the document."

"Listen, I really appreciate your taking the time to run all those tests."

"Let me know if Jae wants the ink tested. That would establish the age with more certainty. 'Course, you'd owe me a second lunch."

• • •

Paul half expected Trina to push on and guess who penned the letter. Forensics people were used to spinning whole scenarios out of small shards of evidence.

But if what she said was true, the letter could be real, a prospect that horrified Paul. It was hard to know which was worse—to discover he was the target of an agency sting operation or that the father he lionized had become the dupe of an evil cult.

But he had to know for sure—now more than ever, after his own near death. The ink was the key, Trina said, and handwriting analysis would add certainty. But Trina's intuition and curiosity could be a problem. The last thing Paul wanted was speculation about the letter all over the office.

But what about Angela Pass? According to her business card, she worked for the Library of Congress, which surely had the means to test the letter. He could write via the secure e-mail he used for dealing with informants, and she would have no way of knowing he was with the NPO. Now that the truth was out about Andy, the letter had no value to Ranold as a test of Paul's loyalty, but the old spymaster would probably still view him with suspicion. If Ranold *had* planted the letter, approaching Angela would be a good way to flush him out.

He dashed off a note to Angela, reiterating his pleasure at meeting her. Trading on the fact that they both had military fathers, he claimed to be working on a commemorative project for his father's platoon. Might she have a colleague who could identify the soldier who had written a certain letter by comparing two handwriting images he could scan and send her—and perhaps also help him get an age fix on the letter from an ink specimen?

Two can play the spy game.

And, Paul thought with a smile, asking Angela for help could fan a spark between them.

• • •

Jae had been surprised at how unwilling Paul was to talk to his father-in-law during his two weeks of recuperating at home. He claimed he was in too much pain. But now that he had been back to work a few days, he seemed to welcome Ranold's calls. Jae took that as a good omen—that Paul's new satisfaction on the job was promoting better relations with her father, which might also herald greater contentment for him at home.

• • •

Koontz urged Paul to ease back into his duties, but by the end of the week he was demanding a new assignment. "I want to keep my momentum," he said. "I can't do that hanging around the office. Put me back in the field."

Paul didn't confess his rage over Andy Pass—or his father— getting sucked in by the promise of "springs of life-giving water" or the threat that Jesus was coming soon. He couldn't purge his mind of the young, overzealous Coker grinning and giving him the thumbs-up before jogging into a bomb shop, or of the earth pitching and bucking as he tumbled down the hill. He relived shooting the burning woman, the white uniform, and the limping man; and he kept flashing back to that moment when his heat ray intersected the arc of the man diving off the porch. Paul's bruises were healing but his anger remained. How he wished he'd killed more, that he'd killed them all.

For a few days he had been distracted. First, there had been his thank-you-for-the-paper-analysis lunch with Trina Thomas, a languorous, wine-soaked afternoon culminating in a kiss that had left Paul relieved he'd had the sense not to place himself any further in her debt.

Angela had responded with delight in having heard from Paul and expressed her eagerness to help out his father's old platoon. He had immediately transmitted images of a few lines his father had written his mother and a sentence from the letter— *"One day you will hold your own child and understand the profound depth and breadth of a father's love"*—along with a snippet of the date at the top of the page for ink testing.

Then he'd given over a few evenings to cat-and-mouse discussions with Ranold, trying to determine whether the old man knew about the letter and his approaching Angela.

But now Paul was stir-crazy.

"Well," Koontz said finally, "we've got a situation in Gulfland. It's strictly fact-finding, but I'll send you with all the authority you need to question anybody at any level. You don't even have to take a weapon."

"I appreciate it, Bob, but don't baby me."

"Fair enough. But this one should be easy." Koontz handed him a folder. "Oil country. A gusher there suddenly stopped pumping and caught fire."

"I'm not an oilman, Bob. Is that unusual?"

"Must not be, other than being a nuisance for the investors, but what's happening now is without precedent. It's not some underground flare-up but a pillar of fire a couple hundred feet high."

"Sounds dangerous. Why can't they put it out?"

Koontz raised both hands. "Foam isn't working, and they can't figure a way to cap it. It's another 'inexplicable occurrence' the crazies will have a field day with. People who see these things talk, and then rumors spread like wildfire. Personally, I think it's got to be some sort of industrial sabotage."

"This I gotta see."

"How does first thing tomorrow morning sound?"

8

PAUL HAD ALWAYS BEEN privately amused by the Gulfland
NPO bureau chief. Most of the chiefs Paul had met were fairly
buttoned-down bureaucratic types. Lester "Tick" Harrelson
was about five-foot-six and 140 pounds. He had a shock of dry
hair through which he was constantly—and ineffectively—running a hand. His tie was loose, and he had trouble keeping his
shirt tucked in. But he was a pro, and his people worshiped him.

Tick and Donny Johnson, president of Sardis Oil and Tick's
polar opposite, met Paul at the gate at Bush International in
Houston. All Tick and Donny had in common were cowboy
boots and hats and a commitment to the problem at hand.
Johnson was a big man with a long gait, and while it appeared he
would be more comfortable in a workingman's clothes, his suit
was clearly custom-made.

"Good to see you again, Doctor," Tick said, introducing him to the oil magnate. "Welcome back. Glad you're back in the saddle. This boy's a hero, Donny."

Donny Johnson looked approvingly at the bruises on Paul's face. He all but crushed Paul's hand when they shook. "Sure could use a hero 'bout now."

"Well, I—"

"Used to call that well my Spindletop. Now it's nothin' but cash money burnin' up."

Tick interpreted. "Spindletop was the original Texas gusher, the one that put us on the map way back when. Pumped a hundred thousand barrels a day, or so they say."

Johnson shook his head. "We do double that now with geomagnetics, but in the old days that was somethin'. Biggest gusher the world ever saw. A miracle, they say—which is what they're callin' my well fire now and gettin' folks all worked up."

"Who's calling it a miracle?"

"That's for you to tell us, mister. Not even forty-eight hours and it's already out over the Internet. And when you find 'em—" he clenched huge fists—"I'm fixin' to beat their brains out."

"Figuratively, of course," Tick said. "Religious activity alone is punishable by law. Sabotage—"

"By law?" Johnson said. "We have our own ideas about law in Texas."

Tick looked as if he'd heard this before. "Let's show Paul what's going on."

The three climbed into a stretch limo at the curb. Though it was only March, Paul was sweating in his wool suit, even in the air-conditioned car. He took off his jacket. "Loosen your tie," Tick said, but Paul declined.

Houston had long been one of the most populated cities in the country and had recently passed Chicago for third place behind Los Angeles and New York. In the distance Paul saw some of the tallest buildings in the world, giving the port city a dramatic skyline. The windows of most of the skyscrapers were reflective, countering the relentless sun, and the glare gave the city an ethereal golden glow.

The Sardis Oil field was a two-hour drive from the airport. "This is not my area, Mr. Johnson," Paul said as they left the suburban sprawl and headed into open country. "My questions may sound stupid."

"Nothin' sounds stupid out here, mister. I've been in oil all my life and I can't explain this."

"Tell me about this well."

"This here's a production well, as opposed to a wildcat well. Wildcats are the ones we sink when we're looking for oil trapped in reservoirs. Once we find a reservoir, we drill production wells. With geomagnetics, we don't need a lot of roughnecks on a crew, but by the time a well like this starts pumpin' oil, we've sunk millions into it."

"How often do oil wells catch fire?"

"Happens, but it's rare. Nowadays, the cause is almost never mechanical. Sometimes lightnin' will strike a well. Sometimes the fire is set. Like now."

"You seem sure."

"The Mexicans were behind it."

"Let's say it *was* a foreign faction," Paul said. "How would they do it?"

"Not just foreign—Mexican," Johnson said. "They work up here, learn our technology enough to sabotage it, thinkin' that'll help their sorry little oil business. Or maybe the A-rabs put 'em up to it. Those boys would just love to see us go back to the Middle East for oil."

"Paul's here as our religious expert," Tick said. "The rumors

about miracles suggest there's a Christian threat—that this may
be a Christian terrorist act."

"Christians, Mexicans, A-rabs—I don't care. Somebody's got
to pay."

• • •

The oil field lay about ten miles off the freeway. When the driver
rolled down his window to check in at the gate, a smoky chemi-
cal smell invaded.

"Whoa!" Paul coughed. "You could get high just breathing
out here."

"No joke," Donny said. "It'll make you sick if you breathe it
too long."

"Downwind you get the real pollution," Tick said. "The
draft, or superplume, from a fire this big goes up thousands of
feet into the atmosphere. The winds up there disperse the
smoke hundreds of miles away—out over the Gulf, if we're
lucky."

The limo wheeled close to the fiery well, which was surrounded by a fence and guarded by two men wearing hazmat
suits and carrying laser Bayous.

"We won't be stayin' long enough to need the suits," Donny
said. "They're too doggone hot. But we've got goggles and masks
and coats."

He tapped on the interior window. The driver lowered it and
passed back a bag of equipment, three long canvas dusters, and a
Stetson hat.

Donny distributed the masks and goggles and coats, then
handed the hat to Paul. "Keeps off the sun and the worst of the
soot."

Even through Paul's hazmat mask, the air was acrid, and it
felt gritty. His shirt soaked through in minutes under the heavy

canvas coat. The fire sounded unearthly—not the familiar snap and crackle of a wood fire but rather an uprush of wind whirling to a keening wail high overhead—what Paul imagined a tornado would sound like up close.

The fire itself impressed him most. About eighteen inches in diameter, it was a column of pure white, its leaping and ebbing flames stretching high into the sky. Through the scrim of heat waves, the white fire looked pearlescent, hypnotic, beautiful.

"Is this a typical well fire?" Paul shouted.

"No way," Donny Johnson said. "Usually all you see is heavy smoke. Nothin' like this."

"What do your techies say about it?"

"They took samples and they'll be back today, but they got nothin' to say yet. No one's ever seen anything like this before. First there was lots of smoke. Then it just shot right out of the ground like a white gusher. We've got witnesses who can tell you all about it."

Paul could almost understand how the weak-minded or impressionable might regard something this mysterious and haunting as a miracle.

Got to be sabotage.

Johnson pointed back to the car. "Let's get these fool masks off."

Back in the car, the men wiped their faces. "How far from this well do we have to be to risk breathing outside without a mask?" Paul said.

"About a quarter mile, and even then you can smell it. Base camp should be okay."

Johnson had the driver take them through a nearby field where more wells dotted the landscape.

"You've tightened security to protect these?" Paul said.

"We've added a couple of armed sentries at each entrance, on top of our regular guards. We also have electrified razor wire atop the fences. And alarms, of course."

• • •

From the comfort of the air-conditioned car, they surveyed the wells for nearly an hour, eating box lunches of spicy gazpacho soup and thick slabs of roast beef and ham on sourdough bread.

"Meat's from my ranch," Donny said. "Better grub than we'd get at the camp."

Finally the limo pulled up to the gate of a fenced-in compound on a stretch of land without a tree or so much as a blade of grass. Inside were three low, oblong cinder-block buildings flanking a larger square one. A fourth oblong building had apparently been recently completed. It still had stickers on its windows and flats of construction materials nearby.

"Field headquarters," Johnson said. "Roughnecks and guards both work seven straight days, then have three days off with their families in Beaumont or Houston. Workdays they bunk out here in the barracks." He gestured to the oblong buildings. "We have two rotating crews, each pullin' a twelve-hour shift, and when they're not sleepin' they stay busy. Each man has his own room with a bed and sink and entertainment center; there's a common room in each barracks so they can play cards and such; and here behind our offices—" he pointed at the square building—"is a mess hall and gym."

"Nice setup."

"Expensive, but we gotta have it. Keeps the men productive. Buncha guys cooped up in the middle of nowhere—well, they don't call 'em roughnecks for nothin'."

"We've got everyone who was working the well that caught fire isolated in the new building," Tick said. "It blew on the third

day of their work cycle so no one's expecting them home yet.
Easier to keep them here for questioning before going through
the formality—" he winked at Paul—"of detaining them in
town."

"I see," Paul said. "Easier to keep a lid on the rumors. You'd
have to release them soon, especially if lawyers got involved.
And once they were home, who knows what tales they'd tell."

Tick smiled. "Their rooms have been searched—company
property, you know—their phones have been confiscated and
their implants disabled. Everyone will be incommunicado until
we get to the bottom of this. I've got agents interviewing them
right now."

• • •

After dropping Johnson at the office, the limo delivered Tick and
Paul to the new barracks. Tick paused at the door. "What role do
you want here, Paul? Being on the new Zealot Underground task
force, I mean."

"I'll observe the interrogations, looking for any religious
angle."

"You know what?" Tick said. "I don't think it's related."

"No? You'd be surprised how cunning and dangerous these
people are."

"They're a new threat we're all going to have to get up to
speed on. You want to question people yourself?"

"Only if I hear something interesting."

"You have free rein."

"By the way," Paul said, "what exactly were we looking for
when we searched the witnesses' rooms?"

Tick shrugged. "Anything out of the ordinary, I guess. I
couldn't begin to tell you what could cause a disaster like this."

The door opened into the common room, where some

twenty men sat on folding chairs under the watch of guards. One quadrant seemed reserved for the Mexicans, who sat huddled. Two long folding tables; a huge video screen, now dark; and a full trash can were the only fixtures. The building was not yet ready for occupation.

Midway down each sidewall of the common room was a corridor. The NPO supervisor, Dirk Jefferson, emerged from the one on the left. He greeted Tick and Paul warmly and drew them back down the hallway, which was lined on both sides with open doors. In each room Paul saw a disheveled cot with its head pushed under the window, separated by a four-foot aisle from a sink and a built-in armoire with four drawers. Everything smelled of fresh paint. Paul assumed these cells were not yet equipped with their entertainment centers.

Out of earshot of the men, Tick filled Paul in. "Johnson had the sense to round them all up right after the well blew. None of them has left the building for forty-eight hours." He pointed toward the corridors. "We're using the rooms at the far end of each hall for questioning. There was some Internet buzz, but we clamped down fast and tight enough to keep the press off it."

A voice bellowed from the common room. "Lay off, man!" Tick, Paul, and Jefferson raced down the hallway to find one of the Mexicans on the floor groaning, clutching his foot, his nose bloodied and tears streaming. One of the guards cradled an injured arm while another had his Taser trained on a burly man.

"What's going on?" Tick barked.

No one spoke until Tick stepped up to confront the injured guard.

"Uh, Lloyd here was picking on the Mexicans," the guard said. "Think he busted my wrist."

As Tick turned to the burly man, the Mexican on the floor said, "Lloyd wasn't picking on nobody, man."

"What's your story, Lloyd?"

The big man raised his eyes to the ceiling and said nothing.

"Let's hear it, Lloyd," Tick said. "Now."

"Someone stomped on this guy's foot and started smacking him around. I was just trying to break it up."

Looking around, Tick said, "We'll get a medic to look at you two. But hear this: The next man out of line—roughneck or guard—is going to face prosecution. And you, Mr.—"

"Lloyd. Stephen Lloyd."

"Have you been questioned yet?"

"No, sir."

"Well, I think it's time. Jefferson?"

9

PAUL HEADED DOWN THE HALL to observe, curious about Stephen Lloyd. Maybe he was a hero, maybe a troublemaker. If Lloyd had intervened in a good cause, assailing an armed guard was still reckless, considering all the help at hand right down the hall. Standing fearlessly on principle could be noble or hotheaded, but it was also typical extremist behavior.

Jefferson sat behind a table, facing the door, nearly hidden by Stephen Lloyd's broad back. Paul guessed Lloyd at six-foot-three and at least 250 pounds. He wore a white T-shirt and light-colored jeans over high-laced tan boots. His yellow helmet lay on his stomach with his hands folded on top of it. He had long-ish blond hair and was, of course, deeply tanned.

Paul nodded at Jefferson over Lloyd's shoulder and leaned back against the doorjamb.

Jefferson checked a paper. "Mr. Lloyd, you are from Childress?"

"Like I told you folks yesterday."

"Long way from home."

"Over four hundred miles. You go where the work is."

"And you're how old?"

"Twenty-five."

"Athlete?"

"High school football."

"Didn't play college ball?"

Lloyd shook his head. "Grades."

"Stephen, why did you attack the guard?"

"He was beating on the Mexicans."

"And why do you suppose he was doing that?"

"Probably thinks they had something to do with the fire."

"Why do people think that?"

"Got me. Guess everybody needs somebody to pick on. No-body wants to think this could be anything an American would do. But I don't think the Mexicans had anything to do with it."

"Who then?"

"Nobody I know."

"You're an oilman. What do you make of this fire? How does it happen?"

"I'm not an oilman. I'm a roughneck. Do what I'm told. Stuff below the ground is beyond me."

"You must have an opinion."

Stephen sighed. "It won't help you much. I think it's some-thing natural. Something in nature."

Jefferson cocked his head. "Something that's never hap-pened before in recorded history."

"You asked."

Jefferson emptied an envelope onto the table. "This your wallet?"

"Yes, sir."

"Your keys?"

"Yes, sir."

"And how about this? What's this?" Jefferson held up a dull gray coin attached to a leather strap.

Stephen shrugged, but Paul saw the muscles tense in his back. "Call it a good-luck charm."

"You carry it for luck?"

"You could say that."

An old-fashioned book was engraved on it, and Jefferson peered at it. "I haven't seen one of these since I was a kid. What's that about?"

"Just a book."

"You're not old enough to remember books. You a reader?"

"Not much."

Jefferson riffled through the wallet, then slid all three items back into the envelope. Stephen relaxed again.

"Let me see that," Paul said.

Stephen seemed to stiffen as Paul took the envelope. Paul pulled out the medallion and turned it over. The engraved book was open. What was that behind it? A quill? *No, that would be in front of the book, not in the background.* Then Paul recognized it— a palm frond—and knew what it meant.

"Why don't you and I take a walk, Mr. Lloyd."

• • •

The afternoon shadows were lengthening. Paul led Stephen away from the building to the skids of leftover cinder blocks and beams. "I recognize that medallion," Paul said.

Stephen jammed his hands into his pockets and shrugged.

"I think it identifies you."

Stephen rubbed his face with both hands, but still the color seemed to drain from him.

"You know, it's not unique," Paul pressed, "carrying some token so people like you can recognize one another."

Stephen put his hands on his hips and closed his eyes, turning his face toward the sun.

"And when you told Jefferson he could say you carried the medallion for luck, you meant that in an entirely different way than he meant it, didn't you?"

Stephen lowered his face and opened his eyes, staring at Paul.

"And when you said the oil phenomenon was something natural, you meant supernatural, didn't you?"

The big man grimaced, as if unsure how to respond.

"Word is it's a sign," Paul said. "A miracle."

Paul felt like a hunter circling his prey. He flashed back angrily on the Christian service in San Francisco, the widow speaking of "signs that the coming of the Lord draws nigh" and the "tasks we must perform—despite the law, despite the danger." And he thought of the greeting—the password—of the believers.

"Listen to me, Stephen. He is risen."

Sweat broke out on the big man's brow. "Who is risen?" Lloyd whispered.

Paul felt they were both teetering on a precipice now. *Will he deny it?* "Christ is risen."

Lloyd covered his mouth with a hand, then pulled it away just enough to whisper hoarsely, "Who did you say?"

Paul parroted the phrases that he could call to mind from the service. "The one who says 'I am the root and the offspring of David, and the bright and morning star.' The one who says 'Let him who is thirsty come.'"

Stephen Lloyd seemed hardly able to stand still. Paul drew on the words of the letter from his own father, which were etched on his brain: "'He will lead them to the springs of life-giving water. And God will wipe away all their tears.'"

Lloyd was gasping. Paul moved to the clincher. "The one who reminds us, in Revelation, 'I am coming soon.'"

"He is risen indeed," Lloyd croaked.

Bingo!

Lloyd clutched at Paul, almost sobbing. "Man oh man, brother, I've never been tested that way. You never know if you'll have the courage . . . I almost didn't make it. . . ." He wiped his eyes with his wrist.

"It's tough being isolated," Paul said. "Stuck out here, bearing witness to such an awesome sign . . . I hope you haven't been completely alone."

"Thank God, no," Lloyd whispered.

"There are others like us?"

"Some. Mexicans, mostly. They tend to keep to the old ways. But the rest of these people. Can you believe 'em? Trying to blame this on Mexicans, Arabs, sabotage. I mean, are you kiddin' me? A pillar of fire, man! If that's not God, who is it?"

They were interrupted by the approach of a limousine.

"Hey there," Donny Johnson called, unfolding his big body from the backseat. In his cowboy hat he towered over even Stephen Lloyd. "How's it goin'?"

"Fine," Paul said. "I'm making an arrest."

Stephen Lloyd jerked back.

"Who? You?" Johnson demanded. He grabbed Stephen's arms. "You're the arsonist?"

"No, no, I—"

"He's a Christian," Paul spat. "I want him in custody—"

"Why, you scum—" Johnson drew back and slugged Lloyd in the gut, doubling him over. He yanked him up by the hair, cursing and pummeling him with his free hand. At the commotion, Tick and Jefferson came running out of the barracks.

"Johnson, stop!" Tick shouted, jumping to grab his arm. Johnson wrenched free, his hat flying, and again set upon Lloyd, pushing him back into the cinder blocks. Before Tick could stop him, Johnson had snatched up a block and started brutally bludgeoning the roughneck.

"You'll kill him!" Jefferson flung himself at Johnson, trying to wrestle him away. "Help me!" he yelled at Paul, who had been watching with satisfaction. Johnson was only doing what Paul wished he could do without losing his job. Paul moved in slowly just as Johnson, finally out of steam, dropped the cinder block.

"What's wrong with you, man?" Jefferson demanded, panting, aiming the question as much at Paul as at Johnson.

Tick knelt in the dust to examine the still figure on the ground, his T-shirt and jeans dark with dirt and blood. He looked up. "I can't get a pulse, Donny. I'm going to have to place you under arrest."

Johnson snorted and his body went slack. He had popped the armhole seams of his expensive shirt. "Lost my head. A Christian, rabble-rousin', sabotagin'—"

"Who told you that?" Tick said.

"Lloyd confessed to me," Paul said. "That gives the Zealot Underground task force jurisdiction. Leave Johnson to me. I want his help. Round up every Mexican on this oil field for interrogation. And march that group in the barracks out here now."

• • •

Seven Mexicans stood shoulder to shoulder in two rows, hemmed in by four large guards.

"Where's the one with the busted foot?" Paul said.

JERRY JENKINS • 83

A guard pushed him from the back row, and he stumbled, limping on a newly molded plastic-foam cast.

Paul grabbed his arm and hustled him over to Stephen's bloodied body. "You see your friend here?"

The man nodded.

"You know what killed him? His alliances. And he told me that he had a lot of company on the Mexican crew. You a Christian?"

No answer.

"You don't deny it? Think you're brave? It's a simple question. Are you a Christian?"

Silence.

"Tough guy, huh? Stephen was tough too, but look at him now. I know—and you know—who's behind the fire."

Paul shoved the man to his knees. "I want names." He pressed his gun to the back of the man's head. "You've got five seconds."

One of the Mexicans behind them sobbed.

"Do I hear a name?" Paul called out. "Your man is about to die."

A Klaxon blasted. They all spun toward the sound, and Paul saw an eruption of smoke in the distance.

Johnson cursed. "Not another one!"

He whirled and bounded toward the limo. Paul sprinted after him, grabbing the back-door handle just as Johnson was sliding into the front seat beside the driver. Diving onto the floor, Paul clawed the back door shut as the limo sped off. He pitched and rolled until the car cleared the rough terrain and reached the road, and then he managed to get settled on the seat.

On the floor in the back lay the gritty dusters they had worn that morning, along with the hat Johnson had loaned Paul. Despite the acrid soot on the coats, Paul put one on. He found the one he'd worn, his mask and goggles stuffed in the pocket. Smoke filled the air as they neared the site.

The car paused at a gate, which was flung open by masked sentries streaked with soot. "Turn off that alarm," Johnson bellowed out the window. "No one lets in the fire crew till I say so! Get a roll call and search everyone right now!"

Already, out along the perimeter fence, guards rounded up the roughnecks—some masked, others bare-chested, shirts tied over their faces. The crew was apparently moving too slowly for one guard, so he whipped out a Laser Taser that fired thin strands of barbed wire in an arc of about twenty feet. When the barbs caught clothing or skin, they transmitted an electrical charge that made the men scream and scramble into position.

The driver shot forward but soon had to slow when the windows clouded over. Windshield airjets could do only so much against oily grit. Johnson didn't seem daunted. He slipped on goggles and a mask and borrowed the chauffeur's cap.

The driver lowered the interior window.

"Give me one of those coats, Stepola," Johnson said. "The biggest one."

"What are you doing, Johnson?" Paul said. "Just call out the fire crew and wait in the car. You're under arrest."

"I'm the law out here, mister, not the NPO." He brandished a Walther Stealth. "Try to stop me, I'll kill you."

Paul held up his hands. "You're insane, walking into a fire."

Johnson opened his window a crack. "There's an updraft. Just wait five minutes," he told the chauffeur. "I'm gonna catch me a terrorist."

Smoke rushed into the car when Johnson opened the door. The chauffeur buried his head in his arm and coughed. Paul, his own goggles around his neck, put on his mask.

"We've got to stop him," he told the driver. He flicked the tip of his thumb against his pinkie repeatedly, trying to activate his molar implants. No signal. Something was scrambling the frequencies. "Can you call for help?"

The chauffeur was putting on a mask. He tried to raise a signal on the car phone. Nothing.

"I'm going after him," Paul said.

"Mister, I'd give him the five minutes. He knows this field like the back of his hand. You get lost, we'll get killed chasing after you."

Paul hesitated, then stayed where he was. *Tick and the others saw the explosion. They had to have called the fire crew.*

Long minutes passed. Paul and the chauffeur, mouths and noses shrouded, sat in silence.

After ten minutes Paul couldn't stand to wait any longer. "Johnson is a rancher. Would he have a rope in the car?"

"In the trunk."

Goggles on, draped in the coat, mask tight over his mouth and nose, Paul made his way to the trunk. He found a large coil of emergency-orange rope, tied one end around his waist, and handed the rest to the chauffeur. "Keep the window open a little so you can spool this out as I go. I'll yank every other minute or so. If you don't feel a yank after more than a couple of minutes, pull me back."

Near the car the smoke was relatively thin, just an oily haze. "Johnson!" Paul called out, scanning the ground. Up ahead the air looked denser. The well had to be that direction. Paul wondered how effective his mask would be in heavy smoke.

The car was soon hidden as Paul penetrated deeper into the cloud. He swiped at his goggles with his sleeve. He cut a zigzag path straight ahead on the road, then cut an arc to the left, swung back to the road, and cut an arc to the right—sweeping the ground in search of a fallen man.

"Johnson!" he yelled, voice muffled.

Paul kept stopping, trying to get his bearings, peering into the fog. Even his sense of time was distorted. *Count out loud.* He chanted numbers, pausing each time he reached one hundred to yank the rope.

"*John*-son!"

On one of his zigzags, he discovered a wider apron of concrete. He had to be getting closer to the well.

The wind picked up and smoke swirled around Paul. In the distance he heard a growing whir. He yanked his hat tighter and resecured his mask, tugging at the rope to reassure himself of his tether. His vision dimmed as the mounting winds caked oily soot on his goggles. He tried to rub it off, leaving them so smeared he could hardly see at all.

The whirring grew louder, faster. *That tornado sound.*

A hint of light, a flare, a sputter. *What's going on?*

Paul frantically scrubbed his goggles with his sleeve, fighting panic. The winds began to wail. *What is it?*

Finally, he had to see it. Shielding his eyes with his arms, he yanked his goggles down.

A blaze of light blasted away the smoke. A white jet of flame shot to the sky. Searing heat. A pillar of fire. Pain. *A white gusher.*

• • •

White jeans, white shirt, white cowboy hat. Everyone else was flamboyantly dressed, so the figure didn't even stand out at the Houston Cheetah Racetrack. The gleaming glass-and-steel structure south of the city was a giant, modernistic bowl with three tiers of tracks, hundreds of betting windows, and seats for the tens of thousands who came to watch the exotically beautiful, fastest-running land creatures in the world.

Ringing the seats and tracks were gardens interspersed with a range of restaurants, from Houston's finest to humbler tourist haunts. At precisely eight o'clock the figure in white found a table at one of the latter, Horatio's House of Ribs, and ordered a full slab, coleslaw, potato salad, and a black cow. Waiting for his food, the figure turned over the paper "Texas History Quiz" place mat and began to jot the day's events: the brutal killing of Stephen Lloyd; the roughnecks' detention at the Sardis Oil field; the unknown whereabouts of its owner, the well-known magnate Donny Johnson; and the second mysterious conflagration.

When the food came, the place mat was right side up, and the figure was checking off answers to the multiple-choice quiz questions.

When the white-clad figure was gone, the place mat was left folded in half, quiz side up—all filled in, every fact correct—with the empty soda glass placed directly over a picture of Spindletop and enough cash to cover the bill.

Before dawn every media outfit in the state had a helicraft circling the Sardis Oil field, capturing the striking image of the two white columns of flame against the dark sky. Newscasts around the world led with the story: "Texas Mystery: Twin Pillars of Fire."

10

PAUL FELT conflicting sensations and dreamed strange dreams. At times he felt afire. Moments later he shook uncontrollably from cold. He was vaguely aware when he was jostled, moved, lifted, settled, strapped. He heard voices but couldn't make them out. He was aware of crying out in pain; then another compressed air injection brought the floating, mellow feeling, rendering him so drowsy he felt he could sleep forever.

The image of a blast of white light was implanted on his brain. Whenever he roused, it jolted him. *Soot. Can't breathe. Smoke. The exploding well. The white gusher.* Terror.

He was moved from a vehicle and was now outside. His skin was so tender he wanted to scream, but he could not make a sound. He was covered, but cold wind sliced through him to the bone. Now he was on a gurney, rolling over uneven ground. On a ramp. Bumping, almost tipping. Whining engine sounds. An airport? A plane? Was he going home?

More voices. Someone was referred to as Doctor and Doc. Were they talking to Paul himself? He could not respond. Another injection and sweet relief. Drifting, drifting . . . and he was gone into dreams of his family. Jae and Brie and Connor embracing him, welcoming him home. Driving to work, but Felicia was now his boss. Then she was in flames, and the Chicago bureau's building crashed into the river.

• • •

When Paul awoke, his head was clearer, his senses acute. His eyes were bandaged snugly, and he felt gauze circling his head. His scalp was cold, and he was sure his hair was gone. Unmistakable hospital smells. The heavy padded steps of thick-soled shoes.

Paul felt the clear, irritating pain of an IV shunt in his right hand. His lips were cracked and dry, but when he licked them he tasted petroleum jelly. An oxygen feed irritated his nostrils. He swallowed and tried to clear his throat. Paul's whole body ached, and though he sensed he had not moved in hours, he was sleepy.

"Water."

But no one was there. He felt for a button, but through the tape he couldn't make out anything.

"Where am I?" he tried, louder.

Someone hurried in. The voice of a young woman. "Are you awake, Dr. Stepola?"

"Am I in Houston?"

"Oh no, sir. You're in PSL Hospital in Chicago."

"PSL?"

She sounded conspiratorial. "Well, years ago it was Presbyterian-St. Luke's, but of course they don't call it that anymore."

She pressed a tiny sponge between his lips and he bit eagerly, sending cool water across his tongue and down his throat. He coughed. "More."

"Slowly."

"Is my hair gone?"

"I'll get your doctor."

"Tell me that. I can take it."

"Temporarily, yes. And it looks rather striking, if I may say."

"Am I burned?"

"You were." He heard pages turning. "But you were lucky."

"Lucky?"

"You had on a hat and mask. Your hands were inside your sleeves. You must have used your arms to shield your face, except for the line from your eyes to your ears."

"What about my eyes?"

Her hesitation pierced him. "I'll have to get your doctor. He wanted to know when you were conscious anyway."

She gave him a little more water and hurried out. Within minutes he heard two sets of footsteps.

"Hey, Paul!" It was Koontz. "You are one tough customer. I'm starting to think you've got nine lives."

"Not funny, Bob."

"It's no joke, buddy. Listen, your wife and your father-in-law will be in to see you soon. And when you're ready for it, the kids, of course."

"Bob—"

"This is Dr. Raman Bihari—a top eye specialist who will also oversee your general care."

Paul felt a hand laid gently on his left biceps. "Dr. Stepola?" A male Indian accent.

"Yes. What's wrong with my eyes? I want the truth."

"I will be very frank with you about your vision. After your burns were assessed and treated, I performed a procedure that allowed me access to your eyes. Your lids had been badly burned, but fortunately, technology has advanced to where we believe they will look and function normally."

"I'm less concerned about my eyelids than my eyes, frankly—"

"Of course, and so am I. The truth is that you apparently took actual flame directly into your pupils in both eyes. There is considerable damage that may only be able to be rectified through transplant surgery. But the body is an amazing self-healing mechanism. My plan is to monitor you carefully, but keep your eyes medicated and covered for approximately two months to see how much natural restoration may take place on its own. Then we will decide on surgery."

"But for now I'm blind?"

"With or without the bandages, yes, sir."

"What's your best guess about my vision returning?"

The doctor drew in a long breath. "I hesitate to speculate. . . ."

"Tell me."

"My guess is that there is a better than 90 percent chance that you will require transplant surgery in order to have any return of vision."

"Then why not just do that now?"

"The odds against success would be just as bad if we didn't wait for your body to heal the retinal area itself."

"And if it doesn't do that?"

"Even the transplant surgery would be futile."

"Tell me. How common is it that the body heals itself enough to make transplant surgery viable in cases like mine?"

"I'm sorry. It is very rare. I never give up hope because you never know, and as I say, the body is amazing. But it is very possible that nothing more can be done."

"What will I be able to see? Fuzzy images? Shadows? Anything?"

"Without significant restoration, you would not be aware even of shades of light."

• • •

Dr. Bihari called in help so Paul could get out of bed. Paul had heard of the other senses becoming hyperacute when one went blind or deaf, but he was astounded at how quickly this manifested itself. It was as if he could hear everything on the floor. He was also supersensitive to touch and felt the draft under his gown.

He immediately became demanding. "I need a robe. I'm not going another step in this getup."

A few minutes later he was changed and back in bed. "Bob, get everybody else out of here and shut the door."

"You want to wait and talk when Jae and your father-in-law—?"

"Do I sound like I want to wait?"

Paul made him pull a chair close. "Bob, I want to know what happened in Gulfland."

"You have a right to know. Another oil well caught fire. Johnson's chauffeur said Johnson went to check it out but never came back. You tied a rope around your waist before you went out into the smoke to save him. That was good thinking, because then the well blew. The chauffeur was trying to drag you back when fire rescue showed up. They followed the rope and found you. After the docs got you stabilized, we flew you back here. You've been in and out of consciousness for about a week."

"What happened to Johnson?"

"Didn't make it. Smoke inhalation."

"I let him go out there, Bob. I should have stopped him."

"We know from Tick that he had a gun and he'd just beaten a man to death. Suicide is not in your job description. You did the right thing."

"Tick told you what led up to it?"

"He said you were sweating a suspect when the horn went off." Koontz hesitated. "Tell you the truth, Tick is catching major heat on this one. The word leaked about the second well. It was all over the news even before Johnson's body was found. And of course, a death like that couldn't be kept quiet. Half the country seems to think this is some kind of miracle, and the other half wants to fire the entire NPO for failing to foresee and prevent terrorism. People upstairs believe Tick botched this. He's been encouraged to take a leave of absence."

"What a mess."

"He's got a daughter to visit in Australia. But he's really torn up about Johnson's death and about you. Your injuries, I mean."

"I don't want his pity. Yours either."

"Easy. All I'm saying is that people care."

"Caring won't bring my sight back."

"Paul, you're getting tired." He heard Koontz stand and move his chair. His voice came from farther away now. "Get some rest before Jae gets here."

"It bothers you that I'm angry? Losing my whole life—job and everything—shouldn't upset me?"

"Paul, it's going to take time to adjust. I don't blame you for how you feel. I want to help. I'll spend every off-hour here, if that's what it takes. And don't worry about your job. No matter what, there's a place for you in my shop."

"Yeah, right."

• • •

Paul wanted to think rather than sleep, but he couldn't bear the pain. When he was given medication he slept soundly. He awoke early that afternoon, still trapped in darkness but feeling the warmth of the sun through the window, even through his bandages.

"Hey there, chief." It was Ranold. Why did everyone feel they had to sound jolly for him? "I've got a young lady here who'd like to see you."

"Jae?"

"Hi, honey." She stepped close. "I've been so scared. I'm so glad you're going to be all right."

"I'm not going to be all right. There's almost no chance I'll ever be able to see again."

"The doctor said that?"

"Don't believe me? Ask him. There are things they can try, but it will take time."

"How much time?"

"At least two months. I'll be here awhile."

"Well," Ranold said, "I think we should hear it from the doctor. Let's get him in here. What's his name?"

"Bihari."

"What kind of a name is that?" Ranold said.

"Indian."

"Great. They can't even give a government agent an American doctor?"

"He sounds knowledgeable."

"Yeah? Well, they all talk a good game."

A few minutes later, Dr. Bihari was forthright with Jae and Ranold about Paul's prospects. Paul heard Jae crying.

"Turn off the waterworks," Paul said, "and stop feeling sorry for yourself."

"Oh, Paul, this just makes me so sad. I know you're strong enough to cope with this, but it will be hard—"

"Hard for whom? I'm the one who's blind. You're only making me feel worse."

"Paul, I'm not up to fighting. I'm just overwhelmed and sorry—"

"You're overwhelmed?"

Paul heard her leave the room, sobbing.

"Dr. Stepola," Dr. Bihari said gently, "situations like this af-
fect the whole family. Everyone will have feelings they need to
express, but that doesn't mean they will be unwilling or unable
to support you. And you may need that support."

"Spare me," Paul said.

"I'm just saying that even a strong man uses all his resources,
including his family."

Paul shook his head, sighing. "Ranold, would you tell Jae
I'm sorry?"

"No you don't," Ranold said. "Believe me, I've learned the
hard way that women don't want to be chased down in a situation like this. She'll pull herself together. Now, Doctor, thank
you. If you would excuse us . . ."

When they were alone, Ranold shut the door and pulled a
chair next to Paul's bed. "I'll see what I can do about getting you
a real doctor, a specialist."

"Bihari *is* a specialist, and I don't want anyone else. He tells
me they're going to use freezing techniques, synthetic skin, laser
debridement of the burned areas, the whole bit. Now please, get
Jae back in here."

"Trust me on this, Paul. I know these things."

Yeah. I can tell from your own stellar marriage.

"Women are emotional," Ranold said. "It can take them a
while to grasp the big picture."

"Which is?"

"That we should all admire you, Son, for risking your life in
the line of duty. You got knocked around in San Francisco, of
course, but you didn't know a bomb was in that house. This
time you knowingly stuck your neck out to save a man—that's

what it means to be a soldier. You've paid a terrible price, Paul. That makes me proud."

Proud? Going blind is what it takes to impress you? "Well, I didn't save him."

"You tried, and that's what counts. Don't worry. Jae's going to come around."

Where is she, anyway?

"And we're going to get the terrorists who did this to you. You can jump right back into the fight when you're better. The agency will always need a mind like yours."

"Don't patronize me, Ranold. That's the same line Koontz fed me."

"Don't be so negative, Paul. You're an expert on these religious fanatics."

I don't understand them at all.

"If nothing else, this should strengthen your resolve to stamp them out. That alone is going to make you a major asset to the agency. And I feel more sure of you now than ever."

"What do you mean?"

"C'mon, Paul, it's no secret you and I have always been a little at odds. And then Pass died, the funeral . . ."

"What about it?" *So you did plant that letter.*

"I wasn't sure how seriously you took the threat. But your work with the task force has shown me the kind of man you are. Now, is there anything you need, or should I just let you sleep?"

"You know, there is something. Can you get me the New Testament on disc? There's a lot I'm trying to figure out about these terrorists—what they believe, how they think."

"That's the spirit. Stay focused. I've been there. Revenge can be a real motivator. I'll see what I can do."

Ranold returned a few minutes later and read a note from

Jae. "'Paul, I'm sorry this is so difficult for me. It hurts me to see you in pain and so angry. I need a little time, but I promise to try to be strong for you. I'll bring the kids to see you soon. Meanwhile, know that my thoughts are with you.'"

11

OVER THE NEXT THREE DAYS, though Dr. Bihari expressed enthusiasm at Paul's progress—except for his eyes—Jae could see Paul plunging into depression. She knew he was furious about his vision, confounded by his confinement, and frustrated by how little he was able to do for himself; and he was spitting nails at her. The doctors called his attitude "displacement"—inflicting his rage and hopelessness on an innocent victim—and assured her it was common and would ebb, ideally, with Paul's growing acceptance of his blindness. But that didn't make it any easier to take when every visit brought a new wave of recrimination.

Paul upbraided Jae for every attempt to help him, along with any other failing he could dredge up from their ten years of marriage. He refused to accept her apologies for what he called her weakness when they first met with Dr. Bihari and her "selfishness" for "abandoning" him afterward. Jae regretted losing control that first day, but the truth was, she was terrified. It had been a long time since she and Paul had been on the same track.

Their early years together had been idyllic. Even Ranold—impressed that Paul was Delta Force but suspicious of his religious studies graduate work—had embraced Paul after he joined the NPO. When the children came along, Paul seemed ecstatic, but it was around then that Jae had caught him in the affair. Paul offered a vapid defense—new-father pressures—but never seemed to show remorse. Jae originally loved Paul's confidence—"I am who I am; take it or leave it"—but not when he brought the same tough-guy attitude to his family.

After the affair she felt she could never trust him again. It didn't help that women were drawn to Paul—waitresses, airline attendants, even some of her friends. And Paul was constantly on the road, exposed to myriad women and temptations Jae was sure he lacked the will to resist. So they had reached an impasse. Jae was consumed by jealousies that Paul did nothing to assuage and that seemed to push him into stubborn withdrawal.

Now Paul was blind. Could a couple already so resentful of each other withstand such a devastating blow? Jae wasn't sure she knew how to get through to him anymore—if she even wanted to—or whether he would let her.

One thing was clear: Jae had to keep a grip on her emotions. She willed herself not to react to Paul's outbursts. She took it as a positive sign when he started asking about the kids, and she hoped their visit might improve his mood.

But as soon as Brie and Connor reached the threshold of his room, they stopped. Jae had tried to explain how he would look, but they seemed shocked.

"Go on, say hi to Daddy. It's okay to touch him, but be careful of his face."

Brie and Connor edged in.

"Hi, Dad."

"Hi, Daddy."

• • •

Paul gave the kids a crooked smile, sensing their uneasiness. "How are my two favorite kids in the world?"

Neither responded. Jae approached and touched his arm. "Hi, Paul," she said.

"Thanks for coming," Paul said, unable to hide his bitterness.

"Just be patient," she whispered. "They're scared."

"Of what? I'm not going to bite. This isn't contagious, you know."

"When will you be able to see, Daddy?" Brie said in a quavering voice, back by the door.

"Don't know," Paul said. "Not too long, I hope."

He heard Connor whimper.

"We're going to be right outside, Mom," Brie said. "C'mon, Connor."

"Jae, keep them in here."

"They're fine, Paul. Let them get used to this."

"They won't till you do. What did you tell them?"

Jae sighed. "Just that you had been seriously hurt and that now you're in bandages. That's a lot for them to cope with. Listen, I brought this thing Dad said you wanted."

"The New Testament?"

"He said it's strictly forbidden. What are you planning to do with it?"

"Well, what do you think? Listen to it, of course. I've got to be on top of these people."

"I wish you would just focus on healing. Why don't I bring you some music?"

"Don't tell me what to think, Jae. You have no idea how I feel."

"I wasn't telling you anything. By the way, Bob Koontz is coming this afternoon. He has some news."

"He said he was going to be here every off-hour. What a joke."

"Oh, Paul, that's a lot to ask."

"I didn't ask."

• • •

Jae bit her tongue and took the disc player out of the box, studying the directions.

"What are you doing?"

"Trying to set up this thing for you, Paul."

"Can't be that hard. Just adjust it to the frequency of my receivers."

She fiddled with the player.

"Just look at the instructions!"

"That's what I'm doing!"

"Why can't you handle simple electronics? Who do you think's going to do it for you now?"

She said nothing.

"Grown woman and you can't even—ah, never mind. I'll get someone else to do it."

"I'm sorry, Paul."

"Are you crying again?"

Jae dropped the box on the bedside table.

"Now what? You're leaving? Where are you going?"

Jae collared the children in the hall and steered them back to Paul's door. "Tell Dad bye."

"Bye, Dad."

"Bye, Daddy!"

• • •

Paul was still stewing about Jae when Koontz showed up.

"So much for every off-hour, eh?" Paul said.

"Hey! You got the New Testament thing. Want me to set it up for you?"

"Jae was going to, but she pulled her helpless-woman act."

Bob got the player working, then rolled the bed table close. "Careful, now. Here, feel this. It's a standard player. I've set the frequency, and the stack of discs is on your left. Can you handle it?"

"I think so. Just test the volume."

Bob turned it on, and the sound reverberated in Paul's head. "Down a bit," he said. "There. Perfect. Where's the On/Off switch?"

Bob moved Paul's hand to the switch, and Paul shut it off.

Koontz sat. "I've got to tell you, Paul, I'm very encouraged about your interest in this research. Very. Tells me you're eager to get back in the saddle. We need you, man. Every day we're getting more and more news of possible Christian groups."

"I'm eager all right. If these eyes would cooperate."

"You can't hurry that, Paul. Concentrate on your study and let the healing happen on its own."

"C'mon, Bob. We both know the odds. I'm never going to get to do the job you gave me."

"Don't say that."

"I'm not going to kid myself, Bob. My career has the same odds my eyes do."

"Well, call me crazy, but I'm optimistic because I know you."

Paul waved him off. "Jae said you had news."

"Get this. As soon as you're able to travel, you're on your way to D.C. The White House. The regional governor is going to honor you in the Rose Garden for bravery in the line of duty."

"Yeah?"

"Big stuff, pal."

"I don't know if I want an award I can't see."

"What are you talking about?"

"The whole thing smells like a PR stunt—something to show the NPO was on the ball in Texas, even if Tick screwed up."

"Don't be cynical. You earned this award. Be proud."

"Of what? A man died and I went blind. I'd call that a lose-lose."

"So what are you going to do? Tell the governor that?"

"No. I guess I won't pass it up."

"Of course you won't! And I'll be there in the front row."

• • •

As soon as Koontz left, Paul felt around for the disc player. The New Testament had figured in recent, major turning points of his life—in that service in San Francisco before the raid, when he had killed for the first time; in the ruse he'd used to extract Stephen Lloyd's confession; and of course, in the letter that, coupled with the death of Andy Pass, had led Paul to join the task force. He still felt Ranold had all but admitted planting the letter by saying that he finally felt sure of Paul.

But did Ranold know Paul had asked Angela Pass to get it analyzed? All Angela had was Paul's secure e-mail address. She had probably already sent him a report on the ink and handwriting samples. Paul would have to devise a way to find out.

The ideas in the letter—the "springs of life-giving water," the "punishment and suffering" for unbelievers, and especially the "I am coming soon" promise—had been echoed in the San Francisco subversives' meeting. Ranold's lackeys had clearly done their homework. Paul felt sure the New Testament was the key to discovering whatever "critical tasks" the rebels were plotting. Maybe the book of Revelation was the place to start.

He kept advancing the disc to find it, but each time he stopped to check his place, he found himself caught up in a fascinating story. Like most religious texts, the New Testament was a teaching tool. It took good stories to hold people's interest. Paul became engrossed by the letters to the first-century churches from his namesake, the missionary apostle Paul. They told of constant persecution, and Paul was amazed that he had totally forgotten that the early Christians were also persona non grata with the government and had to meet in secret and worship virtually underground. He decided to go back and start listening from the beginning.

Involved as he was, midway through the four Gospels that preceded the letters, Paul dozed. Laser debridement of the burned flesh on his ears and nose, where the synthetic grafting would take place, was excruciating, despite the painkillers, and left him exhausted. The disc finished playing, and it was late afternoon by the time he awoke.

• • •

With his heightened hearing, Paul found the ringing phones, the clatter of food trays in the hall, and the visitor chatter tormenting. He was so close to the nurses' station that his ears throbbed with the gossiping, arguing, and questions. He longed to pull his pillow over his head, but his ears were too tender. He could do nothing but lie there and stew.

One voice grew distinct from the rest: a deep, rich, baritone singing, humming, musing, and greeting staff as it wended its way down the hall. Paul wasn't up to what sounded like an energetic visitor, and he tensed when the voice seemed to hover outside his door. Then Paul heard a cart roll in and rattle to a stop. He fought the urge to turn toward the sound, hoping whoever it was would assume he was asleep.

"Are you awake, sir?" asked the baritone voice. "Might I trouble you for a moment?"

"Well, I don't have much choice now, do I?"

The man approached. "Where might I touch you in greeting, sir, if I have your permission?"

"You don't. What do you want?"

Paul felt a light squeeze on his shoulder from an extremely large hand and wrenched away, but that didn't seem to deter the man. "The name's Stuart Rathe. Stuart with a *ua* and the last name spelled R-A-T-H-E. The nickname's Straight, and you may feel free to use it. I saw your name and title on the sign outside. How might I address you?"

"Rip van Winkle."

"They tell me you should be sleeping at night and up most of the day. Paul, is it? May I sit?"

"Stop asking if you're just going to ignore the answer."

Straight dragged a chair next to the bed. "So you're the blind man."

"You caught that, did you?"

"Well, I hope it's temporary. Meantime, I would like to offer you my services. Anytime you've had enough of me, simply say so and I will be on my way without the slightest offense."

"I'm saying so."

"The nurses sent me. I am here to help in your recovery, not to tire you out. May I continue?"

"No."

"I, sir, am fifty-nine years old and an African-American. I am six-foot-four and weigh 225 pounds. I lost a foot in a car wreck with a drunk driver eight years ago, but more importantly, I lost my family too. Fortunately there were no other vehicles involved, but unfortunately that makes *me* the drunk driver. You can imagine, sir, how such an experience sobers a man. My life has never been the same. I retired as a professor of history at the University of Chicago, and now I volunteer here every day."

"Doing what?"

"Whatever patients want. I talk to them. I read to them. Sometimes I play the sax for them. I play games with them. My cart is filled with games. Checkers. Scrabble. Parcheesi."

"I don't imagine chess."

"It's one of my favorites. I play in clubs and tournaments. Is it your game too, Paul?"

"A long time ago."

"Well, I have a game that will work for you. Nice big pieces you'll recognize easily by touch. If that interests you at all, I am here every day."

"So am I."

Straight laughed. "My time is almost up, but let's make a date for a game tomorrow."

"Can't guarantee I'll feel like it."

"Just let me know. What's that you're listening to?"

Paul started. He hoped the title wasn't showing. Only family and coworkers would understand. "Ancient texts," he said. "Trying to understand the motivations of people who would risk their lives to promulgate fiction."

"A worthy task, friend. I'll be interested to hear what you make of it."

12

VIOLENT MOOD SWINGS became Paul's routine. He awoke daily to realize afresh his blindness. He'd had his bed moved close to the window so he could reach the curtain, and he'd instructed that his blinds never be shut. He loved the warmth of the sun magnified through the window, but it also reminded him that he enjoyed zero visual sensation of the light.

The bandages on his eyes were now thin discs of gauze, held in place by one layer of a mesh strip secured at the back of his head. His hair had begun to grow back. The patches were situated so he could open and shut his eyes, which he was encouraged to do as much as possible.

Though Paul had been urged not to let direct sunlight linger on the worst of his burns, he began each day by turning his face directly toward the warmth. Try as he might, he couldn't sense the difference in brightness from facing the window versus facing the door. Every day he hoped some tiny ray of light would sneak through the bandages to herald the return of his sight. But no.

Shortly after breakfast, he faced what he called the torture chamber, where the burned mask on his face and ears was frozen and debrided with a laser to prepare for the grafts of synthetic tissue. No matter how Paul psyched himself up and how much medication they gave him, this was by far the worst part of his day. It didn't help when the personnel who inflicted the torture reminded him that most other severely burned patients had much larger areas to treat and that such treatments used to be done by hand and had been many times more excruciating.

The physical pain, worse than anything he had ever experienced, was the least of it. He burned with rage, convinced he was the only patient in the unit who had to face the ordeal with an unsupportive family.

It galled him that though Jae visited the hospital every day, she came mostly in the evening, after dinner, with the kids. They'd stay for an hour or so, and then it would be bedtime and she'd take them home. So all day he'd sit there, miserable and bored, alone. Why wasn't she here? She had to chauffeur the kids to and from school, but what else did she have to do all day? What was so precious about her daily routine? Paul wasn't about to beg her to spend her days with him, but he deeply resented her absence.

True, he wasn't very good company. Often he was harsh with Jae and the kids. He had been furious when Brie and Connor were still afraid of him by their fourth visit, and he yelled at them, making Connor cry. He had fought with Jae about that—he was still convinced they were picking up on *her* fears—and it seemed to make a difference. Now they came all the way into the room and even close to his bed or chair, so he could touch them before they ran to play in the hall. But his whole family still seemed to tiptoe around him, wary of his temper. He was sick of feeling guilty for

JERRY JENKINS • 111

his anger. What did they expect? Some kind of phony good-boy, model-patient cheer? *Of course I'm angry. Who wouldn't be?*

Night and day, Paul was haunted by the same dream. Jae and the kids were running down the hall to him while he squatted, waiting. But just as one of them jumped into his arms, he was jolted awake and found himself still blind.

Bob Koontz visited about once a week, and while he always reiterated that Paul had a place on his team, Paul couldn't conceive of it and Bob couldn't describe it.

The main thing that kept Paul going was his daily afternoon visit from Stuart Rathe. Straight's rich voice and easy laugh gradually lifted Paul's spirits and gave him something to look forward to. Straight talked and listened, walked him around the wards, and set up the chessboard in different lounges so they could play several games a day. Though he had been a club and tournament player in grad school, it had been years since Paul had devoted much time to the game. Playing with Straight engaged Paul's mind and reminded him how much fun chess could be. Paul was surprised how he could visualize the entire board and the locations of each of the pieces by just brushing them with his fingers between plays. If anything, his blindness helped him focus on strategy. But Straight was good. Paul was able to beat him only about one in five games.

One day Straight noticed two bowls on Paul's bedside table, one full of paper clips and the other holding only a few. "What's this about?"

"I'm trying to count," Paul said. "This ancient text I'm listening to mentions blindness so often that I started wondering how many times I heard it. The nurse set me up with this system. I start with one bowl empty, and then I put a paper clip in it each time I hear a reference to blindness."

"So, how many times?"

"So far, forty-nine in just the first four sections."

"And what does it say about being blind?"

"Well," Paul said, "most of it is about blind people being healed. But there are also several references to figurative blindness, like 'the blind leading the blind.' And there's one passage where a man is arguing with self-righteous religious leaders, and he calls them blind guides who strain at a gnat but swallow a camel."

"Wonder what that means."

"I think he's saying they're worrying about details and missing the big picture."

"And what's the big picture?" Straight said.

"I'm still figuring that out."

"Well, keep listening. Sounds like it's helping you cope."

• • •

As their routine got established, Paul grew comfortable enough to ask Straight for a favor.

"Would you write a note for me?" he said one afternoon. "It's a business thing that I didn't get squared away before I got hurt. You'll have to look up the work address, if you don't mind, because I left the card in my office."

"No problem. Fire away."

Paul dictated:

Dear Angela,

It must seem strange that I wrote you about that letter and then dropped out of sight. As it happened, just days later, I wound up hospitalized after an accident in Gulfland. I was burned and am now—temporarily, I hope—blind.

I was grateful for your kindness in helping me with the

analysis, and I would like to thank you by taking you to lunch.
I will be in Washington in May. Would you write and tell me
of your availability?

> *Until then, with all best wishes,*
> *Paul Stepola*

"Gulfland, huh?" Straight said. "I saw on the news that they had some peculiar goings-on."

"Did they?" Paul said.

"Yeah, wildfires or something."

Straight paused but didn't press for details, and Paul was glad.

"Now Washington is a place where I've got people," Straight said. "That's a nice town."

• • •

Angela wrote back immediately. Paul eagerly handed over the letter as soon as Straight walked in the door and asked him to read it aloud.

Dear Paul,

How shocking to hear of your accident. If it's something you'd like to talk about, I'd be interested to know what happened. I'm enclosing the brand-new audio edition of The History of Delta Force, *which we just got in at the Library of Congress. I hear it's terrific, and I hope you enjoy it.*

Yes, of course, I would love to see you when you're in Washington. Just let me know the particulars, and I'll keep my calendar clear. Meanwhile, take care of yourself and get better soon. After losing my husband, Brian, to colon cancer two years ago, I know how hard it is to keep up your spirits when you're in the hospital. So hang in there! Your new friend in Washington is thinking of you warmly and wishing you well.

Love,
Angela Pass Barger

"Whoa! *Love?*" Paul said. "She signed it *love?*"

Straight paused. "That's not atypical of cordial notes, Paul. I do it myself. How old is this woman?"

"Thirty or so, I guess. And incredibly beautiful." Paul couldn't hide his elation. "And she's single. I can't believe it."

"I thought this was business."

"Frankly, I hope it can be more."

Straight was silent.

"You don't approve?"

"Leave me out of it."

"C'mon, Straight. Speak your mind."

"You need me to remind you you're a married man?"

"But what kind of a marriage? How often have you seen my wife?"

"Coupla times."

"*You* spend more time here than she does."

"Paul, she's wrangling two children."

"Who are in school every day."

"And what do you think she's doing with her time, Paul?"

"What do you think?"

"Well, it wouldn't surprise me if she was looking for work."

Paul hadn't even considered that. No doubt Jae could see the handwriting on the wall. She didn't believe Koontz had a job waiting for Paul any more than Paul did, no matter what was being promised. She was fully expecting to be, in essence, the single parent of three. Even his care would fall to her.

"I get it. She assumes I'm going to be dependent on her forever. She doesn't have the guts to tell me, so she just leaves me sitting here fuming every day."

"All I'm saying is that you ought to be patient with your family. I just wish mine was still here. You don't want regrets, Paul."

"Straight, I dread the day I have to go home. I miss my kids, of course, but they're already pulling away. They're never going to accept me as a father if I'm incapacitated, especially with Jae handling it this way."

"That's why you wrote this Angela woman?"

"Well, not entirely. Straight, I've never had much trouble in that department—women, I mean. But now that I'm losing Jae, it makes me wonder if other women will see me the way she does. Disabled. Dependent. Useless. So I *loved* Angela's response. She sounds like a woman who could deal with my blindness even if it was permanent."

"Paul, let me tell you something now, and I want you to hear me. You're still the same man you were before you lost your sight. Life's dealt you a blow, but you're a man with deep resources. You're the kind of a person who can work through this. Go easy on Jae. Put yourself in her shoes. Does that book you're listening to have anything to say about situations like yours?"

Paul thought a moment. "Matter of fact, it does. This miracle worker heals a man of blindness and says to him, 'Go your way. Your faith has healed you.'"

"Paul Stepola! You remembered that? You are one good student!"

"Tell you the truth, Straight, I just surprised myself there."

"Oh, Paul—there's more to the letter from Ms. Barger."

P.S. I'll give you the details when I see you, but our expert says that ink is at least thirty years old. And the handwriting samples definitely match. Hope this helps.

"Straight, would you mind if we didn't play chess today?" Paul said. "I think I'd better rest awhile."

• • •

Was it possible? Paul had become so convinced that Ranold's newfound faith in him related to the letter that he had abandoned any thought that it might be genuine. Old paper could be scrounged up. Old ink could be procured by the agency, no doubt, and there was probably a way to fade it. But the handwriting matched—"definitely," Angela said.

Still, it was difficult for Paul to think the letter had actually been written by his father. That he was not the hero Paul so desperately wanted to believe in, but a flagrant, fantasy-worshiping Christian. That he spoke the same incendiary language as the bombers in Pacifica and the firebugs in Gulfland, pledging allegiance to ideals that caused the murders of Coker, his team, and Donny Johnson—and, very nearly, of his own son. *Because of the very beliefs you tried to foist on me, I am blind.*

Paul had worked his way through the New Testament discs a couple of times. He still suspected that the book of Revelation held the key to the Christian uprising, but so far he hadn't managed to tease it out. In fact, he'd had trouble concentrating on Revelation because it was so richly detailed and graphic. In a few weeks without sight, he hadn't yet learned to absorb as much by listening as he would have seeing a printed page.

Now he skipped again to Revelation, hearing the familiar introduction in which John, in exile, receives a visitation from a man with "a voice that sounded like a trumpet blast" and feet "bright as bronze." He held "seven stars in His right hand, and a sharp two-edged sword came from His mouth."

What was the code—the hidden message?

13

BY THE FIRST OF MAY Paul was home and into a routine that did not endear him to Jae. Straight visited every day, and they spent hours playing chess and talking. Occasionally Straight would bring his sax, and if he was still there when the kids got home from school, they seemed fascinated by his music. At least a couple of nights a week, Straight took Paul to chess clubs.

Often Jae felt relieved to have Paul out of her hair, occupied and relatively happy. She was grateful for little things Straight did around the house, such as minor repairs. But most of the time she felt terribly alone. It was as if Paul were using Straight as a distraction to avoid confronting his blindness, and as a buffer to keep his distance from her and the children. *He acts more like a guest than a father and husband.*

Twice a week, Jae drove Paul to the doctor. She had come to dread those trips because they inevitably led to arguments. Paul refused to let her come in the examining room or even talk to Dr. Bihari. "I am not that weak, Jae. I don't need you calling the shots."

"Don't I get some say in your treatment?"

"Treatment? Bihari still doesn't believe transplants would make a difference. And there's nothing else to try."

"Why not get a second opinion?"

"To give me false hope? Or to confirm I'm a lost cause?"

"I'd think you'd want to investigate every possibility."

"Don't forget, I have more of a vested interest than you. It's my life."

"Isn't it *our* life?"

Paul shrugged. "Not necessarily."

"What are you saying?"

He hesitated. Then, "No one's making you stick with a blind husband."

"Have I said a word about leaving?"

"You don't have to. I can hear the 'poor me' in your voice."

Jae changed the subject. "We never did get your mother's basement cleaned and the house fixed to sell. Why don't I go see what's left in there?"

"No. Don't."

"There's not that much left. And it's already May. Summer is probably the best time to put the house on the market."

"Jae, I said leave it. I don't want anyone poking through my mother's stuff. When I'm able, I'll sort the rest of it."

"I could move the boxes here. There ought to be room for them in our basement."

"What's your problem with the house, Jae—money? You want to sell it because you're saddled with a husband who will never work again?"

"Of course not."

"Then let me worry about the house and my family's affairs."

• • •

In truth, Paul couldn't bear the thought of Jae discovering the letter from his father. Paul weighed that disillusionment on the same scale as losing his sight. Of course, the blindness was the more devastating—profoundly altering every aspect of life—but strangely, there was a challenge in fighting to master new skills, gauging the compensations made by the other senses. He could measure his progress and regain some sense of control. But the virtual loss of the father he'd thought he had left a hollowness, and there was nothing to fill it but rage.

• • •

One afternoon Paul came across something exciting in the New Testament. At the beginning of Revelation, John's visitor offered an appraisal of the different Christian cells or churches in the ancient world. Each was promised its own reward if it remained faithful. In Sardis, believers were told, "All who are victorious will be clothed in white. I will never erase their names from the Book of Life."

Paul's heart raced when he remembered Stephen Lloyd's medallion, which was imprinted with a palm frond and a book. And Lloyd had worn a white T-shirt and light-colored pants, which even at the time had struck Paul as inappropriate for the dirty work of a roughneck. Obviously these were symbols. The Christian underground was communicating using the imagery of Revelation!

Sardis was also the name of Johnson's oil company, which was harder for Paul to compute. But surely it was no coincidence. Maybe the name inspired terrorists to target it. *Poor Donny. His own corporate logo may have gotten him killed.*

But even if Paul had stumbled onto the key to the Christian code, he was still stymied by their potential plots—their so-called appointed tasks. The book of Revelation was filled with page upon page of acts of judgment from heaven—twenty-one in all, from famine and disease to stinging locusts and horses' tails with the heads of snakes. The bomb in San Francisco was arguably an effort to simulate an earthquake, but with so many scourges it was hard to guess where or how the subversives might strike next. In the hated letter, Paul's father spoke of "punishment and suffering beyond anything we can imagine or have ever managed to inflict upon each other."

So far.

Still, a lead solid enough to take to Koontz continued to elude Paul. Stephen Lloyd's medallion was clearly symbolic, but he had guessed what the book was before he read even a word of Revelation. So it wasn't necessarily part of an arcane code. He called the nationwide phone directory and was dismayed to find so many Sardis variations listed, including a century-old landmark restaurant in New York. And the light-colored clothes— well, it was Gulfland. He'd been there in March, but in the summer temperatures often exceeded a hundred degrees.

The more he thought about his theory, the more far-fetched it seemed.

• • •

Paul had been home a few weeks when it came time to go to Washington for his award. The agency had provided two first-class airline tickets. With Jae along, it would be difficult to connect with Angela Barger—whom he'd been fantasizing about ever since she had written to him in the hospital.

Then Brie and Connor both contracted the Peruvian flu, which had swept through their school. "I'm sorry, Paul," Jae told him. "I want so much to go to the ceremony. But I can't see leaving the kids with someone else when they're this sick."

Paul pretended disappointment. "What should I do with the extra ticket?"

"Go with Koontz."

"He's already there. He had to go early for a conference."

"Well, we don't have to use it. I can take you to the airport, and the airline will get you on and off the plane. Daddy will pick you up on the other end."

Paul had failed to consider the logistics. Could he really manage by himself? He recalled anxious days in the hospital room when he didn't know who was entering. Flying alone, feeling his way to the washroom, all eyes on him—even imagining it was painful.

"Maybe I just won't go," he said.

"Of course you'll go."

"Hey, you know Straight said he had family in D.C."

"So take him, Paul. He'd love it."

• • •

Straight thought it was as great an idea as Paul did. Paul would stay with his in-laws, and Straight would stay with his own relatives.

Paul was surprised how jumpy he was on the plane, though the flight was smooth. With his heightened senses, he heard every whine and knock, wriggled when the landing gear was raised and lowered, and started with every spot of turbulence. By the time they landed, he felt wrung out and disgusted at his own fear and helplessness. All the hopes he had recently entertained of leading a seminormal, somewhat independent life seemed ridiculous.

As they drove from the airport to the Decentis', Paul became newly aware of the acuteness of his sense of smell. "Cherry blossoms, Straight. Tell me what they look like."

"Like you remember them," the older man said. "Cherry

trees everywhere, busting out with pink-and-white blossoms. The festival must have been spectacular this year."

Paul lowered his window and the fragrance washed over him. "That aroma almost makes up for not being able to see them," he said. "Actually that's not true. I'm having trouble getting used to this."

"To what?"

"To life with only four senses. I'd almost trade these four for the one I lost, but—"

"Don't give up hope, Paul. The doctor just said the time wasn't right, not that it would never be right."

"It's getting to me, Straight. I thought I'd feel good being out, but I don't. I just feel like more of the world is passing me by. My kids don't respect me anymore. I'm some invalid they have to treat kindly. Jae can't accept that I'm blind. She's always pushing to talk to the doctor, as if she could wring some magic out of him. Life just goes on around me, without me, in spite of me. It's like I'm a trespasser in my own home. That makes me furious, and when I blow up, I'm just pushing Jae and the kids farther away. I feel worthless and hopeless, and I'm so helpless I can't even fly on a plane. I was actually scared today, Straight.

"Even this honor is depressing. It's like a last handshake before the government throws me overboard. They might keep me afloat for a while, but it will be out of charity and, come the next budget crunch, I'm gone. 'You've done enough'—that's what a medal means."

Straight let out a huge sigh. "Oh boy, have you got a bona fide case of the blues! Have faith, man. What about all that stuff you've been quoting about blindness from that ancient book? Didn't that healer touch two blind men's eyes and say, 'According to your faith let it be to you,' and their eyes were opened?"

"Yeah, so where's my healer, Straight?"

"The point of the story is to have faith. Without it, they wouldn't have been cured."

Paul didn't remember quoting Straight that particular passage, but thinking about it cut into his melancholy. For a moment he actually wondered what it would be like to be a Christian. He'd been obsessing about the subversives, listening to his New Testament over and over, trying to penetrate their thinking. What was it that made a person reach toward God? Adversity—well, he had that in spades—though for people like Andy Pass and Paul's father there was no excuse. Now, as an exercise, he tried to put himself in their shoes.

If I were my father, reaching toward God, what would I expect to get? What would be in it for me? Sullenly, feeling foolish, Paul invoked the words of the letter, *If I am seeking the truth, what will I find? Will God show himself to me? Will I experience a love transcending all earthly gifts? Will accepting it be the most fulfilling decision of my life?*

He willed himself to believe it, to surrender—just for an instant. Then he snapped himself out of the spell, feeling impossibly foolish. His face felt so hot he believed it would look bright red in the mirror. If he could see.

He cleared his throat to shake his embarrassment. "Uh, Straight, you know I could still get you a ticket to the ceremony. You'd like to see the White House, wouldn't you?"

"Oh, no, no. Now you just have a wonderful time with your father-in-law. I've got plenty of things to do."

• • •

At the monthly event where the regional governor bestowed various awards, Paul sat on the platform with his father-in-law on his left and Bob Koontz on his right.

Following nearly a dozen awards to athletes, young people,

and citizens' groups, the governor said, "We have saved our most prestigious honor for last. In March, Dr. Paul Stepola, an operative with the National Peace Organization, was severely injured in the line of duty, requiring skin grafts for his burns and costing him his sight. He was charging into a fire set by terrorists, giving no thought for his own safety, to rescue one of Gulfland's most prominent citizens. An explosion nearly killed him."

Beside Paul, Ranold stirred, as if jutting out his chest. Then when his father-in-law was introduced and asked to bring Paul to the lectern, he could feel the older man quiver.

"For valor in the face of danger, it is my great honor to present to Dr. Paul Stepola the Pergamum Medal."

Paul heard cameras clicking and basked in the applause and cheering. Ranold led him back to his chair, where Paul listened to the governor finish the festivities with a ten-minute speech on the supremacy of the state. He concluded: "For generations the world lauded people, personalities, individuals. Some were deified. We should rejoice that we live in a world that has evolved intellectually to where we recognize that the state reigns. Long live the United Seven States of America! Long live the Columbia Region! Long live the free state!"

After the festivities Ranold took Paul's arm and steered him to the Rose Garden. It was as if Ranold wanted to be seen with him, to show him off. *So it was never the letter at all. He really thought I had proved myself.* Still feeling useless, Paul marveled again at the new respect his injury had kindled in his father-in-law.

"I don't think it ever impressed me how this place smelled," Paul said. "I can point to the flowers from here, just from the fragrance. Tell me how the rest looks."

Ranold didn't answer except to say, "Oh, good." Then he pulled Paul close and whispered, "There's someone here I want you to meet."

He moved ahead a little too quickly, and Paul nearly stumbled. He was just regaining his balance when Ranold introduced him. "Paul, here's a rising star at the Washington NPO bureau. Agent Balaam has been coming on strong with the Zealot Underground task force."

A large bony hand gripped his. Paul was astonished when the voice was a woman's. Her warm breath hit him full in the face, so she had to be at least his height.

"Congratulations on your award, Agent Stepola."

"I've come to appreciate Agent Balaam for the creative interventions she's come up with to cripple the leadership of our local Christian terrorists."

"Interventions?"

"You wouldn't believe how much ground that movement has gained," the woman said. "Your Gulfland fires, I'm sorry to say, have helped them recruit."

My Gulfland fires?

"So we've been training our sights on the heads of local cells. In some cases we've sent a signal that it's unhealthy to be a Christian."

Paul hated her voice. *Am I threatened that she's a woman? jealous that she's working when I can't? envious that she's Ranold's protégé?* No, it was her smug self-satisfaction that got under Paul's skin.

"This will make you feel good," Ranold whispered. "Last week we had an accident at Asclepian Zoo. An after-hours visitor on some kind of a drug trip happened to climb the wrong fence and was killed by a giant python."

"That's horrible," Paul said.

"Normally it would be, except in this case it meant one less terrorist. The occasional well-timed accident can be a very effective tool. This one's thrown a scare into plenty of believers, according to our moles."

"We've got operatives planted at both the Smithsonian and the Library of Congress," Ms. Balaam said. "It won't be long before we get a grip on the terrorist cells there. They're not going to gain a foothold."

"See, Paul, there will definitely be work for you in the agency," Ranold said, "whether or not you regain your vision. The battle is heating up. These people have been proliferating right under our noses."

Despite the law, despite the dangers . . .

• • •

On the way to the airport, as planned, Straight took Paul to the Dover Inn, one of Paul's favorite lunch places. Paul waited on a wooden bench while Straight parked. He smelled Angela before he heard her—rainwater and lavender.

She took his hand. "I'd have recognized you anywhere," she said.

He was struck by the lyrical quality of her voice. "What would you have done if I had not been the only blind man here?"

"Well, this is the first time I've seen you in wraparound shades, but the rest of you is memorable enough."

The three enjoyed a casual lunch, laughing and reminiscing about Angela's father. She discreetly waited to bring up the letter until it was time to leave for the airport and Straight had gone to get the car. "Here's that ink sample," she said. "Though I don't suppose you've been able to do much more with that memorial project since you've been hurt."

"No, but I've been giving it a tremendous amount of thought. I really appreciated your analyst's report. It opened my eyes—pardon the expression." Angela giggled and brushed his hand. Paul turned up his palm and clasped hers. "That's proba-

JERRY JENKINS • 127

bly my first blind joke. But seriously, it's been a great morale booster, as well as a pleasure, to be with you today."

"The pleasure is mutual. It's been a while since I've been out to lunch with an attractive man."

"I want to tell you something." *What am I doing?* "Is there anyone within earshot or am I talking too loudly?"

"There's no one nearby. I'm the only one who can hear you."

"This is highly irregular for me," Paul said, "but I just want to mention that government agencies sometimes scrutinize their own backyards just as closely as they do the general public."

"Is that right?"

"Some even plant moles at places like the Library of Congress. A subversive cell would have difficulty thriving too close to Big Brother."

Angela sounded amused. "So if I've been using my lunch hour to plot the overthrow of the government, I'd better be careful—is that what you're saying?"

"Well—"

"Don't worry." She gave her musical laugh. "Here comes your friend. Hi, Mr. Rathe!"

14

PAUL DECIDED ADRENALINE must have kept him going through his first full day out of the house. Waiting for takeoff in a first-class aisle seat next to Straight, he was exhausted and claustrophobic. It didn't help that Straight mentioned the plane was full. Paul turned down a preflight drink and sat with his chin tucked to his chest, trying to doze. His reverie was interrupted by an announcement that weather in Chicago would delay their departure.

"Daley International is experiencing heavy thunderstorms," the captain reported. "So, folks, let's just relax. We want to see which way the front's going to move. Then we'll file our flight plan and get cleared for takeoff."

Relax? Paul felt his pulse and respiration increase. He tried to slow them by rehashing the visit in his mind—the awards ceremony, Ranold's pride, meeting that up-and-coming Washington agent in the Rose Garden—but that just boosted his anxiety. His fear returned, and he had to stay focused—on Angela's fragrance, her voice, her touch. *Keep calm. Have faith.*

But what was faith? Paul couldn't deny the New Testament was having an effect on him. Jesus urged people to have faith, to believe in Him. Most atheists chose to believe He was a fictitious character, but Paul's professors had been more generous. They allowed that He was a historical figure and perhaps a wise teacher, but needless to say, they scoffed at any claims of deity. He couldn't be the Son of a God who did not exist.

And yet Paul had found Jesus' teachings revolutionary, His pronouncements paradoxical. If you want to be exalted, humble yourself. If you want to be rich, give your money away. If you want to lead, serve. Somehow Paul was finding it harder and harder to dismiss the man as just a teacher. He claimed to be the Son of God, said He was sent by His Father and would return to His Father. He also said He would come back. The letters of the apostle Paul argued for the real reasons behind His death on the cross and treated the Resurrection—long since decried by skeptics—as historical fact.

Could it be? Paul had a vague recollection of a truth postulated by C. S. Lewis, a twentieth-century atheist scholar turned Christian. Something about how Jesus had to be one of three things: a liar, a lunatic, or who He claimed to be. You couldn't have it two ways. You could not call Him a wise teacher unless you believed His claim to be the Lord of all.

Again Paul found himself playing at the edges of belief, ruminating on the what-ifs. His own father had clearly been a believer. Paul thought he knew enough of his dad's character through his mother's recollections. She never said he was stupid. And Paul knew beyond doubt that Andy Pass had been no intellectual lightweight. But when Paul allowed himself to consider that Jesus might have died for his sins, he found himself overwhelmed with grief.

Was he a sinner? He had been unfaithful to his wife. He had lied. He had been selfish, caring more for himself than for his family. He had killed people. The weight of it was too much. He did not remember suffering guilt before; he hardly even knew what it was.

Until now. He wanted to shake himself back to reality, to get out from under the awful shame by reminding himself that these were myths, fairy tales. Maybe this project, this new study for the sake of his NPO mission, had been a terrible mistake.

The plane had sat on the runway for more than an hour, making Paul even more agitated. He couldn't mention any of this to Straight. Besides, from the sound of his breathing, the big man was dozing. *Must be nice.* Delays were unusual in the age of supersonic travel. Paul decided on a walk in the first-class section, counting the seats to keep his bearings.

• • •

The Smithsonian's old National Air and Space Museum was Angela's sons' favorite place to visit. They spent many rainy Saturdays marveling at the Wright brothers' boxy spruce-and-muslin plane—which the pilot had to fly lying flat on his belly—and the ancient *Spirit of St. Louis,* with its gas tanks up front so Lindbergh had to peer through a periscope to see ahead. At least the first manned spacecraft from eighty years before had windows so the astronauts could see where they were going. Angela's favorite flying machine was the scarlet Breitling Orbiter balloon, the first to fly nonstop around the world just before the turn of the century, about six years before she was born.

She made her way past the quaint moon-rocks display and upstairs to the Albert Einstein Planetarium, which still boasted the old-fashioned Sky Vision shows. The shows made her sons impatient, accustomed as they were to the Spacetime Astronomy Center's telescope turrets, made of powerful magnifying lenses that seemed to thrust you physically into the cosmos. But she loved the digital-projection surround-sound system that was state of the art before the war, which gave the illusion of flying through an outer space echoing with dramatic music and swirling with supersaturated colors.

She bought a ticket for the three o'clock show and chose a place in an empty section. At that hour on a weekday, the theater was only half full—mostly tourists, she guessed. The magical star field was projected on the ceiling—inaccurate, they knew now, but still fascinating. It was no wonder that, from earliest times, human beings had looked for God in the heavens.

A couple entered, taking seats on each side of her. The three clasped hands and, as the powerful bass line of the soundtrack boomed, shared a silent prayer.

Angela whispered, "There may be a bust soon. That death at the zoo may be the beginning of a purge."

"Who's behind it?" the woman said. "Balaam?"

"I don't know. But they've infiltrated." Angela revealed Paul's oblique warning.

"This guy pops up and warns you out of the blue?"

"He served under my father. He was in Washington to receive an award for being injured in the line of duty."

"He's got to be NPO. Angela, you need to get out of town. They may be watching you because of your father, but clearly you're on their radar. Even this could be some kind of a trap, to see who you'll try to warn."

"I doubt that, but it makes sense for me to leave."

"Get your kids and head out today," the man said. "We'll

handle the school and work arrangements and make sure Detroit is ready for you."

"And the book-drop operation . . . ?"

' "Maybe we should hold off awhile—just till we see what this heat seems to be about. Whenever it's safe to move, don't worry about your part of it. We'll get it covered."

• • •

"Didn't they know it was raining in Chicago?" a man asked as Paul paced the aisle. "Why did they let us board? If this were a normal plane instead of a two-hundred-seater, a storm wouldn't hold us up. I'm never flying one of these puddle jumpers again."

Others joined in, griping and me-tooing. The chorus of complaints drove Paul back to his seat. Straight had roused.

"What time is it?" Paul said. "People are talking like we've been here for hours."

"Just after four," Straight said. "Not so late. Funny, it's already getting dark. We're in for some rain here too."

"I hope not."

The captain came back on. "Folks, thanks for your patience. Our storm in Chicago is moving toward Detroit, but another weather system is coming from the south. Our best bet is to get going and outrun it. We're cleared for takeoff."

The passengers, including Paul, clapped and cheered. Maybe he could forget his private torment.

• • •

While Paul was in Washington, Jae had decided it was time for him to move back upstairs with her. Since he'd come home from the hospital, he'd been set up in the den. He'd learned to master the first floor and could even find his way out into the yard and back. But he'd made no effort to attempt the stairs and rejoin her in their bedroom.

When Jae had broached the subject, he had protested that he was still up and down all night, dozing an hour or two, then waking and listening to his discs until he could get back to sleep. He didn't want to disturb her, he said. She had been reluctant to ask again. A second no would be humiliating.

Better to present Paul with a *fait accompli*. She knew moving his things might be provocative, but it would also give her a chance to see what kind of a stand Paul would take in their marriage. *I want to see what's coming—if we have a next step.*

Jae threw all Paul's bedding and clothing in the washer. She heaped his toiletries and medicines in a basket. On the end table was the disc player that had defeated her in the hospital, along with the tidy stack of discs. Where was the box for the New Testament set? It was raining hard outside, making the den so dark she had to turn on the lights to look for it.

She finally found it on the floor under the skirt of Paul's favorite armchair. There she also came upon a note crumpled and soft from fingering, from Angela Pass Barger. Her eyes skipped over it in horror. Impossible! How could her blind, seemingly helpless, definitely depressed husband have met a new woman, corresponded with her, and made a secret plan to meet her in Washington? And right under the nose of Jae's father?

No wonder Paul wanted Straight to go with him. He must have been Paul's accomplice all along. Who else could have read him the note? It amazed Jae that she had been so naive and accepting—waiting on Paul hand and foot, enduring his mood swings and angry outbursts, defending his temper to the children. All the while she had hoped he was coming to terms with his blindness, he had been trolling the waters of a different future.

It was the same old story, Paul and his other women. And he always acted like her jealousy was crazy. She dumped out the basket of medicines and toiletries on the end table, too angry even to force tears. She had already cried enough for a lifetime.

• • •

"Just in time," Straight said as the plane ascended. "We could have been stuck a couple more hours."

But even when they reached cruising altitude, high above the clouds, the flight was bumpy. Passengers were restricted to their seats, which heightened Paul's claustrophobia—not that he would have dared venture into the aisle anyway with the plane pitching and jerking. Straight must have sensed his discomfort. He laid a steadying hand on Paul's arm.

"Spot of turbulence," the captain announced brightly. "Don't think it will last. We'll stay south of Detroit, and we can expect a smooth ride."

"How can he be so cheerful?" Paul said. "He's driving me crazy." In truth, Paul was driving himself crazy, trying to put out of his mind the jarring teaching of the Gospels. It was like trying not to think of an elephant.

• • •

The cherry blossoms were still a draw, Bia Balaam thought. Even in this age when it was possible to have a virtual version of any life experience, tourists flocked to Washington for the simple pleasure of walking under the delicate canopies of scented blossoms. Recognizing the commercial appeal of the tradition—and with the help of cutting-edge horticulture—Washington had extended the cherry blossom season from just a few weeks in late March and early April to all of April, May, and June. Now more than ever, celebrating the cherry blossoms was part of the nation's rite of spring.

Tourists near the Washington Monument scanned the skies

and scrambled for cover. The breeze bore the strong taste and odor of ozone. An expectant hush, an electric tang in the air, got everybody revved up and anxious, wishing the storm would break.

Bia slipped the pen-sized titanium cartridge from her pocket, popping the lid with her thumb, and tapped the button. Her umbrella shot up, unfolding like a parachute above her head. But the rain did not come. One block, two blocks . . . Bia felt foolish with the umbrella up, but there was no one around to notice.

Finally a few soft pelts. The downpour quickly intensified and her umbrella grew heavy. But Bia didn't smell water. Her legs and feet were dry, and no rain pooled on the pavement. Instead she saw drifts of pink-and-white petals.

She shook them off her umbrella. The air grew thick with cherry-blossom petals, their fragile sweetness giving way to a cloying smell of decay. Through the blizzard of petals, she saw the trees were bare.

Brushing the rotting petals off her face and hair, she moved off the sidewalk to examine the trees. The branches were stripped of blossoms and the leaves were brown, as if a sudden winter had aged them. But it wasn't cold. The warm air crackled with static electricity and smelled of decomposition.

Holding her umbrella by the tip, she hooked a branch with the handle and bent it down into her hand. The end was shriveled. The bark was slowly mottling and withering all the way up the branch to the tree's trunk. The tree was dying before her eyes.

For nearly two hundred years, since the Japanese presented them as a gift to the nation's capital, the cherry trees had been a beloved symbol of renewal and one of Washington's most compelling attractions. Now in the time it had taken Bia to walk a few blocks, they were destroyed, shriveling to dust.

What force of nature could possibly have wreaked such havoc, and so quickly? Scientists would be scratching their heads over this one, but Agent Balaam already knew what her boss would say. He would recognize that it wasn't natural and wasn't a miracle, as some would claim. No, it was a shockingly bold and utterly despicable act of terrorism—worthy of ruthless, immediate reprisal.

• • •

The pilot was wrong on all counts. The turbulence never eased, and the stubborn storm hovered directly over Chicago for hours, forcing the plane to circle. The passengers' initial joking about white-knuckle flights had faded into uneasy silence. Paul hoped his terror didn't show.

Even the pilot finally sounded stressed. He communicated in short, tense bursts. "Bumpy patch . . . aah . . . holding for clearance . . . safer to bring her down when it clears . . ."

At last he came through with a complete sentence. "Okay folks, we're gonna try to land."

"*Try* to land?" All around him, Paul heard sounds of horror. Could they be in real trouble? Was it possible he could die? What if everything he had been listening to was true? What if there was a God and a plan of salvation and consequences for not connecting with it? He shook his head. He wasn't about to become a foxhole convert. That made no sense. He wondered if it would even be valid.

The plane rocked and bucked as it circled down, buffeted by high winds. Disoriented, Paul twitched with anxiety, which escalated to panic when a woman behind him cried out. This had been a mistake, thinking he could fly. *God, help me.*

He didn't mean that, he knew. Anyone might have said it. Just an expression. *Get a grip.*

Straight's deep voice cut through his terror. "The sky is spectacular. It goes from pitch-black to an inky green where clouds roil up on the horizon."

Paul vise-gripped the armrests. "Enough play-by-play."

"You all right, Paul?"

"Kindà jumpy." Paul's heart was pounding so hard he wondered if it would burst. *I don't want to die. I'm not ready.*

"Rough ride," the captain barked. "Assume the brace position, head down, arms over it."

Screams, cries, shouts. Someone retched.

"Bend over! Cover your head," a flight attendant yelled over the hubbub.

The plane lurched and dipped. Screams became wails. Paul pressed his forearms tight over his ears to muffle the sobs and howls of fellow passengers. His breath came in hard gasps.

Quivering, the plane plunged, sucking down his lungs and stomach. *The point is to have faith. What makes a person a believer? If I were my father, reaching toward God, what would I expect to get? If I sought the truth, what would I find? Would God show Himself to me? Would I experience a love transcending all earthly gifts?*

God, save me, Paul cried silently, and he knew he was not pleading only for his physical life.

Thunder cracked and made Paul bolt upright, turning toward Straight amid the screams. He reached out but met only air—like the other passengers, his friend was bent in the brace position. A huge bolt of lightning flashed in the window, filling the cabin with blazing light. Paul felt the jolt in his fingertips, up his arm, to his face and hair.

Suddenly, with the resounding thunderclap that followed, his fear was gone, replaced by a swelling awe.

I saw that!

15

WHAT JUST HAPPENED? Paul's arms and face still tingled, and behind his bandages his eyes pulsed with the bright aftershock. Had his sudden burst of faith restored his sight? Could that fearful prayer have been valid? He felt nothing.

He had made no bargain with God, made no promises. Had he decided to receive Christ, to become a Christian? His namesake in the New Testament had told a jailer that all he had to do was call upon the name of the Lord Jesus Christ, and he would be saved. There was no doubt Paul had called upon God. Or had he simply blurted something in fear? His eyesight was restored, but it made no sense. It seemed way too easy.

Could faith come out of nowhere? Could one simply express it and reap huge benefits?

And was it really possible for someone like him? Paul recognized he had been wrestling with the question of faith since

Wintermas, when Andy Pass died and he discovered his father's letter. His contempt for the weakness of the two principal men in his life; his outrage over their betrayal, which led him to join the task force; the hatred filling him as he listened to the worshipers in San Francisco; his loathing for Stephen Lloyd at the moment when he confessed—all were battles against faith. But Paul had been guilty of more than hostility. He had even killed in an attempt to eradicate faith like a contagious disease—with no regrets, as he'd told Koontz—taking satisfaction in a job well done.

How could faith have taken root in him, the enemy? Who could be more unworthy? The New Testament Paul said *he* was the "chiefest of sinners." Well, now he had competition.

Seedlings had been sown when Paul listened to the New Testament, even as he believed his mind was actively rejecting it. Had it gained purchase when he turned the lines from the funeral service and his father's letter over and over in his mind? Could it have emerged from pretending he had faith, imagining how his father might have experienced it? Or even from his father's wish that he grow up to seek the truth and to become a man of God?

All Paul knew was that something had changed—something even more profound than regaining his sight.

The plane righted itself as another thunderclap boomed. Straight sat up, putting a hand on Paul's shoulder. "You okay?" he said.

"I'm sorry?"

"Paul, you seem agitated, like you're not well."

"Straight," he said, "I saw that lightning!"

"You saw it?"

"I didn't imagine it, man."

"But your eyes are bandaged, under dark shades."

"I know what I saw!"

"I hope you're right, but don't get your hopes up."

"It's true. I want to rip these bandages right off and see what I can see."

"Don't," Straight said. "Whatever happened, your eyes will be sensitive, and you don't want to risk further damage."

"What happened is what you told me before, in the car—" Paul dropped his voice to a whisper— "'According to your faith let it be to you . . . and their eyes were opened.'"

"Hmm."

Then it struck Paul. The reason he hadn't recognized the quotation was that he had never recited it to Straight. Straight was familiar with the Bible! His friend had to be a secret believer! The way he gently aimed Paul back to the book, frequently asking innocent questions about what it said on this or that subject . . .

If Straight is a believer, am I?

The airliner touched down. Some passengers applauded weakly, but most were too spent to do more than stand and listlessly hunt for their bags. Paul jumped up, jubilant. He had one goal—to get home and get back into the New Testament. All the passages about blindness and sight were one thing. There was so much more there, more he needed to hear again until he understood.

• • •

Paul burst into the house, and he and Straight dumped his bags in the front hall. Paul rushed to embrace Jae—for the first time, he realized, since he'd been injured. He gushed the news of his sight. She stiffened, and he fell back, stung. *She doesn't want to get her hopes up.*

"I know it's impossible to believe, but it's true, Jae. I looked toward the window, and there was this incredible lightning, and I saw it!"

He took his sunglasses off his bandaged eyes. "I can see the lights in this room. There's one lamp. . . ."

"Paul, keep your voice down. I don't want the kids to wake up and hear this. You remember where the lamps were. Maybe Straight should take you to the emergency room—"

"No, no. I can't explain all this to strangers and spend the night there getting tests. We'll see Dr. Bihari in the morning."

"Paul, maybe it's some neurological shift—"

"I'm not going, Jae. Forget it. It's my eyes, not my head. . . ." Suddenly he was out of gas, deflated emotionally and physically. "And I'm just so tired. It's been such a crazy day. That plane ride was a roller coaster. . . ."

• • •

First thing the next morning, Jae took Paul to Dr. Bihari. It took several minutes for his eyes to adjust to the light, and the doctor was clearly dubious. He rolled back and forth in front of Paul on a small stool. "Tell me what you think you can see."

"Everything is fuzzy," Paul said, "but I *can* see. Last night I could tell which lamps were on at home, and this morning I could see outlines of furniture. . . ."

"Paul, you've lived in that house many years."

"You don't believe me," Paul said. "Test me."

"Of course. Now don't strain, and also, please don't get your hopes up."

How many times am I going to hear that? Of course my hopes are up!

"Limited, intermittent vision is not unheard of," Dr. Bihari said. "But be careful not to jump to conclusions."

Paul was able to make out only the large single letter at the top of the chart and the next line of fairly large letters. "But you have to agree, it's something."

"It's more than something," Bihari said. "I need to do one more thing, and I warn you it will cause some discomfort."

"I'm game."

The doctor examined Paul with an extremely bright light. Paul blinked and squinted but forced himself to keep his eyes open long enough for the doctor to find what he was after. "I am astounded," Dr. Bihari said. "Your corneas, irises, pupils, and choroids show permanent damage. If you can see anything, it should be clouded with the blurry shapes of scar tissue within the eye itself."

The doctor asked Jae to lean in close. "You see the disfigurement of the lens, just behind the iris in both eyes?"

She nodded.

"But you do not see that, Paul?" the doctor said.

"I see only what I've told you. It's blurry but it's becoming clearer. Now, how about those transplants?"

"They may not be necessary. I don't understand it, but I wouldn't want to mess with nature yet. Let's see how much better this gets."

•   •   •

Jae was confused. She didn't know how to feel. She ought to be overjoyed, but she was furious with Paul about the letter. Now she didn't know how to confront him. He'd be angry and claim the correspondence was innocent, though it was signed "love" and he had obviously schemed to connect with the woman. If the relationship was platonic, why hadn't he mentioned it? How could Jae believe in him again? She was sick of his deception— sick of worrying, of checking for signs, of being consumed by doubt and suspicion.

Even if Paul confessed—a big if—what could she do? Was she ready to kick out a man who was just beginning to regain his sight? Could he function alone in a strange new place? Forcing him out now would be unforgivable, the final blow in their marriage. Jae wasn't ready to take that step. She needed time and space to think things over and—if nothing else—to prove to Paul she meant business.

The only solution was to pack up the kids and leave. That would have to wait till they got out of school in a few weeks. Then she could pitch the departure as something positive—an adventure, a summer vacation. *I owe them that after all we've put them through.*

Until then, she'd hide her feelings from Paul, which proved easier than she expected. His routine stayed the same: listening to discs in the den all morning with the door closed, waiting for Straight; holing up with him all afternoon; and then going out to chess clubs several evenings a week. For the first time ever, she was grateful for his neglect.

• • •

For Paul, the gradual restoration of his sight was a mystery that turned his world upside down. If he now had faith in God, what did that mean? What would be expected of him—surely his life, his work, even his marriage would have to change. Given who his father-in-law was, Paul couldn't imagine how to explain the change in himself to Jae. What if it spooked her, made her tell her father? Paul's life would be over.

First he had to come to grips with this himself. He'd been studying the New Testament as an outsider. He had listened to the words over and over, yet there was so much he didn't understand. Jesus' teachings were antithetical to everything Paul had ever been taught. He said to love your enemies and be kind to those who mistreated you. How would that play in the NPO?

Another hurdle for Paul's intellect was the assertion that

Jesus had lived a perfect life, without sin, so He could become God's sacrificial lamb for all the sins of the world. That made Christianity unique among religions, at least the ones Paul had studied. What other religion based salvation on a gift, something someone else had done? What other religion featured a hero who not only rose from the dead but also supposedly still lived? Most religions seemed focused on man's attempts to reach God, but Jesus was clearly God's attempt to reach man.

Paul's namesake, a highly educated man, seemed to write directly to him in a New Testament letter: "For the message of the cross is foolishness to those who are perishing, but to us who are being saved it is the power of God."

Was I perishing? That's the apostle Paul's contention. Unless I believed this, I would die without God.

The passage continued, "For it is written: 'I will destroy the wisdom of the wise, and bring to nothing the understanding of the prudent.' Where is the wise? Where is the scribe? Where is the disputer of this age? Has not God made foolish the wisdom of this world? For since, in the wisdom of God, the world through wisdom did not know God, it pleased God through the foolishness of the message preached to save those who believe."

Paul listened to that passage over and over. He was reeling. He had been looking for intelligent reasons to consider this all just nice-sounding words for the religious mind. What he thought sounded foolish was *meant* to be foolish, to confound the wise. Well, he was confounded.

Then there was the promise that Jesus would come back to earth someday. He had told His disciples that He was going to heaven to prepare a place for them and that He would return to receive them to Himself. And He added, "If it were not so, I would have told you."

Paul had studied the book of Revelation, which described the

conditions of Christ's return and the promise that He was coming soon. Both Paul's father and the San Francisco worshipers
believed that time was nearly at hand. How did that fit in with
Paul's new embrace of faith?

Paul needed a spiritual confidant, someone more seasoned,
with whom he could share his doubts and questions.

• • •

The next time Straight came over, as soon as they were behind
closed doors, Paul said, "We need to talk. I need to ask you a
question."

"Shoot."

"You remember in the car, when you quoted me that passage
about the two blind men? '"According to your faith let it be to
you." And their eyes were opened.'"

Straight seemed to stiffen. "Yeah?"

"I've been thinking about this, and I know I never told you
that story."

"Huh."

"So how did you know it?"

Straight leaned back in his chair and put his hands behind
his head. "You think you're the only person who reads?"

"The Bible is contraband, Straight. Forbidden. I have access
to it because of my job."

"You looking for a confession, Paul? What do you want
from me?"

"I want to know if you're reading the Bible."

"And if I am?"

"I want to know."

"Are we friends, Paul? You don't seem to have any friends
but me."

"We're friends."

"You're asking your friend to confess a capital crime to an operative of the National Peace Organization."

"So it's true?"

"My life is in your hands, Paul."

"Is it true?"

"It's true."

A shiver ran through Paul. *I knew it!* And he needed Straight's wisdom.

"Are you going to turn me in, Paul? Are you going to do your duty, or are you going to aid and abet the enemy?"

Paul let his head fall back and closed his eyes. "I couldn't ever see you as the enemy, Straight."

"That's a mighty important decision."

"I know. This changes everything."

"Yes, it does. Are you sure?"

"I don't know."

"God spared you and restored your vision. You don't have any question about that, do you?"

"Not anymore."

"You know, Saul asked the Lord who He was. Remember the answer?"

"It works on me every day," Paul said. "He said, 'I am Jesus, whom you are persecuting.' For a long time, I resisted that. I said that even if I was persecuting underground Christians, I wasn't really persecuting Jesus."

"But there's a bond between us and Him, Paul. Persecute us, persecute Him."

"That's exactly what I came to."

"Have you told Him yet?"

"Told Him what?"

"That you believe in Him? He restored your sight, and He's proving to you every day who He is. You telling me you can ignore that and treat the New Testament as a bunch of stories, just like those of all the other religions you've studied?"

Paul found himself trembling. "No."

"You know what to do."

"I think I sort of already did."

"Sort of?"

"I was scared to death on the plane, Straight. I called upon God to save me. And then all this happened. But I didn't earn it. I don't deserve it. It doesn't seem fair."

"I wouldn't want it to be fair, Paul. I'd never have earned this either. You remember what Paul wrote to the Romans about what he called 'the word of faith, which we preach'?"

"Vaguely. I haven't memorized it."

"He said, 'that if you confess with your mouth the Lord Jesus and believe in your heart that God has raised Him from the dead, you will be saved.'"

Paul fell quiet. For his entire life it had been important to understand the logic of things and to know for certain how the world worked. He had learned to trust the mind and distrust the heart, and the world made sense accordingly. But now, in just days and hours, all was turned upside down. He had experienced things he could not explain, things not logical. His mind reeled and he was confused. His sight was no more miraculous than that God would save him when he didn't deserve it. And yet, from deep inside, somewhere other than his mind, there was something else . . . a sense? a voice? a whisper? Whatever, it was nodding, whispering *yes*, saying, *You do not deserve this, yet I am here with you.*

Paul's eyes welled with tears. He had to take the final step.

"Yes," he whispered. "I do believe."

16

THE LIBRARY WOULD HAVE BEEN impressive anywhere. The walls of its thirty-by-sixty-foot expanse, from the sparkling white floors to the vaulted, glinting twenty-five-foot ceilings, were lined with old-fashioned books printed on paper. Long cherry tables with inlaid detail and matching leather-cushioned chairs dominated the left side of the room, and the right was a honeycomb of carrels, each with its own Internet connection.

"I'm amazed how warm and cozy it is down here," Straight said.

"Perfect environment for books and furniture," his host said. "After World War II, you know, they found caches of looted artwork in European salt mines. It was the best place for them: bone-dry, clean and pure, temperature steady between fifty-five and seventy-five degrees. No insects or mice—nothing down here to sustain them—and they haven't found us yet. I do worry about stowaway roaches though, especially in the books."

"It's a precious collection," Straight said.

"We're transferring it all onto electronic media. I love the old volumes, but they're fragile, and the point is to get them back into circulation."

"How many people live here?"

"About a hundred and fifty permanent and fifty to a hundred passing through at any given time."

"It's amazing you can feed and house so many."

Straight's host shrugged. "We've got fourteen hundred acres down here, fifty miles of tunnels. The water and ventilation systems are huge—had to be, to accommodate the mining machinery. Even back then they could pump in a hundred thousand cubic feet of air a day. These mines were worked successfully for almost two hundred years."

"What happened? Salt run out?"

"Oh no! It was a money thing—cheaper to ship it in from Canada. We're still surrounded by seventy trillion tons of it— enough to supply the world for millennia."

A couple in their late fifties entered, accompanied by a younger sturdy blond man. "I was boring the professor with tales of our city," the host said. "It's been a while since he's been here. Stuart, you know Abraham and Sarah—" they embraced him— "and this is Isaac."

"I'm not their son," the younger man said, shaking Straight's hand.

"I didn't think so."

Straight's host, Simeon—who had been Clarence Little when they were growing up and had become his colleague at the University of Chicago—was the man Straight credited for "getting me saved and saving my life."

"Let me introduce three more recent arrivals," Simeon said. "Silas, Barnabas, and Damaris, who may have some insight on your proposal. Folks, meet the professor."

Straight greeted the two men but paused when he got to the woman called Damaris. "No names," Straight said, "but I believe we recently met over lunch in Washington, D.C."

"We did," Angela said.

• • •

The committee of seven took their places on one side of a long table, facing Straight. "I've become involved with a very unusual convert," he began, "one in a unique position to help us. But there are also huge risks. His father-in-law was one of the original big guns in the NPO. The convert himself is an agent."

He described how he had met Paul. "The nurses had asked me to check on him. His bitterness was interfering with his healing, and he had alienated his family. But he was also listening to the New Testament on disc."

Straight recounted conversations they had shared and what he considered the figurative opening of Paul's eyes. "Then I witnessed a miracle. On a flight back from Washington—this was the same day as the cherry-blossom miracle—Paul regained his sight."

The committee exchanged glances. "That's when I left Washington," Angela said, explaining how Paul had warned her and how she'd come west with her sons to be picked up by the underground in Ohio. "I was one step ahead of Bia Balaam, who was responsible for the killings following the blossom miracle."

"*Bia* means 'force' or 'might' in Greek," Straight said. "In Greek mythology, Bia set up the torment of Prometheus."

"That's fitting," Angela said. "Her specialty is intimidation. She masterminded my father's death and a snake attack at the

Asclepian Zoo, and now the latest atrocities—a Christian leader crushed in the machinery at the Bureau of Engraving and Printing and two others gassed with pesticide in a National Botanical Gardens greenhouse. That's five leaders killed in Washington alone. Others, like my Uncle Jack, have been forced underground."

"Obviously, those last two killings were designed to link us to the cherry blossoms and tap into the public outrage," Silas said. "And that's what has me worried. Bia Balaam is just the talent. She's a creative sadist, a monster who comes up with these dramatic and frightening deaths to undermine our groups—and she's been all too effective. Not only has she crippled our leadership, but we've also had defectors, maybe even moles.

"But it's the puppeteer pulling her strings that we really have to worry about. So far Washington has done a masterful job of keeping our existence out of the press and the public eye, even when they expose and kill us. They've tried to cover up clear acts of God by blaming them on pranksters, as in the case of the Reflecting Pool; industrial sabotage, as in Texas; or even random terrorist cells, as in San Francisco. But the more of these acts they pin on us—as they seem to be doing with the cherry blossoms—the more they'll rouse public opinion against us. Then they'll be able to mount a much more systematic offensive. That's what I'm afraid is coming next."

"A contact in the NPO could keep his ear to the ground," Isaac said. "He could warn us when and if that kind of crackdown was imminent, as well as help prevent tragedies like we've seen this year. These deaths and the lack of public outcry are stifling our movement. Cowards who would avoid us we wouldn't want anyway. But there may be hundreds of thousands out there who would rally to our mission."

"A contact might also help us carry out our mission more effectively," Silas said. "Someone who could circumvent the government could keep us in touch with each other—help us share resources, like the electronic and physical materials you produce here, as well as ideas on how to disseminate them. At the very least, we want other believers to know they are not alone."

Abraham stood and leaned forward, hands flat on the table. "I don't know, Professor," he said. "I'm troubled by this whole idea, asking a man to become a mole in the biggest government security agency in the world. He'd be putting his life on the line every day. He could flip on us—make a name for himself, exposing us and engineering a raid that could end our cause."

"I know him," Straight said. "I trust him. I'm not a fool. If I thought there was a chance in a million he wasn't who I think he is, I'd never have brought it up. We need help in high places. You don't get much higher than this guy."

Sarah reached out to Abraham, and he sat again. "I don't like the alternative," she said. "Had it not been for the deaths we've seen, I might not recommend that we take such a risk. But it's clear the government has declared war on us."

Barnabas spoke for the first time. "There's something we're forgetting. This man's sight was miraculously restored. The professor here, whom most of you seem to know well, observed him daily and witnessed his recovery. How can we doubt such an obvious gift from God?"

"Abraham," Simeon said, "I've known the professor most of my life, and I would never doubt his judgment. But the risk is great. Why doesn't one of us meet this man? I could go, or—"

"No," Abraham said. "I'll meet him myself, if the professor can make the arrangements."

• • •

Angela left the library with Simeon and Straight. "What's next for you?" Straight said. "Staying here?"

"A few more days," she said. "I'm not so well known that I have to get out of circulation for good, like some here. I was overseeing book drops in Washington—working out of the Library of Congress to get Christian texts planted in the reading rooms and computer archives along the East Coast. Now I've been training for a new mission, and I'll probably head west. There are plenty of places I could be useful."

They entered the main thoroughfare of the mine, as wide as a four-lane highway. Straight ran his hand along the white salt wall. "Like marble but more translucent. It glows."

"Those darker streaks are dirt that got trapped when the salt was forming eons ago," Simeon said.

"Beautiful."

Angela stopped at the left turnoff that led to dormitories and family suites. "Professor, I assume Paul will hear nothing of this meeting."

"Of course not. I know everyone's anonymous here." He took her hand. "Glad to see you again. May God keep you safe and bless you on your new mission . . . Damaris."

Straight followed Simeon to the right turnoff, where permanent members of the community lived. Simeon kept a pair of modest rooms for sleeping and sitting, furnished with castoffs from the old mining operation—old lockers and an upright filing cabinet where he kept his clothes—and the few relics of his old life he'd bothered to smuggle in, like his sophisticated decasonic sound system. Knowing how much his friend loved music, Straight always brought him a couple of new discs.

Simeon poured coffee from his old-fashioned electric pot, stirring two sugars into Straight's cup.

"Ever get claustrophobic?" Straight said.

"No, man." Simeon swept a hand toward the ceiling, far above the twenty-foot-high wooden partitions that formed his walls. "The roof is so high that we never feel closed in. And look at the scale—those columns holding up the roof are sixty feet wide. Human beings are dwarfed. You miss the outdoors, of course, but I get out once in a while. We have everything we need—worship, fellowship, and peace. For someone like me, who loves books and study, this is a great place."

"It's incredible, the work you all do here. Maintaining a library. Copying old books. Printing and circulating flyers. Training teachers to establish or lead Christian communities. Sending missionaries. Maintaining a network of Christian groups, spreading the news. Being a haven for victims of persecution. It's a lot."

"Just keeping the faith, man."

• • •

"Missed you yesterday," Paul said. "Get your business straightened out?"

"Sure did," Straight said. "You were on my mind. I was thinking about you going back to work."

"You know when you told me I was making a mighty important decision?"

"Yes."

"You know what I was thinking about?"

"I think so."

"I was thinking it means I'm going to have to quit the NPO."

"Not so fast."

"C'mon, Straight. If you know the Bible, you know the story of Saul before he became Paul. He persecuted Christians. What am I doing if I stay with the agency? That's my job."

"You told me your job was to advise and interpret and interrogate. Have you persecuted anyone?"

"I sure have. I've been responsible, directly or indirectly, for five deaths. I can't do this anymore."

"There may be another way of looking at it."

Paul shook his head slowly. "I don't see how I can go back to the NPO."

"I know someone who could help you make that decision. Someone who understands the ramifications. I can't really say more. Want me to set up a meeting?"

"I guess so, sure."

• • •

The following evening Paul had dinner with his family, then announced he would be going out with Straight.

"What?" Jae demanded, almost out of habit.

"There's someone he wants me to meet, something to do with my work."

"You're still on sick leave, but you're working?"

"It's somebody who might be useful down the road."

"Hmm. Well . . ." Jae shrugged and noticed Paul's surprise. He had no idea she already felt so betrayed that a late night with Straight was just one more slight.

The minute school ends, I'm out of here.

• • •

Straight picked Paul up at nine-fifteen and drove downtown, parking near Michigan and Chicago. It had been months since Paul had seen the Water Tower. For more than 150 years, it had stood as a monument to the end of the great Chicago Fire. Now it lay on the ground, bathed in colored laser beams as a memorial to the great Chicago Earthquake of 2 P.3.

Straight and Paul walked north all the way into Lincoln Park, which was deserted at that hour. Straight steered Paul to a bench under a statue of the father and son mayors, Richard J. and Richard M. Daley. Fog had rolled in off Lake Michigan.

"Lucky it's a pretty straight shot out of here," Paul said. "I'd hate to be off the path, trying to find my way."

Light footsteps approached.

"Right on time," Straight said.

A figure in a hooded jacket emerged from the mist. He passed the bench, then doubled back. "Hello, friend," he said to Straight.

"Hi. Paul, this is Abraham."

A hardy man of about sixty, with a white mustache and beard and wisps of white hair poking out of his hood, slid onto the bench next to Paul, boxing him in beside Straight. Despite the hour, the man wore dark glasses.

"Dr. Stepola, thank you for meeting me," Abraham began. "I come to you with a proposition. We are responsible for many lives, and as you well know, we are involved in activities punishable by death."

"Back up. Who's *we?*"

"We call ourselves the Watchmen. In the book of Isaiah, God tells His chosen people, 'I have set watchmen on your walls, O Jerusalem. They shall never hold their peace day or night. You who make mention of the Lord, do not keep silent, and give Him'—that's the Lord—'no rest till He establishes and till He makes Jerusalem a praise in the earth.' We believe that is going to happen, Doctor. Soon."

Paul turned to look at Straight. "So I've gathered. And I'm struggling to understand."

"Please have faith, Paul," Straight said.

"Doctor, we believe the time of the Lord's coming is near because there have been so many signs."

"What kind of signs?"

"I'm sure you've heard what happened with the Reflecting Pool in Washington. Then there was the earthquake in San Francisco—"

"I knew that couldn't have been a bomb. It was like the top of the hill imploded."

"Exactly," said Abraham. "Yet it was like no earthquake ever seen. Then there were the pillars of fire in Gulfland and, recently, the withering of the cherry blossoms in Columbia. Most of these miracles have biblical antecedents. And there have been many other miracles, signs that the end is drawing near."

"I heard from a wise man that the Lord might come in my lifetime," Paul said. "And I have had a miracle in my own life. Two actually—the reversal of my blindness and the gift of faith."

"That is the gift we share among ourselves, in worship, study, and fellowship."

Paul looked at Straight. "I need that."

"We all do," Straight said.

"We also offer that gift to others, as Jesus instructed: 'Go therefore and make disciples of all the nations,'" Abraham said. "And Paul, our numbers are growing exponentially. We're not just a few isolated fanatics, as the government would have you believe. I can't tell you how important it would be for us to have someone in your position on our side."

"So you are actually organized."

"You can understand that I will not explain how right now. But yes, there are Christians all over the country, with a nerve center here in Heartland. We are a movement, a veritable army of God."

"But what exactly could I do? My job is to hunt down Christians."

"You could save lives, friend," Straight said. "I would never suggest this if we didn't need you."

"You know the government has been suppressing news of the miracles," Abraham said. "You could help with leaks to the press."

JERRY JENKINS • 159

"Risky. Very. I don't know how I'd manage that."

"You'll have access to government information on the Watchmen factions in each region, so you could warn us about raids or put groups in contact with each other."

"Riskier yet. I'm not sure about any of this. This is no easy decision."

"I know," Straight said.

"There are also false Christian cults," Abraham said. "You could help alert the legitimate Watchmen to them. With your background, you'd be able to recognize their characteristics."

Paul had been wondering how he could accept this challenge and still appear legitimate to the NPO. It wouldn't take them long to notice if he was ineffective in flushing out Christians. But if he exposed false cults, the organization wouldn't know the difference. "Are there enough of these weirdos to make me look good?"

"Probably."

Paul ran a hand through his hair. "Well, you've heard the expression 'don't kid a kidder.' I'd have to be crazy to go undercover in a spy agency."

"God would help you," Abraham said. "He would give you the strength, show you what to do. Let God lead you to the right decision."

"I've never had a death wish, but if the NPO brass found out about me . . ." Paul drew his finger across his neck.

"I don't want to talk you into anything," Straight said. "But doesn't it seem there's a reason God has put you in this position?"

"I've wondered."

"Think on this awhile; pray over it," Abraham said. "Go back to work and see how it feels."

"I could do that."

Straight put a hand on Paul's shoulder. "If you decide to do this, you'd be a double agent. Did you ever imagine that?"

17

PAUL WAS BACK TO WORK by the second week of June. A big Welcome Back banner hung over his desk, and his coworkers high-fived and backslapped him as if he were a conquering hero. Paul was warmed by the reception, despite the stab in his gut. He was an impostor, regardless of whether he committed to working with the Watchmen. He'd worked undercover before, but not against his "own people." This was literally a life-or-death proposition. He couldn't help wondering if it was a mistake to return as if nothing had changed.

Koontz had breakfast catered in the conference room for the staff. He feted Paul, concluding, "He regained his sight for a reason: to see his way clear to lead the way in stamping out the subversive menace."

Paul pasted on a smile and held up both hands to stem his

coworkers' applause. How he might have enjoyed this just a few weeks before.

Afterward Koontz privately asked Paul, "So how are you feeling? How's your energy level, your stamina?"

Paul shrugged. "I'm snapping back."

"Really ready to get back in the saddle?"

"If I wasn't, I wouldn't be here."

"Be honest with me, Paul, because your next case is no picnic. We can put it off, put someone else on it."

"No, Chief. I want whatever you've got."

I'm fooling everybody but myself.

"We need you at your best. You'd leave Wednesday morning for New York City—if that's not too soon."

"I love New York."

"Strange things going on there, Paul. I almost envy you." He handed Paul a folder labeled "Demetrius & Demetrius." "Heard of 'em?"

Paul shook his head.

"Wall Street brokerage firm. Precious metals. Apparently a whistle-blower tipped off the cops that the company attempted a run on the silver market, trying to corner it. Which, as you know—"

"Is illegal."

"Of course. Anyway, this whistle-blower claims that bizarre occurrences—"

"Here we go again."

"Right. Bizarre occurrences are stopping the run, not the law. It's complicated stuff, and we've inherited the search warrants from local authorities, including authority to search the main vault. There's been a report, from the older of the two Demetrius brothers, Ephesus, that a woman on his staff accused him of manipulating the market. He dressed her down, and she supposedly responded with a note containing a Bible verse. He took it as a curse and fired her. It's in your file."

"A curse?"

"Manhattan is one of the most superstitious places on earth. All those high rollers tied up in speculations—at least in Vegas they call it what it is. In New York everybody's trying to get an angle on the market, so they'll use seers and psychics and horoscopes—anything to give them an edge. So yes, a curse, ridiculous as it sounds, has the company spooked.

"The company had been aggressively buying silver, but right after the curse it stopped cold. Its own traders were confused, available silver plummeted, and the market went squirrelly. Ephesus Demetrius has gone missing, and the last two guards to visit the vault were found on an elevator nearly catatonic, their hair instantly turned white. Some are claiming something supernatural has happened. So it's your turn."

"I'm on it."

"Could be unpleasant, Paul. Just so you know. Personally, I think Demetrius the elder absconded with the money. Either way, your job is to eliminate the religious angle."

• • •

That night Paul called Straight and asked if he had contacts in the Christian underground in Atlantica.

"No, but we know about them. And there's something you'll need. I'll bring it over."

Straight sounded thrilled, but he didn't ask if that meant Paul had made a decision about joining the Watchmen. Paul was grateful that since the meeting with Abraham, Straight had never again broached the issue, apparently recognizing that Paul had to choose for himself.

Meanwhile, Paul checked his file for the so-called curse

verse. It was Job 27:19: "The wicked go to bed rich but wake up
to find that all their wealth is gone."

Ephesus had mocked her, calling her a witch and challeng-
ing her to make his wealth disappear. She denied having that
ability but warned that greed and duplicity would be punished,
if not by the government then by a higher power. She castigated
him with Revelation 21:8: "The corrupt, and murderers, and the
immoral, and those who practice witchcraft, and idol worshipers, and all liars—their doom is in the lake that burns with fire
and sulfur."

Ephesus had said, "Doom? Prove it." He fired her then
promptly disappeared. Local authorities were seeking her for
questioning. In the meantime, the vault seemed to hold the answer, but since the guard incident no one had dared approach it.

Was it booby-trapped? Or *had* something supernatural happened? As an NPO agent, Paul could never ask that question.

• • •

Straight showed up an hour later with a handful of green compound leaves.

"What are those?" Paul said. "They look like they're off a
weed tree."

"They are. Leaves from an ailanthus tree."

"Never heard of it."

"It's native to China, but it's hardy and grows anywhere."
Straight handed Paul the two- and three-bladed leaves.

Paul sniffed them. "Peanut butter!" he said.

"Don't try eating them. They don't taste like they smell.
They're going to taste good in heaven though."

"Say again?"

"The ailanthus is also known as the tree of heaven. The
Christians in Atlantica use them as an identification symbol.

There are a lot of references in the Bible to the tree of heaven. 'Blessed are those who do His commandments, that they may have the right to the tree of life, and may enter through the gates into the city.' That's heaven. 'In the middle of its street, and on either side of the river, was the tree of life, which bore twelve fruits, each tree yielding its fruit every month. The leaves of the tree were for the healing of the nations.' "

Paul vaguely remembered that from his discs. "A tree in heaven," he said.

"And just for us. Listen up now: 'To him who overcomes I will give to eat from the tree of life, which is in the midst of the Paradise of God.' You can't beat that, Paul."

• • •

The flight from Daley International to Giuliani International took a tick over an hour on the supersonic projectile. Paul used the time to study the Atlantica file and to pray. Bizarre, he thought, that talking to God was now so natural. After a lifetime of assuming He didn't exist, now Paul talked to Him about everything. Especially about Jae and the kids.

He also prayed—in futility, Straight told him—about his remaining sense of guilt over killing people he knew were now his brothers and sisters in Christ. "I'm not diminishing your sin," his friend had said. "I'm telling you that once you've confessed it and asked forgiveness, God casts aside your guilt as far as the east is from the west. I know it's not something you can simply put out of your mind, but to wallow in it is to fear God didn't do His part. That's a lack of faith, Paul. If God could save you and heal your blindness, He can forgive you, and He has."

Paul wished he could feel it.

Today, though, his prayers took on a new urgency. This was his first foray into a new dual role. Paul hoped that, as Abraham had promised, God would give him wisdom and show him what to do. But he would keep his options open. It might just be impossible, and he hadn't actually committed to the cause yet. Such a move would endanger more than just himself. There were his wife and kids to consider. He prayed that someday they would also become people of faith. But in the meantime, who was he to plunge them into such danger?

• • •

Paul took a cab to the Pierre Hotel, marveling at the dark beauty of Manhattan. He had visited New York a couple of times as a youngster, but it seemed all the new buildings designed since then were black. It gave the island, particularly midtown, an ultramodern look and feel. While some of the ancient landmarks—the former Empire State Building (now the Atlantica Tower) and the former Chrysler Building (now the Northeast Building)—retained their gray-granite charm, sleek black skyscrapers with black tinted windows dominated the skyline.

After lunch Paul took the bullet train to the Wall Street financial district, which boasted some of the most spectacular examples of the new architecture and color scheme. He got off a block and a half from the Demetrius & Demetrius Building so he could take in the full scope of the celebrated structure. It didn't disappoint. The main part of the building rose thirty stories and supported another six-story pyramid that made the entire complex look like a magnificent nontapered version of the Washington Monument, only in black.

Staring up at the building, Paul was jostled and whirled to find himself face-to-face with a street person. It had been years since he had encountered one, what with modern anti-delusional medications, strict no-loitering laws, and aid programs more profitable than panhandling. But a few renegades always slipped through the social safety net—drug addicts or alcoholics in flight from treatment. In a shabby fedora and a huge grimy trench coat despite the June heat, the scruffy character looked incongruous against all the gleaming black glass, a rumpled stowaway from another century.

Flushed with a compassion he had never known before, Paul shoved a bill into the open hand and headed into the cool glass lobby.

18

THE DEMETRIUS BROTHERS' EXECUTIVE OFFICES were located in the pyramid atop the building. The lobby guard told Paul to take the glass jetvator to the thirtieth floor. From there he could switch to another bank of jetvators or, to get the full dramatic impact of the design, walk the rest of the way—five floors up a glass staircase—to the office of the younger Demetrius brother, Arthur.

The first two floors of the pyramid were filled with back-office operations. Hundreds of clerks and clerical workers hunched over computers and high-speed calculators, ignoring the spectacular views outside their maze of cubicles. No one seemed even to have the time to chat, all were so busy keeping up with the mass fortunes of the brothers Demetrius.

Paul found the next two floors equally fascinating, but for a different reason. Here fewer people just as obsessively filled vast offices and sat before banks of flat screens, trading slavishly with brokers all over the world. Word was that the place never shut down. Three shifts worked around the clock to keep up with all the international markets.

The fifth story of the pyramid boasted an extravagant reception area that divided the floor in half. Marveling at its marble and gold and silver and mahogany, Paul couldn't imagine a more opulent piece of realty anywhere in the world. Discreet signs pointed to the right for the offices of Ephesus Demetrius, Chairman and Chief Executive Officer, and to the left for Arthur Demetrius, President and Chief Operating Officer.

The sixth and top floor, Paul knew, comprised the utilities for the entire structure.

In the bowels of the place, beneath the street level, sat one of the largest vaults in the USSA. Supposedly it was jammed with more precious metals than any repository outside Fort Knox.

The receptionist confirmed Paul had an appointment with Demetrius the younger. He was asked to wait in the reception area, where his attention was drawn to pristine first editions of rare books displayed in elegantly carved wooden bookcases. As Koontz had suggested, a number of the titles had to do with divination—finance-oriented interpretations of the I Ching and the tarot, as well as Western, Asian, and Indian astrology, among other systems. Before he was able to examine the books, an assistant escorted Paul to the Arthur Demetrius side of the floor.

"Both wings of this level are identical," the assistant purred. "The brothers enjoy equal space and facilities."

They passed several offices and conference and meeting rooms until Paul found himself in yet another reception area, this one apparently the last buffer between Arthur Demetrius's office and the real world. The assistant handed Paul off to the personal secretary, who ushered him into Arthur's private office.

Paul tried to keep from gawking. This office alone was as big as the first floor of his home. It was not only professionally decorated, but it was also landscaped. Trees. Bushes. Flowers. Tables, chairs, a sofa, two fireplaces, bookcases, credenzas, pillars. The half-moon, granite-and-smoked-glass desk was centered between a bank of windows that looked out over Battery Park and the Hudson River for as far as one cared to see. An enormous telescope added even more potential. On bright sunny days like this one, Paul was certain he would have been unable to concentrate on his work.

The floor on either side of the desk was not marble but Plexiglas, and one could watch the traders at work below. How much of Arthur Demetrius's day was spent keeping tabs on his most important mercenaries?

The secretary pointed to a luxurious leather chair that sat in a grouping about ten feet in front of the desk. Paul sat, briefcase in his lap. Then he put the case next to his feet and crossed his legs. That seemed too casual too, and he knew he should stand when Demetrius entered. But where would he come from? Behind? From the side, which Paul guessed led to private quarters?

Paul reminded himself that he was in charge here. He was the one with the agenda, the warrants, the questions. This place may have been intended to intimidate the competition, but it should have no effect on him. At least the marble floor would make it impossible for the man to sneak up on him.

Fortunately, Arthur Demetrius entered from his private quarters where Paul could see him coming. His soft leather shoes made hardly a sound. He was tall and lithe, bronzed, and wearing an exquisite black pin-striped suit, white shirt, and gleaming white tie with a silver stickpin. His watch and a ring on each hand were also silver. His hair was black, short, and curly; his eyes dark; and his teeth perfect.

"Dr. Stepola," he said as Paul rose, "do I need a lawyer?"

"Oh, I don't think so. We should be able to cover what I need without acrimony."

"What can I do for you?"

"I just have a few questions, sir. Our reports show that you and your brother, on behalf of the firm, had a particularly active silver-buying period last month. This abruptly ceased, causing much speculation in the marketplace. Rumors of an attempt to corner the market, that sort of thing."

"You get right to the point," Demetrius said, clearing his throat. "First, we have a long history in the precious-metals market, and we have broken no laws. I would hesitate to discuss our strategy and don't believe I am obligated to."

"I assure you," Paul said, "finance is not my area. I don't work for the Securities and Exchange Commission. My role for the National Peace Organization has more to do with investigating claims of the supernatural."

Demetrius did not blink, his face impenetrable as stone. "I am a capitalist, sir, and I make no apologies for that. My brother and I would never have to work another day in our lives, but we love the chase, the challenge. But we also know and understand the law, so no, we are not trying to corner the silver market. As for the supernatural, you'll have to explain where that comes into play, and while you're at it, who believes in it."

Sifting through his file, Paul thought about the divination books. Funny that trying to read the future didn't count as believing in the supernatural, according to Arthur Demetrius. Paul assumed all the Wall Street firms had similar books in their arsenals of business tools.

"Let's start by talking about the vault. Is it true that two of your uniformed guards, the last to visit your vault, were discovered in an elevator in a state of shock?"

"I don't know what you are talking about."

"Mr. Demetrius, what would they have seen in that vault?"

"Our vault contains precious metals, of course, and cash, securities, original bonds, that type of thing."

"Is it true these guards are under the care of mental-health professionals and have not returned to work?"

"I told you, I don't know what you are talking about."

For the first time, Paul noticed something in the man's eyes. "All due respect, sir, but the story of the guards has swept your company, fueling speculation that something supernatural *has* occurred."

"Nonsense."

"Are you aware that the alternative explanation, which a significant portion of your workforce believes, is that your brother absconded with the contents of the vault, and that is why no one has seen him for days?"

"Ridiculous. Why would he steal from himself?"

"And that the guards saw an empty vault and collapsed out of fear of being blamed, since it was full the last time they opened it?"

"You're wholly mistaken."

"Where is your brother?"

"Abroad. We take turns traveling a great deal."

"Where?"

"We go many different—"

"Where is he now, as we speak?"

"His people could give you that information."

"Has the vault been opened since the incident with the guards?"

"I deny any knowledge of the incident, but no, to my knowledge the vault has not been opened for several days."

"Why not?"

"It's not unusual for it to be used infrequently."

"Then it's not true that no one, including you, has dared go near the vault since the guards saw whatever it was they saw?"

"That is correct. It is not true."

Paul shuffled papers in his file for effect. A faint hysteria was starting to color Arthur's responses. "Well, it says here that the mystery of the vault and your brother's disappearance, on the heels of an alleged curse, caused your local NPO bureau to invite me here from Chicago."

Arthur stood. "Come, Doctor, let me show you something."

"But I have more questions—"

"I will answer everything, but please, come."

Paul followed the man to one end of the drapes to the left of his desk. "The only door that opens to the outside," Arthur said. He pressed a button and the glass turned, allowing access to a small balcony enclosed in a wrought-iron fence with spearlike posts.

It was windier than at street level, and Demetrius's hair fluttered. The sun glared off the black windows. Paul had to stand close to Arthur to hear him, and Demetrius seemed to want to confide in him.

"Listen," he said, "you must know that this is not the first time I have been asked these questions. The local NPO office has been through all this, and there *is* an explanation."

"Well, sir, this is now under my jurisdiction, and I need to hear it."

"It all stems from an act of vengeance on the part of a disgruntled employee. Maybe more than one. Anytime you have a business so openly successful with people at the highest levels enjoying the spoils, there will be resentment and jealousy. You understand."

"Vengeance? You mean the curse?"

"There is a religious faction here," Demetrius said, sighing, "clearly violating the law. Maybe because we're a big company in a big city, they are bolder than they might be elsewhere. One woman did make serious threatening remarks to Ephesus. She was out-and-out trying to persuade others to believe the way she does until Ephesus finally fired her."

"Sir, proselytizing is a crime. Why was this not reported to the authorities?"

Demetrius shrugged. "Our business depends on quick response. We didn't need the police or a government agency nosing around, slowing us. It seemed easiest to simply be done with her."

"Nosing around? Are you hiding something? Where can I find this woman?"

"I have no idea. I have been asked and asked about the whereabouts of both the woman and my brother. My employees have been quizzed at length about these two allegedly freaked-out guards. The investigation has turned up nothing and has resulted only in the interruption of our business."

"Might your brother have harmed the woman to keep her from turning him in?"

"No! Dr. Stepola, the reports that brought you here are nothing but rumors. Wall Street is full of them, and fortunes are made and lost based on them. The lies of the religious faction are a result of one of their own being fired. They are trying to undermine us."

Paul glanced down the angled wall to the roof of the supporting skyscraper, which extended a little more than four feet beyond the bottom of the pyramid. "I don't want to see you undermined, sir. Firms like yours, acting within the law, keep this country going."

Back inside, Paul pulled an envelope from his briefcase and

put it in his inside breast pocket. "Is it not true that it was common for you, before the recent incidents, to be in and out of the vault daily?"

Demetrius pursed his lips. "I never kept track. The vault is on a timer and can be opened only at 8:00 A.M. or 8:00 P.M. I have had no business in there recently."

Paul looked at his watch. It was past five. He pulled the envelope from his pocket and handed it to Arthur. "I have here a warrant to search the vault. I will return by eight o'clock this evening, and I will require your presence to open the vault."

Demetrius studied the document, and Paul thought he heard the man's rate of respiration increase. "Of course, I will comply," Arthur said, standing, and again, Paul heard something in his voice. The pitch, the timbre—something was different. What he had detected, Paul decided, was stark terror.

"I assume you won't mind if I look around on my way out? I'd like to get a sense of your operation."

"We have nothing to hide. In a few minutes the two-to-ten shift breaks before the Tokyo markets open."

• • •

Paul moseyed around the trading floor a few minutes, then moved one floor lower to an almost identical operation. Many traders were finishing conversations and transactions. He headed toward an exit but was overtaken by an unusual odor.

Peanut butter.

Paul followed the aroma to a tiny tree in a glass cubicle, where a thin, dark-haired woman he guessed to be about his own age was arranging her things and packing her purse. Paul fell into step with her and others as they headed for the jetvator.

At ground level Paul followed the woman into the crowded

streets. But then she was gone, caught in the rush-hour swirl. He scanned the crowd frantically, shouldering his way deeper into the throng hoping to catch a glimpse of her, but to no avail. *Just my luck—she's probably day shift, heading home. She could be blocks away on the bullet train by now.*

Someone plucked his sleeve. He tried to jerk away, but the tug was insistent. He turned and found the same street person he had given money to clutching at his coat, pointing past him with a filthy hand. *There she is!* "Thanks," Paul said, darting after his quarry. *How did he know?*

Slowing, he pulled alongside her, apparently without engendering suspicion, but said nothing until they had passed the Stock Exchange. The old Georgian building with its marble columns now sported a mammoth mobile of the spinning planets. Behind it, a zodiacal chart loomed.

"Hey, excuse me," he said. "You work in the district here?"

Without slowing, she gave him a New York look. "Maybe. Why?"

"I understand the blinking sign on the Exchange there, with the stock prices and all. But what's the zodiac thing? Looks like it shows the relative positions of the planets every few seconds."

She slowed. "That's for superstitious investors. Gives them an instant read on their fortunes."

"Kinda silly, isn't it?"

"I think so."

This is the moment of truth. Will she talk to me? "Name's Paul," he said, reaching for her hand with an ailanthus leaf in his.

She cautiously gripped his hand and her eyes grew wide. She peeked at the leaf and froze, then continued walking.

Paul hurried to catch up with her. "I'd like a minute," he said.

"Across the street and left, there's a deli."

A few minutes later they sat across from each other in a booth. Paul introduced himself more formally.

"Call me Phyllis," the woman said.

"I've just come from your office, where I was interviewing Arthur Demetrius."

"I thought so." She looked at him suspiciously.

What should I say? "Officially I am here as an NPO agent, investigating the possibility of a supernatural occurrence."

She laughed. "And what would the NPO do if there had been a supernatural occurrence?"

"Probably the same thing they did in Washington, Gulfland, and San Francisco."

She raised her eyebrows. "Why should I talk to you?"

He pulled out a handful of leaves from his pocket. "Because of these. I know what they signify: 'Blessed are those who do His commandments, that they may have the right to the tree of life, and may enter through the gates into the city.'"

She said nothing.

"'To him who overcomes I will give to eat from the tree of life, which is in the midst of the Paradise of God.'"

She appeared to relax. "You seem to know what you're talking about. What do you want with me?'"

"Well, first, why would a believer work for Demetrius?"

"I'm trained in finance," she said. "It's no worse than anywhere else. All the financiers worship money. Plus, I'm not alone. There are almost thirty of us believers there. We're nothing compared to the total, but we've made progress. Things are a little more open here than in the rest of the country, and we're careful. People get to know we're believers, and they want to know about things like the oil well fires in Texas and the cherry blossoms. They want to know what these things mean. We believe they signal the beginning of the end, and we say so."

"Risky."

"That's our lives. Yours too if you're working for Uncle Sam."

Paul shrugged. "Can't argue with that."

They sat in silence for a moment. "Tell me, Phyllis," Paul said finally, "what do you think is going on at your firm?"

"I think it's God."

"What do you mean? I should tell you, I'm new at this."

"At the NPO?"

"At being a believer. What did God do?"

"Well, Ephesus was a greedy man. Arrogant. He ridiculed Dolores and challenged God. He thought he was above the law and beyond God's reach."

"Dolores? The missing one? Did you know her?"

"Not well. She was one of the new ones hired to buy up silver. She didn't like what Ephesus wanted her to do."

"Did he hurt her?"

"I don't know. I pray she ran away when word of this 'curse' got out, so she wouldn't be arrested as a Christian. If he did something to her, we'd never find out. He's rich enough to cover it forever."

"What about the guards? That story true?"

She nodded. "I knew them both. And I haven't seen them since."

"What do you think they saw in the vault?"

Phyllis shrugged. "God. Some evidence of God."

"What about Arthur?"

"Arthur idolizes his older brother. But he was never as ruthless. We pray for him."

"You what? For Demetrius?"

"Of course. We're supposed to love our enemies."

"That can't be easy though, can it, Phyllis?"

She hesitated. "No, but when you think about it, it's a privilege."

"I think I'd be tempted to pray he would come to a bad end," Paul said.

"Oh no, sir. We pray for his salvation."

19

PAUL AND PHYLLIS AGREED she should head back to the office a full five minutes before he did. It was a little before six-thirty, and while the sun was still high behind the skyscrapers, it had turned a burnt orange and cast long shadows in the street.

As Paul approached the building from the west, he was struck by the jewel-like glow of the pyramid in the twilight. He squinted to make out the balcony that had blended in with the glass the first time he had seen the place. It appeared as if a dark figure was up there now, leaning against the wrought-iron barrier. It could only be Arthur.

When Paul got off the jetvator on the first floor of the upper complex, he found himself in a crowd on their way back to the trading floors above. Letting the others stream past him, he paused to check out the magnificent view of the early evening sun on the black glass towers beyond the windows. Suddenly from above there was an ugly thud and a scream. Paul jumped and looked up just in time to see a dark form tumbling down the side of the glass pyramid.

Everyone around Paul froze. People gasped. The body rolled, skidded, and then slid all the way down to the flat roof of the skyscraper. People pressed up against the glass to look. Some clung to each other. Paul fought through the crowd and searched frantically until he spotted a fire door, sprinted toward it, and burst out onto the roof.

The crumpled body was dark-haired and wore a black pin-striped suit.

Running to him, Paul was inexplicably overcome with grief. Why should he care? With Arthur Demetrius in a heap, Paul realized that here too was a man God had loved. Arthur may have thumbed his nose at heaven, but he was still a lost soul, someone who needed forgiveness and salvation as much as anyone else. As Phyllis had said, it should be a privilege to pray for him. But surely now it was too late.

Paul knelt over him, fighting his own baffling emotions. "Arthur! Oh, Arthur! Why?"

The body was sprawled, facedown and still. Knowing it was fruitless, Paul pressed two fingers to the man's neck, checking the carotid artery for a pulse.

Paul reeled, off balance, and tumbled to his seat at finding not just a heartbeat, but a robust and fast one.

Impossible. No one could have survived that fall.

Paul struggled to his feet and bent close to listen for breathing.

None.

He checked the neck again. No mistake. The man's heart was beating, hard and strong. Paul had been trained not to move a severely injured victim, but he had to get the man breathing again. He slid one hand under Arthur's shoulder and, cradling his head and spine with the other, gently rolled him onto his back.

Arthur's lungs released a huge *whoosh* and his eyes fluttered. Paul was about to call emergency services, but he hesitated. "Arthur," he said, full of emotion, "lie still. Breathe deeply. Don't move."

Arthur's eyes were open now, and he stared at Paul as if he'd just awakened. His lips moved, but no sound came.

Paul shushed him, then glanced at the windows where employees were still pressed against the glass, mouths agape.

"Alive?" Arthur whispered.

"You are," Paul said. "Hold on."

"How?"

"It's a miracle," Paul said.

Arthur's eyes grew wide and he reached for Paul. He wrapped his arms around Paul's neck and pulled himself to a sitting position. He began to weep, and great sobs shook him.

"What happened, Arthur?"

"I jumped, Doctor," he rasped. "But I didn't even clear the ledge."

"Why?"

Arthur's voice was weak and labored. "I am so sick of this. Ephesus . . . maybe he killed her, I don't know. He's gone."

"Killed who?"

"That woman . . ."

"Arthur, listen. You can't believe you or Ephesus were ever cursed."

"He mocked her, dared her. . . . What if he did something? What if she's in the vault? The guards went mad. . . ."

"If Ephesus committed a crime, he will be punished. But you don't know that he did. Why try to kill yourself?"

"I was afraid . . . the guards . . . I was evil too, ruthless about the silver. . . . Once the truth comes out, I'm ruined."

"Arthur, clearly you weren't meant to die."

"But why? Why was I spared? I don't deserve it."

Paul thought of what Straight had told him: *I wouldn't want it to be fair, Paul. I'd never have earned this.* He held his breath a long moment before venturing, "People have been praying for you."

"I knew it!" Arthur whispered. "Something has been tormenting me for days." He clutched at Paul. "And you . . . you're one of them?"

Paul nodded.

Arthur bent and straightened his legs, then stretched his arms over his head.

"Don't get up yet. Give yourself a minute."

Paul turned and glanced at the clearly shaken crowd gathered at the windows. They shrank back when Arthur insisted on getting to his feet with Paul's help. He stood there, wobbly, trying to get his bearings. The onlookers finally backed away when Paul started to walk Arthur back through the emergency door.

The men made their way to the jetvator and ascended to Arthur's office. The staff averted their eyes as if they had not seen him jump. Paul helped Arthur to his private quarters, where a small den separated his bedroom and bath.

As they sat in easy chairs facing each other, Arthur looked exhausted. Paul leaned forward. "Is there someone I can call for you? Your wife, anyone?"

"No wife anymore," he said. "I have no one."

"You have God. He wouldn't even let you kill yourself. What does that tell you?"

Arthur buried his face in his hands. "Maybe He has a fate worse than death for me. I made the Christians out to be idle critics, condescending. They had ideas about what Ephesus and I should do with our resources. They sickened me.

"Oh, Dr. Stepola, I don't want to see what's in the vault. What if it *is* that woman . . . or what if it *is* something supernatural?"

"You cannot escape it, Arthur. But whatever is in that vault cannot compare to the coming judgment. Jesus said not to be afraid of those who want to kill you. They can only kill your body; they cannot touch your soul. Fear only God, who can destroy both soul and body in hell."

"Surely God will destroy me then."

"Jesus said, 'The thief's purpose is to steal and kill and destroy. My purpose is to give life in all its fullness.' " Paul stood. "Now you need to relax and collect yourself. It will soon be eight, and I'll be back, needing you to open the vault for me."

"Can I just give you the access codes and tell you how to do it?"

"The warrant calls for your presence."

Arthur slumped.

• • •

When Paul returned, Arthur looked like a man on his way to his own execution. He trudged ahead of Paul to a jetvator dedicated to the vault. To get the car to reach the subbasement, Arthur had to have both eyes scanned, have both hands read by print machines, and turn two keys simultaneously. Voice and DNA recognition technology opened the jetvator, and then he had to go through all that and more to open the floor-to-ceiling vault itself.

"I have sixty seconds from the tone at 8:00 sharp to get the codes entered on the keypad. I have enough time to make one mistake, but not two. The vault will not allow a third try for twelve hours."

Arthur trembled as the massive door slowly swung open. He told Paul that, apart from a small vault interior, the first floor would be filled with currency, stock certificates, bonds, some files and folders. "Mostly paper. The lower floors are filled virtually to the ceiling with silver bars—sterling silver bullion—92.5 percent silver and the rest copper, to give it enough hardness to stay together."

"May I?" Paul said, standing before the gaping entry.

Arthur nodded, still clearly panicked. "A light will come on."

That was an understatement. In truth, the place lit up like day. Paul looked back briefly and Arthur looked calmer. With nothing amiss so far, he moved in to join Paul. After his first step toward the back, however, Paul stalled. Something was in the air, nearly blocking the light, and yet it reflected brightly. It appeared at first to be a fine mist, but it seemed to hang heavy, sparkling in the air. The front shelves, full of paper products, looked like they were covered with tinsel. Paul pulled a handkerchief from his pocket and covered his mouth.

Paul heard Arthur gasp and turned to see him slowly sweep his hand through the air, catching the powder in his palm and rubbing it between thumb and fingers. He covered his mouth as well.

"Vaporized silver!" Arthur said behind his hand. "Gone to powder."

"How does that happen?" Paul said.

"It doesn't. It's impossible."

"What's that inner door, Arthur?"

But the man was overcome, quivering.

"Where does it lead?"

"To a cache of pure silver in special containers," Arthur said, his voice flat. "We call it native or free. Nothing has been added to it yet. It's almost white."

Paul pulled open the door, and a fresh cloud of silvery vapor surged out to mix with the rest. With his handkerchief pressed firmly over his mouth and nose, Paul entered. His body went rigid. He knew Arthur was behind him, and there would be no protecting him from this.

There on the floor of the special room sat a man who looked very much like a statue of Arthur. His eyes were open. He did not move. And he was covered, every millimeter from head to toe—hair, face, shirt, tie, suit, socks, and shoes—with silver dust.

Paul retreated slowly. "Arthur, is that your brother—?"

"Ephesus! Ephesus!" Arthur screamed, pushing past. "You have become what you loved so much!"

He embraced the silver-covered cadaver, and it slid from his hands and toppled to the floor.

• • •

Paul spent the next few days dealing with Arthur Demetrius and cleaning up the mess. He prevailed upon the security company to override the timing of the locks on the vault, had Ephesus Demetrius's body moved to a morgue, and had a metallurgist examine the silver residue to see if any was salvageable. It was not.

Arthur was a broken man. He spent most of his waking hours weeping, praying for forgiveness, and asking Paul to tell him more from the Bible. He took his greatest comfort from Jesus' words in John 5:24: "I assure you, those who listen to My message and believe in God who sent Me have eternal life. They will never be condemned for their sins, but they have already passed from death into life."

"God has been trying to reach me," Arthur said. "And whom should He send to explain Himself? An NPO agent who could have me sent to jail."

"What I've learned," Paul told him, "is that God's love

transcends all earthly gifts. God so loved the world that He sacrificed His only Son, who died on the cross to save us. Accepting that love has been the most important and fulfilling decision of my own life."

Finally, late one night in his opulent town house, Arthur asked Paul to pray with him, and he received Christ. Paul comforted him by telling him of the underground believers in Atlantica and gave him an ailanthus leaf.

"I want to contribute something concrete. I assume this underground needs funds."

"I'm sure that's an understatement. I can connect you with people who would be happy to hear from you. You're going to want to meet with them personally, so you can also learn and grow."

• • •

In his report to Robert Koontz, Paul blamed the underhanded dealings at Demetrius & Demetrius on the elder brother. Apparently he had diverted silver and funds, and a huge shipment he bought never made it to the company. He died in a freak accident when he was locked in the vault past two opening times and was asphyxiated. The younger brother was exonerated and would continue to run the firm.

"So no religious shenanigans," Koontz said.

"No shenanigans," Paul said.

"The guard business? That was because they saw the body in the vault?"

"Right."

"What about that curse? Is the place infested with subversives?"

"There can't be many, Bob. The woman who supposedly cursed them was a recent hire with no real ties to her coworkers.

She's vanished—to avoid arrest, most likely, though the police found no evidence of foul play. As for us, I think we just keep an eye on the company and see if Arthur Demetrius complains any more of proselytizing or other underground manifestations."

• • •

Straight was euphoric. He embraced Paul and said, "Look what you've done! Talk about a quick study. First time out, you go and make a convert."

"I couldn't believe it when I felt that pulse and realized he was alive, Straight. To actually feel the power of God working in another person—well, it was incredible. And somehow I was given just the right words."

"You were led."

"Definitely."

"And how about the big picture? Have you decided if you're on board?"

"The answer is yes, Straight. It seems to have been decided for me."

20

"STRAIGHT WANTS TO TAKE ME to a regional chess tournament this weekend."

"You've got to be kidding," Jae said. "You were stuck in New York till last Sunday, and now, rather than spend a weekend with your children, you want to go play?"

"It's not a question of 'rather.' Tournaments, when you get to play real people in the flesh, not just on-line, don't come along that often. Straight thinks I'm ready."

"Well, whatever good ol' Straight thinks."

"Look, I'm proud that I've gotten good enough to play tournaments again in such a short time."

"Yeah, real impressive, Paul. But let's face it, you've had nothing else to do for months. If you can waltz out of here with a clear conscience, then you and Straight just go ahead and enjoy yourselves."

"I can tell you don't want me to go."

She shook her head and put her hands on her hips. "Thank you for clarifying the obvious. Where is this tournament, anyway?"

"Toledo."

"Toledo! More than two hundred miles away."

"What difference does it make how far it is?"

Would it make a difference to you, Paul, to know your family is leaving you next week?

• • •

"Maybe we shouldn't have come," Straight said when Paul told him of the argument.

"Maybe. Lately she doesn't even seem to want me around. It's like she's given up on me. But I guess I can't blame her. I've been no prize either." He grew quiet.

"Paul?"

"I'm worried about my family, Straight. The kids, especially. What does it mean for them that I'm a Christian? It's one thing to put my life on the line, but do I have the right to drag them into it? I can't put Jae and them at risk by telling them the whole truth, even if it would make me feel better.

"It would be so much easier if I could tell Jae all that's been happening to me—how I got my sight back, what I've been studying, making the decisions to become a believer and to become a double agent. But her father is as rabidly anti-religious as they come. He once said, referring to Christians, 'I hate snakes.' And he heads up some kind of covert service at the NPO."

"Nothing like having your head in the lion's mouth. But, Paul, you're going to have to figure this out. Do you want to protect Jae and the kids from physical danger and lose them for eternity?"

Paul had to catch his breath after that one. "Even before I got

JERRY JENKINS • 193

hurt, Jae and I had grown apart—mostly my fault—but I always thought there was a chance we could reconnect. Now that seems impossible. I can't imagine ever again getting close enough to Jae to trust her with this.

"You know that verse in the New Testament that says, 'He who loves God must love his brother also.' Well, I've been having trouble loving my own wife."

"These are the toughest questions, Paul. As for Jae, things may be difficult now, but you have the same job: to honor her and serve her. Keep it up, and you'll be amazed at the change you'll see in her. It's an investment. You do this because it's the right thing, not for what you get in return. But you *will* get what you give. Invest kindness, service, love, and understanding, and you'll get it all back in spades."

"Guess I'm wondering when—if—that will ever happen."

"Faith means trusting God to sort it all out."

"Well, in the meantime, I hate being at home. I feel so alone—like a triple agent in my faith, at work, and in my own house."

• • •

As they neared Toledo, Paul's eyes kept darting toward the outside rearview mirror. "Hmm . . ."

"What's up?"

"Don't make it obvious, but you see the gray sedan back there?"

"Yeah?"

"How long has it been behind us?"

"Maybe almost all the way from Chicago," Straight said.

"Take the next exit."

"The truck stop?"

"Yeah, perfect. And do it at the last minute."

When Straight swept out of the traffic and up the ramp, Paul noticed the sedan switch lanes too late. "Let's casually head inside, get a bite, and see if that car waits for us farther down the interstate."

Sure enough, the sedan took the next exit and stopped at the top, apparently waiting for Straight and Paul to pass again before getting back on the highway.

"I don't like this," Straight said.

Paul shook his head. "Neither do I."

When they got back out on the road, Paul instructed Straight to take the next exit past where the sedan sat, head left across the bridge, and reenter traffic going the other way. By the time the sedan followed suit, he had Straight do the opposite, and soon they were on toward Toledo, several miles ahead of their pursuer.

"Guess we shook 'em."

"Better not get too comfortable," Paul said.

"Think they're going to pop up again?"

"Maybe. Get off here and let's take back roads to the hotel."

Though he tried to cover his worry for Straight's sake, Paul was shaken. The tail clearly hadn't been NPO; trained agents would never have been so obvious. Unless they wanted to be seen. But why? And if their pursuers weren't NPO, who were they? Paul couldn't fathom it.

There was no sign of the gray sedan when they got to their hotel. Straight checked in via retinal scan, but because of Paul's injuries, his didn't work. A handprint sufficed and they were given their infrared keys.

Straight still seemed nervous, his eyes shifting here and there. "Paul," he said, "let's freshen up, meet in my room for a practice game, then have an early dinner so we're ready for the tournament in the morning."

• • •

After a shower, Paul felt almost normal again. He was ready for a game, but when he got near Straight's room he slowed. The door was ajar. That didn't have to mean anything, but then he found the light off. It wasn't like Straight to leave his room unlocked, especially after their scare on the highway.

Paul carefully pushed the door open. His acute sense of smell detected sweat. He stepped in cautiously, making no sound on the carpet. Could Straight be napping? Not with the door open. Paul squinted in the darkness at the closed bathroom door. No light beneath it either.

Suddenly the bathroom door flew open, and two large figures swarmed Paul, slamming him against the wall and wrestling him to the floor. Paul put a death grip on a meaty wrist, but before he could do any damage, yet another man joined in.

He was no match for the three. He relaxed his grip and large, rough fingers pressed his hands against his sides as a pillowcase was forced over his head. A strap followed that—it felt like leather—wrapped around his torso and fastened in back, immobilizing his arms.

Paul heard squeaky wheels and felt something brush his thigh. The men lifted him and set him into what felt like a canvas cart.

"Fetal position," one said.

Paul thought about trying to wrestle free, but he was at too much of a disadvantage. They covered him with sheets and blankets, and he heard Straight's voice.

"See you down there." Then, "Trust me, Paul."

He felt the cart move—toward the door, he assumed. Was it possible Straight was a double agent? If so, Paul was dead.

"Are we alone?" he asked.

"Quiet."

"Where're we going?"

"Don't make this difficult, Paul."

Paul heard the door open and felt it bang the side of the cart as Straight pushed him into the corridor. They were going the opposite direction from where Paul had gotten off the elevator, so when they stopped and he heard a button being pushed, he assumed it was the freight elevator.

Doors opened, the cart was pushed on, doors closed, and Paul heard a whine and felt downward motion. When the doors opened again, he smelled the underground garage and heard electric- and hydrogen-powered cars coming and going. The cart slowed as it was wheeled up a ramp. A metallic door slid open, and the cart jostled over an uneven space. The door slid shut.

Everything was quiet save the sound of a truck engine, and they began to move. Straight removed the sheets and blankets. "Can you sit up, Paul?"

Paul planted a foot and tried to rock up, but he needed help. Straight pulled him to a sitting position, then unfastened the leather strap. "You okay?"

"I could have killed one of you in that room."

"I believe that," Straight said, tossing the strap aside and lifting the pillowcase free.

There was zero light in the back of the truck. "So it's just the two of us now?" Paul said. "Where's the muscle?"

"In front with the driver. Now take my arm and step out of there. There's a bench over here. It'll be a long ride."

"Where are we going, Straight?"

"You'll see when we get there, Paul—but let me just say it will be more than you ever could have imagined."

"I need to know—"

"You need to have faith, Paul. Just relax."

After about two hours, Paul guessed, the truck finally

stopped, but the engine continued to idle. Straight put the pillowcase over Paul's head. "I'll accept a blindfold," Paul said. "But don't restrain me. If you can't trust me—"

"You're not in charge here, Paul. It's not about me and my trust. This is for the comfort of those you are visiting. Now don't make me get help."

From outside, Paul heard what sounded like a huge metal gate sliding open. Straight knocked twice on the back of the truck, and the door slid open. Paul felt the cool evening breeze through the flimsy pillowcase and was aware of the glare of overhead lights. He was led down off the truck, across a gravel pathway, and inside. The way the door rattled and the way their quiet conversation echoed and rang, he deduced it was a metal structure.

They moved him across a squeaky wood floor, and he heard an elevator noisily rumble open. "Careful," Straight said, guiding him onto what felt like a floating platform. "There's just enough room for the five of us, and you won't fall through."

Paul felt cool air rush from below, and though the car began a rickety, metallic descent, the wall felt like wire mesh. They seemed to descend forever. "How far are we going?" Paul said.

"A good ways. More than eleven hundred feet."

When the elevator finally bounced to a stop far below the surface, Paul sniffed and found the air cool, dry, and briny.

Straight said, "You two drive on ahead and tell them we'll be along."

Drive? Eleven hundred feet underground?

Straight walked Paul a couple hundred feet then guided him into another truck. They rode a long time before Straight helped him out of the restraint and the pillowcase. They were on a broad thoroughfare, where huge, cloudy translucent pillars rose to a vaulted roof. A salt mine.

"Southwestern Detroit or northeastern Ohio, right?" Paul said.

"If I wanted you to know, I wouldn't have tossed you in the back of a truck, would I? This salt bed covers tens of thousands of miles. We could be in any of several prewar states."

They rolled past huge, dilapidated equipment that made Paul wonder aloud how it had been delivered to this level. The tires alone had to be seven feet tall.

"In pieces," Straight explained. "Assembled down here. When the mines were active, just before the end of the war, there was all kinds of that stuff down here."

The farther they rode, the better lit the mine was. Every few yards, signs along the walls warned of radioactivity. "Phony," Straight said.

They passed what looked like massive banquet halls or ballrooms.

"People live down here?"

"More than you would think. You're going to meet three of 'em."

"And nobody knows they're down here?"

"Nobody who doesn't need to know. They're not thrilled about your knowing."

Paul heard nothing and saw only whitish walls. "How far in are they?"

"About another quarter of a mile. This labyrinth goes for miles and miles."

"What's all this?" Paul said, pointing at a network of pipe and cable overhead.

"It used to supply electricity to all the mining equipment. They connected to the cables the way electric trolleys used to on the surface. We have vastly expanded this to provide power for daily living. This is a city beneath a city, Paul. Any outsider gets this far and sensors let our guards know. All activity in our little community ceases. Lights go out; refrigerators, freezers—you name it—stop humming. Snoops get tired of walking in the dark, so they head back up and out none the wiser."

"Anyone ever get far enough to encounter your lookouts?"

"Never."

"What if somebody did?"

"We don't like to think about that, but we have a plan."

"And . . . ?"

"Like I say, we don't like to think about it."

"You'd have to kill them. And then what?"

"Procedure calls for taking the body to the surface, putting it in the vehicle it showed up in, and moving that vehicle some- where so the body would not be traced to the mine."

"How do you justify that?"

"We don't, Paul. We pray it never happens."

"How do you keep people from nosing around?"

"We're way off the beaten track, and you have to really want to get here. There's absolutely nothing of value that anyone knows about. The gates work only on our highly encrypted code, and as soon as we're inside the fence, our vehicles can be hidden. There are signs warning of high voltage, dogs, and again, radia- tion. When the mine first shut down, a group planned to dump radioactive waste here, which would have worked well. They never did it, but our signs scare off people with bad memories. I daresay most of the locals believe this *is* a radiation dump site."

"That would keep me away."

They finally turned a corner that opened onto a long, straight corridor. "About another three hundred yards that way you take a left and you'll come into the community. Up here on your right should be our hosts."

Paul was struck that the area looked like a lunchroom for a small office. Nondescript chairs, a table, a fridge, a microwave, even a coatrack. As they entered, three people rose. In the center was Abraham, the man Paul had met in the park, hoodless now but still wearing shades. "Doctor," he said warmly, embracing him, "welcome to our community. This is my wife, Sarah—" a woman who looked to be in her late fifties, with salt-and-pepper hair, smiled—"and this is Isaac."

"Not their son," Isaac offered so quickly that Paul guessed he said it often. He and Sarah, like Abraham, wore dark glasses. His hair was reddish blond with a little gray visible. Paul judged him to be in his forties.

"We all use code names here," Abraham said. "Many of our residents are fugitives. Almost none of us know the true identities of those we live and work alongside. It's a matter of security."

"That's why all the cloak-and-dagger stuff getting me here?"

"I can understand if you found it a bit off-putting. But we transport everyone in and out of here, with few exceptions, the same way. Imagine if law-enforcement agencies got wind of this place."

Abraham gestured toward chairs for Paul and Straight. He, Isaac, and Sarah wore small crown-shaped pins identical to one he'd seen on Straight's lapel. Some kind of Christian insignia? Paul had never thought to ask Straight about it—in fact, he'd barely noticed it—but he would now. As Isaac sat back down, Paul noticed that though he was powerfully built, one arm dangled, unusable.

Isaac caught him looking. "Shot," he said. "Got my shoulder blown out during a government raid in Pacifica. I was the only member of my group who survived."

Paul stifled a gasp. Pacifica—did he mean San Francisco? *Dare I ask?*

"We were thrilled by the success of your efforts in New York," Abraham began.

"What I witnessed there was amazing," Paul said. "And as you predicted, God showed me what to do."

"The professor says it helped bring you to a decision on our proposition."

"It has. And my answer is yes. I'm with you all the way."

Abraham beamed. Sarah leaned against her husband, raising a hand to brush away tears. Isaac reached with his good arm to grasp Paul's. "Thank you," he said. "We know you're in a far more vulnerable place than any of us, living within the camp of the enemy. You're an answer to prayer, and we will continue to uphold you in prayer."

"Paul, one of our people has begun daily prayer and study with your new convert," Abraham said. "And we owe you a special debt of thanks. He has already made a substantial donation that will let us implement some new efforts we have planned. We spoke a little of our mission when we met in the park."

"Yes, to offer believers fellowship and guidance, as well as to spread the word."

"That, and to help coordinate the work of local Christian groups. But our mission actually goes deeper than that. What do you know of the Rapture?"

Paul looked at Straight, puzzled.

"You might call it the opening phase of the events described in the book of Revelation," Straight said. "In an instant, in the twinkling of an eye, Jesus will appear in the clouds and with a shout and the sound of a trumpet will summon all who are ready—the true believers—to meet Him in the air and welcome them into heaven."

"Literally lift them off the earth?"

Straight nodded, smiling. "And the Bible tells us it will happen at an unexpected hour."

"What happens to everyone else?" Paul asked.

"Those who are left behind and survive the chaos—imagine what happens during rush hour when people disappear from behind the wheels of their cars—will try to survive a period of tribulation, when God sends twenty-one judgments from heaven in a last-ditch effort to get their attention. Many will receive Christ, but more will still reject Him, in spite of everything they've experienced. Since the true believers will be in heaven, there will be no one left to teach them except people who should have known better."

"And since religious texts have been banned for decades," Isaac said, "there might be nothing for them to learn from without our help."

"What do we do?"

"We've started planting copies of the Bible and Christian tracts throughout the world, in countless locations and in every conceivable medium, to ensure that God's Word will never be eradicated from the earth. We've begun to issue print, digital, video, audio—even international sign language video—editions so it will be accessible to all despite technological change, illiteracy, or environmental upheaval, such as power outages arising from natural or man-made disasters or even the privations of the end times. Some of the places we plant texts are predictable—after all, you want to put them where people would naturally look, even while safeguarding them from the government. For example, the American Library of Congress, which has outreach all over the world, runs our book-drop program, getting Bibles or tracts, often bound inside other books or monographs, placed in every single library in the world."

"The Library of Congress," Paul repeated, thinking of Angela Barger.

"I used to work in the recording business," Abraham said. "One of the new programs we want to start involves having one in every-so-many-thousand discs issued contain a New Testament track or maybe even be an entire New Testament disc, instead of what the customer ordered. The same goes for downloads off the Internet; you might expect Thelonius Monk and get Thessalonians."

Paul laughed. "Corinthians instead of *Carmen*. Galatians instead of Garth Brooks. Ingenious."

"We have to keep thinking up new schemes to stay ahead of the government," Abraham said. "One of Sarah's pet projects involves textiles with texts woven in."

"It would be quite easy," Sarah said, "and think how valuable it could be in less developed parts of the world."

"And your friend the professor is working with medical professionals to tap into the nationwide hospital communications network."

"Straight! I always thought you were overqualified to be an in-patient baby-sitter."

"Oh no, Paul. My volunteer work is important too. That's why you're here, don't forget."

We have our appointed tasks—which are critical—that we must diligently perform. . . .

Abraham said, "So you see, Paul, our work is vital. We are fighting to win hearts to Christ in what is surely the most repressive time in human history—when world governments have not only banned religion but also are technologically capable of enforcing that ban by spying on every citizen. We maintain a library, train teachers, and offer other support services to believers today, but we must also lay the groundwork, through our mass-communications program, for a future we will never see that could begin at any moment. We code-named the new effort *Soon*.

"Let's pray." They all clasped hands, Paul taking Isaac's crippled one. "God, our Father, we bring to You Your son, Paul, who is embarking on a journey so dangerous that his life is in Your hands. We pray Your guidance and protection, Your wisdom and strength for him as he serves You. In the name of Christ, amen."

Abraham raised his head. "We wanted you brought here, Paul, so you would feel that you are truly one of us, a soldier in the growing army of God. Since He is with us, none of us need ever feel alone."

21

PAUL WAS BLINDFOLDED and restrained again once they were a short way from the meeting site. His mind spun like a turbine, thinking of a city in a salt mine, modern catacombs, a refuge from persecution, and a mother ship for Christian groups. The Rapture, when God would call believers to heaven. Operation Soon, a bold initiative to keep the Word of God in circulation through the end of time. Isaac, who may have been the man Paul tried to murder in San Francisco. And those lapel pins . . .

When they were settled on the bench in the truck, Straight freed him.

"When you gave me the ailanthus leaves, it fit my theory that different Christian groups use different identification symbols."

"Yeah?"

"Why didn't you tell me about those?"

Straight hesitated and spoke slowly, seeming to choose his words carefully. "Well, ah, before you committed to joining us, it didn't make sense to give you a lot of background on Christian identification symbols."

"Fair enough. But you can tell me now. Those crowns you and the people in the salt mine wear are your identification symbols, right? And they come from the third chapter of Revelation, when God tells the church of Philadelphia: 'Hold on to what you have, so that no one will take away your crown.'"

Straight raised a brow. "Well, yes . . ."

"So my theory was right. I figured the resistance was using imagery from Revelation, especially the beginning, the part about the churches. For example, they might have attacked Sardis Oil in Gulfland because one of the churches of Revelation was in Sardis. The believers connected to that operation picked a medallion depicting a book and light-colored clothes as their symbols. I never worked it out enough to report it to my boss. But it's true, isn't it?"

Straight shook his head. "It's scary how close you came, Paul. But remember, the events in Gulfland and other places were miracles. Christians never targeted or attacked anything. So no, your theory wasn't quite right."

"What did I miss?"

"Think about it. How many churches—or lampstands or stars—come up in that section?"

"Seven?"

"And what seven divisions could Christians be grouped under?"

"Well . . . we are the United Seven States of America."

"Right. And the affiliations aren't random. You know history is my game, Paul. Check the history of those seven churches of Revelation and you'll find that each bears a distinct correspondence to one of our seven states."

Paul decided that was the most amazing thing he'd heard that night—even considering he had been abducted and dragged down into a mine.

"Take Ephesus," Straight said. "It was a port city called the 'market of Asia' because it was the most important financial center on the Mediterranean. Besides banking, a major industry was making silver shrines to the goddess Artemis. The Bible tells us that, in addition to believing in false gods associated with silver, so many Ephesians believed in magic that when their divination books were burned, it was as if fifty thousand pieces of silver had gone up in smoke.

"Ephesus remind you of someplace?"

Paul stared, dumbfounded.

"Thought so," Straight said. "And—just as an aside—remember, in Acts Paul is called upon to revive a man who fell from a third-story window in Troas." Paul sat back, speechless. "See, Paul, once you start looking for signs that the end is upon us, they're everywhere."

•　•　•

Paul dozed, exhausted. The next sound he heard was the truck's back door opening. They were in a parking garage.

"There's a cab outside," Straight told him. "It'll take you back to the hotel. I'll be along later. See you at the tournament in the morning."

"I almost forgot we came here to play chess."

Paul found his way to the street, deserted in the wee hours except for the taxi. The driver knew where he was going and had already been paid. The hotel lobby was empty except for two men reading newspapers. Two men, just sitting in the lobby in the middle of the night? The odds were astronomical. Paul busied himself looking at brochures of local attractions. Neither man turned a page. Had Paul been found out? He moved to the counter and asked for messages. None.

Paul took the elevator to his floor, but rather than go to his room he slipped into a stairwell from which he had a view of his door. The men never showed. He dead-bolted, chained, and propped a chair against his door, finally able to relax. They couldn't have been NPO. Too obvious.

Paul napped a few hours, showered, then headed down to meet Straight. He saw no more of the two men. *Amateurs.*

• • •

Paul couldn't imagine concentrating enough on chess to have any kind of success Saturday morning. In the hotel ballroom he found his name on a plasma screen, one of fourteen players in the Novice division. Straight was playing a couple of levels higher. Players in the various levels met with tournament organizers for instructions, and Paul eyed the competition. Many players looked antisocial, even unwashed. Some carried dog-eared paperbacks of chess strategy.

Paul was intimidated and played too quickly, losing two of his first four games and finding himself in the middle of the pack. That was actually better than he had expected, but he was convinced that both of his losses could have gone the other way had he been thinking clearly. He found Straight's stats and saw that he was faring the same in his bracket. Paul was grateful for the competition Straight had given him over the last several months. He hadn't faced anyone yet who could have held his own against Straight.

After a snack, Paul settled down and became the talk of the tournament when he won nine of his next ten, including seven in a row, and won his division. The cash prize was minuscule and wouldn't pay for dinner, and the trophy was but a toy, but

Paul found the experience invigorating. He was surprised at his stamina—that his mind had stayed sharp, that he could actually relax and concentrate.

It seemed Straight, who finished fourth in the tougher division, was even happier about the win than Paul was. "I'm really proud of you, man!"

• • •

Brie and Connor seemed fascinated by Paul's small, cheap trophy, but Jae quickly excused them. "You can talk to Dad later," she said. "Run along upstairs and play."

"What's going on, Jae?" Paul said when they were gone.

"Oh, Paul! Where were you last night?"

"What do you mean?"

"Where were you until you came back to the hotel alone just before dawn?"

"You had me followed?"

"And I called your room. Till well past midnight. And I had people pounding on your door till all hours."

"I don't believe this."

"Were you with another woman?"

"What?"

"Just admit it, Paul. Don't you think I know by now? I read her letter."

"Her letter?"

"Paul, you met her in Washington. And now Toledo too—how can you flat-out lie to me?"

"Angela Barger? You went through my things? I can't tell you how offended I am, Jae—"

"Oh, you are? Well, here's how offended *I* am. School's out next week, and I'm taking the kids to Washington for the summer. That'll give us both time to think."

"If you'd stop yelling and listen for a minute—"

"Listen to what?"

"Jae, that is totally unjust—"

"Truth hurts, Paul?"

"We can work this out."

"We're going, Paul. It's set. The kids are excited."

Jae asked Paul to call only on Saturdays and only to talk to the kids. "When I want to talk to you," she said, "I'll be in touch."

And she was gone.

• • •

Alone in the house, Paul hated himself for letting the argument get out of hand. He was ashamed at how things had deteriorated. So his new life didn't cure everything.

By midweek he had found a distraction, a memo in the office about a case in Las Vegas. Sixteen people had been discovered dead, all of drug overdoses, before an altar under a cross. The deaths had been traced to a self-proclaimed prophet who called himself the reincarnation of Jonah. Friends of the victims claimed "Jonah" spun a story about having been swallowed by a whale off the coast of San Diego a few years before, then belched up onto shore three days later, suffering superficial burns from the creature's stomach acid.

While inside the whale, Jonah claimed God had told him to build a congregation that would have direct access to heaven through the miracle of hallucinogenic drugs. The prophet, according to friends of the victims, also espoused free love, saying God told him this was His intention from the time of creation.

Several hundred people in and around Las Vegas were reportedly linked to the Jonah cult.

"A seriously dangerous nutcase," Paul told Straight over dinner. "Imagine if I could bring him down and round up the others. I could save some lives and also get rid of a cult."

"You're going to Sin City?" Straight said.

"Early next week. Boss thinks this looks solid."

Straight sat back and studied Paul. "Better get yourself some blinders, boy. You're pretty young in the faith to be going there, especially with your family gone. It's all gambling and sex."

"I can handle it."

"Famous last words. Sounds like you've decided."

"I have."

• • •

That weekend, with time on his hands, Paul decided to finish the task he'd neglected so long: clearing out his mother's house. Before heading over, he called a realtor to come and look at it on Monday before he left for Las Vegas.

Parking in the drive, Paul sat staring at the compact brick home where he had grown up. The lawn was cut, thanks to the landscaping service, but the shrubbery and flower beds were wildly overgrown. He hadn't been here since Wintermas, more than six months before. It was the longest stretch he'd ever gone without visiting the house, including his time at college and in the service. *How much has changed—everything I've ever believed in or even thought I did—since then.*

Paul left the car and opened the front door. The air was thick and hot and stale. He moved through the empty rooms and stopped at the door to the basement. It had been six months, but he distinctly remembered locking the basement door—pushing in the button, testing the knob, sealing in the letter, which was either an NPO plant or, as he'd felt then, worse—a shattering betrayal by his long-dead father. Now the door stood ajar.

Paul strained for sounds, then quietly pulled the door to

him and locked it. He quickly circled the rooms of the small house, upstairs and down. Nothing. He returned to the basement door, silently unlocked it, and, listening again, made his way downstairs.

The basement looked empty, but he detected a tinge of something out of place in a house that had been shut up for so long: fresh air. He scanned the windows set at the top of the concrete walls. The one closest to the storage space was open.

The boxes were still in the storage space where he had left them, but they had all been rifled and dumped, their contents strewn on the floor. He knelt and discovered the old greeting cards congratulating his parents on his birth.

Who did this? A vagrant looking for valuables? One of his NPO colleagues, stage-managing a search to look like a break-in? Or—more likely—Jae, opening the window for air, then forgetting it while searching for who knows what after finding Angela's note?

For two hours Paul sifted through the mess, finally acknowledging his greatest dread: His father's letter was gone.

22

PAUL SPENT THE REST of the weekend packing what re-mained of his mother's keepsakes, then made a last walk-through. Nothing seemed out of place upstairs, making him even more suspicious about the basement mess. Monday he showed the Realtor around and handed over the keys.

By two o'clock Tuesday afternoon, after checking into his hotel downtown on Fremont Street, he stood in the middle of the Vegas Strip.

The Strip dominated most of Las Vegas Boulevard just out-side the city limits. It was lined with the biggest hotels in the world, offering twenty-four-hour entertainment, slot machines, cards, roulette wheels, and every other form of gambling anyone had ever conceived. Much of the half million-person population worked in the tourism industry that carried the town. Paul was amazed that so many people would travel so far to the heat of the desert to lose their money.

The instantly recognizable skyline featured two gigantic neon images: Apollo, the god of the sun and music, and Dionysus, the god of wine and carnal pleasure. New to Paul were the suggestive holograms in front of each establishment, featuring what looked like live people engaged in various explicit acts.

Paul had been carefully studying the New Testament, Revelation in particular, the last sixty to ninety minutes before falling asleep each night. He thought about the parallels Straight had drawn between the churches of Revelation and the major population centers of the USSA. If there was any question about which ancient church correlated with Las Vegas, it was dispelled by Paul's destination: Thyatira's.

Paul was jostled during the long walk to the place, the afternoon crowds as thick as they would be all night. He was surprised to see streetwalkers in the light of day and knew they would be even more pervasive after the sun set.

Similar to the others, this casino boasted a hologram depicting a woman who appeared to be losing her clothes as the image turned and danced. But always, just before the most revealing moment, gossamer veils strategically covered her.

Thyatira's proprietor, a woman who called herself Jezebel, supposedly knew the Jonah character personally. Most of what Jezebel did with her casino was legal in Vegas. But Paul would be on the lookout for irregularities in case he needed to pressure her. He needed her to get to Jonah.

Thyatira's was the largest casino hotel in the world with more than six thousand guest rooms and a main floor with more acres of gambling paraphernalia than any two other establishments combined. The slot machines and gaming tables all had alluring women depicted on them, and the bordello-like décor with garish reds and pinks accommodated the hundreds of flesh-flashing waitresses servicing the tables. The dealers were all provocatively dressed women.

Paul stopped cold as he gazed out over the floor. One of the girls looked familiar. He moved a few steps and she turned. That profile! Could it be? Impossible.

Paul juked and darted through the crowd, pushing and elbowing and excusing himself, but he kept losing sight of Angela. It had to be her, and yet how could it be? What would she be doing this far from home? Paul had never determined whether she knew the truth about her own father or whether she herself was an underground believer. Regardless, he had never pegged her for the kind of woman who might be found at Thyatira's.

When Paul reached the main entrance, people were coming and going in a mad rush as if the place had just opened. Angela had seemed to vanish. It didn't add up. It simply could not have been her.

An entourage swept past surrounding a handsomely and somewhat conservatively dressed woman of about fifty-five carrying a leather portfolio. She wore a lavender suit—tight, short, and flattering—but nothing like the suggestive attire of her employees.

Paul rushed to catch up, but as he edged close enough to call out, her muscle cut him off. "She's not available," a beefy, suited man said.

"She's available to me," Paul said, flashing his credentials.

The man nodded. "In the office. Follow me."

By the time they had made it to her office, her bodyguard had whispered in her ear and handed her Paul's card. She spun and her eyes found him. "I'm not really here today," she said.

"I'm afraid this can't wait, ma'am. I just need a few minutes. If you're not really here, there should be no interruptions."

Jezebel glared at Paul and turned to her secretary. "I'm not here," she said, and Paul followed her into her office. He sat on a leather love seat and she in a chair facing him.

"So what does the NPO want with me? I run a legitimate business."

"I need to know your association with Jonah."

She rolled her eyes. "If you're after him, we're on the same side."

"It's known he uses so-called legal prostitutes for his rituals, and no one employs more than you do."

"Don't say 'so-called,' Agent Stepola. Everything in my place is legal and aboveboard."

"Fair enough. Does he employ your girls?"

"He's lured some, yes."

"You lose any in the recent tragedy?"

Paul had finally gotten to her. Jezebel started to speak, then caught herself. "He's dead serious about this stuff, you know," she said.

"Stuff?"

"The religious mumbo jumbo. It helps if his constituents buy into it because it means more money for him. But it's more than just a gig with him."

"Ma'am, did you lose somebody?"

Jezebel actually teared up. She tried to speak but just held up two fingers.

"You lost two?"

She nodded and reached for a tissue from her desk. "I told them and told them not to get swept up in it. Most of my girls, far as I know, don't even do drugs. Or if they do, it's only recreational. First sign of a junkie, they're out of here."

Jezebel balled up her tissue and backhanded it into a basket ten feet away in the corner. "Look, I knew Jonah when he was a two-bit pusher named Morty."

"Morty what?"

"Morty Bagadonuts was what he called himself then. I think the real name is Bagdona. Mortimer's always been a lowlife, but he had an angle. He had a string of girls at the hotels on Fremont until he realized the potential on the Strip.

"I don't let him have full access to my girls, but what they do on their own time is their business. Legalized prostitution is a tough enough game. Makes no sense to make the girls push dope too. But if you can get them hooked, they have to deal. That's part of Morty's religious thing. There's the dope—for a price—and there's the free love—but it's not really free either. He says God told him while he was in the fish that those are the two ways to Jesus. So pay, shoot, play, and pray."

"And he's really into it? It's not a scam?"

"I'd worry less if it was. C'mon, I sell dreams. You think my real name's Jezebel? Mary Anderson, Cleveland. You can look it up. People come in here believing they're going to beat the house, even though they know—they *know*—everything is tilted our way. Yeah, we need only a few percentage points off the top for every multimillion-dollar twenty-four-hour period, so we let 'em think they're winning. But both of us know it's a con.

"And our girls are also trained to persuade these marks they really are the most impressive men they've ever seen. In another setting, other circumstances, it could be true love. The more they believe it, the more they pay for it. So Morty found a tall tale people would literally buy into. More power to him. But really making *them* believe this stuff? Getting my girls to take enough dope to snuff 'em? No, uh-uh, that crosses the line. He's got to pay."

"Where do *you* think Jonah is?"

"I think Jonah as we knew him, the robe and all, is history. But Morty's not far. No way he's going to abandon this gravy train. He rents a penthouse at the Babylon under his own name.

Nobody there knows Morty is Jonah. When he's doing the Jonah bit he wears a dirt-colored robe, a long wig, and a fake beard. So many people bought into his story that he broke them up into what he calls congregations. There are literally too many to all meet in the same place without it getting around. So they're in little pockets here and there, and he uses different girls in different places for the rituals.

"But when he makes the rounds of the casinos, recruiting, he's just a balding, middle-aged redhead with stubble and bloodshot eyes. If you want to find him, the Babylon is the place to start."

"He's responsible for sixteen deaths we know about. The cops must be all over this."

She snorted. "They were all over the news, carrying out bodies, making pronouncements. So far they haven't connected Morty with Jonah—or if anyone has, let's just say payoffs are not unheard of in this town. I wouldn't even be talking to you if it weren't for the girls. The only way I can see to deal with him is on his own terms. Someone needs to take him out."

"If I can persuade you that he will be prosecuted to the full extent of the law, will you help me?"

Jezebel studied him. "You look all squeaky-clean like you might actually be trustworthy."

"Like you said, we're on the same side here."

Jezebel gave Paul a list of six employees who had done part-time work for Jonah. None had been seen for days. "They're adults, but I'm worried. If you find them, keep them safe."

"Deal."

• • •

There were various ways to get around Vegas, from the limos of the well-heeled to rental cars, taxis, an elevated monorail, and sidewalks. Paul chose to blend in and used the monorail that ran the length of the Strip. He always disembarked a few blocks from his destination and tried to look like a tourist, gawking at the gargantuan hotels and casinos, moseying here and there.

At the Babylon, the second-largest establishment after Thyatira's, he bought trinkets at a couple of stores and carried his shopping bags around the gambling floor and in and out of the theaters, trying to get the lay of the land.

Paul found himself studying every face as he moved around the Strip, staying within the shadow of the Babylon. The blood-shot-eyed redhead Morty was his main target, of course, but he found himself constantly on the lookout for Angela Barger too.

Once, while on a monorail car so crowded he had to stand shoulder to shoulder with others, Paul thought he saw her again. He couldn't be sure because she had her back to him, but it looked as if she was talking with two or three ladies of the evening—who were not, of course, limited to the evening in that town.

Paul fought his way to the front and got off as soon as he could. He ran back to where he thought he had seen Angela. The hookers were still there, but she was gone.

He approached, shopping bags still dangling from his hand.

"Looking for a date, stranger?" one of the women said.

"No, I'm sorry," he said. "I don't mean to bother you, but—"

"You a cop?" another said. "'Cause we're working and we're licensed."

"No, I'm looking for the woman who was just here talking to you."

"She more your style?"

"Well, no, I—"

The girls giggled and looked at each other. "She's not even a working girl, honey. You don't want her."

"Yes, I do. Did she tell you her name? Do you know where she is?"

They shrugged. "You're blocking traffic, man. If you're not buying, move on."

"Just tell me where I can find her," Paul said.

One of the girls laughed aloud. "Try a church. Oh yeah. They don't have those anymore."

23

WHEN PAUL FINALLY CRASHED into bed after midnight, three things were rattling in his brain: how dangerous Morty/Jonah was, how badly he wanted to see Angela again, and what the hooker had said about church.

Paul listened to his New Testament discs for an hour, slept fitfully, and was up early. Vegas still advertised itself as the city that never sleeps, and the activity and crowds seemed hardly abated even at six in the morning. Paul wasn't looking forward to a day of quizzing working girls to try and track down Jezebel's employees and, of course, Angela Barger.

Paul had zero interest in even attractive, alluring women who made sex their business. He felt a strange emotion, however, as he made the public rounds. As he talked to various women, finding it easier one-on-one than with a pair or three, he actually felt compassion for them. Paul ran that through his mental grid. If God loved everyone and cared for every soul, and if He, as Straight had quoted to him over and over, "does not want anyone to perish," He must love these women too. Living in out-and-out sin, selling their bodies, and yet worthy of love and compassion and forgiveness. Then it struck him: If Angela was a believer and made a professional woman think of the ancient concept of church, perhaps that's what she was feeling for them too—and talking to them about.

Many of the women brushed him off as soon as they realized he was not a customer. Others were kind and tried to be helpful. None admitted knowing Jezebel's girls, and few recalled seeing anyone of Angela's description.

God, Paul said silently, *I know she's here. Help me find her.*

That afternoon Paul saw a working girl who looked so doped up, distracted, and forlorn he almost avoided talking with her. "I'm looking for someone and wonder if you could help."

"What's your pleasure?" she said without enthusiasm.

"I'm looking for a dramatically pretty blonde, about thirty, who might have come around talking to working girls."

"About God?"

"Possibly. Yes."

"She talked to me. Told me I could get off the streets, that she knew people who would take care of me, protect me from my employer, help me find Jesus."

"When did you see her?"

"Yesterday afternoon, late."

"Where?"

"About six blocks north."

"If I gave you my number, would you call me if you see her again?"

"You gonna get her in trouble? What she's doing is dangerous—and illegal."

Paul contemplated the irony of that, considering the source. "No, she's a friend. I just need to find her. Will you call me?"

"I'll think about it."

"I'd really appreciate it. And look, even if you don't call me, it's probably worth listening to what she has to say."

"Yeah?"

"Definitely."

"If you say so . . ."

Paul turned to leave.

"Hey, mister?"

The girl dug in her tiny purse and pulled out a card. "She didn't tell me her name, and I don't blame her. But she invited me to a meeting tonight at a place called the Meadows. Here's the address. It's in the basement of a bungalow."

Paul jotted it down quickly. "You going?" he said.

"Nah. I gotta work till midnight. She said to come at ten and if anybody else was going in at the same time to just walk around the block and come in alone. She gave me this too. I guess it's like a ticket. You can have it. I'm not gonna use it."

It was a flat, smooth white stone. Paul guessed it was a token, like the ailanthus leaf, that underground believers used to identify each other. Just the night before he had heard a verse from Revelation that would have inspired it: "And I will give to each one a white stone, and on the stone will be engraved a new name that no one knows except the one who receives it."

That would make it the emblem of Pergamum, which Paul supposed correlated with Washington, D.C. He was definitely on Angela's trail.

"Sure you don't want this?" he said. "What if you change your mind?"

"I won't. You don't know my employer."

• • •

The rest of the day proved futile in spotting Jonah, but Paul couldn't get his mind off the possibility of seeing Angela that night. He rented a car, then called Bob Koontz from his hotel.

"When you going to need backup?" Koontz said. "You closing in on this guy or what?"

"I got a pretty good lead on his alias and where he stays, but he's playing hard to get right now. Trust me, I'll find him."

"Let me know when you need a team, and we'll have 'em there in minutes."

"Thanks. Meanwhile, could you run the name Mortimer Bagdona, alias Morty Bagadonuts, and send me whatever you find?"

"Sure. I'll have somebody from the local bureau run it over to you."

"Okay, but I don't want them trampling all over my case."

• • •

Paul considered how best to approach Angela's meeting. He wondered whether any men had been invited, and if they had, were they employers? The old pimp concept was gone with the legalization of prostitution, but men still played a huge role in these women's lives. From the looks of the girl who had put him on to Angela, he was certain she was a junkie and that her employer was a pusher.

So it was unlikely that men would be welcome at the meeting. What would he look like, showing up with a white stone? Maybe his presence would be intimidating. What if he was turned away at the door, before he even got a chance to see Angela? He decided to stake out the house and watch for his opening.

At nine-thirty he parked a few houses from the bungalow and slouched behind the wheel. He saw a young woman—a hooker?—jump from a cab halfway down the block, then wait till it pulled off before heading for the house.

No lights were on upstairs, and the basement windows were boarded up. Looking around, the woman made her way up the driveway. Paul gave her a moment, then followed. A large dark mass at the end of the driveway was angled into the yard—a van. He hugged the shadows of the house for as long as he could and then slipped behind the van.

Peering through the driver's-side window, he could see the woman standing at the basement door at the back of the bungalow. She didn't have to knock. Someone inside must have been watching—someone who didn't see him—because the door opened.

"Welcome, welcome," a young woman said. "Were you followed?"

"No, I was super careful."

Not careful enough.

From behind the van, Paul watched eight more women arrive. Seven looked like working girls—two arrived together—and one looked like a runaway.

• • •

Angela was thrilled at the turnout. She smiled at each woman, remembering most by name, which seemed to make them more comfortable.

"First," she said, "I applaud your courage in coming tonight. I don't plan to keep you long, because we realize it's as dangerous for you as it is for us. So let me get right to the point. Tonight can change your life.

"As I told you in town, I believe in God. I believe in Jesus. We're here from far away because God has put it on our hearts to reach out to working women like yourselves. If you were happy with your life and your lifestyle and whomever you report to, you wouldn't be here. We are offering you a way to get out of this lifestyle and turn to God. We have a shelter where we can hide you, feed you, and teach you about becoming a believer in Christ. I have some literature I want to pass out, which you should feel free to study.

"Now here's the exciting news. I know this is all new to you, and you may feel that you have a lot of loose ends to tie up before you could even consider such a thing, but hear me out. You may be like many of the women in your shoes who have told us they were ready to make the break immediately. You may be in trouble with your employer right now. He doesn't know where you are, and unless you come up with a very creative and convincing lie, you're going to suffer for having been here tonight.

"Here's our offer: Leave everything behind. Disappear. We can transport you to our center tonight, and we have clothes and food and everything you need to start over. We'll put no pressure on you, we won't force you into any decisions, and we'll never ask you to do anything against your will. You will be presented with the claims of Christ on your life, and we hope you'll see that God loves you and that Jesus died for you. If at any point you decide this is not for you, you are, of course, free to go. And we will never ask you for a dime.

"Now, while you're thinking about it, I'd like to ask my compatriot who met you at the door—let's call her Freda—to tell you her story."

Freda said she had been a prostitute in Washington, D.C.,

when someone invited her to a meeting "just like this one. I'll tell you, I couldn't wait to go. Somehow I was ready for a change, and I knew I was putting my life on the line just being out of touch with my employer. I came and I listened. Know what? I discovered I believed in God already. I had all my life, no matter what the government or my parents or teachers or society said. I just knew there was a God. I mean, come on. Look around.

"But I didn't feel worthy. I was a druggie. Had three abortions. Been married twice. Had a record a mile long. Made a bunch of money and blew it all. I was so dependent on my employer that I thought I'd die before he did. Ladies, I came running after this with all that was in me. I was ready. And when I found out I didn't have to change a thing, that I could come to Jesus the way I was, man, that was it. He did all the changing in me.

"If this all sounds too good to be true, trust me, it's true. Your life may not get any easier. Think about that. You can live in public as a prostitute, but we Christians have to sneak around in the dark. But you decide. What's the better life? Life with Jesus and your sins forgiven? Or going back to the streets and selling yourself for someone else's benefit? I hope you'll all take that ride tonight. If you don't, all we can ask is that you trust our motives and don't tell anyone about us. We mean only the best for you, and we appreciate your confidence. And for at least the next month, you can find us here every night."

Angela was gratified to see that all the women were hanging on Freda's words. She was a powerful speaker who pulled no punches and really hit the women where they lived, a tremendous asset to the ministry.

"Questions?" Angela said.

"What time's the bus pull out?" one girl said, and the others laughed.

"Soon as we're done here. We have a driver, and Freda will go with you. How many would like to go?"

Five immediately raised their hands. The runaway waited until they were counted, then asked, "Is this only for hookers? I'm not one yet, but if I stay on the street I'm not gonna have any choice."

"This is for you too, dear," Angela said.

"Then count me in."

"Willie?"

Angela's partner appeared and told the women he'd be escorting them to the van. They went in groups of two, while Angela talked to the three who had decided not to go.

"We're really packed in, Angela," Willie said, after delivering the last group. "Do you want to go and swing back to get me?"

"Oh no. We're still talking anyway. I'll be fine till you get back."

Two of the women left after the van pulled out. One lingered another ten minutes, clearly regretful she hadn't had the nerve to make the break. Angela didn't persuade her, ultimately, and she left promising to come to the next meeting. "I think I'll be ready," she said. "Pray for me?"

Angela saw her out, watching until she turned, with a wave, to head down the driveway. There was no moon, and Angela felt spooked by the impenetrable shadows. She imagined she heard something. *Is someone in the yard?*

With a shudder, she backed into the house. As she was locking the door, she heard a light knock. She jumped back. The knock came again.

"Hello?" she said softly. "Did you forget something?"

"No." A man's voice. "I'm just here to see you."

"I'm not, uh—seeing anyone right now," Angela said. "It's late, and—"

"Angela, it's me, Paul Stepola."

"Paul!" She yanked open the door. "Are you here as NPO?"

"No," he said. "I'm here as one of you."

Once inside with the door locked, he gushed his whole story, about his healing, the New Testament, Straight, his conversion, seeing her at Thyatira's and on the street, everything.

Shaken, she rushed to embrace him. "You scoundrel! You scared me to death."

"Your security's not so hot," Paul said. "I've been out here the whole time. You need to be more vigilant."

"Clearly."

"Tell me what you're doing here, Angela."

"Well, I had to leave D.C. for a while, and this seemed like a place where I could do some good."

"A missionary effort."

"Exactly."

"Where are your boys?"

"Believe it or not, they're here. We have young people with us who serve as nannies."

"But surely they're not here where you might be raided."

"No, no. They're in town. We're at the Fremont Towers."

"Angela! I'm just up the street. How're you getting back?"

"Willie and Freda will take me after they drop off the girls."

"Call and tell them you're riding back with me, and let's get dessert or something."

"I'd love that, Paul. And you can tell me what *you're* doing here."

24

IN THE RESTAURANT, Paul couldn't stop staring at Angela. He loved her look, her compassion, everything about her. He had felt drawn to her from the first time he saw her and now, the way things were with Jae . . .

Angela was beaming—"high," she said, from seeing all those girls make the right decision and also from seeing Paul again, having learned from Straight that he had become a Christian and that his vision had been restored.

She was aware, of course, of the horrible Jonah incident. "It just makes our work all the more important," she said. "I keep looking for girls who have been associated with him, but so far no one has shown up—or they don't admit they worked for him. They're all terrified of him."

Paul told her about the young woman who had directed him to the meeting and given him the white stone.

She nodded. "I know that girl. Name's Lucy. At least that's

what she goes by. I've talked to her more than once. She's got a really bad-news employer too. She's petrified of him. He doesn't split the money with the girls. He gets them addicted, makes them buy their drugs from him, also makes them sell, and then takes all the cash and gives them a tiny bit to live on."

"Charming."

"Yeah. Lucy seems so sweet and so lost. I'd love it if she would break away and come see us. But even when I'm talking with her, she's looking past me, worried Mort is watching. We even had to go around the corner before she would take my card."

"Wait—what? Who's she worried about?"

"She's one of Morty Bagadonuts's girls. I don't think that's his real name, but he's notorious. Lives in a pent—"

"Penthouse at the Babylon, yeah." Paul told her what he knew.

She looked ashen. "Lucy's Mort is Jonah?"

Paul nodded. "You could help me nail this guy."

"I'd be happy to."

Until the wee hours of the morning, they concocted a plan, and at one point Angela reached across the table and took both his hands in hers. Looking deep into his eyes, she said, "This is exciting. You're brilliant."

And Paul realized she had no idea he was married. He had never mentioned a word about his family.

He took Angela back to her hotel and walked her to her room. She looked up at him expectantly. "Until tomorrow then," he said, and she reached for him.

She pulled him toward her by his shoulders, and he offered her his cheek. Giving him a peck, Angela whispered, "Chivalry lives."

• • •

Back at his hotel, Paul stopped at the desk to pick up Koontz's package with the background on Bagdona. As he headed upstairs, he felt a confusing jumble of excitement, guilt, and surprise. For most of his marriage he had succumbed to—or even actively sought—temptation from women for whom he cared little, with Jae waiting at home. But tonight—while estranged from Jae—he'd been with a woman he'd dreamed of for months, who more than fulfilled those fantasies, and who was single to boot. Yet he had upheld his marriage vows.

How ironic that, after a mere peck on the cheek, he was consumed with remorse for betraying Jae, as well as for misleading Angela. He had played out a lie, loving Angela with his eyes and his body language, even his tone. She was a widow with young kids, and she had every reason to believe he was available. She acted as if he were exactly what she had been looking for. He would have to set things right.

If nothing else proved God was working in his life, that did.

• • •

Mortimer Eugene Bagdona, no surprise, turned out to have a record of racketeering throughout California before coming to Las Vegas several years before. His mug shots were more than six years old, but they gave Paul something to go on.

Bagdona called himself an import/export jeweler, but apparently he had never actually plied the trade. His last known residence before settling in Vegas was Chula Vista, California. Paul wondered if local law enforcement would put together the proximity of that city to San Diego and at least suspect a link between him and Jonah. Not likely. Somehow, Morty Bagadonuts had never been busted for drug-related activity.

The next day, through Angela, Paul found two of the girls from Thyatira's who had worked part-time for Jonah. Both had been scared off from the extra work by what had happened the week before. They knew two of the women who had died.

"At first it seemed like normal work," one said. "We danced in these rituals with very specific instructions from Jonah, we turned tricks, and we passed out dope. We were allowed to do a little ourselves if we wanted, but it was just to encourage the congregation—that's what he called the guys (they were all men)—to buy more and more. He really pressured us to come with him full-time, but who would now?"

Late that afternoon, Angela was to try to get next to Lucy. Paul had advised her to play it by ear to decide how much to reveal to the woman. Angela was simply to indicate to Lucy that she had a good chance of getting her away from Mort.

Paul met Angela just after noon at a small restaurant off the Strip to set the plan in motion. She seemed excited.

"This may sound like fun," he said, "but it's dangerous."

"I know, but everything I've been doing in Vegas is life-and-death, Paul. And you won't let anything happen to me, will you?"

"That's the last thing I want, Angela. I wish I could guarantee it."

She took his hands again, and his blood started pumping. *We'd better talk—soon.*

Paul handed Angela a set of button covers to slip over the ones on her blouse. "Make sure this one goes over the second-to-top one," he said. "It looks like all the others—"

"Pretty."

"Yeah, but can you imagine? A set like this costs a fortune. That one is a transmitter connected to the frequency of the receivers in my molars. As long as I'm within ten miles of you, I can hear what's going on."

"That makes me feel secure."

"It should help, but, Angela, really, you need to decide if you want to go through with this."

"Me?" she said. "Are you kidding? The chance to catch a guy like this? You couldn't talk me out of it."

"The first thing we want to know is whether Mort is still in town. There's no sign of him at the Babylon, but if he's skipped, why is Lucy so scared? Get her to tell you the last time she talked to him, and better yet, the last time she actually saw him."

"Will do."

"Don't say a word about my knowing who he really is. Lucy has to know he's Jonah. He's likely used her in the rituals. Just say I'm a friend of yours who's going to keep him occupied long enough so she can break away."

"She hasn't seemed willing to do that yet, Paul."

"Only because she's scared to death of him. Why did she keep your card *and* the white stone? Even that had to be risky. Wouldn't she have just tossed them if she didn't have in the back of her head that her opportunity might come?"

"See? You *are* brilliant."

Paul wanted to tell her she was too and that she was beautiful. He just couldn't.

• • •

Paul parked about three blocks from where Angela expected to find Lucy. The fidelity of the equipment was so good he could hear Angela's breathing. "I'm not seeing her," she was singsonging under her breath. "I'll just keep looking. I hope you can hear me."

A few minutes later Paul heard a male voice. "Well, hello, little cutie."

Someone talking to Lucy? Paul was tempted to maneuver into position to see.

"I said hello, little stuck-up."

"Yeah, hi," Angela said.

"What're you, too good for me?" the man said, and others close by laughed. Paul had a sinking feeling. Was he going to have to rescue Angela even before she found Lucy?

"What's your problem, friend?" Angela said, with a bravado that impressed Paul.

"Just looking for a little action, that's all."

"Do I look like a hooker to you?"

"Well, no, I—"

"Then leave me alone."

"Yes, ma'am. Sorry, ma'am." More laughter.

"Hear that, Paul?" she said a moment later. "I guess hooker is in the eye of the beholder."

Paul wished she had ignored the creep. If he felt humiliated in front of his friends, there was no telling what he might do.

Paul was growing anxious. *Come on, come on!*

Finally he heard, "I see her. About a block and a half ahead of me. I'll keep you posted."

A few minutes later Angela whispered, "I'm just walking right past her. She might have a customer. Yep, they're negotiating. I'm past her now, but, Paul, she noticed me. I saw her eyes widen. She looked like she wanted to talk. Maybe she'll run the guy off."

The silence was a little too long for Paul's nerves, but Angela soon came back on. "He's gone. I'm heading back. Hang on."

Paul had been on a lot of stakeouts, but none had ever made him this jumpy. He knew if he tried getting approval to enlist a civilian in an operation like this, he'd be denied and reprimanded. But he told himself Angela wasn't working for the NPO. She was working for him. Yet somehow that didn't make him feel any better. Either way, he'd put her in danger.

"Hey, girl, how you doing?" Angela said.

"Hi," Lucy said. "Things are slow. The way I like them. I'm so sick of this."

"You run that guy off?"

"Quoted him double when I saw you. I hoped you'd come back."

"What's up?"

"Your friend find you?"

"Friend?"

"A guy told me yesterday he was a friend of yours, looking for you. I hope I didn't do something wrong. I gave him that rock and the address."

"Yes, he found me."

"Whew! I hoped I wasn't getting you in trouble."

"You're not so skittish today."

"We're out of his view."

"Whose?"

"Morty's. Lots of times he can see me from his penthouse, but we're around the corner now. If I don't get back in sight in a while, he'll come looking for me. You'd think I was his only girl."

"He's got lots, doesn't he?"

"Lots."

"You think he's watching you now?"

"When I'm within view, yeah."

"You're sure?"

"He's back at the Babylon. He was gone a few days."

"You ready to bail on him yet?"

Lucy paused. "I'd be risking my life."

"You're risking your life out here, Lucy. C'mon. What if I told you I could make this work and he'd never find you?"

Paul listened closely, but Lucy wasn't answering. It sounded as if they were moving.

"Where you going?" Angela said.

"I just don't know."

"You hate this life. It's time for something new. What are you afraid of?"

"Him, of course."

"Lucy, listen to me."

"I don't know. Can I get back to you?"

"Lucy, I'm not going to push you into something you don't want to do. This is all up to you. It's your freedom we're talking about."

25

PAUL AND ANGELA RENDEZVOUSED in his car and discussed how she and Lucy had left it, that Angela would find her again the next day at the same spot—out of Mort's view. Paul was glad Lucy had volunteered that Mort was back at the Babylon, but she seemed less certain she would leave him.

"Experience tells me she's going to pass," Paul said.

"Oh, I think she's ready, Paul. It's a major, major deal for these girls to make a decision like this. She's right on the edge. It won't take much to push her over."

Before Paul dropped Angela off, he had a nagging feeling they were being watched. He had noticed nothing in the mirrors. Could it have been someone on foot, something in the corner of his eye? He had learned not to worry until he was sure, but he had to wonder about Lucy and how stable a contact she was.

• • •

Angela was right about Lucy's readiness. As Paul sat listening to their conversation the next day, it quickly became evident what was wrong.

"Why the shades, Lucy?"

"Sunny day."

"Yeah, that's unusual here, isn't it? It was the same yesterday and your sad, beautiful eyes were on display. Let me see."

"No."

"Come on . . . oh! Lucy! What did he do?"

Lucy's voice was quavery. "It was just one shot, a backhand. His ring caught the bone."

"What was that about?"

"I was out of sight too long yesterday."

"And you're still not ready to leave? Lucy, you have to get away from him. We can get you to a shelter right now."

"I can't go . . ."

Paul sat shaking his head, assuming Angela was shaking hers too.

"You think I'm stupid."

"No, I don't, Lucy. I'm sorry. But I can't let you go back to him. You need to let me get you off the street now. Just say the word, and you're out of here."

Lucy hesitated. Then, "I'm not ready, ma'am. Maybe soon, but leaving Morty is one thing. Not knowing where my drugs are coming from . . ."

"You know you've got to get off that stuff."

Pause. "Yeah, but . . ."

"There's no easing off it, hon. You have to make a clean break, start over."

"Spoken like somebody who's never been a junkie."

"I know. But we can help. Lots of girls at our place have

been where you are. They'll become your family. They'll walk you through this."

"I'm not saying I'm not tempted. But this is the only life I've known for more than five years."

"Five years? You were a teenager when you started?"

"Uh-huh."

Fainter, Paul heard a car and a male voice. "Say, ladies?"

Lucy sounded dead. "Oh no. Oh no. It's—"

"Wonder if you'd be kind enough to give me some directions?"

Paul put the car in gear.

"I'm new here," Angela began, "but my friend might be able to help—"

Lucy, whispering, "Don't! It's Morty."

Paul backed up and pulled into traffic, wondering if he would do better to leap from the car and run three blocks, gun drawn.

Why didn't I just stake out the Babylon last night and bust him as soon as I saw him?

Traffic was gridlocked. *Should have called Chicago, played it by the book, got some help.*

"Can you see me clearly?" the man said pleasantly.

"Yes, sir." Angela's voice had gone from helpful to resigned dread.

"Then you had better do what I say or I will use this."

"What do you want?"

"Get in the car as if you know me and nothing's wrong."

"Where are we going?"

The voice was angry now. "Stall and I'll drop you where you stand. Lucy, stay put."

Paul heard Angela slide in and shut the door. He honked and edged up onto the sidewalk, drawing shouts and gestures.

As he sat within view of Lucy he caught sight of a late-model black sedan pulling away. No way he could pick through the traffic, and even if he could, there was little he could do if Mort had a gun on Angela.

"Where's your boyfriend?" Morty's voice caught Paul's attention again.

"Don't have one. I have a family." Angela sounded as if she was trying to cover her terror.

"You don't say. Well, you've been playing a dangerous game for a woman with a family, talking to my girls. But I need women like you. . . ."

"Why?"

"I need to connect people with God."

"And how would I do that?"

"I'd teach you. Hey, you're gorgeous. Ever think about making some real money? Lucy makes more than you ever dreamed of."

"I thought you were talking about bringing people to God. Oh, the Babylon. You staying here?"

Good, Angela. You'd have been a great agent.

Paul heard the car stop, doors opening and closing. "We're going to walk to the elevators, and you're going to come up to my place. One hint you're not thrilled, you'll regret it. Follow?"

"I can tell you right now I'm not interested in what you're offering."

"You might want to change your mind about that. I know who you are."

Paul called Koontz. "I'm going to bust this guy, hopefully within the hour. Get local NPO to the Babylon, but tell them not to move till I say. Mort Bagdona is Jonah. He has a hostage. It's all going down pretty fast."

Paul checked the side arm strapped to his leg, then called

the number on the card Angela had originally given Lucy. Willie answered.

"Paul Stepola. You still standing by to rescue Lucy?"

"Tomorrow, sure."

"I need you to do it right now."

"But we have a meeting tonight, and—"

"Lucy's available for pickup right now. I'll get Angela back to you later. Got it?"

"I guess, but—"

"Willie, trust me. I'll explain later. Do this now."

• • •

"You've been a bad girl," Morty was saying, "infringing on my territory."

"I don't follow."

"Sure you do. You're trying to pull people away from me. You've got your own idea of what God wants."

"Who told you that?"

"Well, not Lucy, if that's what you're wondering. But she should have. That was a serious breach of loyalty. That's why she's going to get what's coming to her too."

"You're not going to hurt me, are you?"

"Not unless you make me. Keep quiet on the elevator."

Paul pulled up to the Babylon and left his car at the curb. He rode the elevator to the exclusive floors and found hotel security. He motioned the man close with a nod and showed his credentials. "I'm on a stakeout and I have backup coming. I need to borrow your handcuffs, and I need a key that gets me into the suites on the penthouse level. Come on, I know you have one. . . . Thanks. Local bureau NPO will be downstairs soon. I'll call when I need them."

The man looked as if he had been deputized by Wyatt Earp.

• • •

"You're in 2200? Bet it's a big place."

Angela, you're a pro. Keep talking.

"Wait till you see it." The door opened.

"Two floors! Do you play the piano?"

"Comes with the place. Make yourself comfortable."

"That's a lot to ask. How comfortable can I be?"

Paul positioned himself at the end of the hall where he had a view of the entrance to the suite and could also see anyone getting off the elevator.

"I told you I'm not going to hurt you unless you make me."

"I won't make you."

"Then you'll join me?"

"In what way?"

"You see yourself as a woman of God. I'm a man of God. I want you on my team."

"Doing what?"

"Recruiting. People need God, ma'am. They really do. And He has told me the true pathways to Himself. I teach you those paths; you teach the seekers."

"I don't think so."

"Well, I do think so. God told me to seek you out, to sign you up. He said He would prepare you. If you refuse, He will be angered, and He will tell me what to do with you."

26

PAUL KEPT RUNNING SCENARIOS through his mind. If Jezebel was right, Morty Bagadonuts really believed he had a pipeline to God, so there was no telling what he might pull. Instinct told Paul he had the man right where he wanted him, in a confined, finite area. The last thing Paul wanted was a high-speed chase.

"I'm afraid I'm going to have to tie you to a chair," Mort said. He actually sounded cordial. No surprise that he could persuade people—he had their best interests at heart.

"That's not necessary. I'll cooperate."

"How I wish that were true," Mort said. "But we're going to be here awhile. I'm hoping to persuade you to join me willingly tonight for a peyote and performance prayer meeting."

"Where's that?"

"West of here."

"And what does that entail?"

"I present to my congregation two divinely prescribed paths to God. A natural, created compound that puts the mind on a sacred plane, and the physical love God created."

"Drugs and sex."

"If you're going to be the queen of heaven, you'll not be so crass."

"You really don't have to tie me, you know."

Paul heard Mort working with what sounded like rolls of tape.

"Eventually we must consummate our union, becoming one under heaven."

Angela didn't respond.

"You're misguided, Angel," Mort said, and Paul was struck that he had come so close to her name. "Your heart is in the right place, but it's not right to try to convert people unless they have no religion. My girls already have faith."

Paul called the main number of the Babylon and asked to speak to the chief of security.

Angela said, "I have faith too, so why are you trying to convert me?"

Paul asked security if room 2202, immediately to the right of 2200, was occupied.

"Two gentlemen are registered in that room, Agent Stepola. Our motion and heat detector tells us they are not currently there."

Paul moved quickly down the hall, using the universal key to slip into 2202. The men were reasonably tidy, and housekeeping had already cleaned the two-bedroom suite. The gigantic flat-screen TV was embedded in one wall, and on the other a wide, chrome column rose from floor to ceiling with a sliding panel in the center.

"By the time we leave for the ceremony," Mort was saying, "you will not feel forced. But you will have been converted. God made the substance that will free your mind."

"Peyote?"

"Precisely."

"That's nothing but mescaline, and natural or not, it's still illegal."

"According to the laws of men. But can you fathom the presumption of man trying to outlaw something God created?"

A call came through Paul's receivers. He rushed to the back bedroom and slipped into the closet so as not to be heard through the wall. "Stepola," he said.

"Sir, the occupants of 2202 are on their way up."

"Detain them. Don't let them into this room."

"Sorry, but we noticed them too late. NPO is here also, by the way."

"Keep them downstairs for now. I've got to get out of here."

Paul hurried to the door and peeked out the peephole. Two suited men were getting off the elevator; the taller one was black. Paul rushed back into the bedroom and crouched by the door. He heard a key and watched as the main door opened and the men entered. The black man turned on the television and settled into a chair while the other kicked off his shoes and flopped onto the couch.

Paul didn't want to startle them, so he thought about phoning from the closet and telling them he was here and why. But he noticed both were armed. Before he did anything, he wanted to know which side they were on. He stayed and listened.

"I'd like to at least see her first," the tall black man said.

"Me too, but Morty said just sit tight."

"All we do is sit, Jimmy."

"What're we supposed to do if she doesn't cooperate?"

"I don't think he cares. He doesn't want to know."

"They in there?" Jimmy said. "I don't hear a thing."

Jimmy moved past the other man, who sat watching the mute TV, and stood by the service door. "They're talking, Danny," he whispered, "but I can't make it out." He returned to the couch. "I'm starving. You want something?"

"Sure. Whatever you're getting."

Jimmy phoned in their order.

Paul was in no-man's-land. It was three against two, and Angela was neither armed nor trained, and she was bound. The problem was, to kill one he'd have to kill all three. Maybe that happened in the movies, but it rarely did in real life.

"He shoulda used us to grab up the girl," Danny said. "But no, we would make too big a scene. He had to do it himself."

"Well, he did, didn't he?"

"Yeah, and we're just yesterday's celery, waiting here—"

Jimmy laughed. "We're what? Yesterday's celery?"

"Or whatever they say."

Paul could hear Mort still trying to sell Angela. "See, with peyote your mind goes to a different dimension, and God speaks to you."

"You're going to have to force them down my throat."

"I wouldn't want to do that. I want you to see that this is a monumental moment in your life. You may have thought you were serving God before, but you'll hear Him speak today."

"Tied up and against my will?"

"That's just a precaution. We've got an hour, and I can't sit here holding a gun on you the whole time."

Jimmy rolled off the couch and stepped into the bathroom. Paul pulled his side arm from the leg holster and crept up behind him, waiting. As soon as Jimmy pulled up his zipper, Paul pressed the barrel of the gun into the base of his neck. "Not one sound," he whispered, reaching for Jimmy's gun. He patted the man down and found no more weapons.

"How many pieces is your friend carrying?" Paul said, and he could feel Jimmy shaking. Jimmy held up one finger. "If you're lying, you get it first. Now I'll follow you out. You tell Danny, very quietly, to put his gun on the floor and kick it to me."

As they shuffled out to stand behind Danny, Jimmy squeaked, "Danny, let me see your gun."

The big man didn't turn. "Hmm?"

"Danny?"

Danny turned and instinctively rose, reaching for his gun.

"Don't," Paul whispered. "I can put you both down in a half second."

"Put your gun on the floor and kick it over here," Jimmy said. "Please, Danny, do it."

Danny, scowling, did as he was told, never taking his eyes off Paul's. With Jimmy's piece in his pocket and Danny's in his left hand, he quietly told Danny to lie facedown on the couch. "Any noise, any signal, that's all the excuse I need."

He had Jimmy take the sheet off the bed in the back bedroom and tear it into strips. "Tie Danny's wrists and ankles together behind him, then connect them with another strip. I'm going to check your work, and if it isn't perfect, you won't be going home tonight."

Jimmy was so enthusiastic he made Danny madder. He tied his wrists behind him first, then his ankles, then lifted Danny's feet and struggled to tie them together, leaving him in a most uncomfortable position, feet up behind him, bound to his wrists. The connector between his wrists and ankles made it impossible for Danny to even squirm.

Paul had Danny open his mouth and told Jimmy to wrap several lengths of strips around Danny's head and between his teeth like a bridle bit. He could emit no sound. Paul tugged at all the bindings.

"Good job, Jimmy," Paul whispered. "Now put your left hand between your legs from behind and your right hand between your legs from the front."

Jimmy squinted as if he didn't understand, but by squatting slightly, he managed it. Paul cuffed his wrists, then nudged him onto the floor where he flopped onto his back. Paul tied his ankles and put a gag on him. Paul frisked Danny one more time to confirm he'd had only the one weapon.

The playing field was finally even. Mort began sounding as if he were at the end of patience. "Listen, Angel, you can have a life like you never dreamed."

"Like Lucy's? No thanks."

"C'mon, missy. She's on the hard stuff. If she'd stayed with the natural, she could be sitting where you're sitting."

"What a privilege," Angela said. "And where does she get the hard stuff, Morty?"

"Jonah. The only reason she gets it from me is that I don't want some scumbag ripping her off. She could get off it if she'd switch to peyote and do what I say spiritually."

For the next twenty minutes, Angela seemed to be trying to engage Mort in small talk to keep him from force-feeding her the drugs.

Paul jumped when he heard a noise behind him, coming from the chrome column in the far wall. The panel slid open to reveal a wide dumbwaiter, and there sat Jimmy and Danny's room-service order. Paul removed the tray and set it on the floor, then pushed the Received button, which closed the panel.

Paul studied the mechanism, realizing that every penthouse suite had to be equipped with the same. He examined the wall that adjoined 2200 and found nothing until he reached the bathroom. There, jutting from the wall three feet inside a utility closet was what had to be the back side of the dumbwaiter that served the next room. It was painted over, but when he lightly tapped it with a fingernail, Paul found it was metallic.

He moved back out into the living area and tried to determine how far from the chrome column Mort and Angela sat. He decided they were far enough for what he had planned, knowing Angela's life depended on it.

Back in the bathroom closet, Paul found the back of the column enclosed by screws and a thin sheet of metallic ductwork. His car key was all he needed to painstakingly and quietly remove the back panel. It opened onto the dumbwaiter, where there was a horizontal floor every five feet or so. A flange on each floor could apparently be programmed to trip a lever, which would open the sliding door in the room and display the delivery.

Paul squeezed a leg between the exposed floors and tested the load-bearing strength of the platform. It floated some but seemed solid enough. He gingerly slithered all the way in until he was crouching, facing the sliding door that opened into 2200.

Kitchen smells wafted through the shaft from twenty-two floors below. And it was steamy. Paul knew it was only a matter of time before someone on a floor below placed an order and the whole mechanism would move. He had to act now.

"We leave in about half an hour, so I want you to willingly take the prescription of God," Mort said. "It will be the most wonderful feeling you have ever had. And God will confirm what He told me, that you are to be mine. And you will assist me on a mission for Him that will bring many souls to heaven."

Paul slipped his weapon from the holster under his pant leg and reached for the lever, his face dripping.

"Receive these in your mouth."

"I won't."

Mort was clearly angry now. "You will or you'll regret it. Open your mouth."

"I told you I wouldn't do it."

"Maybe you'd like a gun barrel in your throat. Open up."

Angela apparently obeyed.

"Now chew them."

Angela whimpered. "No!"

"All right," Mort said. "I'll fill your mouth with water, and you'll have to swallow to breathe."

Paul waited a beat, hearing Mort leave the room. He pushed the lever and the panel slid open. Angela was taped to a chair. Paul put a finger to his lips. Her eyes bulged and she spit out the dope. Paul slid behind a door between her and where he heard water running.

The water stopped. Mort returned, glass in one hand, gun in the other. Paul was behind him now.

Mort knelt before Angela. He stuck a thick finger into her mouth as she tried to squirm away. "You spit them out?" he said, incredulous. "I had hoped we wouldn't have to do this the hard way."

Paul edged close and raised his weapon over his head. He brought it down so hard on Mort's forearm that he heard both ulna and radius crack as Mort's gun went flying. Mort screamed and flopped onto his side, staring terrified into Paul's gun.

With his free hand, Paul freed Angela. "Call security," he said. "Tell them we've got Jonah and two of his lackeys in custody and to send up the NPO."

27

BEFORE PAUL COULD HUSTLE Angela away, the press showed up. Paul called Bob Koontz, who predicted he would be feted in Washington again. "Great job, buddy. I can't wait to hear the details."

Finally back at her hotel, Paul walked Angela to the elevator and could see she was still deeply shaken. She melted into him and wrapped her arms around his neck. Fearing she might collapse, he held her tight. She pulled his face to hers and kissed him hard. He froze, not responding, much as he wanted to.

Angela pulled back, smiling. "You're shy in public," she said. "I need to shower and change for the meeting tonight. Would you mind giving me a ride?"

"To the meeting? Are you sure you're up to it?"

"Today was grueling, I have to admit. But the outcome more than confirmed my mission here. And Paul, thank you for rescuing Lucy. You saved her life."

• • •

That night, as Paul drove her to the bungalow, Angela slid over and sat with her hand on his leg. "We've been through a lot together," she said, gazing at him. "Nothing like a shared trauma to let you really know someone."

If only that were true . . .

"Angela, we need to talk."

"I could talk to you forever."

"You're a wonderful person. Brave, beautiful. I—"

"The feeling is mutual, Paul. I'm sure you know that."

"Thanks, but I haven't been totally up-front with you."

"Uh-oh," she said. "This sounds like a brush-off, and we haven't even gotten started yet."

"It's not a brush-off, Angela. It's an I'm-not-available."

"What? Now you're going to tell me you're married?"

"I am."

Angela pulled away.

"I'm sorry," Paul said. "I should have said something."

"What, you didn't think to? You couldn't tell what was happening, or didn't you think I might fall for you?"

"Fact is, Angela, I fell for you too."

"That's supposed to make me feel better? At least it wasn't one-sided?"

"I'm sorry. I don't know what else to say."

She sat shaking her head. "So you NPO guys don't wear your wedding rings on the job."

"Protocol."

"How convenient. So how was I to know?"

"I should have told you."

"You sure should have."

"Forgive me, Angela."

"That's the least of it, Paul. This is going to take some getting used to."

They sat in silence for most of the rest of the way.

"Drop me off a couple of blocks south," she said finally.

He stopped, but she didn't get out immediately.

"You have a family too?" she said.

"A girl and a boy. Seven and five. Jae and I have been married ten years."

"So you're *very* married."

"I am."

"You had no business even letting yourself fall."

"Don't I know it," Paul said.

"Well, good for you. Feel bad. Regret it awhile. Miss me. And go back to your family. I'll survive."

• • •

Paul drove slowly back into the city and to his hotel, then sat in the parking lot, thinking. Angela was everything Jae wasn't, at least everything Jae hadn't been for a long time. And he'd had her in his arms. Why was he staying in his marriage?

Jae had been unfair, but maybe she had a right. Paul thought back to when they were new to each other, when they would drink each other in with their eyes, live for each other. That had lasted a few years, until he had begun to yield to the thrill of adventure. It had seemed fun at times, but he had to admit that, ultimately, it was a shallow, bankrupt thrill—a sugar rush instead of a decent meal.

Straight was right. With Paul's new faith and new life came new responsibility. Paul had an idea what kind of a husband he should be. What was he going to do about his marriage? There were no options. He had to work it out. Rebuilding with Jae sounded like a chore when his heart wished he could start over with Angela. This would be a true test of his faith.

The news on the car radio trumpeted the arrest of Jonah, the religious figure who had duped hundreds and had been responsible for the overdose deaths of sixteen. Paul decided to see what it looked like on TV. Besides bringing down a monster, he was grateful for what it would mean to him as a mole within the NPO. The brass wouldn't know the difference between Jonah and his misguided followers and the real believers.

The walk from the elevator to his room seemed to take forever, and he realized how bone-weary he was, both from the tension of the day and his talk with Angela. He felt as if he could sleep twelve hours. Maybe he would.

He pushed open his door, but before he reached for the light he noticed the thick silhouette of a man sitting on his bed. Paul dropped to a crouch and pulled his weapon.

"Put it away," a familiar voice growled. "You wouldn't shoot your own father-in-law, would you?"

Paul held his breath. "Tell me Jae and the kids are all right."

"Sit down. They're fine."

Paul collapsed into a chair. *Then what? Did Jae show him the letter? Have I been tailed? Am I busted?*

"You're going to tell me who she is. And then you're going to get rid of her."

"Excuse me?"

"You think I'm ignorant, Paul? You used a woman in this operation today."

"She was working locally. Had a contact with my suspect."

"Yeah? Well, you know what? She was in the background in some of the TV reports. Looked real familiar to me. Know why?"

"I can't imagine."

"I've seen pictures of her before."

Paul fought to maintain composure. "Really?"

"Uh-huh. What's her name, Paul?"

"I never share names of informants."

"She's an informant now?"

"She was in this case."

"What was she in Washington? and Toledo?"

"Sir?"

"You know what I'm talking about."

"No! I don't know what you're—"

"You certainly do, Paul."

"You're so smart, you tell me."

"Don't use that tone with me, boy. That's Andy Pass's daughter. We had her on file."

What?

"How do you know she's not a subversive like her old man? You'd better clean up your act, Paul. This is *my* daughter you're cheating on."

"I'm not cheating at all—on anyone."

"Fix it, Paul."

Of all the things to be caught for . . .

"But that's not why I'm here," Ranold said. "There's trouble brewing in Sunterra. Shaping up to be a terrible crisis."

"What's going on?"

The old man scooted up so he could rest his back on the headboard. "Christians. The regional governor himself made an appeal to the agency. The Zealot Underground task force will be involved, but you don't have the know-how or manpower—or the guts—for a major operation like this. It's Special Projects."

Ranold grinned. "I always knew this day would come, Paul, ever since we saw those first little snakes in the woodpile.

Congress and the agency lacked the will to crush them then. The new generation is a bunch of liberal pantywaists—careerists and politicians with no firsthand war experience—and they were scared of public outcry. At least they knew they needed a tough old wizard behind the curtain. That's when I founded Special Projects.

"I set the best protocol they'd let me: Lop off leaders for intimidation, set up a task force, leak selectively to the press to avoid creating martyrs. I warned all along they were trying to shoot a bear with a popgun, and now they see I'm right. In just six months, snakes have overrun our country. Terrorists don't slink away—they proliferate.

"So while you task-force types have been investigating and making arrests, I've been watching for the right opening to drop the bomb on the pit of vipers. This is it, Paul. Congress has granted me emergency powers, and I'm calling out the army. Sunterra is where we smash this insurrection once and for all."

"Ranold, I'm . . . *shocked* is the word, I guess. I figured you were handling something major but—"

"You didn't know how bad things had gotten. Paul, you were out of commission a long time. What you've seen is just the tip of the iceberg. We're finding Bibles everywhere, along with what they call 'tracts'—little brochures with the 'gospel' in them. Plenty are turning up in your own backyard, all over Michigan and Ohio. We don't know where they're printed. And the same stuff's flooding the Internet. We've got laws against that, but they're almost impossible to enforce."

Paul nearly burst with pride over what his brothers and sisters were accomplishing—just as he had been told in the salt mines—but he maintained a disconcerted look.

"The movement is bigger and stronger—more ruthless and cunning—and more widespread than you know. That's why it's time."

"What's happening in L.A.?"

Ranold turned and put his feet on the floor, warming to his topic. "The zealots there are pervasive and bold," he said. "And I'm sure you know how important the film industry is to our government."

Paul massaged his eyes. "Important enough that all the studios have been conglomerated into one."

"One government-run studio, right. L.A. Idea Co. And why? Because movies are more than our most important propaganda tool. They are also among our most valuable exports, both in terms of culture propagation and income. Well, the zealots are trying to sabotage the business. But they've made a fatal miscalculation."

"What are they doing?"

"You'll see. We're heading out there tomorrow."

"Does Koontz know?"

"Of course. And you'll still report to the NPO through the bureau chief in L.A. Nepotism breeds dissension, Paul. Besides, for this operation, I've decided to play the role of General Decenti— military consultant, old soldier called out of retirement to advise. That's the beauty of Special Projects. I'm spared the burden of public scrutiny and—" he smiled—"the law. It lets me run the show as I see fit. For the day-to-day, I've put Balaam in charge."

"That agent I met at the awards ceremony?"

"I told you she was a comer, Paul. She's made a real contribution on my team, strategically and in detention situations, even if she hasn't been tested in the field. But I'll be keeping you close. We'll travel together, and we'll bunk together."

Ranold stood. "I got a room two floors below. Flight's at oh-eight-hundred."

"Dad, you need to know there is zero between me and Andy Pass's daughter."

"Whatever you say. But unless you're trying to get next to her for information on the underground, you're playing with fire."

• • •

Paul phoned Ranold's room a few minutes later to be sure he was there. "What time did you say that flight was?"

"Oh-eight-hundred. Meet you for breakfast at oh-six-thirty."

"Roger that."

Paul phoned Angela but got Willie instead. "She's still talking with some of the girls."

"Willie, this is really important. Tell her not to return to her hotel. Have someone else pick up her stuff and her kids and find them someplace new to stay. Got that?"

"Yes, sir, but—"

"This is not negotiable, Willie."

• • •

Paul's final call was to Straight, who was horrified about the coming raid. "I have to tell you, Paul, we've been expecting some kind of backlash. One of our Washington people even guessed there was some major muscle behind Balaam. But we never thought it would come down this hard or this soon."

"I need contacts with believers in L.A., and I need them fast," Paul said. "I wish you could be there with me."

"Interesting you should say that, Paul. Now that the battle has been heating up, I've often wished that I could be more on the front lines. But not just yet."

Straight promised to have everything Paul needed within twenty-four hours.

28

BREAKFAST AND THE FLIGHT proved exhausting for Paul, the victim of his father-in-law's bluster. Everything was about how Paul should be thrilled at this opportunity for visibility.

"We're staying at Tiny Allendo's in Beverly Hills," Ranold said as they got off the plane at LAX. "You've never seen a place like his."

Allendo was the studio chief. "We're *staying* there?" Paul said. "That sounds like a conflict of interest."

"He works for the government too, remember?"

"He's paid on profits, Dad. That's why nobody else who works for the government lives in Beverly Hills."

A stretch limo pulled up with *Decenti* on a card in the window.

"That's Tiny for you," Ranold said as the driver put their bags in the trunk.

Ranold asked the driver to take them through Hollywood on

the way to Allendo's home. "You're going to get an idea what's happening here," he told Paul. Paul enjoyed the vibrating massage of the passenger seats and the array of radio and TV signals available through his molar receptors.

"Pull off here a second," Ranold told the driver. He pointed out to Paul a billboard that announced one movie, yet the hologram depicted another. "Disgusting."

The billboard advertised a new erotic thriller, but the holographic image was from *The Ten Commandments* where Charlton Heston as Moses throws down the tablets in disgust at the sin of the Israelites. It played over and over, the tablets breaking to pieces and Moses chastising the people.

"What's that about?" Paul said.

"What do you think? It's the zealots. They're convinced Hollywood is immoral, and they're determined to change it. We can't let that happen."

That Hollywood and her product were immoral was hardly news. Even in Paul's previous life he could hardly stomach the new movies. All were now holographic and most were interactive, but there was hardly a thing he could enjoy with his family. Nothing was off-limits now.

"It's high-tech vandalism," Ranold raged. "And because this industry is government run, that's a federal felony."

"How hard would it be to stop this?" Paul said.

"That's why we're here."

"Billboard mischief?"

"We can't find the source, Paul! We can override it only temporarily with interceptors, but we can't stop it. That'll be your job. At least part of it. That's only the beginning."

"I hope so, because you said—"

"I said it was a crisis, and it is. This is just one manifestation. Driver, take us to where we can see the Hollywood sign."

It seemed every house in the area was trying to top the one next door. All had fountains and swimming pools. Many had several golf holes and misted landscaping. "You should have seen this city before you were born, Paul. Smog so thick you wouldn't have been able to see the houses. Thank technology—primarily electric-powered cars and trucks—for cleaning that up."

A few minutes later the limo pulled over again, and Paul peered into the Hollywood hills where the famous white sign had been standing for roughly a century. For the last twenty years its letters had consisted of laser light images, and there the vandals had struck again. One of the *L*s had been snuffed, and the sign now read *Holywood*.

"Same people?" Paul said.

"Well, of course it's the same people," Ranold spat. "The problem is not only that these people exist, but also that they are out of control."

• • •

Tiny Allendo was not, of course, tiny. His was an ironic nickname for a man six-foot-eight with wavy black hair, supposedly bright blue eyes, and an easy smile. Paul wouldn't see those eyes until late in the evening, because Allendo wore wraparound gold-mirrored shades, even indoors, until past dark. He dressed in black on black, was a paragon of style, and proved a generous host. Nearing fifty years old, he looked ten years younger. He enjoyed carrying the conversation and, while pleasant, was unable to hide an underlying rage about what was happening in Hollywood.

Tiny had a staff that rotated in sets of eight, and after the butler, whom he referred to as simply a doorman, welcomed Paul and Ranold, they were shown to their respective rooms— in opposite wings of the sixteen-thousand-square-foot home—

by valets who unpacked their bags and hung up their clothes. They were invited to relax until brunch, which was to be served by the pool at ten.

Though Tiny was technically a government employee, Paul was not comfortable with the arrangement. The marble-and-stucco home was the most lavish Paul had ever seen. Everything was sleek and ultramodern and custom-made, from the furniture to the draperies and linens. Paul's private bath was as large as his living room at home. Lights came on when he entered a room and went off when he left. A valet stood at the end of the hall, waiting to be paged if he needed anything, anything at all.

Paul didn't know whether to dress for the pool or for work. He decided he was there on business and should look the part, even if he was dining poolside with one of the wealthiest men in Hollywood. He put on light slacks and a sport jacket. His only concession to the weather and the location was a pullover rather than shirt and tie.

His valet escorted Paul to the pool, and he arrived the same time Ranold and his chaperone did. Ranold showed up in a three-piece suit, looking wholly uncomfortable and promising to buy pool gear that day for a swim that evening. The pool was filled with at least two dozen bronzed and bikinied lovelies.

Tiny had changed into a skimpy gold thong to match his sunglasses, black flip-flops, and a white dress shirt as a cover-up. He enthusiastically welcomed his guests and directed them to sit facing him at a round table, placing his female secretary and his young male assistant at his sides. The five of them were served a light brunch of fresh seafood by the hovering staff.

"And you two are related somehow, do I have that right?" Tiny said.

Ranold explained the relationship and waded through the formalities of greetings from Washington.

"I'm grateful you're here," Allendo said.

"In just days, you'll be even more grateful," Ranold said. "Washington will be working within the National Peace Organization bureau headquartered in Los Angeles, to which Paul has full access, owing to his advisory role with the Zealot Underground task force. Agent Bia Balaam and I, representing the Congress of the United Seven States of America, have all the resources of the federal government at our beck and call. I assure you, Mr. Allendo, that these attacks on Hollywood will never have the chance to spread. We will not leave here until we crush the efforts of these zealots to destroy the movie industry."

"That's a relief," Tiny said. "This is more than a nuisance, you know. These people are trying to overthrow us. And regardless what they think about our product, is it just me, or are these people breaking the law simply by practicing religion?"

"Of course they are," Ranold said. "That's why it is imperative that the uprising be quashed and the underground dismantled as quickly as possible. We have marshaled a formidable army contingent. By this evening it will have encircled not just Hollywood but also the entire city of Los Angeles."

"You're not serious."

"Quite. It's a huge area, of course, but not such a difficult job. Our men will interface with your local NPO bureau, which, under the guidance of our Agent Balaam, has already been investigating, infiltrating, and attempting to apprehend those responsible for the attacks against your operation."

Infiltrating? That was what Balaam had bragged about doing in D.C. too.

Allendo proved a dainty eater for a big man. He dipped his hands in a water bowl to wash the drawn butter from his fingers and dried them on a towel. "The press would love the operation, Mr. Decenti, so—"

"You may call me General Decenti."

"Very well. How do we keep this from the press?"

Ranold dabbed his mouth with a napkin. "So far, we've managed to control the spin rather well."

"The billboard vandal is just a hacker with access to one old movie," Tiny said. "And the Hollywood sign defacers are pranksters. Their disinformation campaign is a failure. We still beam our message throughout the world."

"Exactly. And we'll continue to spoon-feed the press what we want them to say."

Allendo smiled and nodded. "How long do you think a press blackout can be maintained?"

"Excellent question," Ranold said. "Not long. The nature of the beast. So we'll make a swift surgical strike. Believe me, Mr. Allendo, we come with a zero-tolerance policy, committed to ferreting out and decimating these zealots."

"I see *movie* written all over a mission like this."

Ranold beamed.

• • •

When they had finished eating, Allendo said, "I have reservations this evening at a wonderful club, the Studio. General, you mentioned wanting to do some shopping this afternoon. Please feel free to use my limo and driver."

"Most generous," Ranold said, "but I have a government car and chauffeur at my disposal."

"And you, Dr. Stepola?"

"I'm having a car delivered from the agency."

"Your car has just arrived," the secretary told Paul.

Allendo walked Paul to the front of the estate, where a solid gold replica of Buckingham Fountain shot water a hundred feet into the air. Shaking Paul's hand again, Tiny purred about how happy he was to have him as a guest. "I just wanted to add that evening companionship is available. After-hours drinks, conversation, that kind of a thing. Merely mention your pleasure to your valet."

"That won't be necessary," Paul said.

"No?"

"No, thank you."

"As you wish. If you're not busy, you're welcome to join me for the rest of the afternoon by the pool."

"Would you excuse me?" Paul said. "I really need to get some calls made and legwork done."

"Of course. But you will join us at the Studio tonight?"

"Yes, certainly."

Allendo disappeared as two unmarked, government-issue sedans pulled up to the walkway that encircled the fountain. Both drivers got out, one a woman of about sixty, the other a man of about forty.

"Tough gig," the man said. "So much for the water shortage, eh?"

"Yeah," the woman said. "You wanna stay at my place and let me have your room here?"

Paul tried to sound amused. "Doesn't seem right, does it?"

"Too bad you don't get a Benz like Triple-D."

"Sorry?"

She pointed to the limousine and driver that waited closer to the house. "Deputy Director Decenti. That one's his."

"Former Deputy Director," Paul said. "He's here as General Decenti."

"Whatever. We're starting with a briefing at nine tomorrow morning at headquarters, sir. Does he want to be in on that?"

"I'll inform him."

As the two drove off, Ranold came out, and Paul filled him in on the briefing.

"Don't expect me to get involved in meetings where the blind lead the blind, Paul. Balaam and I are meeting with the regional governor and his people tomorrow morning, and then I'm getting together with the army's commanding general. You take care of your own little schedule, and when I want you to debrief me, I'll let you know. How's that?"

"Perfect."

• • •

Paul headed out for a driving tour to get the lay of the land. Wartime floods had once swallowed up L.A.'s coastal communities, but now the gleaming city of five million looked prosperous. New technology allowed the skyscrapers to withstand frequent tremors, even the most severe.

From one particularly high point on the expressway, Paul could see the Pacific beaches to the west and the snowcapped mountains to the northeast. The NPO office was in the civic center complex between the historic white twenty-six-story city hall and the convention center. Paul stopped nearby to get a map.

The map roughly depicted the city's eight major areas: South Central, Central, Downtown, the San Fernando Valley, the Port of L.A., West L.A., South Bay, and East L.A. According to Straight, the people in the salt mines under Detroit had relationships with underground factions in each of these areas. Before heading back to the Allendo estate, Paul drove around, praying for his brothers and sisters in the city.

• • •

That night Paul and Ranold squeezed into Tiny's extravagant roadster. They wore somber suits. Tiny was in a black-and-gold caftan. The Studio turned out to be the new tenant in the historic Grauman's Chinese Theatre, now a dazzling nightclub and bar that featured interactive movies, music, dancing, and dinner.

In a sunken center circle the threesome dined on sushi and other delights that had been flown in from Asia that very day. On tiers above them patrons not dancing or hitting on each other participated in the Studio's trademark entertainment: virtual-reality movies. For a hefty fee, one could enter a special glassed-in room and step into any movie he chose, play a part, and purchase a copy of the scenes in which he had participated.

Paul noted that most of the people his age and younger chose erotica or porn, and no one seemed self-conscious about what they were seeing or doing. Older people inclined toward the classics. Paul wondered what it would be like to stand next to Humphrey Bogart while he interacted with Ingrid Bergman in *Casablanca.*

Ranold said he would like to be "John Wayne, just once."

To Tiny the stuff was old hat, but he insisted that Ranold and Paul satisfy their curiosity. Ranold couldn't quit talking about being Rooster Cogburn in a gunfight. Paul actually reached over piano player Sam's shoulder in Rick Blaine's nightclub and played "Chopsticks," then slid onto the bench himself and took Sam's place, for ten minutes becoming the piano player in *Casablanca.* He declined to purchase his scene.

When Paul returned to the table, Tiny and Ranold were occupied with the latter's exploits in *True Grit.* Thinking it was safer here than at Tiny's house, Paul slipped into a quiet hallway to call Straight. He brought him up-to-date, and Straight said he would pass along the information, primarily about the military presence, to the nerve center in Detroit. Straight also gave him leads to the Christian community.

"Where do I start?" Paul said.

"Kirk Quinn," Straight said. "Goes by Specs because he actually still wears glasses. He's a lone wolf, a computer techie, but he knows everybody. He can put you in touch with whoever you need. He's the mastermind behind most of the mischief out there. But be careful, Paul. If you're under Decenti's thumb, let the various factions pass messages back and forth for you. Limit your direct contacts. Obviously, you're going to be watched."

29

IN THE MORNING, as Paul waited for his car, army personnel pulled up in a security vehicle the likes of which Paul had only read about. It could purportedly withstand a missile attack. It looked slow and heavy until Ranold, lavishly welcomed by all on board, got in and it raced away.

Paul drove his NPO-issue electrosedan back into the city. Bureau personnel went through the formalities of welcoming the religious adviser from Chicago, but Ranold had been right. It did seem like the blind leading the blind. These people apparently had no real leads and seemed demoralized that Ms. Balaam was in charge of the operation. She had already been out there laying the groundwork and had raised hackles, Paul gathered, by implying that the locals had proven incompetent to check the rebellion. She was treating them like lackeys who had to redeem themselves.

The L.A. bureau chief, a sixtyish no-nonsense woman named

Harriet Johns, displayed a fancy chart of the city's eight major areas, pointing out the most likely places subversives might choose to meet. They had traced underground activity, she said, to an abandoned college not far from Los Angeles International Airport, which had been a Catholic university. They also believed a small cell might inhabit an abandoned nightclub in South Central.

"As *Washington* advised," she said with an edge, not mentioning Balaam's name, "we've got informants inside both cells. But they haven't been terribly effective yet. And we might not have time to pull them before a raid."

NPO would leave an infiltrator vulnerable? Paul worried even more about his encountering one.

He offered to check out potential meeting sites and to look for signs of subversive activity, and he left. Paul was quietly gratified that he had more information than the task force. Unfortunately, according to what Straight had given him, the task force was right about the abandoned university and South Central. Paul called him from the car.

"I know that college location," Straight said. "It was once Loyola Marymount University. The government turned it into a reprogramming center after the war. Taught people how to get along without the encumbrances of religion. Wasn't that nice of 'em?"

"Hey, Straight, do the believers here have a talisman of any kind?"

"Yes. A penny."

"The old English coin?"

"American. Worth one percent of a dollar. Used them up until the end of the war. Abraham Lincoln's on one side, and it says 'In God We Trust' on it. Dark brown 'cause they've got some copper in 'em."

"Does that relate to Revelation?"

"It's a little more obscure than the other symbols. Lincoln was known as Honest Abe, of course, a virtue we want to be known by. And the 'God' line on there is one thing that took the penny out of circulation. But because of the color, the penny also represents gold."

"Sure is a lot of that out here."

"Well, the believers aren't the ones who have it. The line the penny relates to is 'I advise you to buy gold from me—gold that has been purified by fire.' "

"So Los Angeles is Laodicea. But I'm still not sure why."

"Laodicea had to bring in its water by aqueduct, for one thing, as L.A. does. And remember what else that passage tells you to buy: 'ointment for your eyes so you will be able to see.' Laodicea was a big maker of eye salve for the ancient world."

"L.A.'s movies could be considered eye products today."

"You got it—not to mention what they used to call 'eye candy'—the beautiful people."

"Incredible. Where would I find a penny?"

"Other than the underground there? Got me. Use their code phrase to make your connection, then see if you can get a penny from them."

• • •

With his map on the seat beside him, Paul ventured out to find his first underground contact. He hadn't seen anyone in glasses since he was a kid. According to Straight, Kirk Quinn was one guy on whom laser eye surgery didn't take. But that hadn't seemed to hamper Quinn's current task. Though no one outside the underground knew who he was, his work was seen and commented upon by millions in L.A. every day.

Paul took the Santa Monica Freeway west to the postwar

incarnation of Venice-on-the-Ocean. There he located a row of single-story brick buildings housing movie postproduction facilities.

Paul parked a few blocks away and seemed to attract no attention walking through parking lots to the buildings. On a simple directory he found "K. Quinn" listed as a freelance editor in suite J, second from the end.

The suite had a locked door with a peephole and a small window in the wall next to it with its shade pulled. Paul pressed the button on the intercom.

"Not taking any work for a while," came the staticky response.

"What if I was a friend of a friend?"

"Still not taking any work."

"I just want to talk."

"Too busy."

"What if I was from the National Peace Organization and had a warrant to search the premises?"

"Then I would cordially invite you in. Hold your card up to the peephole."

The door opened almost immediately upon a short, pale, balding, midthirties man with, sure enough, black horn-rimmed glasses. The place was a royal mess—dishes, cups, and electrical equipment everywhere.

Paul saw a hot plate and a dirty saucepan. "You *live* here too?" he said, shaking hands with Specs.

"Creative wall making," the man said. "Through that curtain are my quarters. Your warrant extend that far?"

Specs pulled a folding chair out from behind the refrigerator and set it up for Paul. He plopped himself on a counter after sweeping aside some clutter. "What have I been suspected of now, and what can I do for you?"

JERRY JENKINS • 275

"You're suspected of being the projectionist who's vandalized billboards and the Hollywood sign."

"*Holy*wood, you mean?" Specs said, smiling.

Paul nodded. "How do you do it?"

"Whoever's doing it, it would all be a matter of hacking. I love the term *projectionist*, though it is, of course, archaic and inaccurate. These high-tech visuals are all run off computers, so if a person *did* want to mess with them, he would have to understand the inner workings of the machines, be able to access the images and manipulate them, then hard-wire them to revert to the— shall we say, fix?—as the default every time someone tries to override the new programming."

"I'll pretend to understand that and ask if that's what I would find on your computers if I were to confiscate them and have them studied."

Specs ran a grimy hand over his shiny head. "If I had the brains to pull off what I just described, don't you think I would also have the capacity to so encrypt the programming that it would be undetectable?"

"I don't know that much about it," Paul said. "But I should think someone else at your level would be able to decipher it."

"That would be the challenge for both sides. Your suspect trying to keep anyone from doing that, and the other side trying to crack the code."

Paul intertwined his fingers behind his head. "So with you unwilling to admit it's you, and with us unable to find evidence on your equipment, it's a stalemate?"

"Given those variables."

"How about another variable? What if I were to tell you that I am your brother in Christ and that the only reason I don't have my penny to prove it is that I have not yet made contact with the local underground leadership?"

Specs cocked his head and folded his arms. "Now there is a conundrum."

"How so?"

"If I were who you think I am, I would want this to be true so badly that I would declare myself. But if you are not who you say you are, my words could convict me."

Paul leaned forward, elbows on his knees. "I am who I say I am, and you can believe it because I say it in the name of the risen Christ, who said, 'My purpose is to give life—'"

"'—in all its fullness.'" Specs shook his head. "So you're that guy? You're really that guy?"

"That guy?"

"You can imagine it's getting around that we have a contact in high places."

"It's me."

Kirk Quinn slowly removed his glasses and set them on the counter. He covered his face with both hands and began to weep. Paul stood and put a hand on his shoulder, whereupon Specs grabbed him and pulled him close, hugging him tight. "We've felt so alone, so isolated, for so long."

"It's an honor to meet you, sir," Paul said. Then, imitating John Malkovich in *Con Air*, "Love your work."

That made Specs laugh. He wiped his face and put his glasses back on, then dug in his pocket and gave Paul a card with his cell phone number on it. "This is constant work, you know. Unfortunately, it's fairly easy to override my protocols for defaulting back out of the fixes."

"I don't follow."

"Well, I know they're going to try to change what I've done, so I make my new program the default. But that's merely a nuisance to them, and they quickly rebuild a new platform for the operation. I have to be constantly on the lookout for that and start over. Often several times a day."

"Why can't they figure out what you're doing and make it impossible for you?"

"The truth?"

"Of course."

"It's not humble."

"Go ahead."

"They're not as good as I am."

Paul was telling Specs about the danger to both Loyola and South Central when he heard a tone in his head. "Excuse me, Mr. Quinn," he said, turning toward the door. He pressed his fingers together. "This is Paul."

It was Ranold. "Wherever you are, get to South Central."

"What's going on?"

"Just hurry. You're going to want to see this." He gave Paul an address.

Paul told Specs to warn the people at Loyola. "I have to run."

Specs nodded. "Soon," he said.

Paul smiled. "Soon." He rushed out and sprinted to his car. Just the other side of the new Marina del Rey, he hit traffic, so it took him an hour to reach South Central. There he found his father-in-law amidst a knot of military men in combat gear, congratulating each other on the success of a shoot-out that had killed five Christians, wounded six, and seen a dozen captured.

When Ranold noticed Paul he rushed over, palm raised. Paul ignored it. "Ranold, how did we get from suspecting a small cell here to this holocaust?"

His father-in-law flushed, leaning close to Paul's ear and hissing, "Listen to me, Cub Scout. Don't ever challenge me in front of my subordinates. And you ought to be proud to be part of this. What's the matter with you?"

"Is it common for the zealot underground to be armed? Did they return fire?"

"You've never been close enough to the action to see anything but a fireball coming at you, Paul. Grow up."

A tall, rangy figure in fatigues detached from the group and sidled over. It took Paul a moment to register that it was a woman. *Got to be Balaam.* When he was introduced to her in the Rose Garden, he had been blind.

"Dr. Stepola," she said, extending the bony hand he remembered. "Glad to have you on board."

Paul took her hand, recalling the smugness in her voice when she had talked about making it "unhealthy" to be a Christian. Her eyes mesmerized him. Like her hair, they were silver and seemed to pulse and shift like pools of mercury. They also seemed to rob his head of thoughts. She looked nearly inhuman.

"You had a tough time in Gulfland."

"Not as tough as those who died. I was lucky."

"Very lucky," Balaam said. "And with the guidance of your father-in-law, this operation is going to be very lucky too."

"I'm sure you're right."

The soldiers were getting into their vehicles, calling out to Ranold and Balaam.

"Join us, Paul," Ranold said.

"I'm chasing a lead. Let's catch up tonight."

Paul returned to his car and sat gasping. He called Straight. "I just heard," Straight said. "Those people weren't armed and had no munitions. Word we got was that they were packing up, trying to get out of there."

"Who's left, Straight? Who do I try to contact now?"

"Quinn should be able to tell you. You met him yet?"

"Just came from there. Oh no."

"What is it, Paul?"

"One of the billboards just went dark."

"Don't worry about it," Straight said. "They go back and forth gaining ground against Specs, and then he regains the ground. Call him."

Paul dialed but got no answer. He had to make sure Specs let the Loyola faction know what had happened in South Central and warn them they could be next.

Traffic was lighter going away from the raid, but Paul noticed all the movie billboards going dark now. Had Specs seen the news? Was this his attempt at a statement, a memorial of some kind? Or was he shutting down for his own safety? Had he abandoned his studio?

Paul forced himself to stop thinking the worst. Specs was merely busy.

Too busy to answer his phone.

30

PAUL KEPT PHONING Kirk Quinn as he sped toward Venice. He drove all the way to the parking lot directly across from suite J. His heart sank when he saw people milling about near the door.

"NPO government business," he announced as he shouldered through. A huge hole had been blown out of the door where the knob had been. The tiny office looked as if a storm had hit. Every computer and monitor had been smashed to bits.

And there on the floor by the back wall lay Specs in a wide pool of black-red blood, lifeless eyes wide under thick lenses, teeth bared, throat slit from ear to ear.

Paul was nauseated and shaking, but he forced himself to pull a notebook and pen from his pocket and ask people what they had seen. "A team of commandos," a young man said.

"They slid up here in three or four army jeeps, and next thing I knew—*boom!* Door flies open, they burst in shouting. I hear stuff being smashed, lots of yelling. Then they're out of here. Couldn't have taken thirty seconds. Is that guy all right, that guy with the glasses?"

Paul had just met Quinn, yet he felt as if he had lost a dear brother. *What a waste. What a tragic loss.*

• • •

The danger should have been obvious—a car issued from the NPO pool, now under the control of an aggressive Washington agent who would trust no one, especially the competition. Paul was a twice-injured operative viewed as a hero in the agency and even more threatening as the son-in-law of Ranold Decenti. No, Bia Balaam would never give Paul a chance to show her up by chasing his own leads and possibly making his own arrests. She would insist on knowing what he was up to at all times, to be sure he was no challenge to her authority.

• • •

With the bystanders' attention still on the mayhem in Specs's studio, Paul dropped to his knees and quickly searched under the car. He found a tracking device behind the right front wheel. Now, where to put it? Down the block was a bright yellow sports coupe that probably saw a lot of action, day and night. Tracking it would keep the monitors busy though now, with the raids underway—and so successful—it was unlikely that Balaam would have more time to focus on Paul.

Back in the car, he called Harriet Johns. "Guess what?" she said. "The army got the billboard projectionist."

"I'm here at the scene."

"That figures. They tell you, one of their own, but we just got

JERRY JENKINS • 283

the word a few minutes ago. Looks like Washington expects us to wait in line too, only one step ahead of the cops and the press."

"That's not how it went," Paul said. "I happened to be nearby and stopped to see what was going on. According to witnesses, the army blew a hole in the door, trashed the place, and then a minute later sped off. The body is still lying here on the floor, covered with blood."

"Sounds ugly."

"It is ugly. And I'm going to have to start beating off the gawkers. Is somebody coming out to clean up this mess?"

"Coroner and cleanup crew are on the way," she said. "Hey, I've got the news on. The billboards are all coming back up. And if you get into the Hollywood Hills, check out the sign."

"Back to normal?" Paul said.

"Better than normal. You've got to see it. I suppose you heard about South Central."

"I heard."

"They took the survivors to King-Drew Medical Center. You want to go by and interview them?"

"Yes, ma'am."

"When you're done, come by and fill me in."

When Paul reached South Central and the prison hospital, he faced stares and glares. This was a place not used to visits from government agents.

Paul interrogated three wounded survivors, but because they seemed so disoriented, he chose not to reveal himself as a fellow believer. In intensive care he came upon Tyrone Perkins, a young black man whose torso was encased in bandages, monitors tracking his vital signs. He was conscious. And crying.

Flashing his credentials, Paul asked the nurse to give them a moment.

Tyrone said, "You NPO?"

Paul nodded.

"I was your guy inside," Tyrone said, tears rolling.

"Our guy?"

"Did it for the money, man. Never thought they'd kill 'em . . ."

"What happened, Tyrone? Those people armed?"

"Not a piece."

"No weapons cache anywhere?"

"No. I'm dying, man, and those dead people are on me. Good people. Killed 'em . . ."

"I didn't want to see them killed either, Tyrone." The young man's chest heaved, and Paul noticed on the monitor that his pulse was dangerously irregular. "I'd better get someone for you."

"No, man!" he gasped. "I deserve to die."

"Tyrone, did you know of other groups?"

"Can't tell . . . not now." His breathing was raspy.

Paul touched his bandaged hand. "If I convinced you I was one of them, could you tell me so I could warn them?"

"What?"

"You want to make up for what happened? Tell me who I can warn."

"Can't trust . . ."

"You can trust me, Tyrone. I know the code phrase."

"Didn't tell nobody the phrase . . ."

"You didn't need to tell me. I know it."

"Say it."

"'My purpose is to give life . . .'"

Tyrone's eyes looked huge. "'. . . in all its fullness,'" he whispered. Paul had to bend close to hear him. "The port . . . Fishers of Men . . ."

"Thank you," Paul whispered. "Bless you."

Tyrone's machines started beeping and staff came running.

• • •

Paul drove back downtown—passing a colossal army caravan heading the other way—and up into the Hollywood Hills, where he saw the famous sign again. It now read "Hurray for Hollywood." Drivers honked and waved as they passed.

The sight filled him with sorrow and rage. He felt sickened by what he'd witnessed that afternoon. *Was I ever that bad?* He feared he had been. It had been a thrill to pull the trigger in San Francisco; he had felt justified executing Christians. He had entrapped Stephen Lloyd, then stood by without lifting a finger as Donny Johnson beat him to death. Even that agent, Jefferson, was offended. "What's wrong with you, man?" he'd asked. And Paul would have shot the Mexican kid in the head too, had the Klaxon not sounded. *I was acting in anger, not from inhumanity. At least I hope I was.*

He was sickened by Balaam's ruthless murder of Specs—and that the sadism of her "interventions" in Washington would get to play out here on a more public stage. Paul prayed he could keep cool enough to make some positive impact on what appeared to be a hopeless situation. And his father-in-law—Ranold was merciless, Paul knew, but how could he endure Ranold's bloodthirsty glee the whole time he would be stuck with him at Tiny's? If Paul couldn't contain his disgust, what suspicions might that arouse? He had already drawn the old man's ire that afternoon. *Maybe Ranold keeps me close by to watch me. Did he get his hands on my father's letter?*

Even so, Paul could never keep quiet about the killings. *I'll have to maintain the courage of my convictions—stay steadfast in my faith—and take my chances.*

How could Jae have grown up in the same house with a monster like Ranold? Paul was suddenly desperate to talk to her.

There was no answer on her portable phone, so he left a message and dialed his mother-in-law.

"Jae's not here right now," she told him.

"Where is she?"

"I don't know exactly, but I'll tell her you called. She's gone for a few days."

"Gone where?"

"She didn't give me specifics, but she'll be calling, I'm sure."

"Let me talk to the kids."

"It's three hours later here, Paul. They're asleep."

• • •

Paul had never felt so alone. It was too late to try to find Fishers of Men down at the port; the markets opened at dawn and closed early. By now it was past dinnertime. Recalling that Harriet Johns had asked him to check in, he swung by the L.A. bureau, certain she'd still be there. Until recently, Paul had viewed her with respect. She had come up through the ranks and had earned the admiration of her agents.

Her bureaucratic-green office was in a corner of the fourth floor, and she welcomed him warmly. "Finally got the full story on the projectionist," she said. "Venice-on-the-Ocean, kind of a beach bum, apparently, but heavily armed. They tried to bring him in, but he wouldn't come without a fight. Had to shoot him."

Some gunshot. How do you slit the throat of a heavily armed man?

"So what'd you learn in South Central?" she asked.

"Not much. I'm surprised you weren't down there."

She grimaced. "I wouldn't be caught dead in South Central in anything but a tank. The raid is going to be reported as a gang war that killed innocent civilians. That's more than credible for down there. The LAPD is picking up the pieces."

"I have to tell you, Chief Johns, I'm puzzled. It seemed to me we had squat in this morning's meeting. But then today we zeroed in on a major target. Am I just out of the loop, or what's happening here?"

Harriet raised her eyebrows and studied the ceiling. "It's the Washington involvement—your father-in-law and Chief Balaam and all the resources they bring to the table. The intelligence sector of the army corps alone culled enough information to get close and intimidate the underground into giving up each other. I've stopped asking questions, Doctor. Maybe I should be embarrassed, but I have to admit that they've accomplished more in the last few hours than we have in the last six months."

"What's next? Other targets?"

"I'm not privy to those, Paul. It's all in Washington's hands. That's what happens when you call in the heavy artillery. We're just foot soldiers now, checking leads."

"Chief, what happened to the infiltrator in South Central? Everybody involved on the task force *has* to know who the infiltrators are. We could kill them without knowing it." Paul dreaded the thought that he might already have been exposed to other infiltrators.

Harriet shrugged. "He was a street person, a druggie. Collateral damage."

"I'd like to think if we had someone inside—like a real agent—we might not be so quick to do this to these people."

"You're missing the point, Paul. *We* aren't doing this to these people. They're doing it to themselves. And as for a real agent infiltrating, what about you?"

Infiltrate? "Me?"

"You could speak their language."

"Pretty dangerous work."

"I thought you were once Delta Force. Isn't *danger* your middle name?"

Paul forced himself to smile and realized it had been a long time since he had. "Tell you one thing, Harriet: If I ever did, I'd insist on being the most well-known infiltrator in history. I'd want everyone on your staff, not to mention the task force, and even everyone in the army, knowing whose side I was on. Underground Christians in this town have a way of winding up dead."

"And there're more to come."

Don't count on it.

• • •

Paul headed back to the Allendo estate. "Just leave it running," one of the chauffeurs said when Paul pulled up to the front door. The doorman let him in and escorted him downstairs to a game parlor. Tiny Allendo was dealing cards at an expansive green-felted table, and he and Ranold—beautiful young women at their shoulders—were smoking cigars. Paul recognized the other two men at the table as executives from L.A. Idea Co. Some of the women he'd seen earlier at the pool were playing billiards.

"Come on in!" Tiny called out. "We're celebrating. Not even I expected this much success since the last time we sat together."

"I don't play," Paul said.

Tiny made a show of letting the cards fall from his hands and spray all over the table. "Then we won't either," he said. "We'd rather share war stories anyway, wouldn't we, boys?"

"I would!" Ranold said much too loudly and boozily. "C'mon over here, Paulie. What a day, huh? Huh?"

Paul sat, unable to feign enthusiasm. "It was quite a day."

"They got the billboard vandal," Tiny said.

"I know," Paul said. "Some kind of computer freak?"

"Crackpot hacker—with guns."

"Was there anything on his computers?"

"Obliterated!" Ranold said. "Smashed to dust. No one will ever recover that sabotage program."

That was a relief. Paul assumed Specs kept a lot of information about his brothers and sisters buried in there somewhere.

"I heard LAPD is going to investigate the raid," Paul said. "You know, to allay the fears of the public."

"They most certainly had better not!" Ranold said. "Where did you hear that? I don't care what those crazies in South Central think about it, we weren't going to stand there and be cut down. Now what's this about LAPD? I'll get on the phone right now—"

"I'm kidding, Ranold. I'm sure they're fully satisfied that the site will be replete with the charred remains of weapons arsenals the likes of which none of us has ever seen before."

"Local doesn't check up on federal, Paul. You know that. We check up on them. I'd like to investigate why LAPD never recognized the threats we found in a matter of hours."

"Hear, hear!" Allendo said, lifting a glass.

31

PAUL TUMBLED into one of the most comfortable beds he'd ever enjoyed but found sleep elusive. He was tormented, wondering how he could stop the killing while serving as a member of the task force determined to carry it out. He began to pray for underground believers all over the country, for his wife and children, and even for Angela Pass, whom he knew he had treated shabbily.

God, why am I here? It can't be to witness the slaughter of my brothers and sisters. Please let me know the purpose You have for me.

Finally he dozed, waking at five-thirty surprisingly refreshed. He told his valet to express his regrets for skipping breakfast due to an early schedule and asked that his car be brought around. Although it was not yet six when he emerged from the house, the gushing hundred-foot tower of water from Allendo's garish gold fountain sent a light spray teasing over his head and face. Paul felt as if he were being spit upon. It was hard to pinpoint what was most distasteful about Tiny Allendo, amid all his wretched excesses, but the fountain had to be close to the top of his list.

Paul had to admit that being waited on hand and foot and having your car parked and brought to you were nice perks. But it wasn't real life. Who lived like this? People who didn't deserve to, he decided.

Checking his GPS screen, Paul made his way to the port. When he arrived at the breakwater that protected the harbor from the sea, he recognized immediately that this would be no easy task. Warehouses and wharves lined a wall that had to be miles long.

As was true nearly every day, the port was hopping. San Pedro Bay was already full of ships from around the world, staging and maneuvering into position to off-load fish and goods. At any other time, Paul would have loved the salty, fishy air. But it seemed he brought trouble to fellow believers, and he hoped he wasn't cursing this band just by looking them up.

Paul's nondescript sedan seemed to draw no attention as he worked his way into the bustling area. He parked on a side street and began walking. None of the signs gave him a clue, but he didn't expect the one in question to blatantly call itself the Fishers of Men. As the sun rose, sweat broke out on his forehead, and his mission seemed futile. Paul guessed he was four miles from his car when a sign stopped him.

He had come to a rusting blue-and-gray metal building that sat on a pier just off the water. The front was unmarked, but a hand-painted sign over the side utility door read "Sapiens Fisheries." *Clever.*

He knocked loudly, sending a metallic rattle echoing over the waterfront.

"It's open!"

The aromas that enticed Paul outside sickened him in an enclosed area. The place stank. The filthy concrete floor led to a steel-and-wood counter that contained scales of various sizes. A forklift stood near a huge sheet of plastic that separated the front from the dock in back, where personnel apparently unloaded cargoes of fish.

The building was dimly lit, and while Paul heard activity in the back, the only soul up front was a thick young man, probably late twenties, in cover-all rain gear and boots. His dirty blond hair, peeking out from under a greasy cap, was wet and matted. He had a reddish beard and almost nonexistent lips.

"Ya don't look like a fisherman," the young man said. "And our permits are up-to-date. So what's yer business?"

"You're fishers of men, are you?" Paul said.

Red Beard hesitated. "Actually, we're just laborers, offloading for a fish broker who serves local merchants—stores and restaurants. Can I help you?"

"Dr. Paul Stepola," he said, extending a hand. "From Chicago."

"Barton James," the young man said, removing wet gloves before shaking. "What can I do for you?"

"'My purpose is to give life . . . ,'" Paul said.

Barton paled. "'. . . in all its fullness,'" he said, smiling. "You scared the life out of me. I don't think I've had anybody come to the side door in years. Thought we were busted. Everybody's on edge now, with what happened yesterday. I lost a friend in South Central."

"That was a travesty."

"An abomination. C'mon back. Meet the others."

Barton pushed his way through the hanging plastic to a storeroom stocked with crates that stank of rotting fish. He smiled at Paul's grimace. "Discourages visitors."

On the dock outside about a dozen people, most under

thirty, were loading a delivery truck. "They're almost finished," Barton said, lifting a plywood sheet that revealed stairs to a hidden area.

He led Paul down a narrow wooden staircase that seemed to end in a boiler room. Behind one of its plank walls lay a large windowless space furnished with sticks of furniture homeless people would have rejected. An old woman in a shawl had an open Bible in her lap. An elderly man appeared to be studying a commentary. He was taking notes.

"Our teachers," Barton said, introducing the married couple as Carl and Lois. "Carl was a pastor before the war. Has a collection of books and Bibles that alone could put him in prison for the rest of his life."

"Bring 'em on," Carl said, winking and holding up his fists like a boxer. "Why, I oughta . . ."

Lois, grinning, waved him off.

"It's wonderful that you have a library," Paul said.

"It's invaluable in our mission. We're in the tract business. We also supply most of the other groups in the West with printed literature."

"I'm surprised they'd need it," Paul said. "It might be hard to lay hands on an original document, but once groups do—say, from you or even over the Internet—can't they just make as many copies as they want?"

"Some kinds of things, yes," Carl said. "Flyers, leaflets, even photocopies of books for distribution—everybody does that— but we do something special here. Have you ever seen a book from the time before computer printing?"

"I doubt it. When would that have been?"

"Seventy or eighty years ago. I assure you they are quite different."

Lois leafed through her Bible and pulled out a small brochure. "This is one of our tracts," she said. "You can see it's two-color—I know computers can print millions of colors—but feel it. Just close your eyes and run your fingers over the page."

Paul did. "The letters are pressed into the paper."

"That's right—and that's why they call it letterpress. It's a very old method of printing, and it's a kind that can be done independent of computers, printers—even electricity if necessary. That's one reason it's so valuable. We believe the earth will soon be very different than it is now."

"After the Rapture."

"Not directly afterward, perhaps. But if you've read all the things that are to come, it's not hard to imagine that electronic equipment will become useless at some point."

"That's true."

"But that's not our immediate reason for using letterpress in Operation Soon. You see, we think that if people come across things like this, whether today or after the Rapture, even if they're not sure what they are, they will preserve them. If something is unusual, pleasing to the touch, and beautiful, it's clear someone went to a lot of trouble to create it. Obviously, it must be of value. So they'll try to read it and hopefully preserve it."

"Good theory," Paul said. "I know I wouldn't throw this away."

"I'm going to show him the press," Barton said. He led Paul deeper into the room and through a curtain to reveal an ancient printing press.

"Hard to find parts, ink, lubrication, that kinda thing, but it works fine."

Paul reached to touch the printing plates, but Barton said, "Don't. The oil on your fingers could mar the impression."

"Sorry."

"You can see we're not as productive as the people in Detroit, but we do our part. Of course, we save the press for special things. We do most of our regular leaflets—and also broadcasts—by computer. And now, with all the trouble, we're making a major push."

Barton showed him large bundles of brochures. "We're going to get these into the hands of the other groups and start flooding greater L.A. with them."

The brochures were titled "Risking Our Lives for Yours." The copy stated unequivocally that the underground Christians in Los Angeles were not armed and never planned to be. "The slaughter of secret believers is genocide," Paul read, "pure and simple. We are no threat to the government or the status quo. We merely believe that God is real, that Jesus is alive, that He died for the sins of the world, and that He is coming again soon. We will persist in spreading this word until none of us remain."

The brochure concluded with several verses from the Bible explaining how a person could receive Christ and be forgiven of sins and assured of a life with God for eternity.

"Of course," Barton said, "the penalty for distributing these is prison."

"And for creating them, death," Carl said.

"I don't know what they're so afraid of," Lois said. "We're just talking about the free exchange of ideas."

"Dangerous ideas, though," Paul said. "You have to admit. I studied religion, and there is a huge legacy of religion-related atrocities throughout the history of civilization."

"But religion and true Christianity are two entirely different things."

"You're preaching to the choir, ma'am. But it's important that we know where our opposition is coming from, what their mind-set is. They are terrified of what true spirituality and belief can do to people. Taken to extremes, it *has* resulted in war."

The workers from the dock began trickling down and were introduced to Paul. They shed their gloves and wet jackets and sat on the floor. "I bring you greetings from your brothers and sisters in Heartland," Paul said. "They are praying for you."

"We haven't heard from them about South Central," Barton said. "A contact usually passes on their messages."

"Quinn?" Paul said.

"Yeah, Specs," he said. Others smiled and nodded.

"I have bad news," Paul said. He told them about Specs, and several gasped. Some covered their faces and wept.

"He's a loss," Barton said, his voice thick. "All he ever wanted was to help people and spread the word. What are we going to do? We can't stay hidden much longer, and we don't want to, but if they're gonna set the army on us, what chance do we have? We're in a position of total weakness. We have nothing on them."

"We have to do something big," Carl said. "Something that will get the attention of the nation. We have to cripple this army, unless we want to see more of us wiped out."

Barton stood. "Carl's teaching the last several months has fired us up to where we're ready to stand out because we believe that much in our cause. If they're going to kill us anyway just for spreading the word about Jesus, we might as well take them on. I agree we have to do something that slows their campaign. If we don't, we're not going to be here much longer."

"The various groups are going to have to come together," Paul said. "There has to be strength in numbers."

"But we're no match for the army."

"Neither was Gideon," Paul said. "It isn't might that makes right, or the government would be right. We have God on our side, and we need Him to give us the victory, just like Gideon."

Old Carl struggled to his feet. "Gideon is a perfect model,

people. Let me remind you of his story." He quickly turned pages in his Bible and read:

> The angel of the Lord appeared to him and said, "Mighty hero, the Lord is with you!"
>
> "Sir," Gideon replied, "if the Lord is with us, why has all this happened to us? And where are all the miracles our ancestors told us about? Didn't they say, 'The Lord brought us up out of Egypt'? But now the Lord has abandoned us and handed us over to the Midianites."
>
> Then the Lord turned to him and said, "Go with the strength you have and rescue Israel from the Midianites. I am sending you!"
>
> "But Lord," Gideon replied, "how can I rescue Israel? My clan is the weakest in the whole tribe of Manasseh, and I am the least in my entire family!"
>
> The Lord said to him, "I will be with you. And you will destroy the Midianites as if you were fighting against one man."

"You see, people," Carl said, "the Israelites had been delivered out of captivity from Egypt, but when they forgot God and disobeyed Him, He turned them over to the Midianites, who tormented them for seven years. Now when God called Gideon a hero and told him to go with the strength of the Lord—a lot of people don't know or remember this—but Gideon lit out with an army of thirty-two thousand men.

"God told him he had too many, that if he won with that big an army, the Israelites would take the credit themselves. So He told Gideon to tell anyone to leave if they were timid or afraid. Twenty-two thousand of them took off, leaving only ten thousand. Remember now, this is to fight against an army of a hundred and thirty-five thousand. But God told him he still had too many. Gideon was to take his ten thousand men to a spring and tell them to drink. The ones who got down on all fours and stuck their mouths in the spring were sent home. Only three hundred dipped the water with their hands. And they became Gideon's army.

"When Gideon attacked the Midianites, they were so frightened that a hundred and twenty thousand of them killed each other, and the remaining fifteen thousand took off across the desert. Gideon finally tracked them down too.

"I don't know how God is going to use whatever is left of the underground believers in Los Angeles to defeat the army. But I believe He would have us be as the men of Gideon, brave and willing to do whatever is necessary. And *He* will win the battle."

32

BARTON JAMES WALKED Paul all the way back to his car. "If you're making the rounds," he said, "greet the others for us. Tell them we stand ready to die for the cause."

"I hope that doesn't become necessary," Paul said.

"I should tell you, we're planning something outlandish for twilight tonight."

"Do I want to hear this?" Paul said.

"Sure ya do. It's not exactly Gideon-like, but it's something. We have access to a robotic plane I can control from the ground. Or I should say from the water. It takes off from and lands in the Bay. We're going to blanket the city with leaflets and hope the craft doesn't get shot out of the air. If it does, we lose an expensive plane but no people."

"It's audacious," Paul said. "I've got to give you that. But if you're caught?"

"Big trouble."

"You said it."

"It's not the type of thing that's going to keep the army from wiping out believers," Paul said. "But I like it. It's in-your-face, and it gets the word out. Any of your people been caught yet?"

"No. Close, but no. Three of our members were chased on foot for about a mile one night, but they escaped without showing their faces and, we hope, without leading anyone to us. Are believers dying in other states like they are here?"

"Not on this scale," Paul said. "Individuals have been martyred, yes. But bringing in the army is an ugly turn. It's as if the government has decided to wage all-out war on us. The fainthearted are going to start bailing on us if they think there's a chance they won't survive."

"There are no fainthearted here, sir," Barton said. "This isn't a movement for fence-straddlers."

"If we can just come up with something Gideon-like, Barton. Something that will pull all these people together and show them that God will work through them, even to thwart the might of the army. What would bring this city to its knees?"

"On my way back I'm going to pray over this city," Barton said. "Pray that God will give you an idea."

"Maybe He'll give *you* an idea."

"I don't have that kind of a mind, sir," Barton said. "And I don't need that burden. But you can bet I'll help carry it out."

"You came up with the one for tonight, didn't you?"

"The truth? It was Lois's idea."

• • •

As Paul sat eating in the parking lot of a fast-food joint, a call came from his mother-in-law.

"Jae asked that I call you," she said. "She asked me to express

JERRY JENKINS • 303

her regret that she missed your call and to tell you that she will call you when she is able."

Really? That doesn't sound like Jae. "Do you know where she is?"

"No, she still hasn't told me."

That doesn't sound like her either. "I suppose Dad has kept you informed as to what's happening out here."

"Oh no. I don't hear from him when he's on the road. He's busy with high-level meetings from dawn to dusk. I'm sure I'll hear about it when he returns."

Paul checked in with Straight, who picked up on the first ring and sounded devastated.

"What's wrong?" Paul said.

"You don't know?"

Straight seemed overcome and couldn't speak.

"Take your time, friend," Paul said, flipping the channels on his pocket computer until he found a news site. *What?* The army had struck the former site of Loyola Marymount University in the Westchester area of Los Angeles, a few minutes from LAX.

"Paul," Straight managed finally, "calls from inside just as it was going down told us about two hundred members there were mourning the dead from South Central. They were in a make-shift chapel, and they had no weapons at the whole site. The leadership saw the army amassing and tried to negotiate. Well, there was no negotiating. They were shot dead at the door; then the army leaders retreated to their positions and obliterated the place. Those people were slaughtered."

Paul stuffed the rest of his food in the bag and raced off, chastising himself for not finding a way to warn the believers at Loyola. He'd told Specs to contact them, but he must not have gotten through in time.

Traffic was snarled within miles of the black smoke billowing over the site of the massacre. Finally, Paul ditched the car and jogged more than a mile to the site. Panting and sweaty, he found his father-in-law beside Bia Balaam with a network news reporter sticking a microphone in their faces.

"We're talking live with Tactical Chief Bia Balaam and General Ranold Decenti, World War III hero and now military consultant to the new National Anti-Christian task force. Chief Balaam, what happened here?"

"Our intelligence-gathering contingent has been monitoring the anti-American subversive activities of a heavily armed and dangerous faction of religious fanatics, more than a thousand strong, who were planning to take over Los Angeles and eventually all of Pacifica. We surrounded the place before dawn, awakened their leadership, and ordered them to stand down and surrender peacefully. They promised to discuss an amicable resolution with their colleagues, and we gave them a deadline of noon to surrender their weapons and be taken into custody without incident.

"When there was no further communication from them, we prepared for the worst. One minute after the deadline, they opened fire on our forces, and we were forced to defend ourselves. Fortunately we suffered no casualties or injuries, and they apparently turned their massive weapons cache on themselves. We were forced to retreat as they bombed and burned the buildings and killed themselves."

"How many dead do you expect?"

"Several hundred."

"General Decenti, what about eyewitness reports from area residents who say they saw military personnel arrive after eleven-thirty, and that you yourself, sir, arrived just before the battle?"

"They are mistaken. I have been here since dawn, and they

must have merely seen me coming from another area of the stakeout."

As soon as Ranold was free, Paul confronted him. "Why wasn't I informed this was even planned? I am here to interrogate subjects and interpret their answers for you and the others as it relates to the overall religious picture. I'm finding out about these sieges when the public does, and there never seems to be anyone left to question."

"First of all, Paul, this is Chief Balaam's operation. Secondly, they are hardly sieges. We would love for these people to respond appropriately and cooperatively and to be able to give you no end of subjects to examine. But they are zealots, extremists. They will not listen to reason. They will not negotiate. The first sign the government is at their door, they start shooting."

"Shooting?"

"That's the same argumentative and self-righteous tone you had in South Central, and you wonder why you didn't hear we were going to strike."

"I deserved to know. Otherwise, why am I here?"

"You want the truth, Paul? I didn't think you were up to it. That's why it's Balaam, not you, running this show. Maybe it's your injury, I don't know, but you've grown soft on me, Son. It's been months, man. Time to get over it. Meanwhile, you must see the value of a surgical strike."

"Surgical? This looks more like butchery. And is this your idea of a press blackout?"

Ranold gave him a withering look. "You're hopeless, Paul. How many times have we talked about using the press to our advantage? Truth is perception. People believe what they hear, especially on the news. The time had come to send a message with a major strike—that this religious subversion is a cancer, a threat to our very way of life. Insurrection cannot be tolerated. We must—and we will—combat it with all our might. You should be proud of what we've done here today, Paul. The rest of America will be."

Paul was speechless. Balaam was still in thrall with the reporters, so at least he was spared her boasting about the strike. He drifted away to look for survivors to interrogate.

But there were none.

• • •

One of the chauffeurs nodded to Paul as he drove through the gate at Allendo's. A houseman was waiting when he pulled up to the front door, now shadowed by the gold fountain, the never-ending geyser. It was all Paul could do to be cordial. His valet informed him, "Dinner remains on schedule for seven o'clock. Mr. Allendo asked that I let you know that he and General Decenti are en route and will be on time."

They were indeed on time, and from the tone of the festivities, it was clear that only Paul had a problem with what had gone on that day. Ranold was right. America was proud of them. Tiny had invited many friends and movie-business associates, all of whom crowded around Chief Balaam, who looked like the blade of a knife in a silver gown.

For the celebration Allendo had told the caterers to pull out all the stops. They came up with a spread featuring every sort of delicacy, most colored Tiny's trademark gold. Ranold seemed to be having the time of his life, wolfing down toast points heaped with golden and black caviar and guzzling champagne from a gold-rimmed flute. But the *pièce de résistance* among the hors d'oeuvres was live sushi, small golden fish that darted through a trough down the middle of the table, which the bravest caught with tiny spears. Paul was revolted.

Bia Balaam appeared at his side, spear in hand. "Caught one yet?"

"No," Paul said. "Can't say that I've tried."

"Maybe it's the sport you don't care for."

"Spearing fish in a trough doesn't seem sporting to me."

"You seem very scrupulous, Dr. Stepola."

"I try to do what's right, Agent Balaam."

"I'm sure you do. But what counts most is the ability to do what's necessary."

"I'll keep that in mind."

"I hope you do. And please also keep in mind that I am *Chief* Balaam."

• • •

At twilight the guests were distracted by the hum of an airplane. "That's awfully close," Tiny said. "Even small personal planes are diverted from this neighborhood."

The sound grew louder until the buzz was directly overhead. "I'm filing a complaint," Tiny said. "Disrupting a party . . . I don't know who these people think they are, or who they think we are. This isn't some barbecue in the Valley."

A cloud suddenly masked the darkening sky. As Paul and the others watched, it seemed to disintegrate and drift to earth. Paper from the sky. Hundreds of fluttering leaflets.

Some guests shrieked. Others caught the flyers and read their messages aloud. They cited miracles, warning of the coming judgment and offering salvation through Christ. Tiny barked and the service staff scrambled, frantically gathering leaflets.

Red-faced, Balaam demanded a phone. Ranold shook his fist at the sky, bellowing drunken threats. Paul was thrilled but afraid for Barton. To hide his feelings, Paul strolled to the fountain. The bottom was clogged with sodden flyers, and the new ones blanketing the surface churned with the force of the spray. And a plan came to him—a plan so clear and complete he believed it was from God Himself.

Paul knew what he and the underground believers of Los Angeles had to do.

33

RANOLD HAD RECOVERED his good mood by breakfast the next day.

"Paul," he said, "we caught a big break last night. Our guys were able to get a bead on the plane that littered L.A. Turns out it was unmanned, which we were able to determine through heat-sensitive reconnaissance. They asked permission to shoot it down, but by the time they had it in their sights, it had spent most of its cargo. Balaam told 'em to just follow it to its owner. The thing led them to San Pedro Bay, and with some careful positioning, we put personnel in place where they wouldn't spook whoever was controlling it.

"Sure enough, a guy came out in a boat to get it. Only mistake our people made is they apprehended him before he got the plane back to wherever he houses it. I suspect we could have rounded up some compatriots too, but as soon as he noticed he was being followed, he stayed in the drink and made us come to him.

"Insolent kid. Cool manner, articulate. Smelled of fish. Still had a supply of brochures, and what do we find but more of this stuff in the plane and on his boat. Other brochures, Paul, more about Jesus and getting saved and the coming judgment. You want somebody to interrogate? You got him."

"Where is he?"

"In a holding room at the armory."

"I'll go now."

"He's not going anywhere. Finish eating and relax."

"No, I'd better get over there before Balaam decides this guy is armed and dangerous and makes him kill himself."

Ranold stared. "The people who have been killed deserved it, Paul, starting with your friend Pass, and you know it. Chief Balaam almost single-handedly cut the legs off the subversive sects in Washington, some especially virulent ones responsible for major sabotage. Killing the cherry trees on the mall— destroying a national symbol and disrupting the city's economy—that was as much an act of war as if they'd blown up the Statue of Liberty. It was out-and-out terrorism, and that's the same fire we've been putting out here in L.A."

"No one proved anyone killed the cherry trees, Ranold, remember? And we still have due process in this country."

Ranold shook his head. "I swear, Paul, I'm starting to believe you're jealous of Balaam. All this criticism, when we've managed to crush two major terrorist cells, eliminate the billboard saboteur, and grab this insurrectionist last night. I didn't get it at first, but it's killing you that she's running the show and doing it well. You may be a hero who's suffered for the cause, but this is bigger than any one ego—even yours. Balaam's in charge because she gets results, so get a grip and do your job before second-guessing your superiors.

"Make that kid tell you where these people are headquartered. Let us root 'em out and eradicate 'em like we're paid to."

• • •

At the armory, Paul was taken to a wing where army guards were smoking and shooting the breeze at the entrance to a long hallway. "Tough case down there, sir," one said, standing when Paul identified himself. "Doubt you'll get a thing out of him."

When he got to the interrogation room, Paul found Barton in a fetal position on the floor, still in his bulky jacket and hands cuffed behind him. His breath came in labored rasps.

"Get this man back in the chair," Paul said to the guard. "And uncuff him."

"He attacked us, sir. I wouldn't advise that."

"Get the cuffs off him and leave us. He attacks me, I'll shoot him dead."

"I like your style."

When Barton was back in the chair, hands in his lap, Paul shooed the guard out and locked the door.

"You attack those men, Barton?"

"Of course not." One of his teeth had been knocked out, and he also bled from the nose. He had a gash above one eye, and blood oozed from the back of his head.

"Want to take off your jacket?"

He nodded and Paul helped him wriggle out of it.

"Talk to me."

"You *turned* on me?" Barton said. "Ratted me out?"

"Of course not. Nobody squealed on anybody. Now keep

your voice down. I got here as soon as I heard. Tell me what's been going on."

"Can't you tell? They aren't going to lock me up. They'll kill me like they have all the others."

"That's a very real possibility," Paul said. "I won't lie to you. I'm trying to figure out how to keep you safe. What have you told them?"

"Nothing about our operation. They haven't been nosing around there, have they?"

"Not that I know of."

Barton pressed the heels of his hands over his eyes. "There's going to be no escaping, sir. What have they got, a couple thousand troops lodging here?"

"That's about right. The best I can do right now is give you better odds. I'm going to get you out of army custody and have them transport you to the NPO bureau downtown. No guarantees, but at least you won't be their trophy prisoner. And maybe there I can help you find an opportunity to escape."

"Sounds like a long shot."

"Not as long as if you stay here."

"Well, I knew the odds. Hey, Doc, how long you been a believer?"

"Not long, actually."

"Long enough to pray for me?"

"You bet your life," Paul said.

He put a hand on Barton's shoulder and prayed God's will would be done in his life. He thought of the juxtaposition of the prayer and the location and had to wonder what in the world anyone outside the door would think if they could see this.

When he left Barton, Paul called Harriet Johns and told her to expect a suspect he wanted held for questioning.

"I'll watch for him, Paul. It will be good to get some of the action back in our ballpark. Your suspect will be here whenever you're ready to interrogate him."

Paul filled out the paperwork, then waited to make sure the transfer got under way. He watched the guards lead Barton, shackled at the wrists and ankles, across the parking lot and put him into a jeep, praying Barton would make it downtown in one piece.

• • •

As a cover, Paul stopped to canvass a few of the sites on the task force list before making his way, circuitously, to Sapiens Fisheries. It was late afternoon by the time he arrived. The group there held an immediate prayer meeting for Barton.

"It was such a risk," Lois said, weeping.

"Barton's young and bold," Carl said. "Now we have to have faith."

"I have an idea how to stop the killings," Paul said, "but we'll need a hydrologist."

"A water expert?"

"Do you know any? Anyone here or in another group?"

Lois said a woman who worked for the county public works department belonged to an underground group off the 405 near the Stone Canyon Reservoir. "Oh, Dr. Stepola, these are a wonderful bunch, mostly older, highly educated types. I know they'd want to help."

"Tell me about this woman."

"She works for the Los Angeles County Water and Sewer District."

"This is too good to be true."

"Her name's Grace Dean, and she's a tough old bird."

"You know her well enough to invite her here?"

"Now?"

"As soon as possible."

A few minutes later Lois told Paul, "Grace isn't sure she wants to break the law, but I reminded her she's been doing that for more than two years since she joined that little band."

"How'd she know I wanted her to break the law?"

"She's not stupid, Doctor. She'll be here within the hour, soon as she gets off work."

• • •

Grace Dean arrived with three others from her group. She was in her midforties, diminutive, and stocky with short, black hair. She proved fast-talking and blunt, and she clearly knew her stuff.

Meeting with her and her people and Carl and Lois, Paul cut to the chase. "If I wanted to shut off the water to the whole city and bring Los Angeles and the army to its knees, how would I do that?"

Grace pursed her lips and studied the ceiling. "For almost 200 years," she said, "L.A. has had to get its water from far away. About 135 years ago the California Aqueduct was finally finished, and it's been bringing a lot of our water here from almost 700 miles north in the Sacramento Valley. Of course, once it gets here, it is redirected to various parts of the county through a huge network of pipes and channels."

"So," Paul said, "if we wanted to cut off the supply?"

"You could make mischief with the aqueduct, but what're you going to do with all that water? It has to go somewhere. You redirect it, you're going to flood somewhere else."

"Where would the best place to flood be, without hurting other people?"

"Oh, there are places," Grace said, "many between here and there. But you'd have to do it in one of the places that's not carefully guarded, which has been an issue ever since terrorists got the idea of poisoning the water supply. But you know, water is such a precious commodity that the city, the county, the whole Sunterra region, and the federal government would train all its resources on the problem. You've seen what they're doing. How long do you think you could get away with vandalizing the water supply? Would you really bring L.A. to its knees, or would you just be a one- or two-day nuisance?"

"I don't know," Paul said. "You're the expert."

"Seems to me," she said, "you'd be better off to have God do something."

"Sometimes I wonder if God has abandoned us," a man said. "Is His hand still on us? Have we gone too far ahead of Him and sped past His reach of blessing? I don't blame all these deaths on Him, of course, but if He was still with us, would He allow His people to be cut down like vermin?"

Carl raised a hand. "I make no apologies for being a man of the Word." He leafed through a well-worn Bible. "Listen to this from Isaiah fifty and verse two. God is speaking. He says, 'Was I too weak to save you? Is that why the house is silent and empty when I come home? Is it because I have no power to rescue? No, that is not the reason! For I can speak to the sea and make it dry! I can turn rivers into deserts covered with dying fish.'

"And then in verses seven and eight the prophet says, 'Because the Sovereign Lord helps me, I will not be dismayed. Therefore, I have set my face like a stone, determined to do His will. And I know that I will triumph. He who gives me justice is near. Who will dare oppose me now? Where are my enemies? Let them appear!'

"And in the next chapter, verses twelve through sixteen, God Himself makes this promise: 'I, even I, am the one who comforts you. So why are you afraid of mere humans, who wither like the grass and disappear? Yet you have forgotten the Lord, your

Creator, the one who put the stars in the sky and established the earth. Will you remain in constant dread of human oppression? Will you continue to fear the anger of your enemies from morning till night? Soon all you captives will be released! Imprisonment, starvation, and death will not be your fate!'"

Paul was thrilled and could see on the faces and in the body language of the others that they were coming to life.

"Now hear this, my Christian brothers and sisters of Los Angeles. 'For I am the Lord your God, who stirs up the sea, causing its waves to roar. My name is the Lord Almighty. And I have put My words in your mouth and hidden you safely within My hand. I set all the stars in space and established the earth. I am the one who says to Israel, "You are Mine!"'"

Carl sat only briefly, then pitched forward to his knees and lay prostrate on the floor. Suddenly others were doing the same, and Paul found himself weeping. It was as if God Himself had spoken aloud, and Paul did not feel worthy to stand or sit.

"You are God," Carl prayed. "We worship You."

And from the others came murmurings of assent. "Yes, Lord. Thank You, God. We believe in You. We trust You, Lord. Help us remember You."

Paul haltingly and fearfully approached God aloud, asking for a miracle. "God," he said, "we're asking that You shut the mouths of the atheists, that You reclaim ground won by our enemies. We pray You will act in such a powerful and supernatural way that even the armies of the United Seven States will know it's You and that they will cower. God, we need You to do something."

As others prayed, Paul felt closer to God than he ever had. He silently thanked Him for the miracle of his own sight and asked God to show him what he was to do next. He couldn't long continue to work both sides of the street. How could he do the most, make a real impact, best serve the cause before he was found out and executed for treason?

Paul lay there, waiting on God, praying for an answer, some nudge, some leading, some word. He knew that merely railing against his father-in-law and Balaam would serve little more than to see him found out and exposed. He wanted to be through with driving throughout Los Angeles, finding and meeting fellow believers, only to share in their frustration and dismay as their colleagues were attacked and killed by the enemy.

Paul was moved to hear the others praying, and he was suddenly overwhelmed with a view of what God could do. It was as if he had a leading from the Lord Himself to mobilize the believers from all the seven states—and especially Sunterra, specifically in greater Los Angeles. He heard no audible voice, but it seemed he could sense the mind of God, that if all the underground Christians would unite as one and devote themselves wholly to God, He would act on their behalf.

Paul felt his whole purpose coming into focus. That was why he was here. There was no more wondering, trying to decide how best to serve while being a clandestine agent. His job was to motivate every underground believer he could find to pray and plead with God to show Himself to the enemy.

Trembling, all doubt escaping him, Paul stood. He didn't know whether to announce this or keep it to himself. He had an overpowering feeling that believers all over the country must pray. God could not—would not—ignore the fervent prayers of righteous people.

"I want to get all the underground Christians to agree in prayer that God must do something in Los Angeles to stop this killing," Paul said. "I believe we are to be specific. Let's all pray that God will stop the flow of water to Los Angeles. Then we have to somehow communicate to the leadership that it is God who did it and that He can do the same all over the country. The killing of believers must stop, and they must be given the freedom to spread the truth of the Bible. I'll call Chicago and have my contact there get in touch with as many underground centers as he can. Then let's expect a miracle."

34

IT WAS ALMOST SEVEN.

Grace and her companions walked out to their car with Paul, who had offered to pick up dinner for the Sapiens group. The mood in the basement room was so buoyant that none wanted to leave, and there was a lot to discuss.

"Grace, your words were a tremendous inspiration," Paul said. "I know you were nervous about helping us, so thank you."

"My commitment is real, but my courage is lukewarm," she said. "When Lois told me what you wanted, it sounded much more dangerous than our Stone Canyon meetings. I still feel pretty new in the faith."

"I'm new myself," Paul said. "I was blind—literally—and God restored my sight before I made the leap. Even then it took me a while."

"It helped that they—" she gestured toward her friends—"were willing to come. They tell me to keep praying."

After seeing the group off, Paul called Straight to fill him in. He applauded the plan and promised to marshal prayer troops. Then Paul called Tiny's to tell them not to expect him for dinner. He heard music in the background—inevitably there'd be guests on a Friday night—and Ranold took command of the phone.

"What were you thinking, transferring a criminal from a secure location to a dicey one?"

"He was my prisoner, Ranold. I saw no reason to leave him in army custody. I'll finish interrogating him in the morning."

"No, you won't. He almost escaped."

Almost? "So, they caught him, is that what you're telling me?"

"That's right, and they made him pay. Appropriately."

"They already beat him half to death, Dad. What more do you expect to get out of him? I'll go talk to him."

"You don't get it, do you, Paul? He's not going to be there to talk to. Get yourself back here so I won't have to suspect you of everything that gets in our way."

"Suspect me?"

"I told you to check your ego at the door. Balaam was not happy that you took it upon yourself to move her prisoner. She saw it as a direct challenge to her authority. I explained you were a hothead, maybe feeling a little left out—"

"Ranold, what did they do to the guy?"

"Not torture, if that's what you're implying. We're too busy to waste time sweating a leafleteer. That was your job. This afternoon we got a tip that the terrorists are planning something big. So we took the press opportunity your man offered, and that's that."

"What does that mean?"

"I said leave it alone, Paul. The last thing you want is more trouble over this. Now are you heading back here?"

Paul gritted his teeth.

"You there, Paul?"

"I'm losing you," Paul said. And he disconnected.

• • •

Paul flipped on the radio and found an all-news station, but it was in the middle of a sports report. Finally came the news he dreaded.

"Late this afternoon, a car believed to be carrying subversive Christian rebel leader Barton James pitched off a cliff on Peace Canyon Road and burst into flames. James had reportedly escaped incarceration at the downtown headquarters of the Sunterra NPO. He was being held on charges of drug and weapons possession and assault on army personnel. Authorities are trying to extinguish the fire on the cliff and have brought in dogs to recover the body. . . ."

Peace Canyon Road. Paul had noticed it on the map when he was driving around to get oriented. There was nothing on those bluffs but dense foliage and coyotes and the few houses still standing after the earthquake. No reason for any official vehicle to choose that route.

Though Paul could hardly imagine eating, he picked up a selection of fast-food staples for the group and headed back to deliver the news about Barton. Carl and Lois looked especially devastated, but everyone was shocked. "It may be utterly the worst time for this," Paul said, "but maybe the best way to mourn Barton is to keep planning."

Paul told about his friend Straight spreading the word among underground believers all over the country. "Every believer will be focused on praying for you here. I'm new at this, and even though I believe God spoke to me, my faith will be tested. In spite of all God has miraculously done for me, sometimes I still doubt."

"That's not uncommon," Carl said. "Remember, Jesus said, 'Anything is possible if a person believes.' And a man asking His help said, 'I do believe, but help me not to doubt!'"

It seemed to Paul as he spoke that the grieving little band was growing emboldened. Eyes moist and shining, they were clearly ready to believe God would work—to count on Him to answer their prayers.

"I had started working on something while Paul was gone," Carl said, "and now I'm going to print it out. Then let's polish this thing till it shines and thank God for all He's about to do."

A clanging on the door upstairs made everyone jump. Carl pointed to a young woman. "Rhoda, please see who it is. And be careful."

The rest prayed, some on their knees, others stretched out on the floor. A minute later fast footsteps descended the stairs. "Excuse me," Rhoda said, pale and trembling. "It's—it's Barton!"

"What?"

"Who?"

"Let him in!"

"Where is he?"

"He's alive?"

"I'm going up!"

"Me too!"

Half a dozen people rumbled up the stairs. They soon returned with a limping, disheveled, exhausted-looking Barton James. Duct tape stuck to his shirt and pants.

"Is it really you?"

"What happened?"

Paul waited behind Carl for his turn to embrace Barton. "Did you really try to escape, or was that—"

"That what they told you? We never even got downtown. We went the other direction, and I knew something was up."

"They said you went off a cliff in Peace Canyon."

"I did," Barton said, collapsing onto a worn couch. "They unshackled me and put me in an old car. They wound tape around me like a mummy to hold me in the passenger seat, then put cans of gasoline on the floor in the back. They opened them and stopped them up with rags. The old car was all the way across the road from the guardrail. They revved up the motor and lit the rags just before they threw the car into gear. I was praying it wouldn't hurt bad and that I would be in heaven before I burned too much.

"The car hit the rail at top speed, but I hardly moved because I was taped so tight to the seat. Then the car was airborne, tumbling end over end, and I was choking with the smoke from the gas. When it hit the ground, someone popped my door open, ripped off the tape, and yanked me out. We rolled and rolled together and finally hid in the bushes as the car exploded and cartwheeled down into the canyon.

"The guy told me the tape had saved me, but I would have roasted alive if he hadn't pulled me out. I lay there half-conscious in the bushes for a while. He disappeared, but I had a good view of what was left of the car. It lay there burning, a deep orange with black smoke. I knew I had to get out of there before they came looking for my body.

"I hiked back up to the main road and kept going till I reached the monorail. I didn't dare let anyone see me, so I just followed the tracks as far as I could, then stayed in the shadows and took the back way when I got down here."

"You didn't!"

"A miracle."

"That had to be an angel."

Lois asked for attention and led the group in singing.

Blest be the tie that binds our hearts in Christian love:
The fellowship of kindred minds is like to that above.

Carl led in a prayer of thanks. He told Barton, "We've been planning a counterattack."

"Tell me!"

Carl summarized what Paul had outlined, and Barton painfully sat up and leaned forward. "Let's do it," he said. "Let's trust God to work."

Carl handed him a copy of what he had written. "I was just about to read this."

Paul read Carl's daring manifesto over Barton's shoulder. It boldly stated that the Christian men and women of greater Los Angeles were praying that God would dry up the water supply to the city to stop the brutal persecution of believers.

We know that the fervent prayer of the righteous avails much, and if the killing of the innocents does not immediately cease, we're trusting God to answer this prayer and send this judgment on our tormentors.

If the army does not immediately withdraw and leave us to worship in peace, we believe this will come to pass. When it happens—and it will happen—you will know God has acted. To prevent it, we call on all affected citizens to rise up and force the powers that be to change their cruel and unjust laws against people of faith.

We wish to live out our beliefs in public with respect and love to and from all. Here we stand.

When the drought comes, remember that Jesus said, "If you are thirsty, come to Me! If you believe in Me, come and drink! For the Scriptures declare that rivers of living water will flow out from within."

"This is great," Barton said. "I wouldn't change a word. Get this onto the Internet to all the groups we know and urge them to pass it on to everyone they can. We'll be laughed at and ridiculed, but God will act; then the laughing—and the killing—will stop."

He and a few others raced to the computers to start posting the manifesto. Paul was eager to get going, knowing that Ranold was probably waiting, annoyed. "They'll be done, and we'll all leave in a few minutes," Carl said. "But we have a little something for you, friend. You've been risking your life for us, and we want you to have this token of our appreciation."

He presented Paul with a penny, which Paul folded tightly in his palm. He was unable to speak. Carl stepped to him and put a hand on his head. "Jude 1:24-25 says, 'And now, all glory to God, who is able to keep you from stumbling, and who will bring you into His glorious presence innocent of sin and with great joy. All glory to Him, who alone is God our Savior, through Jesus Christ our Lord. Yes, glory, majesty, power, and authority belong to Him, in the beginning, now, and forevermore. Amen.'"

Paul mouthed a thank-you and ventured back out into the night.

• • •

He drove back toward Beverly Hills thanking God for sparing Barton. "And thank You too for giving me the idea of how You can show Yourself to the people of Sunterra. As I believe, with all my heart, You will."

Paul was within half a mile of the Allendo mansion when he heard a tone and answered.

"Paul?" It was Jae, and she sounded different.

"Yes! Hi!"

"Did I wake you?"

"No. What's wrong?"

"Nothing's wrong, Paul. I just wanted to hear your voice."

"You did?"

"And now I want to see you."

"I don't know when I'll be home, Jae," Paul said, "but I hope you and the kids will be there."

"I want to see you tonight, Paul."

"Jae, I would love that. I've missed you. But I'm still in L.A. and I am working—"

"I'm at LAX, Paul."

"Are you serious?"

"Come get me at Helios Air."

• • •

Nearly an hour later Paul rushed from the car and into Jae's arms, full of questions. She held him fiercely and kissed him deeply. "I don't ever want to be apart from you again, Paul."

He put her bag in the car, and they pulled away from the airport. "I have so much to tell you," she said.

"I'm glad to see you, Jae. But what brings you here? And why now?"

"Let's go somewhere we can talk."

As Paul drove, Jae told him about the kids and described the fun they were having in Washington. "But they miss you, Paul. They keep asking when Daddy will come visit. I've told them that you had to work after being out sick for so long. They're afraid you might get hurt again, and I promised you'd talk to them about it."

"I will."

What about my father's letter? Did you take it? Paul strained to detect anything unusual in Jae's tone. *What is this visit about?*

Finally he pulled into the parking lot of a fancy restaurant a few miles from Allendo's. He waved off the parking valet, then flashed his badge to rebuff the security guard who came to shoo them away. When they were alone, Paul turned to face Jae.

She took both his hands in hers. "Paul, I am so sorry. I didn't trust you. I was convinced you were cheating on me."

"I wasn't."

"I was tormented by that letter from Angela. I couldn't believe it was innocent—not after the last time. The detectives never confirmed who you were seeing in Toledo, but you didn't even offer an alibi—not that I would have believed it. Still, I didn't really want to leave you. If I had, I would have filed for divorce, not just moved to D.C."

"That's what I kept telling myself."

"I knew Angela Pass Barger had to be Andy Pass's daughter. Remember how you refused to let me come with you to his funeral? That made me sure my suspicion was justified. I knew the NPO had taken pictures at the funeral, so I begged Daddy to get me one."

"And he did? That's way out of line."

"I'm his daughter, Paul. It's not like I asked him to track her down or intimidate her. When I saw how young and beautiful and vivacious she was, I thought our marriage was over. And then she was with you on TV after that Las Vegas bust."

"This is all circumstantial, Jae."

"Well, it made a good case. But still, I couldn't let our marriage die. She mentioned the Library of Congress in her letter, so

I tried calling her there. They said that she had quit a few months ago. So I flew to Las Vegas to find her and confront her."

Paul smacked himself in the head. "Oh, boy. Did you find her?"

"No. I showed the picture around at the Babylon, where you made the arrest. One of the hostesses—or whatever they are— knew about her. Said she was doing some kind of social work with the prostitutes."

"That was some detective work, Jae."

"That's when I put it all together."

"You did?"

"I figured you'd met her at the funeral and realized she could be a great source. Even if she wasn't a zealot herself, she might know her father's associates. Then I remembered something in the letter, which I hadn't paid much attention to, about hand-writing samples or something. That helped clinch it for me— you were using her to get information. No wonder you wouldn't tell me about her."

"A lot of what I do has to be secret. . . ."

"Oh, Paul, I know. I guess jealousy got to be a reflex for me. So I decided that—whatever she was to you, even if you fell for her—I was going to fight to save our marriage. Ten years is a long time—too much to throw away. Do you love her?"

Paul sighed. "I can't deny I found her attractive. But I swear, Jae, I was never—not ever—involved with her."

"For the sake of the kids, can we put the past six months be-hind us? Can we try to make each other happy again?"

"Jae, that would mean the world to me."

But Paul couldn't shake the feeling that this was a little too tidy.

35

WHEN PAUL FINALLY PULLED UP to the Allendo mansion, the man at the gate said, "General Decenti asked to be informed when you arrived. He would like a word."

"It's three in the morning," Paul said.

"He said the hour was of no concern."

"Give us a few minutes," Paul said, "and do me the favor of not informing him that my wife, his daughter, is with me. I want to surprise him."

"I'll ask him to meet you in the parlor in ten minutes."

• • •

Once inside, Jae said, "Paul, I'm so sorry for my part in all this. I hope you can forgive me."

"I was wrong too. I haven't been a model husband for years."

"I wasn't a model wife, either. I was obsessed with your

fidelity—or lack of it. And then when you were hurt, I felt you shut me out and I resented it. I didn't take into account how devastating it must have been to be blind."

"All I could think of was my own misery, Jae. I didn't consider the effect of my blindness or my anger on you and the kids. I want to be a better husband, a better father. There's a huge change I want—need—to explain to you. But I'm not sure I can find the words right now with all that's going on. It's a battle zone here."

"As long as it's not a change in your love for me, Paul, I can wait."

"Trust me, it's a change that makes me value you more than ever. I promise you that."

• • •

As Jae unpacked, Paul headed downstairs, wondering if he had a right to be happy, relieved, or suspicious. This had all happened so fast.

He found Ranold in a burgundy smoking jacket, pajamas, and slippers.

"Where in the world have you been?"

"I was not under the impression that I reported to you."

"Maybe not, but you will answer to me. I myself was out this evening. I'm not too shockable, Paul, but tonight I got hit with a bombshell—a bombshell about you."

Paul's blood slowed. His head buzzed. He felt his eyelids twitch—imperceptibly, he hoped—struggling to slam shut against Ranold's stare.

This is it.

Paul forced himself to stay focused on his father-in-law. He willed his voice to stay even and strong. "About me?"

"I met a woman named Grace Dean. Heard of her?"

The cat-and-mouse game. Paul's answer could mean life or death for her and for himself. He did not flinch or respond.

"She's a hydrologist for Los Angeles Water and Sewer. But you knew that, didn't you, Paul?"

He can't wait to see if I'll break down. "This is your story, not mine, Dad."

"This afternoon Grace was asked by an acquaintance she knew only as Lois to come and talk to her group, a terrorist zealot cell, about the layout of the L.A. water system. Grace was afraid, didn't know what to think. She had visited a similar group near Stone Canyon Reservoir off and on, but this was the first time she'd been asked to aid in what might be a terrorist act. She called a few friends from her own group to accompany her. One happened to be our informant.

"Our plant was heading out for a business meeting. Grace said not to worry and got someone else. Of course, our informant called us. But by the time we got someone to Grace's office to follow her, she was gone.

"She lived alone, so we just waited at her home. Potential sabotage of the Los Angeles water supply was too big for an NPO underling to handle. So Chief Balaam, who has a talent for this, went personally. I didn't want to miss a thing, so I went along. And what do you think happened?"

Paul pursed his lips as if he couldn't care less. "Pray tell."

"I've always wondered why people who slit their wrists tend to do it in a full bathtub. Do they *want* to watch the water turn redder as their lives ebb away? That's the end Grace chose. She even left a note describing her despair at being duped by religious extremists who offered friendship to a poor, desperately lonely spinster but in fact wanted to exploit her knowledge for their own illegal ends. She slit open both arms vertically from wrist to elbow—that's when a suicide means business, you know. Of course, she needed some assistance. She squealed like a pig, by the way. Just like a pig."

Paul fought to stay impassive. *Monsters!*

"Here's where you come in, Paul. Before opening her veins, Grace was repeatedly submerged to, shall we say, aid her memory. Balaam blindfolded her with a silk scarf—a nice touch. Each time Grace came up she gave us a little more about the cell near the port. She only had first names, but she had a good description of the ringleader, the one who had all the questions for her about the water. Seems he was from Chicago—an outside agitator. Get this. He called himself Paul and told her he had been blinded but that God had restored his sight. She even saw his navy blue sedan."

Paul's memory flashed to Stephen Lloyd hugging him and gasping, "Man, that was the first time my faith was tested. I almost didn't make it."

"Paul, do you deny being that man?"

"No," Paul said. He stood with fists clenched, trying to keep from erupting.

"No, you're not? Or no, you don't deny it?"

"Hi, Daddy!" Jae said. She rushed to her father, flung an arm around his neck, and kissed him on the cheek.

"Jae! Honey, I—"

"You both seem so serious. What's going on?"

"Just business. What are you doing here?"

"I missed my husband. I hope it's all right with the host if—"

"I'm sure Tiny will be delighted. I'll clear it with him in the morning. But, Jae, this is a working investigation site. It's not as if you can spend time with Paul—"

"I'll stay out of his hair. And I'll likely have to head back before he does anyway. But I just wanted to see him."

"Well, that's good. So you two are patching things up."

"Totally patched."

"Well, terrific. Now, Jae, if you will excuse us, we need to finish some business here, and Paul will be right along."

"Good to see you, Daddy."

"Yes, of course. Delighted."

When Jae was gone, Ranold swore and started in again on Paul. "We can't have our wives joining us on operations like this. Especially like this. You weren't here when I got back around ten, so I called the L.A. bureau chief at home—what's her name? Johns?"

"Harriet."

"Naturally, I told her to consider herself fired and that I'd make it official when I could reach the head of the agency in the morning. She insisted she had not authorized any undercover work for you, let alone a major sting we hadn't approved. Of course, the locals resent us and would love to steal our thunder, but Johns persuaded me she wasn't stupid enough to pull a stunt like that—especially with L.A.'s water supply at stake—and with my own son-in-law, no less. She said she had mentioned that you would make a good infiltrator, nothing more."

Paul was dumbfounded.

"Paul, you have humiliated me—and even more, yourself—with your arrogance. What made you go off half-cocked like that on your own? Did you think you could compete with me? with Balaam? She's twice the soldier you are because she follows orders—shows creativity, sure, but does what she is told. *You're* the one who should be fired. There is no room in the agency—especially now—for loose cannons. How do you justify this?"

"I can't, really."

"What insults me is that I know you thought you could get away with it because I'm your father-in-law."

"I have never, ever tried to trade on your position in the agency."

"So you just thought you could make a big score all by yourself? You thought you had to go an extra hundred miles because you failed in San Francisco and Gulfland? I can understand that, Paul. But we all have missions that go belly-up. A real soldier accepts it and moves on. Or was it your bleeding heart? You disapproved of our tactics and thought you'd bring in these renegades in cuffs instead of coffins. Well, that's not how it works with terrorists." He shook his head. "You're self-righteous and naive. It makes me sick—and it could have cost you more than just your job. You'd deserve to rot in jail if these maniacs had sabotaged the water and you had let them slip through our fingers.

"Fortunately, Grace said she told you there was no way they could do it without a miracle. She had no reason to lie by then."

"Then why was she murdered?"

"You think she could have told us more? Anyway, reluctant as she was, she was part of them. And I told you, it was clearly a suicide."

"With one arm slit from elbow to wrist she managed to slice the other too?"

"We left no tracks, Paul. Don't worry. Some may wonder how she managed it, but no one will suspect us."

"What about the cell at the port?"

"Took forever to find it, but we raided the place, of course. No one was there, but we found an ancient printing press, computers, lots of contraband books and tracts. Think about this, Paul: Had you been there with those people, trying to pull your big lone-wolf ruse on them when the raid went down, you might have been killed. At the very least, you'd have some explaining to do.

"We'll watch who comes and goes there tomorrow. Then on Sunday it will be the first target of a major strike. Intelligence uncovered seven other large cells, and we'll see if Grace's friends have anything to add. Sunday is these people's big meeting day, so we can likely catch all of them at once. Even if massive simultaneous strikes don't knock out the underground, they will certainly cripple it.

"The question now, Paul, is what I should do with you."

"Whatever you see fit."

"It's hard to assess the degree of harm you've actually done. Your meddling did put us onto a new target and give us insight into the kind of attacks the terrorists might plan. Only Balaam and I know what a fool you made of yourself. It would appear a conflict of interest if I were the one to discipline you. I won't humiliate you further by letting Chief Balaam mete out your fate. Rather, I am going to report you to your superior, Chief Koontz, and place your punishment in his hands."

Paul felt as if he could melt into a heap. "Seems fair," he said.

"I'll give you a chance to redeem yourself Sunday. You will stay at my side during the raids and, I hope, acquit yourself enough to mitigate the severity of my report to Koontz. Until then, you're suspended. You may not use an agency car. Perhaps if Tiny is kind enough to help you with transportation, you can take Jae out for a little sight-seeing tomorrow.

"Now I'm going to bed, and I suggest you do the same."

• • •

Sleep was the last thing Paul could imagine. He was horrified at what had happened to Grace, frantic to warn the Fishers of Men to stay away from the port tomorrow, and desperate to alert the rest of the L.A. underground to avoid their usual meeting places Sunday. Further down the list—but terrifying, he had to admit— was the realization of how close he'd come to being caught. It could have happened so easily.

Paul felt unaccountably blessed that Ranold had been so wrong. It wasn't like his father-in-law to jump to conclusions. *If he'd had my father's letter, he would have read the situation differently. Jae must have taken it.*

What time had she called? Was it possible Ranold had her phone to try to pull him out of Sapiens before the raid—not to save Paul so much as to spare himself the embarrassment?

Ranold said he'd gotten home at ten, which might or might not be true. Grace had left the port just before seven. If they had extracted the information from her by nine, Ranold could have set the raid in motion and then put Jae up to calling. He could have sent her to the airport. The rest of her story might even be true, but Ranold could have flown her in earlier in the day.

How long were we there talking about Barton and the manifesto? Then how long was I on the road?

With everything else going on, the timing was too much for Paul to work out right then. Warning the others was his priority.

Paul stepped outside. He might be under surveillance, but he had to call Straight. The fountain was gushing, as always, so Paul positioned himself as close to it as possible. He'd get soaked by the spray, but the burbling and splashing would cover the sound of his call. To avoid rousing more suspicion by going back indoors dripping wet, he slipped off his shirt and pants and tossed them to safety where they'd stay dry.

Like Paul, Straight was stunned at what had happened.

"The big problem is how to reach any of these people," Paul said. "They've got to be warned to stay away from Sapiens Fisheries tomorrow and told to get the word out to every other cell in Los Angeles. And Grace Dean's friends from the Stone Canyon group are about to get snatched for interrogation if they haven't been already.

"And here I am, totally out of commission—certainly being watched by Ranold and possibly by Jae."

"She didn't plant a bug on you, did she?"

"I didn't even think of that with all this madness. Luckily—" Paul burst out laughing—"even if she did, I'm standing here in my shorts, sopping wet, with my head stuck in a fountain."

"I wondered what that sound was," Straight said.

36

TINY ALLENDO OOZED CHARM in the morning and acted as if Jae's presence made his month. "Your timing is impeccable," he said. "This evening at poolside I am hosting an elegant prestrike dinner, to which you are invited. The governor of Sunterra and his wife and some major players in town will be here, along with Chief Balaam and your father. Oh, and Juliet Peters."

"The movie star?"

"The same," Tiny said. "I'm thinking of casting her as Chief Balaam in the movie. You know, beautiful blonde fights her way up the ranks of the NPO, finally gets her big break leading a crack strike force. I'm not sure about the love angle yet— maybe the handsome leader of the zealots, whom she takes prisoner. Maybe a jail-cell seduction . . . she comes in wearing a gold cat-suit and stiletto-heel boots to show she's all woman doing a man's job . . . but it's a triangle. The real Mr. Right is the wise old agency chairman. He's thirty-five years her senior, but he's a tiger—a silver fox. Seasoned. Tough. Rich as King Midas.

"At the end the zealot turns out to be a brute. The silver fox saves the blonde, and she sees he's so much stronger and better than the cute young muscle man. Or maybe it's the other way around, and it's really the old guy who's evil. It all depends on which costars Juliet wants."

Paul could barely hide his revulsion. "Thank you for your hospitality to Jae," he said.

"Until this evening then," Tiny said, bowing.

• • •

Tiny had offered Paul and Jae the use of his car and chauffeur for the day. Ranold must have engineered it because Paul hadn't asked, and he declined to tell Jae that the reason they were imposing on Tiny was that her father had suspended him. Paul had barely slept, anguishing over the fates of Fishers of Men, Grace Dean's three friends from the Stone Canyon group, and the other groups targeted Sunday. Had Straight and the others been able to warn them? Somehow Paul had to connect with Straight that morning, but what would he do about Jae?

He had been genuinely happy, if confused, to see Jae, but he still hadn't talked to her about his father's letter, and she had volunteered nothing. He had no idea whether she had found the letter and, if she had, what she might make of it. On top of that was her call last night, which might well have been timed to yank him out of Sapiens one step ahead of the army.

Even without those suspicions, no way could Paul risk telling Jae he had flipped to the other side and was now working to rescue the very people her father was bent on exterminating.

The news would shatter not just her image of him but also the bedrock values of her upbringing. With so many innocent lives at stake, he didn't dare gamble on her understanding.

The day had broken hot, and by ten the temperature was already flirting with ninety degrees. Paul was soaking but not just from the heat.

Jae needed an evening gown for the party that night. Tiny's chauffeur took them to the famous Rodeo Drive, now a ten-story mall of exclusive stores for those who enjoyed actual shopping more than on-line virtual try-ons.

"This is wild," Jae said. "I never thought I'd actually see it in person. But I doubt we can afford anything here."

"Let's splurge. How often do you get to have dinner with Juliet Peters?"

"A gold catsuit and stiletto-heel boots . . . that movie sounds beneath her. But, Paul, I know how much you hate shopping. . . ."

"I was hoping you'd say that."

"So why don't you have the chauffeur take you somewhere? This is my one big chance at Rodeo Drive, and I don't want to worry that you're miserable."

Paul was a hairsbreadth from taking her up on it, desperate to see what was going on at the port, when it struck him: *This is a test.* Maybe Jae was in cahoots with Ranold and maybe she wasn't. But Ranold had arranged for the limo and driver right after stripping Paul of his agency car. If the man behind the wheel wasn't an operative assigned to check on him, Paul would be shocked.

"You know, Jae, I'm pretty sick of driving around. I've been stuck in a car all week. It'll feel good to be in an air-conditioned mall on a day like this. If I get bored, I'll wander off on my own."

• • •

The mall was an architectural marvel of curved copper beams and gold-tinted glass. Jae checked the registry of stores, *ooh*ing and *ah*ing over the famous names. "I'm going to start at the top and work my way down," she said. "Think you can stand that?"

"Lead on."

Over her shoulder Paul spotted a tenth-floor store that looked like an oasis: Cicero's Games. They got off the jetvator and Jae headed for an interesting shop. Paul left her at the door and headed over to Cicero's. Inside, beyond the usual banks of life-size interactive games, was an entire section devoted to old-fashioned board games like Scrabble and chess. No clerks or customers around. Pretending to examine the merchandise, Paul called Straight.

Straight led off with good news. Someone in the salt mines knew Carl and Lois because of their letterpress-printed tracts and had been able to warn them away from Sapiens. They in turn had provided leads to many of the other Los Angeles groups. The bad news was that the three friends of Grace Dean from the Stone Canyon Reservoir group had yet to be found.

"It's hopeless by now," Paul said. "They may have already been tortured to death."

"Nothing is hopeless," Straight said. "Last I heard, God was still on His throne."

Straight reported that underground factions in every state were fervently praying for God's judgment on Los Angeles and the protection of its believers. "Your contacts are paying off," Straight said. "From Abraham, Sarah, and Isaac in the Detroit underground to Arthur Demetrius in New York, the word is being spread. San Francisco and Washington are hopping, eager for God to avenge their martyrs. And get this: The media is starting to pick up on that Christian manifesto. The whole country is going to be watching L.A., Paul."

Thank You, Lord.

Paul went to collect Jae, and they made their way down to the ninth and then the eighth floor, where Jae stopped off twice to see evening gowns with Paul gamely looking on. On the seventh floor, Paul homed in on an electronics store with state-of-the-art video players in the window. All were tuned to a breaking-news network.

"Let's check this a second," he said.

The Christian manifesto was splashed across every screen. Police spokesmen claimed the warning was a hoax and urged citizens to ignore it. But talk-show hosts took calls from all over, and the warning was all anyone wanted to discuss. The underground's threat to cut off L.A.'s water had frightened many and also had become fodder for jokes, giving pundits no end of fun spinning and laughing at outrageous scenarios.

"What in the world . . . ?" Jae said.

By the time Paul and Jae reached the ground floor, the manifesto had become a nationwide phenomenon.

• • •

They arrived at the Allendo estate a few hours before dinner and strolled the grounds in the sweltering heat. Jae kept her distance from the fountain so it wouldn't ruin her hair, but she stared at it from inside the fence that separated the pool from the rest of the grounds.

"Who are all the young women?" she said.

"Party favors," Paul said.

"And did you—"

"No."

"And Daddy?"

"Don't ask."

Paul found himself silently praying at every spare moment. Now that the warnings had reached the Sapiens group and were, ideally, rippling through the rest of the L.A. underground, he finally felt able to concentrate on his own situation. If the targets were empty when the army came storming in Sunday morning, he knew full well heads were going to roll. They would look for the leak, and someone would pay. Paul was relieved that Ranold had never told him which specific groups were in the crosshairs, but he still worried the breach might easily be traced to him. He had wanted to remain a mole in the agency until he chose to leave. Something like this would make his decision for him. He would have to be gone before they caught on.

• • •

Allendo was resplendent in his usual black on black, gold-mirrored shades in place. Tiny didn't seem to sweat, while Paul felt as if he were swimming. The governor's entourage arrived at ten to six, when Ranold also made his appearance for pictures and handshakes. He proudly introduced Jae to all the dignitaries. The governor's wife appeared relieved to see Jae and insisted on staying at her side and sitting next to the Stepolas at dinner.

Bia Balaam arrived preening in another silver gown—this one satin and skintight, clinging awkwardly to her angular body—with matching stiletto heels. Jae nudged Paul. "You'd think she overheard Tiny's ideas for Juliet Peters. I can't believe that woman is NPO."

Balaam snubbed Paul and Jae, apparently disgusted by Paul's connection to Sapiens Fisheries. *You don't know the half of it.* Paul was gratified that Jae had evidently taken an instant dislike to the woman.

Giddiness was in the air, as if everyone was in on a delicious secret. Ranold laughed quietly with Balaam, the military men, the governor, and Tiny and his friends.

Jae whispered, "There's sure a lot of laughter for what should be a sober day. You'd think they were planning a surprise party."

"Peculiar, considering people might die," Paul said.

The governor's wife agreed. "I know we're targeting terrorists, but I find it hard to approve of jocularity at a time like this."

Suddenly everyone's attention shifted to the French doors leading from the house, where Juliet Peters shyly entered with none of the apparent ego one might expect. She was a curvaceous blonde in a white strapless gown, her trademark platinum mane reaching to her impossibly tiny waist.

"Juliet, dearest," Tiny said, "at last. Now let's all be seated for dinner."

Offering Juliet his arm, Tiny escorted her to a place at the table between his own and Bia Balaam's.

Paul and Jae were at the far end of the table, nearest the pool. Tiny's "party favors" continued to cavort in the water during dinner, and Paul envied them, longing to plunge in and cool off. The servers kept the wine flowing, but Paul concentrated on his tall glass of ice water.

What if there were more targets than Straight's people had been able to reach? What if he had to go along and see his brothers and sisters killed? He fought to hold fast to his faith. He had to believe God would heed an entire nation's prayers and make Himself known.

• • •

"So," Juliet Peters said, as the waiters came around with dessert, "have we all been sufficiently warned of the judgment of God?"

She smiled and sipped water from her glass.

The others laughed.

"Yes," Ranold said, sounding on the verge of a guffaw, "better stock up on water!"

"Indeed," Allendo said. "I bought extra-long straws so we can drink out of the pool if necessary."

Paul could hear the rush of the fountain from the front of the house, which showed high above the roof, and the splashing of the young women in the pool. *Spare us,* he prayed.

Bia Balaam locked eyes with Paul, but he tore his gaze away, fearing she could read his thoughts. As if sensing his anxiety, Jae grabbed Paul's hand under the table.

Juliet Peters coughed. Someone cried out, and Paul looked up just in time to see one of the women at the pool plunge down a slide and slam into the dry bottom with a sickening thud. Her friends screamed.

The fountain had ceased.

The water glasses on the table were not only empty but also dry. Even the sweat on the glass serving pitchers was gone.

Tiny Allendo jumped up so quickly his chair pitched backward. He stared at the pool, then whirled and looked at the fountain.

Paul studied the table. Even the liquid in the food had evaporated. The fruit tart had shriveled. The sorbet was colored powder. The wineglasses held a gooey residue.

Tiny's voice sounded weak and timid. "Bottled water!" he croaked.

Waiters ran into the house, then came out, looking stricken. "The bottles are unopened, sir, but empty."

Paul looked at the grass on the beautiful sprawling lawn under the lights. It was withering. By tomorrow it would be brown.

Balaam was on her feet, tottering out to her vehicle in her

heels. Ranold stood, fingers fluttering, lips trembling. Tiny called out to his people, "Get to the store! Bring back all the water you can!"

But Paul knew what they would find. More empty bottles. God had more than answered the prayers of the faithful. He had done more than shut off the water supply to Los Angeles.

The mighty Lord and Creator of the universe had withdrawn every drop of water in the wicked city. The word would spread throughout the land, and underground believers would rise up with confidence and strength, boldly proclaiming the message of faith. The powers that be would stop killing the people of God, or they would all wither like the grass and die.

• • •

The miracle would be known around the world within minutes. To those aboveground, it marked the beginning of what would become known as the Christian Guerilla War. To those underground, this was clearly the beginning of the end, the mark of what—and who—would be coming.

Soon.

For the latest information on Left Behind products,
visit www.leftbehind.com

For the latest information on Tyndale House fiction,
visit www.tyndalefiction.com